9/00

WRECK BOOK
WITHDRAWN
DATE DUE N.G.

	FEB 15		
OC 5 '00			
OC 30 '00			
NO 25 '00			
JA 5 '01			
JA 19 '01			
FE 3 '01			
FE 21 01			
NO 28 '01			
P 24 2001			

THE ADVOCATE

THE
ADVOCATE

BILL MESCE JR.
STEVEN G. SZILAGYI

BANTAM BOOKS
New York   Toronto   London   Sydney   Auckland

THE ADVOCATE

A Bantam Book / September 2000

Map by Jeffrey L. Ward.

BOOK DESIGN BY GLEN M. EDELSTEIN.

Library of Congress Cataloging-in-Publication Data
Mesce, Bill.
The advocate / Bill Mesce, Jr., Steven G. Szilagyi
p.   cm.
ISBN 0-553-80118-X
1. World War, 1939–1945—Fiction. I. Szilagyi, Steve. II. Title.
PS3563.E74627 A65 2000
813'.54—dc21
00-039764

Published simultaneously in the United States and Canada

Bantam Books are published by Bantam Books, a division of Random House,
Inc. Its trademark, consisting of the words "Bantam Books" and the portrayal of
a rooster, is Registered in U.S. Patent and Trademark Office and in other
countries. Marca Registrada. Bantam Books, 1540 Broadway, New York, New
York 10036.

PRINTED IN THE UNITED STATES OF AMERICA

BVG   10   9   8   7   6   5   4   3   2   1

To the three brothers,
Bill Sr., Tommy, and "Shiekie":
They served.

You were right in that remark that you made last summer.
I was booked to make a mistake.
I have lived too long in foreign parts.

—Henry James,
Daisy Miller

ENGLAND
AUGUST 1943

PART ONE:
THE ANGELS

CHAPTER ONE

THE SENESCHAL

THE OLD MAN'S RITUAL WAS UNCHANGING. Each morning he brewed his tea from a tin of faded leaves and took a biscuit, fresh-cooked the night before but now crusty, from the bun warmer on the stove. He sat hunched over his tea and biscuit, at the scuffed table he'd built himself back in the days when the lumber he'd cut had seemed as light and limber in his hands as child's clay.

The mutt sat eager and panting at his feet in his own morning canon, envious eyes glued to the food in the old man's hand.

When there was but one bite left to the biscuit, the old man paused to study the morsel reflectively. This was the dog's cue to stand, wagging his tail frantically, bright eyes locked on the treat. The old man looked from the dog to the biscuit and back to the dog, as if weighing some great decision. Then, he leaned over, he and his chair creaking together, and held the biscuit over the dog's head.

The old man raised one finger, and the dog, knowing his part well, forced himself to sit and be still. They held this frieze until the old man felt the animal had earned his reward. "Oop wi' ye," the old man commanded, and the dog launched himself onto his hind legs, balancing in a waltzing step until the man dropped the piece of biscuit into the widespread jaws.

When the biscuit was gone, the dog looked up at the old man, tail wagging, and smiled with a mouth full of yellow teeth.

"You *are* the spoil'dest beast!" the old man said, and smiled back with teeth just as yellow. He ruffled the dog's limp ears, then massaged the top of the animal's head with his horny knuckles.

The old man finished his tea and brushed the crumbs from the table. He left the chipped teacup where it sat. By the time the woman awoke, the leaves would be dry and could be returned to their tin.

He wiped his hands on his ragged jersey and poked his head through the curtained doorway of the bedroom. The cross mounted on the far wall stood guard over the woman snuggled in the center of the down-filled bed. It looked like a shadow in the gray light from the window facing the Channel.

The stone walls of the cottage were cool, gathering in the moisture of the clammy morning. A breeze off the sea fluttered the thin curtains. While the dog watched patiently from the doorway, the old man tiptoed clumsily to the window. He tried to close it, but the sash was swollen with the damp and it resisted and groaned. He stopped, not wanting to wake the woman, and pulled the curtains closed. He reached for a hand-made quilt atop the neat pile of bedclothes at the foot of the bed and gently drew it across her shoulders.

He cut some cheese from the brick in the larder, took another biscuit from the warmer, and wrapped both in a damp cloth before tucking them into his haversack along with a small jug of water. He took his crook from where it rested against the wall, and his cap from the hook by the door. He was halfway out the door before he remembered his binoculars on the wireless table.

Try as she might with her hand-tatted doilies, vases of marigolds, the menagerie of ceramic animals, the woman had been unable to soften the bleak presumptuousness of the transmitter, or the grim black ranks of aircraft silhouettes on the recognition chart tacked to the wall, lined up like cemetery crosses. He slung the glasses round his neck, blew out the lantern hanging over the table, and went outside.

The dog spurted past him in the doorway, trotting to the edge of the cliffs where he paced back and forth near the steep drop. He left his urinary mark of proprietorship on the knots of weeds and shrubs growing twisted in the Channel winds. The gulls circling off the chalk bluffs ignored his perfunctory barks and continued with their breakfast, dropping mussels on the boulders strewn along the pebble beach, then diving to pick at the meat amid the shattered shells. Bored with the dawn and the birds and the surf, the dog trotted off to find the old man by the chicken coop behind the cottage.

"Damn . . ."

The hens were out, bucbucbucing in a nagging cluster. A gap had been clawed between two of the floorboards. Bloodied feathers hung on the splintered edges and trailed along the shallow fox tracks that vanished into the thick pasture grass.

The old man turned an angry, disgusted look on the dog. "Where the bloody 'ell were you?"

The dog dodged the old man's attempt to cuff him. He trotted off to a safe distance, then followed the old man toward the tool shanty, his head bowed low and sheepish.

"Better be sorry," the old man grumbled. "Be bleedin' 'shamed o' yerself. That's yer modrern dog for ya. Not like inna olden times. Those were real dogs, dogs a man could count on!"

The old man laid out a roll of rusting chicken wire, frowning when he saw the scant few feet left. He gauged by eye how much he'd need and cut no more than that. These were not days that tolerated waste or excess.

"In olden times, a man and his dog went out side by side. Out inna wars together, side by side. Tough 'ey was. Slayin' infidels."

The old man went back to the coop. He nudged the hens out of the way with his boot and started tacking the patch of wire over the hole.

"Not like 'is easy farm work yer modrern dog's got. Yuh, slay a few infidels 'n' yer olden dog wouldna bother wi' no li'l ol' fox. 'Neath 'im it was. Not like yer modrern dog, lays about all day, lettin' the sheep stray halfways to London, does." The old man turned sharply to the dog. "Buys 'em a rail ticket almost is what 'e does. Yup, that's yer modrern dog. 'N' 'en 'e wants yer biscuit, too, don't 'e?"

The dog grinned in dumb apology.

The old man leaned over, nose to nose with the dog, and wagged a reprimanding finger. "Old age don't let you out of nothin', ya know."

The dog whipped his tongue out; it caught the old man in the eye.

The old man blinked and sighed and rubbed the dog's muzzle. "Spoil'dest beast I *ever* seed!"

He shooed the hens back into the coop with his crook, then headed for the sheep pen. The dog was already there, maintaining an air of diligence as he trotted back and forth beside the rail fence, barking officiously.

"Oh, e's onna job *now*, is 'e?" the old man said dryly as he swung open the gate. He started prodding the animals out, occasionally giving his staff a brisk swing, feinting at the sheep. "Ha, take 'at! Slashin' away at 'em! Infidels!"

Heading off the leaders, the dog steered the herd away from the vegetable garden in front of the cottage and guided them toward the grassy hillocks a safe distance from the cliffs. The flow of animals broke up the last licks of morning mist.

The old man trudged after them. A warming breeze blew over the herd, bringing him the familiar odors of moist soil, dewy grass, and sour wool, and the soft tinkle of collar bells. He could see the dog handily controlling the rambunctious elements beginning to stray from the flock. At the rear, dancing lambs, enjoying their first summer, kicked their heels.

The old man selected a spot of thick grass atop a low knoll and sat, unmindful of the dampness seeping through his trousers. Wary of the dog, the black, teardrop faces of the sheep peeped up from behind each other's sooty shanks as he herded them into a small depression below the old man.

The old man pulled off his jersey and bundled it into a cushion beneath him. The dog left the sheep to the business of grazing and lay beside the old man, panting with a laborer's pride.

"Old age don't let you out of *nothin'*," the old man repeated, stroking the dog's long, shaggy fur. He shifted on the bundled jersey, leaning up against the crook. The breeze, the sounds of surf and birds, were lulling. Under their caress, the old man's eyes began to close.

The dog's bark, sharp and agitated, reminded the old man of bloody feathers, and his eyes snapped open. The sheep were scattered below him in the hollow, gaping at the barking of the dog. No other threat was in sight.

The old man saw that the dog was barking toward the cottage. Pulling himself stiffly up by his crook, he saw the lazy curl of smoke from the chimney, the woman out back where she'd been hanging the bedclothes on a line for airing. She was waving and calling to him. She pointed toward the Channel.

He raised the binoculars and rolled the focus wheel. He scanned the gray stretch of water until he found the barest charcoallike wisp hanging low over the horizon line.

A finger of smoke reached down from the wisp, its tip hardening into something silvery, glinting in the dull morning sun. The wisp grew larger as it neared, and soon the old man could pick out the stubby silhouette of a single-engine aeroplane. A fighter, no doubt, and by its coloring, a Yank. It was heading toward the old man, moving fast and low, no more than 150 meters above the water. The smoke he saw came in a steady, thin stream from the bulbous, black-painted nose of the plane.

Half-tripping, half-shuffling, the old man charged down the slope, trying to avoid the dog, who circled and yipped, tangling himself in leg and crook.

Wheezing and sweaty, the old man and the dog arrived at the door of the cottage. From inside came a ratcheting grind as the woman cranked the wireless generator.

"There's more!" she called to him.

He raised his glasses again, sweeping until he saw two more of the silvery flecks materializing above the line of the water. They were in staggered formation, perhaps another fifty meters higher than the first plane, closing swiftly with the cripple, sniffing along its fragile trail of smoke.

The old man drew himself up straight and forced himself to take long, calming breaths before he stepped inside. He did not want the woman to see how winded he was.

" 'E's 'urt." The woman said it urgently.

"I know." He tossed his crook on the table and crossed to the wireless. She had already flipped the power switch for him. He pulled the kapok-cushioned headphones on, wincing at the hissing and crackling of static in his ears. As he fiddled with the frequency controls, he looked out the window at the approaching aircraft, then to the recognition poster above the generator. He picked up the heavy microphone, cleared his throat self-importantly, and pressed the transmission button.

"This is Observer Three Baker Three to Three Baker Control. Come in Three Baker Control, over."

All three aircraft were still some miles out, but there was no mistaking that silhouette: beer-barrel fuselage; stubby, elliptical wings.

"*Three Baker Three,*" came a young, cool, woman's voice. "*This is Three Baker Control. Proceed, over.*"

The old man moved the family Bible aside to consult the direction markers taped to the wireless table. "I have three American P-forty-sevum Thunderbolts heading my position, course two seven zero. One aircraft is trailing smoke." Then, as the trainer in the village had taught him, he carefully repeated the message.

"*We are alerted, Three Baker Three. Will alert Air/Sea Rescue. Keep us copied. Three Baker Control out.*"

The dog followed the old man and woman outside, to the verge of the cliff. Although the smoke from the lead ship had grown thicker, the faint buzz of the approaching engine remained smooth and steady. The first of the two trailing aircraft had closed to within a mile of its injured mate. The old man nodded approvingly.

" 'E'll be awright," he told the woman, noting how her fingers were knotted tensely together. "We seen much worse."

He shifted closer to her to block her view down the coast toward the point. After three years, there wasn't much left of the plane on the rocks below except the tail section; a canted cross wedged upright in the rocks with its metal bleached bare of markings by sun and sea.

" 'At's 'ow 'ey do it, see?" He pointed to the follow plane closing with the smoking leader. "When one of 'em is 'urt like 'at, 'ey come back wi' 'im. Escorts. 'Ey look after each other like 'at."

The first follow plane was less than a hundred meters behind the cripple, still above it and off to the right of its tail. Then the high plane gently dipped its wing, flashing American stars, and slid into a shallow dive.

The old man saw twinkling spots of light on the wings of the diving plane, and the shell casings showering from under the aircraft. A moment later, muted by the heavy air, the stuttering of the guns reached him. The black cowling of the crippled Thunderbolt blew free with a dull crump. Licks of flame spat back from the engine, sweeping along the fuselage with thick, oily smoke, the stream pierced by the glittering shards of Plexiglas as the canopy shattered.

The crippled plane dropped toward the water and, in another easy motion, the attacker pulled smoothly out of his dive and began to climb and bank. The sun glinted on the aluminum skin, whiting out the stars on the wings.

The old man could see the outline of a figure in the cockpit, sun burning in the lenses of the goggles pushed back on the leather-clad head. The shining glass eyes turned toward the old man, and the Thunderbolt slid into another dive.

He had watched it all, but it had not registered. Suddenly, he understood.

"Run," he croaked to the woman.

"I—"

"Run!"

They reached the doorway as the Thunderbolt opened fire. The old man shoved her through and to the right while he dove left. He hugged the stone wall hard enough to take the skin off his cheek. He squeezed his eyes closed as the stones at his back shuddered under the pounding of the heavy bullets.

The Thunderbolt picked up its nose and the front windows of the cottage imploded. The room flew apart. Dishes, cookware, furniture—all rose up and disintegrated, the air hazing with powdered wood and crockery. The plane nosed up another degree; the roof erupted in shredded thatchwork and splinters of beam.

The guns were drowned out as the roaring engine of the Thunderbolt reached down and washed over the small cottage, over the old man, grabbing them both by their ancient foundations, threatening to tear them stone from stone, bone from bone.

The old man's arms curled round his head and his knees came up to his chest. He squirmed against the cold stone of the wall and waited to die.

CHAPTER TWO

THE JUSTICIAR

AFTER HE WAS GONE, I CLIPCLOPPED my way back to the Annex. Don't know why. Scene of the crime and all that, I suppose. I was feeling a bit mournful just then. Oh, not for poor old Harry. I'd hardly known him, really, though I'd known him well enough to know that that pile of respectable granite walls and marbled halls, the stained glass transoms and slate roofs of the Annex, had been a sad sort of pinnacle for him.

I stood across the lane where I could see past the gate to the court beyond. I looked to a high corner of the yard, to the brace of tall, dusty windows that marked his quarters, and then to the other side of the yard to the single, narrow window that signaled his office. Find the tallest staircase, the farthest end of the hall, the least attractive view, the tightest quarters and longest walk to the loo: There you'd find poor old Harry Voss.

Poor old Harry. The deep, frowning furrows of his forehead, the few strands of hair trying vainly to breach the freckled bare pate, and that plow-horse trudge of his were guaranteed to pluck your pity strings, even at a first glance. He'd already looked worn and worried when he landed in England, no doubt over the security of his threadbare law practice, his household, and the well-being of the two warm-eyed brats and the pear-shaped woman he'd left three thousand miles behind.

The white helmeted Military Policemen at the Annex court gate flicked me one of those steely-eyed glares that I think they'd borrowed from the busby-topped guards at Buckingham Palace. I gave them a little smile, just a polite acknowledgment of their attention because I knew that despite my having stood in the same spot for half the week they'd failed to recognize me. So, I smiled, they glared, and I looked up at poor old Harry's window and shook my head.

Poor, poor old Harry.

Having seen Harry's clerk—as I'd seen most of the other players in this drama—across the cobbles of the court, I could imagine poor old Harry's pain and sorrow when he discovered young Corporal Nagel each morning dutifully waiting at his station in the outer office; this despite Harry's fervent prayers the night before that one of Fat Hermann's 250-kg. high-explosive delights might go astray and find the young Idahoan in his bed. Resigned to another unanswered prayer, Harry would grunt a perfunctory good morning to Nagel, usher the corporal off on his morning toddle to the Annex canteen, then settle in his tiny office. He would neatly hang his khaki jacket on a hanger hooked to the back of the door, loosen his tie in a way that provided the least wrinkling, roll his sleeves with equal attention above his hairy forearms, careful to keep the folds straight and even.

In longer time than it should have taken, Corporal Nagel would duly return and hover over Harry with a cardboard tray of coffee and doughnuts wobbling in his anamorphic hands.

Harry had a plodding way about him. I can see him pushing himself slowly away from his typewriter table and sighing (he was a sighing sort) at Nagel's return. He would pluck at his khaki shirt where it stuck in little damp spots to his sweaty paunch, and look sadly over the tops of his half-moon reading glasses at the tall pimply-faced corporal, gangly and stooped like a broken umbrella arm. Harry told me that the simple act of removing a coffee and a powdered doughnut from the tray and setting them down on the desk was, for Nagel, the kind of operation that required the fierce and painful concentration of a bomb-disposal expert. Doing his best not to make any sudden moves that might startle the lad, Harry would delicately slide his legs as far as he could from where the sloshing cup of coffee was coming in for a bumpy landing.

Corporal Nagel could be relied on for at least one annoyance per day and this particular day he was in proper form. "What's that you have in your mouth?" Harry asked.

"Sir?"

Harry pushed his glasses back up on the damp bulb of his nose and tugged at where his shirt was sticking under his arms. It was quite close in the small office. Harry's one window was permanently wedged open at a height of twenty-one centimeters, and no amount of banging or threats could move it farther up or down. The room, an awkward conversion of what Harry described as "some old biddy's boo-*dwah*," still boasted very civilian floral wallpaper, which only added to a sense of hothouse suffocation. To remedy the stuffiness, Harry had been provided with a small desk fan whose scimitar blades adamantly refused to turn. This, Maintenance explained without offering any solutions, was due to the warm humidity and/or cold damp—depending on the current state of the fickle English weather.

Harry took a deep breath and began again: "I said, what's that you have in your mouth? What are you chewing?"

The corporal's jaws froze. His eyes took on the fixed, wide-look that cows must have in that first moment after the butcher's mallet falls on their heads. "Chewing?"

"Corporal, would you like me to pry your mouth open and see what's in there?"

"Bubba gum, sir. Fleers."

Harry reached for the Lucky Strike smoldering in his ashtray and took a long, tranquilizing draught. "Bubble gum."

"Yessir. My mama sent it. She—"

"Nagel, I don't *care* where you got the bubble gum. Just don't chew it in my office." Harry harrumphed and drew himself up in his chair. One hand unconsciously moved to fiddle with what there was of his hair. "Appearances to the contrary, Corporal, this is a *law* office. You do not chew gum in a law office. You can chew gum in the hall, you can chew gum in the latrine, in the street, or in bed, but you do *not* chew gum in my law office. Clear?"

"Yessir. May I request permission to go out in the hall, sir?"

"No, you may not request permission to go out in the hall. You may request permission to go to work. You may request permission to work on this!" Harry nodded at the sheet of erasable bond wilting in his Underwood. "Do you see what this is?"

Nagel craned his head round for a look and Harry noticed how appetizingly exposed that left the corporal's jugular. Harry's stubby fingers had produced a page spurtled with smudges, erasures, and type-overs.

"What is it?" Nagel asked.

"This is what you were *supposed* to be typing yesterday afternoon while I was over at the Provost's."

"*That's* not what I typed yesterday."

"I *know!*" From his desk, Harry grabbed a fistful of foolscap covered with notes and shoved it at Nagel. "This is what you were supposed to be typing yesterday! This is what you are going to type *now!*"

Nagel studied the notes, trying to camouflage a slow chew of his gum as musing. "Hmph," he said. He started to reach for the page in Harry's typewriter. "I guess—"

"I guess *this* is *garbage!*" Harry tore the page out of the carriage, crushed it in his sweaty palm, and dropped it in his wastebasket. "And Nagel?"

"Sir?"

"Get rid of the gum!"

Having shooed Corporal Nagel back to his own outer office, Harry took another draught of his cigarette, then picked up his doughnut and kicked his wheeled chair over to the narrow window. He propped his heels on the sill among the piles of overstuffed folders and bound briefs, laid the back of his chair against the desk, and regarded the grim view of chimney pots and barrage balloons through the little panes, each crisscrossed with adhesive tape to minimize flying glass in the event of a nearby bomb blast. He took a bite of the doughnut, then reached back to his desk for his coffee. He leaned forward slightly to take a cautious sip.

"Ahhh!" Harry's head shot back from the hot coffee and some spilled on his trouser leg. "Ohhh!"

"Watch that coffee, Major," Nagel called helpfully. "It's hot."

Harry was still stomping round his office trying to keep the hot stain on his trousers off his skin when the telephone rang. "I've got it!" he barked and scooped up the receiver. "Major Voss."

"Hello, Harry-boy."

The purring, mocking voice was instantly familiar.

"What do *you* want?"

"That's no way to talk to your betters, Harry."

"Arf."

"What's on your desk?"

"Today? Or for a while?"

"Maybe a little while."

"Besides eighteen tons of paperwork?"

"Yes, Harry, besides eighteen tons of paperwork."

"Mostly flyweights. I've got a half-dozen D and D's, that statutory—"

"But if you had to, you could dump everything on somebody else?"

"Well, most of it. If I had to. They're pretty routine. But I'd prefer—"

"I may have something for you, Harry-boy. Meet me in the yard in five minutes."

Harry looked down at his stained trousers. "Five minutes?"

"Plan to spend the day, Harry."

"The day? I thought there was a case management—"

"Five minutes, Harry." The caller rang off.

Harry slipped his glasses into his shirt pocket and brushed the crumbs from his shirtfront. "Nagel? Nagel!"

"Yessir!"

Frowning into the little mirror he kept in his desk drawer, Harry used a pocket comb to drag his meager ration of hair into a more strategic pattern. "I'm going to be with Colonel Ryan for the rest of the day, so if anyone calls, take a message. *Get their number!* OK? Corporal?"

"Yessir."

Harry rolled down his sleeves, tightened his tie, and took his jacket from the hanger on the door. He stood in the doorway to the outer office and scowled at Nagel, who was wrestling with a fistful of jammed typewriter keys.

"Nagel? *Nagel!*"

The corporal looked up, his skeletal hands fiddling with the logjammed keys. "Sir?"

"Those notes better be transcribed by noon, Corporal. Captain Brezwhatever the hell his name is—"

"Brezinzki."

"—is coming by for them at noon. They'd better be ready."

"Yessir."

"Or when you thank your mother for the gum, you can write to her from the Aleutians."

"I understand, sir."

"That'd be a first." Harry headed for the door. "After Captain—"

"Brezinzki."

"—picks up that better-be-finished transcription, you go out."

"To lunch, sir?"

"To lunch, to dinner, to have tea with the Queen, I don't care. I don't want you in this office without a chaperone. Take the rest of the day off. Go out and assimilate the local culture. Go stand in a queue at Covent Garden."

"What's a queue, sir?"

"A Chinaman's hair." Harry sighed and left.

Outwardly, Rosewood Court hadn't changed much since the arrival of the Americans, but then the Victorian architects who had designed the clustered block of town houses and pieds-à-terre a century earlier had had the distinctly Empire view that the world outside its gates was more or less irrelevant to those inside. Consequently, brick-and-granite buildings of the square had been built with their bland backsides to the street while their gargoyled cornices and balustraded verandas faced each other round a cobbled square, so the trashmen and postmen and deliverymen could discreetly carry on their dealings with house servants at the rear entrances, while the ladies and gentlemen of Rosewood Court had only to face one another.

Those selfsame ladies and gents were gone now, withdrawn to their country estates within the previous year or two while their Court residences had been "donated" to the Allied war effort, and a great deal of the yard's antiquarian charm seemed to have departed along with them. The ornate, two-tiered fountain bubbling in the Court's center was the first thing to go, along with the prize-winning roses and their trellises, all to make room for the jeeps, staff cars, and 4x4's that soon clotted the yard and left the venerable cobbles stained with rainbows of motor oil. The gatepost ormolu lions were no longer considered sentinel enough; they were joined by rotating shifts of iron-faced Military Policemen.

And then there were the signs: "Maintenance," "Paymaster," "Personnel," and so forth, each accompanied by smaller signs listing various departments subdivided into listings of individual personnel. The grand pater of them all was a monstrous thing two meters square set by the gate that announced Rosewood Court had been rechristened:

UNITED STATES ARMY GENERAL HEADQUARTERS

ADMINISTRATION ANNEX

(Air Corps Inclusive)

London

Harry, still plucking at the coffee stain on his trousers, stood on the veranda of a row house branded "Judge Advocate General———Building B." (Building A was, with the peculiar logic of the American military, located clear across the Court.) Pulled up before the steps was a Chevrolet saloon decked in U.S. Army olive drab with Colonel Joseph P. Ryan sitting in the open rear door pinwheeling one hand to wave Harry on. "C'mon, Harry-boy!" Ryan bellowed. "Move that fat ass!"

Harry jounced down the steps, a sight that provoked a horselaugh from Joe Ryan. Harry hurried to slide in beside Ryan before the young buck sergeant at the wheel could go through the door-holding rigmarole that embarrassed Harry so.

Ryan momentarily put on a serious face to salute the MP's as the car sped out the gate, then immediately switched to a smirk focused at the blot on Harry's trousers. "Accident, Harry-boy? That's the first thing that goes at your age, bucko; the kidneys." He said it with a hideous Irish brogue he reserved for such sporting occasions.

"My age?" Harry said. "As I recall, you are the one who's older by—"

"I can get you an office closer to the latrine if you'd like, laddie. 'Tis no tribble at all."

"I'll settle for a new clerk. Get Nagel assigned to Goering's staff and you'll shorten the war by six months. At least."

"Oh, at least."

They tilted their heads in salute to each other's wit and shared a chuckle.

"Now," Harry said, "do you mind cutting the blarney and telling me what's going on?"

"Oooh, look at those eyes flash!" Ryan's mock gravity played as badly as his brogue. "Such an evil, suspicious mind! Evil! Perfect ingredients for a good lawyer."

Harry leaned back, folded his hands neatly in his lap, and blandly looked out the window. This was his way of telling Ryan he'd wait as long as he had to for whatever Ryan had to say.

The saloon wove slowly through Home Defence roadblocks. Old men in white helmets and HD armbands were directing traffic. The saloon's tires hissed through water streaming from a broken main. Harry saw where a stick of the previous night's bombs had crashed among a row of flats. One explosion had blown a round walk-to-roof hole like a Chinese door in the facades.

Ryan craned across him for a better look. "Hear that one last night?" he asked boyishly. "I thought only sex made the earth move like that!" His tanned face puckered up in an appreciative whistle.

Now, Harry saw rubble behind the exploded facade: bricks, broken furniture, painted fragments of wall. A piece of cloth—a sheet, or maybe a woman's dress—hung high on a point of jagged timber. A squad of men followed an eagerly sniffing collie about the heaped debris until the dog stopped and began pawing at the toppled bricks, then the men went to work with picks and shovels. An ambulance crew emerged from the wreckage of a basement carrying a shrouded stretcher. A slim, gray arm dangled from under the stretcher blanket. Harry looked away.

Ryan nodded at the stretcher bearers. "How'd you like that job?"

"I assumed you asked me along for this little jaunt because there's some business you want to discuss?"

Ryan immediately switched into a businesslike demeanor. "This rape thing; that the heaviest thing you have on the boards? How's the rape shape?"

"I told you: statutory."

"How statutory?"

"Completely."

Ryan permitted himself a thoroughly unbusinesslike smile. "Boys will be boys."

"Well, this time it looks like girls will be girls, too."

Ryan laughed. "I hope these kids of ours liberate Europe with the same energy they're liberating the chastity of the locals. You won't have trouble passing this off to someone?"

Harry fidgeted in his seat. "I'd prefer to keep—"

"Don't want to lose that one, huh, Harry-boy? Be a nice big deal, hm? Look good on the old curriculum vitae, hm?"

Harry fidgeted some more and Ryan chuckled. "—get your name in the Newark Evening News, everybody running over to your wife's house going on and on about reading how her husband defended the virtue—"

"Oh, brother."

"—of some poor British maiden who succumbed—succumbed, I say—"

Harry had gone back to staring out the window, ignoring Ryan.

Ryan laughed again. He tugged at Harry's sleeve. "Who's your best friend, Harry?" and flashed his charming, gratingly ingratiating smile.

Having suffered through Colonel Joseph Patrick Ryan and his bonhomie at several press and social functions, I must say the man set my teeth on edge. He was much too assured of his own charm, of his frightful good looks, of his ability to succeed on a polished flair for knowing the right thing to say and the correct gesture to make. The square, handsome face was always nicely tanned, lined as if for the express intent of emphasizing a wide smile incorporating annoyingly even white teeth and sparkling green eyes. He carried a full, coiffed head of red hair ever-so-gently gray-flecked at the temples, and had the trim figure of a Wimbledon senior, which he emphasized with uniforms tailored by a deft Savile Row hand. Watching him stroll along next to the squat, slogging form of Harry Voss only heightened Ryan's physical attributes, and made his habit of finding the most irritating approach to a situation to inflict on Harry seem all the more like a form of bullying. But then he would flash Harry his you-can't-possibly-stay-angry-with-me little-boy smile, pour on a double dosage of Joe Ryan charm, and toss Harry some little plum to turn sour to sweet. Harry would fuss, fume, but always ultimately forgive.

"Who's your best friend, Harry?" Ryan asked again.

"Sometimes I wonder."

"Me, of course!"

"I've got to start making more friends."

Ryan laughed. The teasing went on, interspersed with occasional bits of diligence as he grilled Harry on the disposition of his various cases.

Then, they were out of London and the staff car was crackling to a stop in a graveled car park.

Harry followed Ryan out of the saloon and across the stones. Beyond the scruffy orchard lining the square Harry could see a wind sock bobbing listlessly from a pole.

"Oh-oh."

"It's two hours by car," Ryan said.

"I'm in no rush."

"A sense of adventure was never your strong suit, Harry-boy."

The ad hoc aerodrome on the other side of the trees was nothing more than a redressed cow pasture. At one end of the field, lean-looking cattle grazed in the shade of the flimsy wooden control tower, thoroughly unimpressed by the statuesque blue shadows of London a few miles beyond. At the other end of the field, pallets of fuel drums were heaped under camouflage netting, and there was a scattering of nonmilitary-looking aircraft with military markings.

"Morning, Lieutenant," Ryan greeted the young man coming up from beneath the wind of an olive drab Piper Cub.

"Mornin', sir, sirs. All ready for ya." He was a blond, smiling youth with a gold second lieutenant's bar on his collar and a cap on his head emblazoned with the insignia of the Brooklyn Dodgers. Harry didn't think the young man looked old enough to drive a motor car, let alone an aeroplane.

The young lieutenant held open the cabin door and Ryan climbed into the backseat. Harry stood frozen under the wing, his white-knuckled hand clamped on one of the wing struts. He gave the strut a little tug: The whole aircraft quivered like a box kite.

"Major, sir? I'd really appreciate it if you didn't do that to my airplane, sir."

Harry lifted a leg into the doorway but then his eyes locked on patches along the fuselage that suggested a pattern of bullet holes.

"Krauts," the lieutenant explained blandly. "But that was a while ago. They don't get through so much anymore."

"See, Harry-boy?" Ryan cackled. "Hardly a t'in' to worry your wee head about."

Harry cleared his throat and climbed up, jamming himself in beside Ryan.

The young pilot bounced into the front seat. He pulled on a set of headphones and aviator sunglasses, flipped some switches on the control panel, and the engine coughed, the propeller swung. A moment later the plane was rocking across a field dotted with cow manure.

"You let me know if you start feelin' sick-like, Major," the pilot called back. "I'll bank 'er over so you can heave out the window. You wouldn't want us all sittin' in it."

Ryan gave Harry a grievous, admonishing look. "That's right, Major. You wouldn't want *that*, now, would you?"

Harry was still trying to think of some bitingly witty retort when the plane started to lift. "Ohhh . . ." Harry said, and closed his eyes so he wouldn't see the neat little fields pinwheeling below.

Joe Ryan laughed.

Ryan would later tell Harry they'd only been airborne less than thirty minutes, but Harry would swear a sacred oath that he'd counted at least several lifetimes pass before he felt the Piper Cub on the ground again, bouncing along another pasture as lumpy with cow manure as the one they'd left outside London. The aeroplane drew to a stop near a pair of jeeps with Royal Army insignia, and the pilot killed the engine. The propeller was still windmilling when Harry Voss reached out the door and grabbed hold of a strut the way a drowning man clutches a life preserver. He pulled himself out of the cabin and set his feet gingerly onto the grass as if terrified it would again spin away beneath him.

"Aw, hell," he said, and Ryan chuckled when he saw poor Harry scraping manure off his shoe with a stick.

"C'mon, Harry," Ryan called. "Stop dawdling."

Harry glared at the squadron of cows clustered in the shade of a tree, then followed Ryan toward the jeeps, trying to scrape his sole clean on the pasture grass as he walked.

There were a pair of Tommies lounging in the front seats of one of the jeeps. One eased himself out and gave Ryan a polite if perfunctory salute. "Colonel Ryan, is it?" he asked. He handed Ryan a map. "Just follow where it's marked, sir. And I've got a chit somewheres for you to sign for the jeep."

Harry climbed into the passenger seat of the other jeep. A copy of a *Spy Smasher* cartoon book lay on the floor. Harry held the magazine up. "This belong to anybody?" The two Tommies looked at each other and both pretended ignorance.

"You navigate," Ryan said and tossed the map to Harry as he slid behind the wheel. There was a manic grin on his face. "Hey, Harry-boy, you think that buzz boy in the plane was something?"

"Joe, just take it—"

The gears made painful sounds and Harry was flung back into his seat. He grabbed the map with one hand, his hat with the other, and rued not having a third with which to hold himself in his seat. It seemed like Ryan had the jeep half off the road more often than not, with one set of wheels bobbing over stones, exposed roots, and small bushes, while the other set slid and spun on the gravel track.

"For God's sake, Joe—"

"Is this our turn, Harry?"

Harry let go of the map and grabbed the windscreen to keep from being hurled out of the vehicle. The hinged windscreen flipped up in his hands.

"Hey!" Ryan barked. "What the hell're you doing? Trying to kill us?"

"You crazy—"

They lurched through a hole and Harry let the windscreen crash down on the hood as he grabbed the sides of his seat.

Harry saw little of the surrounding country: a blur of small farms; low, earth-colored barns; scattered livestock. The trees by the roadside became fewer, the fields less cultivated, the lush heather coating the low hills gave way to low, scraggly grass. Harry smelled salt air. He wiped a squashed fly off his face and prayed their itinerary wouldn't include a bobbing boat ride.

Ryan turned onto a short straightaway and violently downshifted to a halt in front of a 4x4 pulled across the road, four Tommies posted round it. It was time for Harry to enjoy Ryan's discomfort; the Brits wouldn't let them pass.

"No admittance, sir," a young lance corporal with a face full of freckles told Ryan. "Sorry. Orders."

Ryan took a calming breath. What was amusing to see happen to others lit a short fuse in himself. "Corporal, you better let me explain. I'm from the U.S. Army's Judge Advocate General's office. In London. From Headquarters. And—"

"Sorry, Colonel, but like I says; whole area's off limits. Orders."

Harry thought he saw the lance corporal suppressing a little grin at the corner of his lips. Belated revenge for the Revolution, no doubt.

"You're not going to let me pass?" Ryan asked.

"Can't, sir. Sorry, sir. You'll just have to turn 'er round—"

"Stop smirking, Harry. Corporal, whose orders are these?"

"Cap'n Ottinger, sir—'e's me officer—'n' some Ya—uh, an American cap'n—"

"Captain, hm? Well, *Corporal*, I'm a *Yank*, too; a Yank *colonel*—"

"Colonel, I'm sorry, but I've got—"

"*Fine!*" Ryan threw the jeep into reverse. "It's a long trip from London to here, Corporal," he called out as he wrestled the jeep through an about-turn, "and it's a long trip back! I'm going to be thinking about you that whole, looong time!"

"Well, I'm a Yank *colonel*," Harry mimicked as Ryan took the jeep down the road. It wasn't often he got to give it back to Ryan, and he was relishing it. "But I got me *orders*, sir," he responded to himself, his Cockney as wretched as Ryan's brogue.

Ryan glanced over his shoulder to the roadblock. "Little bastards are all having a good laugh. Ha ha. You think it's funny, too, Harry?"

"Well—"

The roadblock still in view, Ryan whipped the jeep off the road. He sent it bounding across the empty field, back past the soldiers in the road.

Harry hugged his seat. "Are you *nuts?*"

"What are they doing?" Ryan had to shout over the noise of engine and wind. The gleam in his eyes and dopey grin on his lips made Harry think of opium fiends.

"They're waving at us. They're shouting something. One of them is running after us."

"I hope it's that little snot corporal. Let the little bastard run. Let 'im get heatstroke. Is he laughing, Harry? I'll bet he's not laughing now."

"Neither am I. He's raising his gun!"

"He'd never fire."

Something pinged into a rear fender.

"You were saying?"

"He's just trying to scare us," Ryan said.

Then, Ryan stamped on the brakes so hard he locked the wheels and almost vaulted them both over the hood. Ryan stood up in his seat, shading his eyes to look at something across the field. Another jeep was coming toward them from over the hills ahead.

Harry reached into his back pocket and pulled out his olive drab government-issue handkerchief and waved it limply in the air.

"Never surrender, Harry," Ryan said, sliding back into his seat. "Even to allies."

The jeep pulled up beside Ryan. Its driver was a pink-faced Royal Army captain not much older than the corporal at the roadblock. He was that very proper Royal Army type that the United Kingdom had been breeding since William the Conqueror: a backbone like a steel rod, slicked hair parted with a razor slash, and probably a birthmark that spelled "Sandhurst" somewhere under his knife-edge-creased uniform. "Morning, gentlemen," the captain said blithely. "Bit of trouble at the roadblock, wot? Indulging in some improper procedure here, are we? Eh?"

"Your boys are lousy shots," Ryan told him.

"Oh?" the captain said, nonplussed. "Didn't they miss? I take it you're Colonel Ryan."

"And Major Voss."

"Captain Ottinger." The captain introduced himself with a tilt of his head and a touch of his quirt to the bill of his cap. "Been waiting for you chaps. Sorry about the security. Orders from your people on high, wot? Why don't you follow me in?"

In convoy, the two jeeps bounced along over the knolls behind the coastal cliffs. Beyond them, to the horizon, sat the blue-gray slash of the Channel. A few minutes later they came to a stop.

They saw the garden, then the cottage. Every square meter—from where they had drawn up to the peak of the thatched roof—was pocked and bullet-torn. In the garden, something small and bloody lay under a tarpaulin.

Harry moaned.

"They didn't tell me about this," Ryan said to no one in particular. "I mean . . . not this."

"Captain Bennett!" Ottinger called, climbing out of his jeep. "He's from your H.Q.," he explained to Ryan and Harry.

An Army Air Corps captain pushed aside the bullet-riddled door which hung from one hinge. He stepped out, squinting into the bright light.

Another young lad, as so many were in those days, early twenties, Harry guessed, trying to hide his baby face behind a meager line of fuzz along his upper lip. Bennett looked over at Harry and Ryan, then back to the scarred cottage. He took off his cap and ran a hand over the close-shaved hair lying atop his skull like a shadow.

"Captain Bennett," Ryan said, climbing out of the jeep. "I'm Colonel Ryan and this is Major Voss. Judge Advocate's Bureau, London."

There was no response from Bennett. He seemed mesmerized by the sight of the cottage.

"Captain Bennett!"

"Yessir," he said blankly, finally. "Colonel Ryan . . . yes."

"And this is Major Voss."

Bennett tried to shake off his daze. "Judge Advocate's, you said?"

Ryan nodded.

Bennett let out a long breath. "Christ . . ." He turned to Ottinger. "Captain—you met Captain Ottinger? Of course. Captain, would you stay with the Greshams?"

Ottinger nodded and went inside.

Bennett stood himself up straight and set his cap levelly back on his head. "I'm from 518th Combat Wing Headquarters. General Halverson's staff. How much did they tell you?"

Ryan looked at the cottage and shook his head. "Nobody said anything about another St. Valentine's Massacre. You better take it from scratch, Captain."

Bennett nodded. He beckoned for Ryan and Harry to follow him to the cliff edge. At the rim, they looked down at choppy water. About ten yards from the pebble beach, an aeroplane wallowed in the low surf. Gaping bullet holes were stitched across the sides of the silver fuselage. The engine cowling had peeled away along one side, and the propeller blades were bent back in twisted mustaches. A metal-wound tether had been tied to the plane and ran to the small beach where a squad of Tommies sat checking the line.

"Thunderbolt?" Ryan squinted at the muscular fuselage.

Bennett nodded.

"What happened?"

"According to the witnesses—"

"Somebody lived through that?" Harry asked, nodding back at the cottage.

"Two survivors," Bennett replied. "Early this morning—this is their story—" He seemed eager to distance himself from the report. "—three P-47's are coming in. One's trailing smoke. That one down there."

"And it crashed?"

"Not exactly. The witnesses say . . . Well, they say one of the other planes shot it down."

"Wait a minute," said Ryan. "You mean one of these other planes, one of these other *American* planes—"

"I'm just telling you what they said. Sir." Hating the message, Bennett had come to hate the messengers as well as those looking to corroborate it. "I've sent for a flatbed truck and a crane. I guess you'll want the plane for the inquiry." He led them back toward the cottage. "The old guy is Charles Gresham. It's him and his wife. He's a spotter for the Home Defence."

Harry fumbled a small notepad from his jacket.

"What he *says*," Bennett continued, "is the pilot of the plane that downed the other 47, he saw him—saw Gresham and his wife, that is—and made a strafing run on 'em."

"They're all right?" Harry asked.

"Shook up quite a bit, but they're in one piece."

Harry fingered a bullet hole in one of the stones in the cottage wall as they stepped up to the door. "Says something for good masonry."

Inside, the front room was freckled with daylight through the punctured roof. Dust motes danced in the columns of light. Every step brought the crackle of broken crockery from underfoot. Ottinger was standing by the short, soft form of Mrs. Gresham. She sat in a far corner in the only intact chair, bleached white and shivering despite the woolen Army blanket pulled up to her chin. Charles Gresham was on his stomach near the fireplace. A medical corpsman was probing the old man's back. With each stab of the corpsman's fingers, the old man winced and groaned.

"I thought you said he was OK," Harry whispered to Bennett.

"Threw his back out carrying the body up from the beach."

"Body?"

Bennett led them past a bullet-riddled curtain into the bedroom. The air here tasted damp and salty. The window curtains had been drawn, but in the spill of light from the door Harry saw splotches of mud and water on the floor leading to a figure on the bed. On the wall above the bed, Harry could pick out a cross in the gloom, suspended upside down, another casualty of the handful of rounds that had found their way into the bedroom.

Bennett went to the night table and lit a hurricane lamp. The blankets beneath the dead man on the bed were black with water and half-dried blood. The smoothness of the dead face—even smoother, now, in the pallor of death—bespoke youth, another fresh-faced warrior. The eyes were partially open, making him look bored and unconcerned and, even in the low light of the lamp, Harry could make out dark circles under the dead boy's eyes. The hair and clothes were still damp, the flight coveralls splattered with large, rust-colored stains. Someone had pulled his flight kit clear and it sat, dripping, in a puddle on the floor. Ryan stepped closer to study the body, but Harry remained in the doorway.

Bennett went to the curtained window, lighting a cigarette. "Positive identification: O'Connell, Dennis F., 015392. Blood type, O positive. Catholic. I left his tags on him for Graves Registration. He's . . . was a second lieutenant with the 351st Fighter Group, 518th Wing, out of Donophan Airfield. That's not far from here, maybe an hour's drive."

Harry kept his eyes on his notebook and note-taking so he wouldn't have to look up and see the corpse. "You, um, did you ID the other—"

Bennett nodded and pulled out a notebook of his own. "Major Albert Markham and Captain Jon-Jacob Anderson. Both with the 351st."

"They're being held?"

"In quarters. Whole field's been sealed up."

"You OK? Harry?" It was Ryan. "You don't look so—"

"The heat, the trip out. I'll, um, be outside."

Ryan nodded and Harry stepped back into the front room to a sight that brought him up short. The corpsman had Gresham on his feet in what looked like a choke hold. He pulled the old man's head up and back, almost lifting his feet off the floor, until there was an audible *crack* of vertebrae slipping back into place. The old man sighed with relief.

"Better, sir?" The corpsman set Gresham down on the edge of the raised hearth. "Good. Me dad's the same way." The corpsman was a flame-haired, ruddy-faced man, large and blocky but with careful, supple hands, and older than Harry thought an enlisted man should be, particularly in light of all the youngsters running round with officer's pips on their epaulets. Harry was unaware, at the time, of how rarely young officers lived to be old officers. "Guess 'e's made me an old 'and at it," the corpsman told Gresham. "You just go easy for a bit."

Harry turned to the other side of the cottage, nudging the pile of smashed metal and tubes that had been a wireless with the tip of his shoe. He knelt and picked out the decapitated head of a porcelain sheep. He set it back down in the debris, stood, his knees cracking, and found himself facing the riddled recognition poster on the wall.

Something he half heard from the bedroom brought him out of his musing and he heard Ryan saying, "Yeah, there was something about Donophan buzzing around the quad. Didn't I hear Lord Haw Haw say something about it?"

"Maybe," Bennett told Ryan. "Krauts hit 'em pretty bad about a week ago. Planted a lot of gold stars that night. They didn't need this on top of it." The lamp went out and Bennett led Ryan back into the front room.

Ottinger was bent close over the old woman. "Yes," he nodded to her soft words. "I'll tell them. Not to worry." He made a show for her of going to the open front door. "Here, you men! Have a care there! Out of the garden now! You're tramping it all up!" He turned back to the old woman and smiled comfortingly. "All right, missus?"

Harry noticed Ryan watching him, and only then did it occur to him that the next move was his. Harry walked over to the old man.

"How's your back, Mr. Gresham?"

"Still 'urts a bit."

"We'll see what we can have done for you. Mr. Gresham, I'm Major Voss of the U.S. Army, and this is Colonel Ryan. Can you tell me what happened here?"

"I awready tol' 'im!" the old man said coldly, pointing at Ottinger. " 'N' 'im!" Bennett this time. "I've had me fill o' tellin' it! 'N' if you don't mind me sayin' so, I've 'bout 'ad me fill o' Yanks today as well, thank you!"

Harry looked over at Ryan. Ryan continued to give him a ball's-in-your-court-Harry-boy look.

Harry's knees cracked again as he knelt by the old man. "Mr. Gresham, I know how you must feel right—"

"Do you, now, laddie? Lemme tell you sumpin'. I been spottin' 'ere for more 'n' three years. I serve me country. I'll die for me King if ol' George asks me. But the first time I gets meself shot at, it's from one o' you!" His finger shot out and stopped just short of Harry's chest. "Do you know how that feels?"

"No. You're right, Mr. Gresham, I don't. But the only way these men are going to be punished, the men who did this to you and your wife, is for me to find out everything I can about what happened. That means you telling me this story, and you're probably going to have to tell it a number of times after this. I'll do whatever I can to make it as easy on you as possible, but . . . I don't think either of us really has a choice, do you?"

The old man closed his eyes. " 'S all so bloody confusin'."

"Look, Mr. Gresham—can you get up? I mean your back—"

"I'm awright."

"Why don't you take your wife outside, OK? Get some air. Captain?" Harry gestured to Ottinger, and he and the corpsman escorted the two old people outside.

Harry sat back down at the hearth and massaged his knees.

Ryan propped a haunch on the splintered table, settling his weight tentatively until he was sure it would hold. "Captain?"

"Yes, sir," mumbled Bennett.

"I think we ought to arrange quarters for the Greshams in London, get them away from here as soon as possible. I want them under protective custody. No visitors, no contacts."

"I'll get on that right now."

"And have a doctor give them a once-over. You know, shock, check out the old guy's back, whatever . . ."

Bennett nodded and left.

"You want my opinion?" Harry asked Ryan.

"More than Betty Grable."

"I think any statement either of those two old birds make is just going to be icing on the cake."

"How so?"

"Who does our labwork?"

Ryan shrugged. "We don't really have a precedent for this kind of thing. If we want, I imagine we could probably get Scotland Yard."

"Good. We get a full team to go over this place. The plane out there, too. They do ballistics comparisons on the slugs they dig out of here with the guns of those two flyboys, uh . . ." Harry flipped through his notebook.

"Markham and Anderson," Ryan filled in.

"Yeah, Markham and Anderson. That should cinch it right there. And those planes've got those whatchamacallits—"

"That's a technical term I'm not acquainted with, Harry."

"You know. The, um, those things. Gun cameras."

"Ah."

"There's your case. Or is it my case? Is that why I'm here?"

Harry had assumed it to be a rhetorical question, but when Ryan hesitated, his face squinched in some painful inner conflict, the confidence Harry had felt coming with the clarity of the case began to ebb.

"Tell you what, Harry. See if Ottinger's got a radio for you. You get on the horn and get what you need out here."

The unfinished quality to what Ryan had said prompted Harry to prod, "And then what?"

"And then you come talk to me."

It occurs to me that—disliking the man as I did—I haven't been quite fair to Joe Ryan. One must give even the devil his due.

I imagine Joe Ryan, at that point, sitting uncomfortably atop the high rail of the fence of the empty sheep pen. Musing, he would look over and see his old friend Harry Voss scribbling his notes, making his wireless calls, tending to all the business that required tending, and feel a sadness. You see, for all the terrible jokes and jibes at old Harry's expense, and his compulsive goat-getting and not-so-gentle mockery, Harry was, indeed, Ryan's friend; that was why Ryan had brought Harry to the cottage by the Channel, and that was why Ryan now faced a dilemma.

I don't know what the original message to Ryan was alerting him to the situation at the coast, and there's no record of it to find, but I would imagine that in those excited, incomplete early moments it was as simple as, "One of our pilots has killed another of our pilots." For all his deficiencies of character, Joe Ryan was bright, certainly cunning; he would have had no problem in imagining the clear path to conviction that Harry had outlined in the Gresham cottage. That was precisely why Ryan had fed the case to Harry. He had, in fact, been feeding Harry such plums for quite some time, including the aforementioned rape case; this was surely to be the juiciest plum of all.

But his dilemma . . . Harry was not, by record, a criminal barrister. Mortgages, small contracts, the drafting of wills and loan documents had been more Harry's line of country. This was less a reflection of some lack in Harry's capabilities than a tribute to poor luck and circumstance; both of which Joe Ryan, in true friendship, had tried to remedy through his position in the JAG.

The case of the dead pilot and his assailant(s) should have taken a straightforward path to the bar and conviction and, quite possibly, the gallows, but for one troubling detail. When the attacking Thunderbolt had turned its guns on Charles Gresham, his wife, and their home, the neat scenario Joe Ryan had projected unraveled like bad knitting. He'd put the plum in Harry's hands, let him feel its pliant ripeness, and now he had to consider pulling it away.

When Harry finished with his business, he found Ryan still atop that sheep pen fence. Harry stood below him trying to read the ill ease clearly on his friend's face. Ryan looked up from his musing and forced a pale imitation of his usual good-fellow smile. "Let's take a walk, Harry."

They stood near the cliff's edge, then turned their backs to the wind like a pair of old cows while they hunched together as Ryan lit them each a cigarette. Ryan took a deep draught and let the smoke seep out his nostrils and slightly parted lips. He nodded over at Bennett.

"Look at him," Ryan said. The captain's face was in a sulking pout as he gave coordinating instructions over one of the jeep wireless sets. "You ever handle a malpractice case, Harry? Ever try to get one doctor to testify against another? To guys like that, this is a second skin. I don't expect you to understand that, considering you can hardly fit in your jacket," and here he tapped one of Harry's straining jacket buttons.

Harry sucked in his gut. "There's a problem with how I'm handling this?"

"Nope."

"What goes? We were in the house cooking along just fine, then all of a sudden I get this feeling you don't think I'm up to this."

"You misconstrue, Harry-boy," Ryan said, delighting in the word. "Miscon-strue! That was never my worry, Harry. Never." He looked over at Harry with a sincerity so rare in him as to be unsettling, then stepped to the edge of the cliff, spat, and watched it fall. "You know what I envy about you, Harry?"

"My good looks?"

Ryan chuckled. "Besides that. You look around, you see the ocean, that little house, those trees. That's the extent of Major Voss's vision. Life is *so* simple for you."

"That's about the nicest way I ever heard somebody called stupid."

Ryan smiled and ignored him. "But *Colonel* Ryan, because *he* is a *colonel*, sits up higher and sees more than that. A lot more; the proverbial big picture. And it's not always a very pretty picture."

"Wake me up when you get to the point. I'd hate to miss it."

"OK, Harry. Having failed to reach you with poetry, let's try plain English. A lot of people on both sides of the Atlantic are not real happy to see us here. Some are locals getting a little sick and tired of seeing this island fill up with young, able-bodied GI's overflowing with candy bars, GI pay, and hormones, while their own—that is, the ones still in one piece—are off in Africa, or Burma, or some other godforsaken mudhole. Some of those unhappy locals are down in Whitehall and they're looking at us strutting around, at Ike on the SHAEF throne, and getting the idea—an idea they do *not* like—that yeah, maybe the sun *does* set on the British Empire.

"There's people back home, too, Harry, and they're not all radio crackpots like Father Coughlin. There's people all up and down the DC Mall who say this is just the same old war between kings they've been fighting over here since King Arthur. Our problem is the Japs, these people say. *They're* the ones dropping bombs in our backyard."

Nothing Ryan had said was particularly revelatory to anyone who had spent any time at all in England in those days, including Harry. But Ryan's unusual glumness kept alerting Harry there must be some sort of relevance here. "What's any of that got to do with this?"

"Mr. and Mrs. Charlie Gresham are what that's got to do with this."

"What about them?"

"Maybe you missed it, but they're citizens of the realm. Subjects of The Empire. Servants of the King. They're English, Harry."

Whatever Ryan's point was, Harry was still missing it. "Joe, how many cases do we get every day where some civilian—"

"You get cases where one of our boys knocked up some nice local girl; where he had too much to drink and cleaned some civilian's plow in a pub brawl; he robbed a liquor store, maybe somebody got knifed, somebody got shot. What you *don't* get are cases where *our* combat personnel, in action, turn their combat machinery against their allies. *Civilian* allies.

"There's people over here who are going to use this to say, Look, see what happens when you let the bloody Yanks run the show? And there's going to be people back home who are going to look at it and say, See? That wouldn't've happened if we'd stayed home and minded our own business.

"Now *me*, for my money, if the limeys want the whole war, they can have it; that's jake with me. Then I could go home. But you wear the uniform. Your job is to do what the guy who signs the checks says to do. And *he* wants this partnership to work."

"I don't see how that changes this case."

"It doesn't. It changes the *handling* of this case."

"How so?"

Ryan looked to the cottage. He flicked his cigarette out toward the Channel, but the breeze blew it back and it exploded in a burst of sparks that quickly died in the wet grass. Ryan nodded at Harry to walk with him along the cliffs, away from the cottage.

"It's got to be quick and quiet, and the person—or persons—who did this have to get *nailed*."

"You talking about going into the railroad business, Joe?"

"Look, Harry, the limeys are going to want blood over this and, looking at this mess, I don't have too many qualms about giving it to them. But it's got to be a solid case, *so* solid that nobody on *our* end'll have any doubts that the triggerman is getting his just deserts. Now, the person—or persons—who did this, Harry, they've got to get their shake. It's got to be done by the book, so this thing can close completely and close clean. And it's got to be disposed of ASAP before it can fester. *And*, it's got to be done on the q.t. No press, no outsiders, everything on a need-to-know basis."

"I understand."

"I don't think so, Harry." Ryan stopped and the two friends faced each other. "I have to consider whether to let you run with this or not."

Harry tried to keep his stolid, professional face on, but he was taking it personally and it showed in his voice. "I guess we're back to my first question. Is it a matter of whether or not you think I'm up to this?"

Troubled as Ryan was, he was still Ryan: He smiled at Harry's discomfort. "Harry-boy, it's not a question of what I think. We're talking about
me handing you a capital case when half my staff has more military-law
experience than you. Hell, Harry, I've got *shavetails* with more criminal law
under their belts! Not that you could possibly get anything else under that
belt!" He chuckled and poked at the equator of Harry's midriff. "I give
this mess to you, I'm going to take some flak for it. The other thing—and
this puts the ball in your court—is not whether or not I think you can
handle it, but do you really *want* to handle it?"

Harry began to speak but Ryan raised his hand. "Understand this,
Harry. Stop getting in a sweat about losing this and just listen. The guy that
handles this, he's not going to get his name in the papers back home. This
isn't the kind of thing anybody wants to see in any papers *anywhere*. But,
the guy who takes care of this, does a good job, makes everybody happy
with it . . . he's going to have some big-time friends on both sides of the
ocean. So, when this is all over and we get to go home and that guy goes
back into civilian practice, well, he's going to have some heavyweight en-
dorsements. And me, without lifting a finger, I get my share of back-pats
because I had the wisdom and insight to pick such a capable joe for the
job. But—

"The guy who handles this and screws up, makes people unhappy . . . I
spend the rest of my life as a corporal shoveling snow in Greenland. And
that'll be heaven compared to what they'd do to the poor fart who actually bobbled the ball."

Harry let his cigarette fall and smothered it with the toe of his shoe.
He could hear sheep bleating off somewhere behind the knolls. "It could
go *that* bad?"

"And I'm putting it in a good light."

"Bleah," Harry said.

They returned to the cottage, where Bennett was propped in the front
door staring blankly out toward the Channel. "Where are they now?"
Harry asked.

"Sir? Who?"

"Markham and Anderson."

"I thought I told—"

"Tell me again."

"At their field. Donophan. They're being held in their quarters."

"Then that's where I want them kept. Separately. And incommunicado."

Bennett's head canted judgmentally. "Don't they get a lawyer?"

"They are not under arrest, Captain. They are just being held at the disposal of the Judge Advocate until we get some answers. So, for now, they don't see anybody, they don't talk to anybody, including each other. If and when we determine grounds for an arrest and charge, they'll get their lawyer."

Harry checked that item off the list he'd made in his notebook. "Those gun films of theirs—get them over to the JAG's in London, ASAP, and have them delivered to Colonel Ryan's office. He'll keep them under lock and key. Colonel Ryan'll also find a place for you to deliver the plane. And I want pictures of this place, every inch. Nothing disturbed until the lab crews are finished, and that includes the body in the bedroom. Until then, tell Captain Ottinger to keep this area sealed off. And I'll need the 66-1's on Markham and Anderson and something about what their mission was today. Better get me O'Connell's file, too. Captain, are you going to remember all this?"

Bennett gave a sullen nod and positioned himself at one of the jeep wireless sets.

Harry loosened his tie. The day was getting quite warm. He thought about the cool interior of the cottage, but then remembered the corpse in the back room.

"I've got some chores for you, too, Joe," he said, turning to Ryan. "I want a complete autopsy on O'Connell, and I want a mechanic to go over that Thunderbird. I don't want some snot defense counsel trying to make out it just got tired and fell down."

"Got it, Harry. Faw down. Go boom. Right. And Harry—it's a Thunderbolt."

Harry took a deep breath. "Now, let me talk to this old guy."

Ottinger had taken a chair from the cottage for Mrs. Gresham and settled her in the shade of a tree. The corpsman brought over another blanket from his medical van. Ottinger took the blanket and laid it over her lap. The old woman still shivered.

"Where's the husband?" Harry called.

The corpsman pointed. "Think he's after his sheep."

Harry found the old man over the next rise, pushing the herd back toward the cottage with his crook. Harry took a moment, steeling himself. He'd managed to keep the war at arm's length. Bodies pulled out of collapsed buildings, rescue workers digging through the rubble, they were only occasional sights and then seen only from a distance. The devastated cottage, the angry old man, and his quaking wife had pushed Harry's nose right up against it.

"Mr. Gresham?"

" 'Aven't seen 'at damn dog o' mine, 'ave ya?"

Harry thought back to the bloody thing under the tarpaulin in the garden. "No, Mr. Gresham."

"Always off somewheres 'e is, doin' everythin' but 'is job."

"I thought we could have that talk now."

"Which talk is 'at?"

"About what happened."

"What 'appens to us, now? Me 'n' Molly?"

"You'll be taken care of. We're going to prepare a place for you to stay in London."

Gresham waved his staff at the flock. " 'N' them? What's gonna—"

"It'll all be taken care of, Mr. Gresham."

"Why can't we just stay—"

"We'll need you in London. For the investigation. Besides, we'll be better able to look after you two there."

"You mean protect me?" The old man laughed.

CHAPTER THREE

DEUS VULT

I'M TOLD THAT WHEN THE DONOPHAN Airfield Military Police received their orders to put Markham and Anderson in custody, they found Markham stretched out on the cot in his tent. The major lay there with a cigarette smoldering in his fingers, still wearing his sweat-stained flight coveralls though it'd been nearly five hours since he'd returned from the morning's mission. He seemed—so I was told—as if he'd been waiting all that time for this moment.

Anderson was with the MP's. They'd found him first, in what was left of the Officers Club. Freshly showered and in clean khakis, an uncharacteristically somber Anderson was treating himself to a solitary lunch of a sandwich and a pint as he potted about the scarred club snooker table. A near miss during the German raid a week earlier had left the Officers Club missing two walls, leaving it more a lean-to than a cozy clapboard cubby, and had cost the snooker table a leg, since replaced with a pile of wobbling bricks.

When the lieutenant heading up the detachment of MP's broke the news to Anderson, the latter—one of those undersized, volatile sorts oft described as "scrappy"—exploded. Anderson declared the situation "a pile o' crap from those brass asses in London!" then apologized for taking it out on the lieutenant who he realized was simply carrying out an order. "Let's go see what the Boss has to say," he declared, and he led them across the field to Major Markham's tent.

The flustered lieutenant stood in the open flap of Markham's tent, unsure how to begin. Markham swung his feet to the ground, and gave him a smile described to me as "forgiving."

"I know, Sandy," he said.

Anderson instantly began fulminating once again about the situation, but Markham tiredly raised a hand. "J.J., please; you're giving me a headache." That was all it took from Markham to silence the steaming Anderson. Markham stubbed his cigarette out on the frame of his cot as the lieutenant fumbled his way through the announcement that the major was to consider himself in custody and so on and so forth. Markham nodded along, as if agreeing to the particulars of a marketing list. When the lieutenant was finished, Markham was holding out his sidearm.

"Do it right, Sandy," the major said. "You take this. Be sure you get Captain Anderson's, too."

There being nothing else, the lieutenant saluted.

Markham gave another one of his forgiving smiles. "You don't salute an officer who's under arrest, Sandy."

"They didn't exactly say you were under arrest, Major."

And then, I'm told, Markham's smile turned more amused, though sadly so. He looked at his watch, nodded at a thought he shared with no one, then stretched back out on his cot and closed his eyes.

Harry could see the ruddy-faced corpsman helping Charles Gresham up onto the tailgate step of a Royal Army lorry. A soldier reached down from the back of the lorry and heaved the old man up, then helped him to a seat on the bench by his wife.

"They're not like your Scots sheep," Gresham called down to the corpsman. "They're randy, they'll bite each other's legs."

"I know me sheep, sir." The corpsman smiled up at him and tossed up to the Royal Army chaperone a cardboard suitcase full of necessaries he'd packed for the couple. "I'll see to 'em."

" 'N' no rich meats for the dog!"

The corpsman raised the tailgate and latched it shut. "I'll treat 'im like me own Spotty." The corpsman stepped back and waved to the driver. The lorry engine sputtered and caught, gears gnashed.

" 'E's not like your Scots dogs!"

"Understood, sir. 'N' we'll see to the chickens, too. You just look after yerself and the missus."

The old man put his arm around the shoulders of his wife as the lorry lurched. " 'N' keep 'em all outta the garden!"

The corpsman waved until the lorry was out of sight. His ruddy face went cold and he turned to the group of soldiers sitting in the shade of the stone cottage, picking through their ration kits for milk-and-nut. The corpsman pulled a trenching tool from one of the troopers' packs and went round to the front of the cottage. He knelt by the tarp in the garden, tucked it gingerly round the small, bloody body underneath, and scooped it into his arms. He headed for the woods.

Ryan and Ottinger had a map spread out on the hood of one of the jeeps. They were doing a lot of officious pointing and proclaiming.

"The kind of cordon sanitaire you're calling for is out of the question!" Ottinger protested. "These men here are all I have, along with the men at the roadblocks! That's not even enough for an effective traveling cordon if—"

"You could request—"

"Colonel, to be perfectly candid, my people simply won't spare that kind of manpower. They don't *have* it to spare."

Harry was seated on a mossy rock amid the deep, waving grasses some distance from the cottage. Looking through his half-moon glasses at the cartridge casing he was rolling between his fingers, he upended the casing and read the engraving on the base for the third time. There were dozens of them lying scattered round his rock and across the hundred yards between him and the cottage, twinkling between the blades of grass under the late morning sun. Harry rose, dusted off the seat of his trousers, and began walking toward Ottinger and Ryan.

"Might I suggest," the British captain was saying, "there's a Home Defence unit nearby at—"

"No!" Ryan snapped upright. "No civilians! Until the word comes down saying otherwise, *nobody* on the outside is to know *anything* about this! You pass that on to your men, Captain: Clam up!"

"You'll get that confirmed from our command, yes?" Ottinger put just enough emphasis on the "our" to be insulting without being tactless.

Ryan indulged his own insulting, tactful moment: a pause showing respect but no great urgency. "Of course. I'll also talk to my people when I get back to London and see what kind of units they can spare to augment. Maybe," and he smiled here, too disarming to be disarming, "we can take the whole load off your hands."

"Appreciated," Ottinger said flatly.

Ryan looked about for Bennett and found the captain standing by the edge of the chalky cliffs. "Captain Bennett!"

The captain seemed to shake himself awake. He noticed the cigarette smoldering between his fingers and tossed it off the cliff. He walked over to the jeep.

"I was just telling Captain Ottinger here," Ryan said, "and I want you to pass it on to our people, everybody who knows about this so far: Mouths shut. This is a security situation. Any breach is going to bring holy hell down on somebody's head. That especially goes for the personnel out at the airfield where these jokers came from."

Harry had, by now, slid himself into the passenger seat of the jeep. "All of which brings a few things to mind," he said, taking out his notebook to tick over a new list. "One, I want the field MP's at that airfield, the ones guarding Markham and Anderson, I want them pulled and replaced by a crew from the Provost. I don't want their jailers turning out to be their best buddies."

"Pretty trusting, aren't you, Major?" Bennett said dourly.

Harry pointed to the bullet-pocked cottage behind Bennett. "Offhand, I'd say Markham and Anderson had pretty much used up their trust quota for the day, wouldn't you, Captain? OK, Number Two: I also want our MP's guarding the planes that were involved until the ballistics boys get to them. Three: These guys fill out some kind of report or something after a mission, right?"

Bennett nodded. "G-2 conducts a debriefing after every mission. That's SOP."

"OK, when you have those gun films picked up, I want the debriefing reports impounded, too. What was that, Three? OK, this is Four," and, relishing the drama of the moment the way one who gets few such moments does, Harry placed the cartridge casing on the prone windshield, carefully balancing it on its base.

Bennett stared at it for a moment. Then he picked up the casing, turned it over, and read the engraving. His eyebrows came together, and he handed the casing to Ryan.

"U.S. Army ordnance," Harry told them. "You can still smell the powder. They're all over out there, I guess from the plane that made the run on the house. I don't want those shells touched until the photo crews get pictures, then I want a detail to scrounge up as many of them as they can find for Scotland Yard's lab people along with slugs from the house and grounds. Captain, I think you should get started on that MP business ASAP."

Bennett nodded. He shuffled off to the radio on the other jeep.

Ryan gave out a proud-dad smile. "You're really something to watch at work, Harry-boy."

"Flattery will get you everywhere."

"One of us should start coordinating the London end of this thing."

Harry climbed out of the jeep.

"That's what I thought," Ryan said, climbing behind the wheel. "Look, Harry, take as long as you need out here, but try to make it back for the case management meeting. I'll hold it off till 1800 if I have to, which won't make anybody happy, but we've got to talk about redistributing your caseload—"

"And get me some support staff."

Ryan took on a look not unlike the one on Harry's face when he'd stepped off the little Piper Cub into cow manure. "I was hoping to keep the number of mouths around this thing to a minimum."

"I believe you were the one who said this should proceed 'expeditiously.' To do that, I'm going to need help with the legwork."

"Hoisted with my own petard, eh? OK, we'll deal with that at the meeting, then me and you can talk it over at The Old Eagle. You want I should send the plane back for—"

"No! I'll hitch a ride back with the lab teams."

Ryan laughed. "See you in the funny papers!" he said and drove off.

Harry was glad Ryan was gone. Considering his concern for limiting the number of mouths—as well as eyes and ears—privy to the incident at the

Gresham cottage, his old friend would have had a heart attack at the parade that followed. There were the serious-looking men in medical white come for O'Connell's body, and more serious-looking men in dark suits spilling out of a convoy of police Wolseys from Scotland Yard's forensics departments, and then a lorryful of eternally serious MP's, now seriously surly when set prowling about on their knees to dig spent bullets out of the earth.

Overseeing the parade had taken Harry into the afternoon. He was now hungry and thirsty, and too uncomfortable with the idea of approaching Ottinger or his men, who seemed to be the only group with the foresight to have brought along something to eat and drink. The late-day heat began to make him feel gritty, headachy, and a little weak-kneed. He took a moment for himself, sitting in the cool front room of the cottage. On the bullet-riddled table, Harry had placed the jagged pieces of the porcelain sheep, picked out of the splinters and dust on the floor, and now he poked at them with a stubby forefinger, moving them together like pieces of a jigsaw puzzle.

The dark-suited serious men worked soundlessly round him, floating about like shadows, taking photographs, prying bullets out of walls and furniture, dropping them with somber little clunks into metal buckets. " 'Scuse, sir," one of the shadows murmured, and Harry rose and stepped out of the way so the shadow could dig bullets out of the table. He almost backed into two of the white coats carrying a covered stretcher out of the bedroom.

"Need another look 'fore we take him out, sir?" one of the white coats asked. Harry shook his head. He watched the stretcher float out the door and into the bright glare outside. A moment later he heard the ambulance engine stutter off.

Then, Ottinger was in the doorway. "Ready for you at the plane, sir."

Harry followed him outside, careful to skirt the squad of MP's digging bullets out of the dirt and clunking them into their upended white helmets. One picked up a pulped squash and held it out to one of his mates.

"Hey, Coop, imagine if that'd been your noggin!"

"Be an improvement!" another said, and they all laughed.

There was a long, flatbed U.S. Army lorry parked near the cliffs. Next to it an Army crane chattered and clanked as it swung its arm out over the chalk rim. Conducting the operation was a bare-chested Army engineer, his arms going this way and that like a rabid Stokowski. The engineer had tied his olive drab handkerchief round his head and a set of technical sergeant stripes were pinned to it over his forehead like an extra set of eyebrows.

"Swing it this way!" the sergeant screamed at the crane. "Right, stupidass, right! No, stupidass, my right, my right! OK, there! Drop it!"

Harry followed the cable from the arm of the crane down to the small beach. The squad of engineers and some of Ottinger's men had pulled the plane almost to shore and gotten a lift girdle round it. One man stood on a wing, attaching the crane hook to the girdle. The others stood on the shore, holding lines attached to the aeroplane's wings they would use to keep the craft from swinging into the cliff face. The cable attached, the man on the wing waved to the sergeant and jumped clear.

The sergeant turned to bellow toward the cottage. "Hey, Major—Oh! There you are! We wuz just waitin' for you, Major. You said you wanted to be—"

Harry cut him off with an impatient nod.

The sergeant, with the intolerance of one absolutely sure he's the only one who knows what he's about, issued a haughty sniff, then turned back to the work at hand. "Awright, you goofballs; up!"

"Go easy," Harry cautioned.

"Hey, Major, I don't tell you how to do whatever it is you do, right? Trust me. Nice 'n' easy for the major, Jimbo!"

The crane motor revved and the exhaust streamed blue smoke as the cable went taut. The plane started to rise, sucking clear of the surf, streams of seawater draining from its wounds.

"*Away* from the cliff, you stupidass! *Away!*"

The crane groaned against the weight and the rear ends of its treads began to peel from the ground. The aeroplane began to swing; Harry closed his eyes. He heard the sergeant curse the men below, the men curse back, and the crane operator curse them all. Then, there was only the growl of the crane's gears and Harry felt a cooling shadow pass over his face. He opened his eyes. He saw the Thunderbolt pendulating above them, spraying water on him and the sergeant.

From the cliff top, wallowing in the low waves, the aeroplane hadn't looked like much, just another piece of flotsam washed in to shore like a twisted piece of driftwood. But now, watching it sway above him, the

Thunderbolt's great bulk and massive engine, visible through the peeled-away cowling, seemed incredibly oversized for the purpose of sending one puny human being into the air.

The engineer sergeant picked absently at the mat of hair on his chest with one hand while he guided the crane operator with the other. The plane swung over the flatbed. The sergeant noted the anguished look on Harry's face and hand-signaled some "Don't worry" braggadocio, hardly justified by the way the Thunderbolt came down so hard that Harry was certain the spine of the lorry would snap.

"Sorry!" Jimbo called from the operator's cab.

"I want to get a look inside," Harry said.

"Better wait'll we get 'er secured, Major," the sergeant advised. "She looks a little rocky up there."

"I want pictures," Harry said. He was standing by one of the wings, looking up at a cluster of bullet holes near the cockpit.

"I seen some o' them suits with cameras over by the house," the sergeant told him. "Should I—"

"Yeah, yeah, I want the whole thing covered. Inside and out."

"Yeah, we wanna get a shot, too."

Harry turned and looked down at the hairy sergeant. "What shot?"

"Ah, we always take one with a job, a little group shot. You know, the boys and me standin' 'round the—"

"Those photographers are here strictly on JAG business!"

"I know that," the sergeant said with his haughty little sniff. "We got our own camera. Hey, Jimbo!" and Jimbo climbed out of the cab proudly holding up a little Brownie box.

"What the hell kind of security—"

"Hey, Major, it's not like we're gonna run it in Stars and Stripes. We know the drill; this is all strictly on the q.t., right? This'll just be for us."

"No pictures!" Ignoring the sergeant's hurt look, Harry held on to the overhanging wing to steady himself. The engineer's idea of security had joined with his own hunger and thirst to send his head spinning again.

Men were pushing Harry out of the way now, as they started strapping the plane to the loading bed. The engineer sergeant boosted Harry up onto the loading bed. Harry stepped up on the wing and the metal boomed hollowly underfoot as the plane tottered. He stepped up to the cockpit and stuck his head in past the remaining shards of Plexiglas. Dials

stared back at him from what was left of the control panel. The violence
of the moment of impact was still there, frozen in time, the punctures in
the side of the cockpit and control panel trailing rigid tendrils of metal
suspended in space. Up on the other wing, the sergeant whistled appreciatively and drew Harry's attention to the back of the pilot's seat. It had
been pierced four times, clear through the seat armor. A few traces of
blood were splattered on the canopy, but anything more had been washed
away by the sea.

The cab left Harry at the Annex gate a few minutes before six. Joe Ryan
intercepted him on a staircase as he hurried to the conference room at
the top floor of JAG Building A.

"Where the hell've you been? What's with this chit for a cab? This is
like a chit from Magellan! You take this cab around the Horn? You couldn't
take one of their jeeps back? Where the hell've you *been*? I haven't heard
from you since this morning!"

Ryan was a believer in the philosophy that one never allows one's juniors to see their leader flustered. Without waiting for Harry's response,
he took a moment to straighten his uniform as well as his usual grinning composure and then, with a whispered, "We'll talk about it later,"
entered through the double mahogany doors of the conference room
with Harry in tow.

The room had once been a comfortable den, now made cramped by
the conference table occupying most of the floor space. The civilian tenants had cleared the shelving of their treasured tomes, but those same
shelves now made a suitable home for the JAG's law volumes, giving the
room double duty as a research library. The weekly case management
meetings held here were intended to keep Ryan apprised of the status of
the London JAG's various cases, but it usually became an opportunity for
his juniors to try to impress him—and each other—over a buffet of coffee and doughnuts.

Ryan took his seat at the head of the table with Harry on his right.
Around the table were the other JAG barristers: another major, three
captains, and two lieutenants, all young, all feeling they deserved better
than to absorb Harry's caseload for the unspoken but obvious reason of
clearing his way for a major case, all hungry for—and feeling worthier

of—that same case. Joe Ryan listened to their complaints, nodded with grave understanding and deep concern, then responded that he was a colonel and they were not; end of debate. Any queries from "outside" about the case reassignments were to be referred directly to him. There would be no idle speculation or conference outside the room on the matter. Period.

Not long after, Harry and Ryan were parked in their usual corner booth of The Old Eagle, a dowdy pub not far from the Annex, at the end of an ignored cul-de-sac lined with similarly dowdy shops that sold old bottles, chipped dishware, and other assorted bric-a-brac. It was that ignored and forgotten air of The Old Eagle that appealed to Harry and Ryan, as it provided a welcome relief from the constant sight of American uniforms, which filled the city in those days.

Harry and Joe Ryan routinely huddled at The Old Eagle, lost among the few old duffers mumbling cricket scores to each other. Harry would nurse a toby of ale while Ryan worked his way through a pitcher, and they ate shepherd's pie and small sandwiches which, for all the culinary deficiencies of the barman/cook/waiter/clean-up man—and English cuisine in general—was still a change from the Annex canteen. Sometimes they would sit and not talk at all, because sometimes that's all old friends need to do.

And it was an old, dear friendship, for all the jibes and teasing. You could hear it in the reflective pause before every "Joe Ryan" part of the story Harry told me.

It went back to boyhood. Harry, son of Russian immigrants unhappy with the czar, and Joe Ryan, son of Dubliners equally unhappy over Victoria's handling of the Irish Question, found each other as fellow outsiders in a Newark, New Jersey slum dominated by Italian immigrants. I surmise it was a chumship founded on complementary parts—the convivial, glad-handing, easily athletic Ryan who glided through his forms with a minimum of effort, and Harry, the plumpish, well-meaning tagalong swot.

I never found what drew them each to the law, but it made sense to me that Ryan would opt for a military practice, providing him with security and prestige without the difficulties of attaining both in private practice. In Ryan, one sensed a man who always opted for the path of least resistance.

Harry the plow horse, on the other hand, set up his little office, asked his wife, Cynthia, to come in on occasion to play secretary and make a good impression on new clients, and worked long hours un-complainingly, assuming that these were the rough early years that would eventually pass. But then came '29 and the Crash, and the rough years were there to stay.

Then there came the war. By then Harry no longer had only himself and his wife to consider, but two young boys. The service, as illustrated by his friend Joe Ryan, could provide his family a comfort—and a security—his little practice couldn't.

One of those evenings in The Old Eagle, with too much ale in him, Ryan had confessed: "I knew you'd be along, then, after Pearl Harbor. I knew you'd be the first one down at the enlistment center once they pushed the age limit up to forty-five. You know, Cynthia came to me when you went to sign up. You know why, Harry? 'Cause no matter what the age limit was, no matter how badly the Army needed bod-ies, you weren't going to be able to get in without someone pulling a few strings."

Harry didn't have to tell me how much he must have reddened on hearing that. "I didn't ask her to talk to you."

Ryan would have given out an irritating chortle when he said, "Harry, she came to ask me to keep you out!" But Ryan, so Ryan said, was Harry's friend. He would have held Cynthia by her shoulders and said, open-faced and sincerely, "I'll do what I can," then turned round and done what his friend needed without being asked: Pull the strings he could pull and put a word where a word was needed. Then he would have turned back to Cynthia, again with great sincerity, and said, "I did what I could."

What gnawed at Harry after that confession of Ryan's was not that he'd helped without being asked, but knowing that with an entire world at war, Harry Voss still could not have passed military muster without a kind word spoken in high places.

So, they came to sit together, Harry and Joe Ryan, in corner booths in far-off places to talk the way they would have talked at home, in this way bringing a little of home across the sea to themselves and, for a brief while, being just that less lonely for it. The ale gone, they would walk slowly and, in Ryan's case, perhaps with a slight waver and an arm draped round Harry's shoulder, as they headed back to the Annex.

There was a narrow building pinched into a perpetually shadowed corner of the Court, not a home as most of the other Rosewood buildings had been, but apartments for short city visits by landed gentry. The apartments lent themselves more easily to individual quarters than the town houses, so the American QM had descended on the building and duly carved it up into an officers' billet.

Harry and Ryan had rooms on the top floor, two of the better apartments whose comforts were somewhat offset by the four flights of stairs it took to reach them, an even harder climb when dragging along a friend sodden with a pitcher of warm ale. Harry put Ryan to bed in his quarters at the front of the building, a room with a delightful view down the tree-shaded lane that fronted the Court. After that, he retired to his room at the rear with, as one would expect of poor old Harry, a less than stellar view of the vehicle parking area in the yard below.

In the early months of their London posting, Ryan and Harry had done the expected, hurrying here and there to see the sights, clicking off photos of one or the other smiling dumbly while standing in front of postcard icons like Buckingham, Parliament, the Tower of London, Westminster, et cetera, each under their respective umbrellas of barrage balloons. The photos went home to Cynthia and the boys, usually with Ryan having scrawled something clever across the back. But Harry soon grew self-conscious over these jaunts, guilty over acting as if he were on holiday while the world was blowing itself apart, and every letter from Cynthia told of some new item gone from store shelves, and each photograph showed her growing rounder with the carbohydrate-rich wartime diet.

The atmosphere of the Officers' Quarters at Rosewood Court did little to break a mood of homesick reflection. Dark and gloomy, even during the height of the day, having only narrow windows front and rear, the exotic woods of the carved ceilings, paneling, and staircases seemed to soak up what little light seeped into that corner of the Court. Nights were worse. Sealed inside blackout curtains, air quickly grew stale and warm, and the electric lights gave off a feeble and flickering glow as electricity was drawn off for higher priorities. A murk rose from the corners like a tide. With it came whispering sounds that might be quiet conversation behind closed doors, a low-tuned wireless, maybe—as Maintenance alleged—mice, or—according to a slightly woozy Ryan—the ghosts of generations of Rosewoodarians gone by.

With a last look out at the dark buildings of the Court, Harry drew his blackout curtains, disregarded cautions about conserving electricity, and turned on every one of his few lights. He fiddled with the knobs of the regal cathedral wireless on his dresser. "Bwono Sayrah," came the voice of "Colonel Stevens," one of the BBC's beacons to the conquered countries to the east. In Italian maimed by a House of Lords accent, Stevens gave the Italians the Allies' adulterated version of the supposedly unadulterated news. What Stevens said and how well he said it was irrelevant to Harry. He just needed a human voice to cover the sourceless murmurings and scratchings out in the corridor.

Harry stripped to his undergarments, pulled back the hand-stitched duvet on his four-poster, and lay on his bed with a copy of The Dain Curse propped in front of him. He read until the letters danced, then turned out the lights and opened the curtains. He lay back down to sleep, left the wireless on, now softly playing music. Soon, he was asleep.

Peter Ricks found his way quite easily to the motor pool garage by following the sound of whoops and hollers. The garage was a long, low shed just a block from the Annex, shadowy despite the tall windows that admitted the bright summer morning. Ricks walked past lend-leased Royal Army trucks and jeeps parked in neat rows on the oil-stained concrete. The smell of gas and grease gave way to one of sweat.

Ricks took a moment to let his eyes adjust to the gloom of the garage before advancing toward an ad hoc gymnasium that had been flung together at the far end of the shed. Someone had nicked some Indian clubs from somewhere, and barbells had been improvised out of pipes and wheel rims. A few sea bags filled with sand hung from the rafters and served as punching bags. A corner of the garage had been roped off and the floor covered with sheets of canvas. The echoing shouts Ricks heard were coming from a crowd of cheering British junior officers crowded along the perimeter of this makeshift ring, the object of their attentions being an enormous fellow with the bulk and coloring of a side of raw beef.

His opponent had skeletal limbs and an ashen pallor that would have looked quite natural on a coroner's slab. The only fleshy part of his body was a roll of beer fat that sat on his hips like a life preserver. But as obviously outgunned as Armando Grassi was, the little man did not back off from his towering assailant. He would wait for the beefy man to swing and—providing the big man missed, which was not always the case—Grassi would use that opening to close and deliver a flurry of blows. Unfortunately, Grassi's small hands, lost in their gloves, did nothing but irritate the big man much like an annoying gnat in need of squashing.

"Armando has this wild, curly hair, jet-black, and it was shooting up in all directions," Ricks told me when he remembered that meeting. "He looked positively rabid. You didn't have to know much about boxing to know Armando didn't know what the hell he was doing. You just had to look at his face." By the time Ricks appeared after just three rounds, Grassi was sporting a massive welt across one cheek, a split lip, and an impressively blackening eye.

Ricks seemed to be the only man in the garage disturbed at Grassi's condition. Even the one other American in the garage—a young PFC Ricks recognized from the orderly room acting as Grassi's cornerman—seemed to be rooting for the big Englishman.

The PFC began to snap to attention at the sight of Ricks; Ricks waved at him to relax. There had been too little time between Stanford Law School and his Army captaincy for Ricks to adjust to the weight of the captain's bars on his shoulders.

"How's he doing?" Ricks asked the PFC.

The PFC was setting out iodine and great wads of cotton. "Primo Carnera he ain't, sir."

One of the British officers had an eye on his watch. He signaled the end of the round by clanging a wrench against a wheel rim.

Grassi shuffled back to his corner. He spotted Ricks and smiled through a bloodstained mouthpiece. "Mornin'," he grunted, holding out one of his gloves for a welcoming handshake. "Ca'n Rick', i'n' it?"

"What do you think you're doing?" Ricks asked.

Grassi dropped heavily onto the stool the PFC had set down in his ring corner. "Wha' i' loo' li'?"

"Suicide," the PFC supplied. He caught the mouthpiece as Grassi spat it out, then started dabbing stinging iodine at Grassi's wounds while Grassi rinsed his mouth from a water bottle. The water he spat out had a pinkish hue.

Grassi wiped at the sweat on his forehead with a gloved hand. "I'm trying to prove Might doesn't make Right."

Ricks looked over at the other boxer. The big Englishman and his cornerman seemed to be doing quite a bit of laughing. "You're not presenting a very good case."

"Oh, wait'll you get a load of my summation."

Ricks started to point to his watch and say something urgent; the timekeeper clanged his wheel rim again.

"Excuse me, Cap'n, this shouldn't take long," Grassi said with groundless optimism. The PFC slipped Grassi's mouthpiece back into place and scrambled out of the ring, pulling the stool after him. Grassi, grunting ferociously through his mouthpiece, charged the big boxer.

The bout lasted a single punch more, delivered quite tellingly by the Englishman. "Poor Armando," Ricks told me later in earnest sympathy. "He saw so many stars they must've been forming constellations."

At a glance, the wide, blocky figure of Peter Ricks would seem more at home in the ring than that of his junior colleague. The square face looked capable of withstanding a blow from a mallet, let alone a fist. But to talk to him even for a few minutes would leave one wondering if, in fact, he wouldn't've been carried out of the ring in even worse shape. Soft-spoken, reflective, unfailingly polite, from a proper, well-to-do, unfailingly polite San Franciscan family of lawyers, Ricks seemed too courteous to punch, and too trusting to defend, never believing someone could be so mean-spirited or so pointlessly brutal as to want to beat him bloody.

Armando Grassi was not soft-spoken, reflective, or polite, nor was he from a family of distinguished lawyers. His upbringing in the woollier parts of the Chicago slums had left him tough enough to climb out of the streets and put himself through law school. It had also left him daring, quick, a trifle tactless, and with a taste for the jugular that even the proprieties of law school never tempered. Perhaps it was the inequities he'd seen between the world of tenements and those who owned them that had ingrained in Grassi a nearly psychopathic compulsion to take the role of David against any Goliath he could find—or imagine he'd found. Or—another perhaps—being saddled with a name like "Armando" had gotten him into enough scrapes to develop a combative attitude. The trait had gotten him into kickabouts with senior officers over junior officer housing, treatment of the mess boys, military court procedure, and a host of other causes. And he was not above taking his crusading stances against America's allies with equal abrasiveness, assailing British military personnel with beer-fueled critiques over the moral bankruptcy of the monarchy and The Empire, aristocratic effetism, English social castes, and the like. These debates frequently resulted in an escalation of tempers, a rashly thrown punch here and there, and—as on this occasion—a duel or two.

Following Grassi's disastrous defense of his principles in the motor pool gym, his cornerman helped him back to his room in the junior officers' BOQ. Ricks followed after detouring by the canteen for a basin of ice. While Grassi sat on the cold tile floor of the shower room letting the fitfully hot spray wash away blood and massage bruises, Ricks waited in Grassi's room, wrapping ice in a towel.

Ricks stayed to the side of the room belonging to Grassi's absent bunkmate, where everything was squared away as stipulated in the Army manual. Grassi's side looked as if a grenade had gone off inside a bin of dirty laundry. His desk was hidden under a pile of files and papers. His locker top clattered with an outrageous collection of scents, lotions, and toilet waters, most of them uncapped, their aromas mixing in a noxious perfume. Over the unmade bunk was a mural of girlie photographs from the obligatory Betty Grable to a surprising Penny Singleton. All looked down at the debris on Grassi's half of the room with delighted smiles.

Ricks shook his head over the sight and kicked a toeless sock. He heard the shower spray die and the slap of Grassi's wet feet coming down the hall. Grassi appeared in the doorway. He had not bothered to wrap a bath towel round himself. His eyes, both the swollen and unswollen one, were half closed. He lowered himself gingerly onto the dirty clothes littering his bunk.

"Does anyone ever inspect this place?" Ricks asked.

"I think someone came down last week. He's probably still in here somewhere. If you see him, let me know."

Ricks did not want to cross into the infected areas of the room, so he tossed his impromptu ice bag over and it bounced once on Grassi's belly before coming to rest. Grassi slid the towel up to the bruises on his face.

"Thanks," Grassi said. "Now, Cap'n, was there something I could do for you? Or are you just a fight fan?"

"I was on my way over to Major Voss's office. It was my impression that we were both supposed to go over there this morning. On assignment." Ricks looked at his watch and his face became pained. "We were supposed to be in the major's office six minutes ago."

"I guess we're late for that, Cap'n. Why don't you go on ahead—"

"Would you just hurry, Lieutenant? Please?"

"Is that an order? Sir?"

Exercising his rank ran so counter to Ricks's genteel upbringing that his response was merely to redden and shuffle his feet.

Grassi was in a merciful mood. He pulled himself painfully off his cot. "Since you asked nice . . ." He opened his locker, drew his bony white body up to its full, stunted height, and regarded it admiringly in the full-length mirror mounted inside the door. He wiggled his hips, swaying his genitalia round, then grinned and jerked a thumb at the beaming pin-ups on the wall. "Now you know what keeps 'em smiling!"

The red-faced Ricks was already halfway out the door. "I'll wait upstairs."

Grassi laughed.

Poor old Harry swung the door of his outer office open that morning to find that, once again, Corporal Nagel had defied Harry's prayers and presented himself for duty. This particular morning, young Nagel, screwdriver in hand, was brazenly stabbing at the bowels of his intercom through its exposed back.

Nagel, intent on the operation, was oblivious to the appalled look on Harry's face. "You're late," Nagel announced.

"Yes, Nagel, I'm late, thank you. Mind if I ask what you're doing?"

"Busted, sir. I'm fixing it."

Like Canute stopped the tide, Harry thought. "Colonel Ryan was supposed to send some staff over to me today. I don't see them."

"Nobody's showed up here, sir. Except me. They must be late, too."

It was a typically Nagelesque belaboring of the obvious and it sent Harry to his office shaking his head. "Get me Colonel Ryan on the phone."

"Yessir," Nagel said and went back to stabbing at the entrails of the intercom box.

"Now would be a good time, Nagel."

Harry found six manila folders on his desk with an accompanying note from Captain Bennett, and a pair of phone messages covered with Nagel's squiggly handwriting taped to his chair.

"Nagel!"

"Oh, sir, a messenger came by yesterday with those files from—"

"What the hell are these messages?"

"Phone messages."

"I don't read Sanskrit, Nagel."

"Sir?"

"I can't make these out!"

"One's from Colonel Ryan."

"Colonel Ryan? When did he call?"

"This morning, just after I got—"

"What's this other one? Something Bill? From S-2? G-2?" Harry turned the paper on its side and squinted. "E-2?"

"Captain Dell. From G-2. He called this morning, too."

"You're supposed to put the date and time—Forget it. Did this Captain Dell say what he wanted?"

"No, sir, just that he'd call back."

Harry started to unbutton his jacket, then stopped and listened. He could hear Nagel still poking around in the intercom. "I'm ready for that call to Colonel Ryan now, Corporal, as in now!"

He had just finished his morning ritual of sleeve-rolling and tie-loosening when he picked up the phone to talk to Joe Ryan.

"Harry?"

"Hold on a second, Joe. Nagel! Are you still playing with that thing?"

Harry heard the screwdriver drop.

"Go get Maintenance to fix it, Nagel. Don't use the phone. Go get them! Now!" When Harry heard the outer door close, he turned back to the phone. "Sorry, Joe. G'ahead."

"Ricks and Grassi there yet?"

At Grassi's name, Harry winced. "Grassi?"

"Sorry, Harry, but everybody's already screaming about taking on your caseload. How do I tell them that, on top of that they get stuck with Grassi? I don't want to risk somebody getting mad enough to take a squawk over my head. Not on this case."

"Grassi, Joe?"

"Look, I'm no fan of his either. In fact, I think the little pain is a Red. If I could find a way to sideline him that didn't draw more attention than it threw off, I'd do it. But listen to me, Harry: You make sure Grassi keeps that yap of his shut. You make sure!"

Ryan was being more than routinely emphatic and they knew each other too well for Harry not to see it as a sign. "Something's happened."

Ryan groaned. "Some newshound's been snooping around up at Wing."

"You're sure?"

"No, I'm not sure. I just know some guy flashing a press pass has been fishing around. The CID boys are checking him out now."

"Did he know anything?"

"He obviously knows something. If he does, what I don't want is him finding out any more than he already knows. And that won't exactly take too much effort on his part. It's all over Wing."

"I like your idea of keeping a secret."

"Don't you start. I've been getting it from Halverson since sunup. What does he want from me? Between Ottinger's crew, those mopes out at Donophan, the MP's, Scotland Yard, Halverson's own staff . . ." Ryan sighed. "Christmas, I'm surprised the story's not on the front page of every rag on Fleet Street by now!"

"It's still early in the day."

"That's not funny, Harry."

"If this gets out and we get caught trying to hold a lid on it, we're going to look pretty—"

"I know, I know. I'm supposed to go over to the PRO's and help draft some kind of statement we can shovel to the press, something for 'em to chew on for a bit. Halverson's going to contact Whitehall and see if we can't get them to go to this bozo's editor and whisper 'national security' and 'official secrets' in his ear. And, speaking of cross-cultural diplomacy, I want you to go to dinner with me tonight."

"That doesn't sound so diplomatic. It doesn't even sound romantic."

"I'm supposed to 'entertain' some Lord and Lady Whosis. That's at the request of the people up top which makes it more than a request. I'll be damned if I'm spending the night with a pair of rigor mortises by myself."

"Sorry, sorry, sorry," Harry said. "Busy, busy—"

"Harry-boy," and there was that annoying brogue, "did this *colonel* give the *major* the impression he was *asking?*"

Now it was Harry's turn to sigh. "What time?"

"I'll pick you up at 1700. Try to look nice. No embarrassing stains. Next topic: You get what you asked for from Bennett?"

Harry fingered the captain's note:

Major Voss—
H/w 66-1's on all concerned incl. 2 KIA's and mission profile.
—Bennett

Harry wondered who the additional KIA's were.

"I've got those files. I'll go over them, then brief Ricks and Grassi before I go to G-2. I need to talk to somebody over there about their debriefing statements, see what else they can tell me about these three guys and their mission. What about those gun films?"

"Anderson's is in my safe. I never got Markham's."

Harry's fingers moved to the phone message from the mysterious Captain Dell at G-2. "I'll find out about that."

They rang off and Harry started to thumb through the six files. In addition to the mission profile, there was one for Markham, one for Anderson, another for O'Connell, and then two more presumably for the Killed In Actions: two lieutenants named Jacobs and McLagen.

According to the mission profile, these five pilots from the 351st Fighter Group had mounted a raid against a fuel depot somewhere in Belgium the previous morning. The attack force had consisted of two sections: Anderson and O'Connell comprised the section code-named Angel Blue, and Markham led the two KIA's in Angel Red.

There was a knock at the outside door, followed by the entrance of a crisp-looking Ricks and a battered-but-unbowed Grassi. Setting the files aside, Harry leaned back in his chair, clasped his hands over the bulge of his belly, and glowered at them over the tops of his glasses. "You gentlemen are late."

"Yessir, my fault, sir," Grassi replied. "I overslept, sir, and when Captain Ricks came looking for me, I—"

"You get that shiner oversleeping?"

"Slipped in the shower, sir," Grassi said blithely.

"Uh-huh." Harry nodded. "Do you think you could manage not to slip in the shower while you're assigned to me?"

"Do my best, sir."

They dragged a pair of chairs into the office and made themselves as comfortable as the cramped quarters allowed. Before they could get down to business, however, Nagel clomped back into the outer office.

"Major? Maintenance won't be able to get somebody up here till— Oh! These must be your fellas!"

"Must be, Nagel. Go on down to the canteen and see about some coffee and doughnuts for everybody." Harry felt that was a complex enough assignment to keep Nagel out of the office for a good half hour.

Grassi clucked his tongue after Nagel left. "Regular mastermind you got yourself—" The reprimanding look from Harry silenced him abruptly. "Sorry, sir."

"Lieutenant, you haven't been in this office five minutes and I'm already tired of hearing you say you're sorry. I've got a case, a priority, and I need footmen. Good ones. Grassi, I didn't pick you, but I've got you and I'm not going to have any more problems with you. Am I?"

Grassi smiled innocently. "Why should there be any—"

"Because if I *do* have one, it'll be the *last* one I have. Understand?"

Harry told them as little as they needed to know about the job. Major Markham and Captain Anderson *might* be involved in the death of Lieutenant O'Connell. He said nothing about the attack on the Greshams. He needed Ricks and Grassi to go out to Donophan, talk to any of the men there who knew the men involved, and work up some sort of character profile. It was swot work and Grassi sighed, anticipating the boredom of it all, but Harry lectured on about how personnel files usually only told half the story and so on and so forth.

Harry watched them scribble away on their foolscap pads. Ironically, the notepad of the immaculate Ricks was a mess of hasty scribbles, with arrows darting here and there, margins jammed with afterthoughts, while the rumpled Grassi wrote in a clear, bold script. But then, that was the thorough Ricks, a seine scooping up everything, ignoring nothing; Grassi was a killer, interested only in the jugular.

"Some of these Donophan people may still be in the hospital," Harry continued. "I understand the field got nailed pretty bad a couple of weeks ago. Also check into any civilian contacts—"

"Girlfriends?" Grassi's eyebrows rose hopefully.

"Whoever you can find." Harry kept his tone businesslike. "And leave whoever is in command out there to me."

"Keeping the choice bits for yourself, eh, Boss?" Grassi said.

Harry rubbed a beginning throb in his head. Joe Ryan was going to owe him big for Grassi. "Now here's the big point. The big point, as in you mess up here and you explain it to Colonel Ryan. While you are conducting this investigation, you will say as little—correction— you will say nothing about this case to anybody. Other than the questions you ask, you explain nothing to the people you interview, you say nothing to other members of the JAG staff, nothing to girlfriends, nothing in letters home, nothing to nobody! This will be a mistake 'I'm sorry' won't cover."

Grassi nodded without great concern, either not understanding or not caring about the direct reference.

"Markham and Anderson—who's their counsel?" Ricks asked.

Harry shuffled the papers on his desk. "No formal charges have been filed yet."

"Does that mean they have no counsel?"

"Right now, their status is that they're confined to quarters pending the results of this investigation. They'll have plenty of time to establish a defense in conjunction with counsel once charges have been preferred."

Ricks was obviously unhappy with the response. Nonetheless, he did not question his superior.

The look on Ricks's face provoked a twinge of guilt in Harry, but he comforted himself with the thought that while some of his tactics were, as they said back home, "dirty pool," he was still within the legal framework of military law. What he could not find comfort for was the conspiratorial wink Grassi flashed him with his good eye. The idea that he and Grassi had some common ethic—or lack thereof—chilled him.

"All right," Harry concluded. "I'm hoping we'll have the ballistics and autopsy prelim by tomorrow and then we can start putting it all together. We'll touch base tomorrow morning first thing. OK, gentlemen, you've got a lot of work to do."

Ricks left, but Grassi lingered in the doorway. "Hey, Boss, did I mention how much I like your wallpaper?"

"Good-bye, Lieutenant."

Then Grassi was gone, and Nagel was back with a dangerously overloaded tray of doughnuts and coffee.

"Where'd they go?" Nagel asked. He seemed offended. "What am I supposed to do with this?"

Harry grabbed coffee and a doughnut, then waved Nagel away. He soon heard Nagel in the outer office renewing his operations with the screwdriver. "Will you leave that thing alone! Call the orderly room at my BOQ and have them send someone up to my quarters. I need my Class A's cleaned, pressed, and returned *no later* than 1600 hours. And when Maintenance comes up to fix your box, would you kindly point out to them that this office was supposed to have been painted *six weeks ago!*"

Harry calmed himself with a bite of his doughnut, brushed the crumbs off the desk, and turned to the stack of files. He sifted through the folders until he found the mission profile. There were several maps in the file: one covering southern England and the northern France/Belgium area; a detail map of central Belgium; a more detailed map of the area between Ghent and Brussels. The maps were crossed with red lines marking flight paths. At intervals along the lines were four-digit numbers: military times signifying the aircraft being at specific points at specific times. Harry searched his memory for anything about Belgium: All he came up with was that it was where Brussels sprouts had originated. He spread the maps along the head of his desk for easy reference, then turned back to the mission profile.

Angel Blue, consisting of Anderson and O'Connell, and Angel Red, with Markham leading Jacobs and McLagen, had been scheduled to leave Donophan Airfield, located down in Sussex, at 0700 hours with Blue in the lead. Keeping as close to the ground as possible to avoid German radar detection, the five planes were to have followed a southeasterly course across the Channel, making landfall on the French coast just south of Boulogne-sur-Mer. They were to have continued on about twenty-five kilometers inland before heading northeast on a course taking them straight on to their target. They would have crossed the Belgian border just north of Tourcoing, dropped their auxiliary fuel tanks a few kilometers short of the target, then closed for the attack. Angel Blue would have pressed in first with Red flying top cover, then they would have reversed positions.

Their target was a fuel depot at the Belgian town of Helsvagen, which sat about thirty kilometers southwest of Ghent; seventy kilometers northwest of Brussels and its renowned sprouts. Helsvagen was a pinpoint so small it appeared only on the two detail maps.

The withdrawal route was a mirror of the attack path. Both sections would leave the target area on a northwesterly course, turning southwest at another pinpoint—Roselare—and head back across France. They'd hit the French coast just south of Dunkirk and head home. The whole mission was to have taken no more than an hour.

As Harry studied the plan and maps and course lines, it occurred to him that all this flying about willy-nilly seemed somewhat extraneous considering the target lay a little over 280 kilometers practically due east of Donophan. He pondered the arcane and often pointlessly complex workings of the military mind.

Something about the course lines tugged at him, and was still nagging at him when the phone rang. It rang quite a few times before he remembered that Nagel was off on his assigned scavenger hunt. Harry scooped the phone out of its cradle. "Voss."

"Major Voss?" The voice was young. "This is Captain James Dell. I called earlier—"

"Oh, right, right. What can I do for you, Captain?"

"Captain Bennett from Wing said you'd want to talk to me. I'm the G-2 liaison and briefing officer for the 351st. I debriefed Major Markham and Captain Anderson yesterday."

"Ah! I was coming over to your offices in a bit. We can talk then."

"Major Van Damm—my CO—he thought maybe it'd be better if I came over there. I have those debriefing reports. They just finished typing them up this morning. I understand you want those."

"I'd appreciate that, Captain, thank you. I want to talk to your Major Van Damm, first. Meet me in my office in forty-five minutes?"

"If you're going to talk to Major Van Damm, you better figure on an hour or so, Major. Trust me."

Harry smiled. "All right, Captain. See you in an hour."

Harry set the phone in its cradle and turned back to the maps. Where was the Gresham cottage? He drew out his notes from the day before, made some rough calculations, and penciled in a small X on the large map; a rough approximate of the coastal crash site. Even allowing for his not being a navigator of any sort, it was obvious that neither of the planned flight paths—the one out of England from Donophan or the one back—came anywhere near Charlie Gresham's cottage in East Sussex.

By the time Harry was trundling out of the Annex, he was facing another problem, although this was one of which he was still unaware. That "newshound" Ryan had referred to had picked up enough of a scent to follow him to his meeting with G-2.

That other problem for poor old Harry was me.

CHAPTER FOUR

EX CATHEDRA

WITHIN HOURS OF THE DEATH OF Dennis O'Connell, the "newshounds"—
as Joe Ryan disdainfully described them—had sensed something was
amiss. The American press officers had informed the members of the
press pools that the affair in East Sussex was simply the routine recovery
of a downed American pilot. But that news didn't fit with the glum faces
behind the podia, and the "No comment"'s that stifled any query for
further information. But what intrigued the hounds most was the question of what sort of routine recovery operation required an impenetrable cordon of American and British troops round the crash site, the
involvement of the Judge Advocate, Provost Marshal, and forensic teams
from Scotland Yard, and the entire staff of the 188th Combat Wing (the
unit that incorporated the late Dennis O'Connell's 351st Fighter Group)
scurrying about like Charlie Gresham's stampeded sheep. And to any
query in that regard came yet another "No comment."

For a journalist, that kind of evasion was a waving red flag in front of
a bull. In short order, the hounds were sniffing about trying to find a
trail that would lead them to at least some part of the truth of the events
inside that cordon in East Sussex. In all that trolling, stalking, and sniffing, the paths of Harry Voss and myself first crossed.

The day following young O'Connell's death—16 August—my colleagues and I were already selecting our perches. Some planted themselves at 188th Combat Wing Headquarters, some in Chillingham where they could eye Donophan Airfield, others at Scotland Yard. I was among a group that posted themselves outside Rosewood Court, home of the Judge Advocate's office; a likely station considering that whatever had occurred the previous day seemed to have involved possible criminal action by American military personnel.

Many of us who had even occasionally covered the goings-on of the Yanks in London had at least a passing acquaintance with Joe Ryan. That was enough to know that the dark glower and strident jogs across the cobbles we witnessed were a noteworthy change from his usual grin-and-wave bonhomie. Then there were the two junior officers (Ricks and Grassi, I later learned, the latter sporting a face like a bruised peach) climbing into a jeep and roaring out of the Court with a serious urgency. We on station across from the gate sensed that all that seriousness and urgency had something to do with whatever was brewing, and that was enough to send my colleagues after them on their respective two good legs.

Which was what held me to the Court; I didn't have two good legs. I stood there, cursing the awkwardness of the wooden contraption that now served as a limb. I was still cursing it when Harry Voss strode out the Court gate and headed toward the complex in Grosvenor Square, which housed the Supreme Headquarters of the Allied Expeditionary Force. As a major from the JAG's offices, Harry seemed of sufficient rank for me to reasonably suspicion him as a part of whatever was stirring all the rumble. But perhaps what made him an even more attractive lead to me was that even I could keep up with that waddling trudge of his: I followed Harry because I could.

I trailed him as far as the entrance to the collection of buildings serving the SHAEF staff. Standing at a discreet distance, so as not to alarm the sentries, I saw him pass through the entrance that would take him down into the shadowy realm of the Intelligence boffins, what the American military nomenclature designated as "G-2." I was now reasonably certain that I was on to something, and poor old Harry had—for the moment—become my unwitting guide.

•   •   •

American engineers had gone down into the cellars under Grosvenor Square, knocked down turn-of-the-century walls, dug and tunneled through London's ancient earth, and interlocked the various chambers in a subterranean complex protected against both Goering's bombs and prying domestic eyes by yards of soil, and old stone walls reinforced with brand-new concrete. Each day those labyrinthine corridors and chambers filled with the dull stutter of stone drills and cement mixers at work behind noise-dampening drapes. Each and every day, the maze of partitions, filing cabinets, desks and tables, drafting boards and map easels expanded along with the war effort.

It was a place peopled by shadows. The shadows sat wreathed in cigarette smoke and hunched over lowered desk lamps and glowing light tables studying photographs, maps, teletypes, ticker tapes, diagrams, telegrams, predictions, calculations, estimations, and all forms and vehicles of information and analysis, then glided from one pool of darkness to another.

Harry's guide deposited him at a small, windowed cubicle, its windows blanked by drawn blinds, before disappearing back into the gloom, leaving him in the care of a bulldog-faced sergeant stationed at a desk in front of the cubicle's closed door; an appropriate Cerberus for such Stygian surroundings.

"Major Voss? Major Van Damm will be with you in a moment, sir."

Harry saw no place to sit and the sergeant offered no chair. Harry fidgeted like a man waiting for a bus. His eyes drifted to a youthful captain, the gnawed stub of a pencil tucked behind his ear, dancing a set of calipers across the scroll-like map overwhelming his desk.

The sergeant cleared his throat theatrically, reminding Harry that this was a place where wandering eyes required a signed authorization. Harry nodded an apology and stepped back to the sergeant's desk.

From somewhere behind him—he dared not turn to see and risk another growling rebuke from the sergeant—he picked out fragments of conversation. He heard a voice—still with an adolescent crack—try to coax a WAC into an evening at dinner. Harry smiled; even in that eternal underground gloaming, with half the world in flames, some things went on as always.

The cubicle door swung open and a cloud of stinging cigar smoke rolled out followed by a blue-faced captain gasping for breath. The captain vanished off into the darkness; the sergeant nodded at Harry. "He's all yours, Major."

The brightness of the cubicle was painful after the dimness outside, and equally distressing was the smell: stale air; old food and coffee; sweat; cheap cigars.

I had seen Major Christian Van Damm at several briefings for the press pools. Even in public and on his best behavior, Van Damm was still prone to that cocky impudence of so many young Americans, an undisguised disdain for the protocols and diplomacies that made the simple unnecessarily complex, and an irritating impatience for any intellect moving slower than his own quicksilver pace. Van Damm, in the privacy of his sanctum sanctorum below the venerable Georgian buildings of Grosvenor Square, sole ruler over his spectral kingdom, allowed his eccentricities full rein.

At Harry's entrance, the major barely hoisted himself to his feet from behind a desk that had disappeared beneath a mass of paper flowing uninterruptedly onto and across the floor, and then up onto caster-mounted corkboards covered by layers of maps. Van Damm shook Harry's hand, gestured at him to shut the door, and crashed back into his chair, a preposterously huge, wing-backed affair, its plush padding covered with a faded pattern of twining leaves. Harry guessed it had been liberated from one of the stately residences aboveground.

"Welcome to G-2, Major." Van Damm punctuated his greeting with a forceful puff on the cigar stub clamped in his tobacco-stained teeth.

Harry smiled a hello, tiptoeing round piles of photographs to the office's only other chair; strictly government issue and not nearly as comfortable as Van Damm's.

"First time down here? What do you think of our little operation?"

"A bit spooky." Having had time to let his eyes adjust to the cubicle's glare, Harry could see that the major was not much older than Ricks or Grassi, though his pasty pallor had thrown Harry's initial estimate higher.

Van Damm chuckled, proudly flashing his stained teeth. "Spooky. That's a good word for it."

"And not so little."

"A growing concern, Major, a growing concern. We're not even settled in here and now they tell us to start reconning some territory out in
Kingston. Ike wants to move the whole shebang out there with him.
He's got this philosophy against the brass getting too settled. We also
serve who pack and move, I guess. I imagine your visit's got something
to do with that little do down on the coast yesterday."

Harry looked pained. "Tell me," he asked, "is there anybody who doesn't
know about this mess?"

"This is G-2, Voss. Intelligence. The Spy Brigade. What the hell kinda
spies would we be if we didn't even know what was goin' on in our own
backyard, huh? Don't worry. It's also our job to keep secrets. 'Course,
that's not Operations' job. Keeping secrets."

"They know, too?"

"And Communications, the Provost—well, that would figure, right?—
and Transport—"

Harry groaned.

"Frankly, I'd be surprised if by tomorrow, all of Wing staff didn't
know! You talk to my boy Dell yet?"

"Captain Dell? Not yet. I'm supposed to meet with him later—"

"He's got those debriefing reports, and those gun films were turned
over to Ryan. Some droop named Bennett—he your man?"

"Bennett belongs to General Halverson, but I asked him to—"

"Well, Bennett was moping around here yesterday trying to get hold
of that stuff but I sent 'im packing. I didn't like his puss. I had Dell hand
it all straight to Ryan. Now, Major Voss," Van Damm said, "what can I do
you for?"

Harry fumbled with his briefcase for his notes and pencil and pad. "I
suppose we could start by talking about the 351st."

"You've got the—hey, is this smoke bothering you?" Van Damm
switched on a small desk fan seemingly oblivious to the commotion it
created among the papers on his desk. He seemed oblivious as well
to the fact that the lazily whirling blades had no place to send the
thick cloud of smoke and merely circulated it about the room. "I was
saying—you've got the wrong boy. I can tell you that they—the 351st—
they were the last of Halverson's groups to be activated, back in May or
June, I think. I can tell you they were his ace group. They were on that

last Essen raid, got themselves a unit citation for that one, and I can tell you they earned it, too. And that is about *all* I can tell you. You need to talk to Dell. He's a good kid. Bright."

Harry repressed another smile. It was odd hearing someone as young as Van Damm refer to another presumed adult as a "kid."

"Dell worked with them directly," Van Damm continued. "He was Johnny On the Spot, on a regular basis."

"I gather you're saying, then, that you didn't deal with the group?"

"Me? Nah, not directly. On an occasional basis. And then only with senior staff."

"Senior staff. Major Markham?"

"Markham, Frank Adams, that adjutant what's-his-face-Corksca-something—"

"Wait a minute. Who's this Frank—"

"Lieutenant Colonel Frank Adams. Commanding officer."

"Commanding . . . ? I thought Markham—"

"Oh, no, no, no. Markham was the air exec, the number two man. Adams ran the show. Markham was the heir apparent."

"What do you mean?"

"There was a lot of good talk floating around about Frank Adams. The 351st was an A-Number-One group 'cause Adams was a crack CO, on top of which Adams and Halverson were buddy-buddy from back before they invented the wheel. Grapevine had it that Adams was being groomed for a slot at Wing HQ, maybe even go bird colonel and get the Wing when Halverson moved up. The way Halverson talked up Adams was the same way Adams talked up Markham. If Adams moved up . . ." Van Damm finished with an eloquent shrug.

"I get the picture. Where's this Colonel Adams been through all this?"

Van Damm removed his cigar and stared at the glowing tip. "I imagine his box should be home by now."

"His box?"

"He's dead."

"Oh."

Van Damm sighed. "So, Markham got the group anyway. Hit Halverson pretty hard, about Adams. I think the whole thing unhinged him a little bit, at least in my opinion."

"What whole thing?"

"Frank Adams and the group going up in one big flash. The bombing. What was it, last week? You heard about that, didn't you? About Donophan being hit?"

"Right, OK. So that's when Colonel Adams was killed?"

"He had plenty of company. Killed and wounded, Donophan lost eighty to eighty-five percent of their combat effectives—" Van Damm snapped his fingers. "Got pasted six ways to Sunday."

Harry nodded and wiped at his eyes. The smoke was making him tear. He pointed at the fan. "Do we really need this?"

Van Damm smiled and leaned forward to flick off the fan.

Harry flipped back through his notes. "You, um, said something about Colonel Halverson—"

"It's General Halverson. Got his star just a coupla days before the 351st got hit. How's *that* for your tragic ironies!"

"—about Halverson becoming 'unhinged'—"

"The man loses his bestest group and his bestest buddy in one big boom. You blame him?"

"No, but what exactly did you mean by—"

"What I meant was that the next day—the *very* next *morning*—I've got the general on the blower, practically *foaming* at the mouth, bending my ear about what he called 'reactive strikes.' Do you *believe* that?" Van Damm shook his head, still not believing it himself. "Not with his other groups, mind you, but with the 351st! What was left of it."

Van Damm's cigar was dead. He weighed relighting it, seemed to decide the stub wasn't worth it, moved some papers uncovering an old cup of coffee serving as an ashtray, and dropped it in.

"So, I tell the general," Van Damm went on, "I says, Look, I'm senior staff, I'm chief Intelligence officer, I've got an obligation to point out that I don't think Markham's playing with all fifty-two cards, OK?" He began rooting through his desk drawers. "The krauts gut Markham's group and now he's talking 'bout going back over there and messing up their brilliantine a little bit? That's what it came down to. Hey, Voss; want one?"

To Harry's dismay, Van Damm produced a fresh cigar from one of his desk drawers. Harry shook his head politely but vigorously. Van Damm shrugged, then carefully began peeling the cellophane off the cigar.

"Tampa Nuggets," he rhapsodized. "Nobody makes a cheap cigar like the good ol' U.S. of A. I have my wife send 'em over. Helps kill the stink down here." He bit the tip off the cigar, spat it out on the floor, then touched a match to the end, basking in the fresh, blue haze. "Hell, last time I had a shower was the last time it rained; went outside and strolled around in it for a few minutes. You'd be surprised how little the brass comes down here to bother me."

"I don't think I—"

"Anyway, where was I? Oh, yeah, so the general says to me, he says, Fine, you fulfilled your filial obligations, Van Damm, you said your piece, now shuddup and do what I tell you. Or words to that effect. Well, Voss, the boss may not be always right, but the boss is always the boss."

"What was it he told you to do?"

"He wanted targets."

"And you gave him this fuel depot in Belgium—"

"I gave him what he wanted: a shopping list. He wanted a spread of easy-to-hit stuff, low-priority targets, highly vulnerable, well within fighter range. I gave him six targets."

"Could I see that target information?"

Van Damm nodded and barked an order into his intercom.

"The general picked the fuel depot out of those six?" Harry asked. "The place in Belgium?"

"Him. Or Markham. The orders came to me from Halverson, but I don't know whose hands are dirty with what."

"You didn't approve of the target choice?"

"I thought the whole mission was a stupid idea! Look, we don't have much experience in this 'fighter sweep' business. We've been doing a lot of talking about it, but so far the fighters have been pretty much relegated to bomber-escort duty. But the first time we let our fighters loose at something on the ground, I'd want to do it when we've got a more definite air superiority and do it with something more than five lousy planes! You want there to be enough so that if things go bad, they can at least protect themselves, fight their way out. And five of 'em ain't enough, *especially* without air superiority."

"You explained all this to General—"

Van Damm rocked in his chair with the unhappy smugness of a proven Cassandra. "About half a second after he told me what he was up to. Emphatically. But, hey, look, I get paid to give opinions; nobody gets paid to take 'em. And now he's out three more pilots, right? If the brass hats want to throw people away like that, that's jake with me, but if you ask me, I think everybody who touched this thing—from Halverson on down—should be strung up by his tender parts for letting that thing go ahead."

"If it was clearly such a bad idea, why do you think Halverson—"

"I dunno!" Van Damm jabbed the red tip of his Tampa Nugget at Harry for emphasis. "I tell ya, I think he just went a little flak-happy over this thing! All Halverson wanted to hear from me was target recommendations, and did I think Markham's plan would bring the boys home."

"Was it sound? The plan?"

"Actually, it wasn't bad as far as it went." Van Damm's intercom buzzed and he stood. "C'mon, it's visual-aids time. I'm gonna give you a crash course in being a member of the Spy Brigade. I hope you brought your decoder ring with you."

Harry took his pad and pencil with him as he followed Van Damm out into the comparatively fresh air of the cellar maze.

The desk sergeant outside held up a fistful of folders to Van Damm. The latter riffled through them, extracted one, and told the sergeant to leave the rest on Harry's chair. Then, with a follow-me nod to Harry, Van Damm steamed off into the dark, his cigar leaving a trail of locomotive puffs behind. They stopped near a group of officers staring bleary-eyed into photographs laid out on a bank of light tables. Van Damm tapped one of the officers atop his head. He was a lieutenant, and even in the harsh glare of the light table Harry could see large bags under his watery eyes, the ghostly pale skin. He wondered if Van Damm or any of his minions saw much sunlight.

"You could use a break, Bennie," Van Damm said.

"Oh, does it show?" the lieutenant said dryly.

"I need a detail map, Bennie. The Channel, covering southeast England, northwest France, western Belgium."

Off Bennie went.

"And see if you can find where that blackboard walked off to." Van Damm pulled up a stool and plopped Harry on it near the light table. He moved the photos that Bennie had been studying out of the way, then drew another set from the file he'd carried with him, setting them out on the iridescent glass.

"Here's what it's all about," Van Damm said.

The composition and scale of each photograph was different, but the subject of each was the same: a crosshatched blob indicating the boundaries and streets of a residential area. There weren't that many crosshatches, which Harry guessed made it a fairly small town. Not far from the town was some sort of construction site.

"Your first Spy Brigade lesson," Van Damm began, setting a magnifier over the photographs. "Aerial photographic interpretation."

Harry leaned forward and squinted through the glass. He was treated to the sight of a mountain-sized pencil point as Van Damm pointed his way through the grainy image. "This up here, this is the town of Helsvagen. Sits on the crossroads between Ghent and Brussels. One of those little jerkwater farm towns out in the middle of nowhere. Just outside the southwest side of town, this is the fuel dump. Most of these pictures were taken back in '40 by the RAF when they were doing recon on Jerry's prep for an invasion of the islands. This fuel dump was one of a bunch of satellite stations supplying the Ghent/Brussels sector. The krauts figured spreading their gas around in these small dumps was safer than putting it all in one basket. They were just building this at the time. You can see them digging foundations. Here's some heavy earthmoving stuff, bulldozers or something. Here's another RAF picture from about two years ago. You can see the finished product."

Van Damm's pencil point traced a neat rectangle that had replaced the construction site. "Here's the perimeter fence." Inside the rectangle were two circles—"Fuel storage tanks"—and several little rectangles along the fence closest to the town—"Barracks, admin building, motor pool."

"That's the most recent picture you have?"

"This place is so low on the priority list nobody's seen fit to risk an air-recon crew for better pictures. We've gotten some intelligence on the place from time to time and, apparently, it hasn't changed much since these pictures were taken. If anything, the krauts have stripped out some of the manpower and heavy AA guns the way they've stripped everyplace else along the Western Wall to feed the Russian front."

Lieutenant Bennie had returned with the requested map and a large chalkboard on wheels.

"You want some java or something, Voss? No? Bennie, get me a cup, wouldja? Thanks."

Harry looked up from the magnifier and rubbed his eyes. "And this place fit the bill for what Halverson and Markham wanted?"

"It was an easy reach for a P-47, and it didn't look like there was much there in the way of AA defense. And, it's just plain easy to hit. I could've hung a Boy Scout from a box kite and sent him in there with a book of matches and knocked that place out."

"I saw their flight plan. If it was that easy, I don't understand why they didn't just zip in and zip out."

Van Damm smiled tolerantly. "Because, my dear Voss, we are in a war, and the enemy looks unfavorably upon Allied aircraft 'zipping' around at will." He spread the map out on the light table and started to sketch in the two course routes that had been planned to take Markham's Thunderbolts to the target in Belgium and back home.

"Uh, Major?" Bennie had returned with a cup of black coffee. "You told me to warn you about drawing on the maps."

Van Damm took the coffee and nodded without heeding.

"You've got a *stack* of them all marked up—"

Van Damm irritably shooed him away. Bennie propped himself on a corner of a nearby desk and turned to the sympathetically nodding WAC sitting there. "I *knew* he'd get mad. He *told* me to stop him, but I *knew* he'd get mad."

Van Damm took a sip of his coffee, grimaced, then nodded at the finished pencil lines on the map. "KISS," he pronounced.

"Excuse me?" Harry asked.

"KISS. The primary rule of military strategy that almost everyone with brass on his collar ignores: Keep It Simple, Stupid. This is how it looks when you *don't* ignore it. They head southeasterly out of Donophan, staying in the grass—below radar—and hit France just below Boulogne. Now, providing they make the coast without being spotted by the CAP's—"

"Caps?"

"Combat Air Patrols. The krauts run regular air patrols up and down the coastal corridor, plus they got E-boats crawling around all the time.

OK, so providing our guys make the coast without one of these patrols spotting 'em, they're certainly gonna be seen by the joes manning the coast defenses. In fact, Markham counts on it. The coast makes the call to the Luftwaffe sector controller that there's five 47's heading southeast. The Jerries alert their people all along this line."

Harry brightened. "But Germans never find Markham and his men anywhere on that line."

"Attaboy, Voss, you're getting the hang of this. Twenty miles in, our guys hit their first IP. This is all open country here. Some farms, lotta swampland. The Jerries have let the Lys River flood as a 'disincentive' to paratroop and glider landings. The upshot is nobody's gonna be there to see 'em make their pivot. So, when our 47's get to Helsvagen, they show up unannounced. Surprise, fellas! Boom! Same thing on this dogleg home. If the krauts at Helsvagen get the word out, they report that the 47's are withdrawing to the northwest—"

"And as soon as Markham and company are out of sight of Helsvagen, they change course and hopefully get home without any problems."

"Bingo."

"Sounds like a good plan to me."

"It had a nice, simple elegance, I think; very much a Markham trademark." Van Damm turned to the chalkboard and found a thimble-sized stub of chalk on the sill. He drew an erratic circle up in the right-hand corner, labeling it "H."

"Helsvagen?" Harry offered.

"You get any better at this and the union says I gotta pay you." Van Damm next drew a rectangle southwest of "H," then two circles along the southwest side of the rectangle. Harry recognized the fuel depot.

"Each of these tanks," Van Damm tapped the circles, "carries about twenty thousand gallons of vehicular gasoline. Each of the planes is carrying twelve 3.24-inch rockets. One of those'll open a Sherman tank like a can of sardines. Markham's boys are fighter jockeys, not bombardiers. This way, they don't have to finagle with the complexities of a bomb run and drop trajectories and all that malarkey. Rockets being a directional weapon, all our fellows gotta do is come in just like on a strafing run. They come up on the tanks just by holding their northeast approach, let go, and then it's good night, Irene. Angel Blue makes

the first approach while Markham takes Angel Red upstairs to fly top
cover. Blue pumps their rockets into the tanks, then they fly cover while
Red lits whatever's left. If it took 'em three minutes to do the job, I'd
be surprised. Since the krauts were considerate enough to build this
place a coupla hundred yards away from the town, there's no worries
about incidental damage to the people and property of the good town
of Helsvagen. Those two hundred Krauts shoulda been sitting ducks."

"So, what went wrong?" Harry asked. "*Something* did." He pointed to
a spot on the English coast. "This is where O'Connell went down."

Van Damm moved Harry's fingertip a few millimeters. "More like
there."

"Which is nowhere near where they should've been coming back."

Van Damm nodded, his brooding eyes fixed to the spot on the map.
"Well, according to their debriefing—Dell'll go over all that with you—
when the tanks went up, O'Connell got his nose a little too close to the
fire. Took a piece of something in the engine. O'Connell panicked—
which, I'm told, is no big surprise coming from him—and scrammed
outta there. I guess he was worried about his engine holding up, so he
beelined his way home. Now, even if his buddies thought he had what
you might call an intestinal-fortitude problem, you still don't leave one
of your own open like that. The others lit out after him to cover him."

"So they aborted their part of—"

Van Damm waved carelessly. "Those tanks were the first things hit
and once they went up, that place was *gone!* One big barbecue. Even if
they'd stayed, there wasn't anything left for them to shoot at. It was that
easy. That's why I put it on the list for Halverson."

"And what happened to the other two pilots? Jacobs and—"

"McLagen?" Van Damm frowned. "That's what I was worried about
from the get-go. That's why I was so steamed at Halverson for letting—"
Belatedly, he realized Harry had no clue what he was talking about.
"They got jumped," he explained, pointing to another spot on the
map approximately halfway between Helsvagen and the French coast.
"Gaggle of kraut fighters bounced Angel Red around here, somewhere
between Waregem and the Schelde. We're not sure, exactly. They were
coming out the way they'd gone in—low—which didn't give 'em any
maneuvering room. The Jerries had 'em nailed to the floor. With just

five of 'em—and one of 'em a cripple—well, Markham did well to come home with as many as he did. SNAFU, Voss: Situation Normal: All Fucked Up. Pardon my French."

Van Damm stood back from the light table, studying the points and lines on the map. He took a few meditative puffs on his cigar, then shook his head. "Whatever else happened yesterday, you got two cases of negligence on top of it: Markham *and* Halverson. I hope you string 'em *both* up by their balls. Pardon my French, again."

The Spy Brigade tutorial over, Harry gathered up the photographs and followed Van Damm back to his acrid sanctum. "Am I cleared for this stuff?" Harry thumbed through the target files on his chair.

"You get higher priority poop on bubba gum cards. Just sign a chit for 'em at the desk outside, don't mess 'em up, and remember to bring 'em back."

"This looks pretty technical."

"The important stuff is clear enough. You have a problem with anything, gimme a blast."

Van Damm snuffed out the remains of his cigar. He reached for a desk drawer and a fresh Tampa Nugget. At that, Harry crammed the files into his briefcase posthaste.

"I want to thank you, Major."

"For what?" Van Damm asked blithely.

"You underrate yourself." Harry buckled his case and patted it like a stuffed treasure chest. "It's been a very informative visit."

Van Damm stood and shook Harry's hand. "If you had fun, tell your friends, bring 'em by. We're open all day, every day, all year round."

Back at the Annex, Captain James Dell was sitting in Harry's outside office, sipping on a bottle of Coca-Cola. At Harry's entrance, the young captain set down his soda and his briefcase, and got to his feet. His arm came up in a nicely deferential salute.

Nagel, however, did not stand or salute. Instead, he whined: "You didn't say you were going to be so long. You should have *told* me—"

"Thank you for your concern, Corporal," Harry said and turned to Dell. "Sorry I kept you waiting, Captain. At ease. Hope you weren't here too long?"

"No bother, sir." He was young, polite, a moon-face sitting awkwardly atop a thin neck, his complexion spotted along his collar line.

Harry had Dell drag his chair into the inner office, then took a moment to steel himself before turning back to Nagel. "I take it Maintenance hasn't seen fit to come up here and fix that thing."

"They told me they were coming right up," Nagel said, gesturing at his dismembered intercom. "They told me that when you left."

"Call them again."

"That just gets them mad."

"Call them again."

"Yessir."

"And hold all my calls."

Dell was standing by his chair in Harry's office, briefcase under one arm, his Coca-Cola bottle at Present Arms. Harry squeezed by him to get behind his desk.

"Relax, Captain. Sit. Just give me a second to get settled. To tell you the truth, I wasn't expecting somebody from Major Van Damm's section to be so . . . formal."

Dell had a little shock of hair on his forehead. He set his briefcase on the floor and brushed the hair away from his eyes as he sat. "I guess the major is a bit of a character."

Harry peeled off his jacket. "A bit."

"But he knows his stuff."

Harry grunted in agreement as he wrestled with his window.

"You want me to try that, sir?" the captain volunteered.

"Forget it. I think they built it that way." Harry gave up on the window. His attention focused on a phone message taped to his chair stating that Joe Ryan had rung him. "One more second, Captain. Nagel! Is this a new message?"

"Sir?"

"This message about Colonel Ryan. This isn't the same one from this morning, is it? I talked to him this morning, remember?"

"Oh, no, sir, that's a new one. He called again right after you left—"

"I told you about putting the times on these things, didn't I?"

"Should I get him on the—"

"No!" Harry smiled apologetically at Dell, and the captain offered a politely sympathetic one in return as he took another sip of his Coca-Cola. "Captain, you know what this is about, don't you?"

Dell squirmed in his seat. "I guess."

"Don't be self-conscious, Captain. If you'd said no, you would've been the only guy in London who didn't know." Harry took his place at his desk and drew out his package of Lucky Strikes, proffering them to Dell. Dell nodded a no-thanks. Harry lit one for himself, drew a clean pad of foolscap in front of him, pulled on his glasses, and picked up a pencil. "There was one thing in particular that Major Van Damm thought you could help me with."

"Do my best, sir."

"Van Damm says that you know the men out at the 351st better than he does, that you deal with them personally."

"Yes, sir, I'm their G-2 liaison. I bring mission information out to them, maybe conduct part of the briefing, handle the debriefing . . . I see them pretty regularly. Or I did till the krauts hit 'em. You know about that, don't you, sir?"

Harry nodded. "How long have you been working with the 351st?"

"Since I came over. That'd be June, mid-June. Not really that long after they were activated." A Coca-Cola burp snuck out of the captain's lips. "Sorry, sir."

Harry let it pass with a smile. "Know the men well?"

"Sort of. Some. Not many, not real personal. I'd see them before they went up, and talk to them when they got back. A debriefing . . . well, a fella's not always at his best sometimes, a time like that. I guess that doesn't really answer your question." He stared down into the neck of his Coca-Cola bottle.

"How about Major Markham? Did you know him well?"

Dell shrugged. Harry could read the signs; there was something on the young man's mind. Dell saw the way Harry was looking at him, waiting, and made the plunge. "I should tell you," he began. "When I went out there . . ."

"Yes?"

"This last time," Dell said, sounding puzzled. "I went out there yesterday to debrief them." He reached into his briefcase and set two folders on Harry's desk. "Those are the debriefing reports."

"And you turned the gun films over to Colonel Ryan."

"What there was. Lieutenant O'Connell's film was ruined by the sea-water. I gave Colonel Ryan Captain Anderson's."

"What about Major Markham's?"

"I don't know. I mean, that's the thing. It wasn't there."

"Define 'wasn't there.' "

"The film magazines were waiting for my pickup. I didn't check them until I got back to London. There was no need to. Like I said, we cracked O'Connell's and—"

"Never mind O'Connell's."

"The magazine for Markham's was empty."

"How often does something like that happen?"

"It's not supposed to happen at all."

"Did Markham have an explanation?"

"Like I said, I didn't know until I got back to London. By then, the MP's were already holding Markham and I couldn't get through to him. So, we only had Anderson's film to go on instead of a BDA run and—"

"BDA run?"

"Bomb Damage Assessment. Post-strike aerial-photo reconnaisance," Dell explained.

"OK. Is that a standard kind of thing?"

"Depends on how bad you want to know what kind of damage you did."

"And Markham hadn't scheduled one of these BDA things to follow yesterday's mission to Helsvagen?"

"I don't know who made the decision, but the order came down from General Halverson that they didn't want a BDA run. The general said the target was such a low priority, and since we did have Anderson's film, it didn't make much sense to risk a recon plane on it."

"I see. Who normally removes the film magazines from the planes?"

"The ground crews."

"And where does the film go from there?"

"I usually pick the magazines up at the admin building. Maybe the CO's got them, maybe the adjutant is holding them—"

"This time."

"The films were waiting for me in the admin building, like always."

"Who had access to them?"

"I don't know. Anybody, I think. It's been a little loose out there since . . . well, you know about the Germans—"

"Yes." Harry stared down at his desk, tapping his pencil point on the pad.

"I guess that doesn't make Major Markham look too good," Dell said. It saddened him to say it.

Harry cleared his throat and looked up at Dell. "Major Van Damm tells me Markham reported his flight was jumped on the trip back."

"Yes, sir. The major reported they were bounced by a gaggle of enemy fighters—Do you have a map, sir?" He used the small map Harry fished out of the attack-profile folder. "Somewhere about here," and he pointed to the same general area Van Damm had designated. "Major Markham really wasn't too sure, though. Nobody was sighting landmarks when it happened. The krauts sixed 'em, coming down out of the sun. The major says he didn't even know they were on 'em until Jacobs's plane flamed. Markham's guys mixed it up with 'em, tried to fight 'em off. Him, O'Connell, and Anderson made it out. McLagen didn't." Dell stared pensively off. The name seemed to bring up a memory.

"Markham say anything about . . . what happened to O'Connell?"

"No. 'Course, we didn't know about what happened when we had the debriefing. I mean, the major didn't know anybody else knew. Just said O'Connell splashed near the coast. Said he tried to radio Air/Sea Rescue but couldn't raise 'em. Interference. I didn't think much of it then, but looking back on it, I guess that sounds pretty lame, huh?"

"Were you friends with these men? The five that went out yesterday?"

"Not really." Dell frowned, trying to puzzle out a proper description. "If they were going to fly, if they were even planning to fly, I sat with them. Before and after. You don't become friends or anything, but you start getting . . . you know. Like doing business with the same people."

"What can you tell me about them? What about McLagen?"

Dell nodded hopelessly. "I don't know, Major. He was one of thirty-odd fellas. What I remember is he was a nice guy. Jacobs? Another familiar face sitting around the debriefing table. Hi, how'd it go? Was it rough? That's all."

"You must've known Major Markham better than that."

Dell smiled, clearly relieved to have something firm to offer. "A really good joe. A helluva fella, if you don't mind my saying."

Harry nodded at him to go on.

"Everybody's nuts about the major. His men, Colonel Adams, Wing staff. Terrific pilot, too. Loves to fly. I mean, this fella *loves* to fly! Up in the air all the time, joyriding between missions, he likes it that much. I think the major has more flight time logged than anybody in the group, including Colonel Adams. That was sad about him, about the colonel. He was a right guy, too. You heard what happened to him? He was a little more GI than the major, but he was an OK guy."

"Major Van Damm was of the opinion that Colonel Adams thought quite highly of Major Markham."

"That's no surprise. The colonel and the major were pretty close. You could see it."

"Pals?"

Dell nodded. "Anyhow, when I'd be doing the debriefing interviews, I always had to do Markham last. That's the kind of guy he is; the minute he's down and out of his plane, he's all over the place, checking on each man, running over to the hospital with the wounded, checking in with Rescue if somebody splashed. . . . I don't want to get too corny or anything, Major, but he really loves those guys. It's not like Colonel Adams didn't care, but Major Markham shows it more. And when somebody doesn't come home . . . Well, you can see it hurts. Every time."

"And Captain Anderson?"

Dell almost laughed aloud. "Tarzan. That's what I called him. Real crazy guy. I mean, not really crazy, not medically—"

Harry smiled disarmingly. "Gotcha."

"He called his squadron 'Anderson's Apaches,' and him and all his fellas had that on their flight jackets and planes. The RAF has radio monitoring stations along the coast, and they follow all the radio traffic. You have to hear this guy, him and his whole squadron. They go into a dog-fight and they start doing these Indian whoops on the radio. Captain Anderson is pals with Major Markham, too, but not like the major and Colonel Adams. Different."

"How so?"

"Oh, like . . . like when you were back in high school? The little kid that always hung around the quarterback? Anything I can do for you, champ?"

"I got the picture."

"Anderson goes everywhere the major does. Markham goes over to the hospital every day to visit the wounded, so does Anderson. Only, Markham goes because he wants to. Anderson goes—"

"Just because Markham does."

"Yeah."

"Now we come to Lieutenant O'Connell."

"Sergeant Sadapple." As soon as he said it, Dell's lips tightened in self-reprimand. "Sorry."

"That's what they called O'Connell? Sadapple?"

"I don't want to talk bad about some fella who didn't come home."

"It's OK, Captain."

"Well, that's how I thought of him." He shook his head, angry at himself. "Ah, I don't know. Maybe I'm not being fair. It's no easy row for anybody to hoe, any of those fellas that go up there. You come back and that night you're looking around the mess table and there's some faces aren't there. What those fellas face up there, no wonder some of 'em, like Anderson, they go a little squirrelly. All of those flyboys are at least a little crazy, Major. They have to be. I sit down with them when they come home and you see it gets to all of them. Some try to hide it, they try to laugh stuff off. One of their buddies goes down and they just go—" he shrugged his shoulders "—and have a drink and chalk it up to a roll of the dice or something.

"They make it a game. They shoot down a plane, it's just another point they rack up. You hear 'em talk about it and it's like listening to somebody talk about how the Giants outplayed the Dodgers. Then I remember that every one of those little swastikas they paint under their cockpits was some fella, and that any one of these boys at the table could wind up a little American flag under some kraut's cockpit. You get all that buzzing around in your head and you can't help but go a little 'khaki wacky.' "

It took Harry a moment to regain himself: Spotty-faced young boys should not have such weighty matters in their tousled heads, he'd been thinking. He announced a return to the business at hand with a clearing of the throat.

"Do you think it would get to you, like it did to O'Connell?"

"Like I said, Major, it gets to all of them. It just doesn't always come out the same way."

That was all for the young captain. He made his exit in the proper military manner, with a crisp salute before making a smart turn toward the door and out, leaving his Coca-Cola bottle behind, tottering on Harry's desk. Harry reached out to still the rattling wobble of glass on wood. The caramel dregs rolling round the thick bottom made him suddenly thirsty. He released the bottle and leaned back in his chair, closing his eyes, allowing a moment to let the image of young Captain Dell's tainted innocence clear from his mind.

He turned to the target profiles Van Damm had provided, spreading them out on his desk, flipping through them. There was an E-boat repair station near Ostende, and a rail causeway that breached a section of the swamps created in Normandy where the Germans had allowed the Dives valley to flood as an anti-invasion measure. Another target was a radio-monitoring station near Calais. All three were much closer to Donophan than the Helsvagen fuel depot. The other two targets that had been passed by were satellite fuel depots similar to the one at Helsvagen: one northwest of Brussels, about halfway along the road to Mechelen, and the other just west of Bastogne. There seemed no obvious reason—other than, in some cases, possibly distance—for the selection of Helsvagen above the other targets. Ah, Harry thought, the vagaries of the military mind.

"Nagel!"

He heard Nagel's chair scrape back from the desk.

"Don't come in here! I want you to call the acting CO of the 351st Fighter Group at Donophan Airfield. Tell him I'll be out there tomorrow afternoon to talk to him. Get directions! And tell General Halverson's Wing headquarters I'm on my way over."

"What about Colonel Ryan?"

"What about him?"

"You owe him a call. Should I get him—"

"No."

"Do I know where you are if he calls again?"

"No. Did you call Halverson's office?"

"If you don't mind my saying so, sir, generals usually like you to make appointments."

"*Make the damn call!*" Harry bellowed back down the hall, and then he was gone.

St. Aloysius Academy for Young Men sat in proud isolation in the rolling country west of London. Ivy-clad granite walls with turrets and machicolations, steeply raked slate roofs, narrow, high windows of stained glass—the Academy looked a combination of castle and cathedral and, in the way it had tutored and counseled English young in the High Tory ideals of empire-ruling, it had been both.

Now, The Empire was a bit in need of repair, and the school desks were stored in the cellars along with the tapestries that had hung in the marble halls detailing grand episodes in British history. According to the sign posted on the whitewashed stakes pounded into the once immaculate sod round the great arched entrance, St. Aloysius had become home to the "188th Combat Wing Headquarters."

Corporal Nagel's warning notwithstanding, a young lieutenant stood waiting on the wide front stairs to usher Harry through the paneled entrance hall and up the marble stairs straight to what had been the headmaster's office.

Behind the monolithic oaken desk where generations of headmasters had once stood beneath the school's coat of arms surrounded by rich, dark woodwork and floor-to-ceiling shelves of leather-bound volumes, now sat Brigadier General Russell Halverson. Harry knew the general from routine JAG dealings in the past, but this Russell Halverson he barely recognized. In better days, Halverson was trim, erect, handsome in an unobtrusive way, and sincerely polite in a cool fashion his British colleagues considered admirably un-American. But this day Harry saw a pale, rumpled, sagging man. Halverson resembled a bronze bust returned to the furnace, its features running under the great heat.

The air in the office was rife with the smell of cigarette ash. The teletype and its alert bell were strangely silent, as were the rank of telephones on the general's desk. Paperwork sat scattered across his baize blotter like autumn leaves. The only movement in the office were the dust motes dancing in the bars of colored light angling down through the stained glass.

"Good to see you again, Major," the general said, rising behind his desk.

"I wish the circumstances were better, sir." Harry was glad to retrieve his hand from the general's unexpectedly soft clasp.

"So do I." He flicked a wry twist of a smile, then beckoned Harry to a comfortable, cushioned chair by his desk. They both sat.

"Thank you for seeing me on such short notice, sir."

Halverson nodded with an officious smile. He pushed a pack of Camels toward Harry and they each lighted one. As Harry went to drop his match, he noticed the overflowing ashtray on the desk.

"How's the case going?" the general asked quietly.

"All right, sir."

"I understand they haven't been formally arrested yet."

"We're still in the investigation process, sir."

"I spoke to Colonel Ryan earlier. He said it looked pretty open-and-shut."

Harry cleared his throat. "Just a few loose ends to tie up. I'd hate to hurt a prosecution by going too fast."

"When are you going to talk to them?"

"If I talk to Markham and Anderson now, I'll have to offer counsel, and once they have that they're going to start building a defense. If I talk to them without offering them counsel, well, we're open to an appeal down the road on the basis that their rights were infringed. Unless they request counsel, I'm not compelled to offer it to them until they're formally arrested. By then, though, we'll have a solid groundwork in place before they can effectively counter. I don't want to talk to them until then."

Halverson nodded deeply, understanding, but then became quite still and concerned. "You may not have much time with this, Major."

"I know."

Halverson leaned back in his chair and drew deeply on his cigarette. "I'd like to ask you a question. Maybe you can explain something to me."

"If I can, sir."

"There's war parties gathering at SHAEF ready to go after Patton's scalp because he slapped a couple of GI's in Sicily. You heard about that, of course. Who hasn't? So, here he is on the verge of giving them the damned island, but he spanks these two kids . . . well, that's something you just don't do." He shook his head. "Meanwhile, about two weeks ago, Ninth Bomber Command in North Africa hit the Rumanian oil fields at Ploesti. They lost over thirty percent of their aircraft—over five hundred men—in a half-hour raid. They're pinning medals on that bunch."

Halverson's face was tired and sad, yet he grinned over the pathetic humor of the point. "I'd really appreciate somebody explaining that scale to me, Major. If you can, maybe you can tell me where I fall on it."

"General, I'm not investigating you."

"It's early yet. I'll bet Major Van Damm thinks you should."

Harry fiddled with his notepad. The foolscap seemed too bright, a rainbow garland at a wake.

"I'm being impolitic, hm? Not to mention impolite." Halverson smirked at his discomfort. "What is it I can do for you, Major? Can I begin by offering you a drink?"

"A little too early for me, sir."

Halverson nodded and reached into a bottom desk drawer. He pulled out a nearly empty bottle of brandy. "It's always later than you think. Did you see my glass anywhere? Ah!"

He took the bottle with him over to the row of windows that ran along one side of the office. Tall and arched at the top, sections of red, blue, and green glass created haloed figures in robes emblazoned with the cross of Saint George. All brandished swords and heraldic shields and pennanted lances. Halverson nursed the first sip, staring blankly through one of the open panes at the trim lawn outside.

"I don't like this heat," he said, absently patting at the moisture on his upper lip with the back of his hand. "You'd think out here in the country it'd be cooler." He took another sip and topped his glass again. "You have questions?"

"Several, if you please, General. Major Van Damm—"

"I find the major tends to the histrionic, don't you?"

"Perhaps. He seems capable enough."

"So did the G-2 section of the Ninth."

Harry stubbed out his cigarette and began to slide his pad back into his briefcase. "General, this is obviously a bad time—"

Halverson held up his hand. "I apologize, Major. That was uncalled-for. These haven't been my best days." He returned to his seat, setting his glass and bottle on the desk in front of him. "You're right about Van Damm. The major has, some might think, a rather flamboyant way of putting his case, but he is capable. Very."

"The way the major explained the command structure . . . Well, I assume that since Major Markham was senior staff at the 351st, you were acquainted with him."

"Somewhat. Markham was Frank Adams's exec. Inevitably, Markham and I met a number of times. Briefings, staff meetings, the odd social occasion."

"What about these other men involved in the mission yesterday? This Captain Anderson—"

"Anderson I'd met a few times, usually official. He was one of the squadron commanders out there. Can't say I really knew the man, though, if you know what I mean. I decorated him once."

"Really?"

"Early on, one of the group's first missions, shepherding some bombers down to Brest, I think it was. Anderson had to nurse two of his pilots home after their planes were hit. He wound up going against a pair of Messerschmitts, bluffing them out with empty guns. I remember Frank—Colonel Adams—saying in passing that Anderson was something of a free-wheeler, tugged at the leash a little too much, but that's all I know."

"And Lieutenant O'Connell?"

Halverson took another sip of his drink. "Never had the pleasure."

"These other two fliers? McLagen and Jacobs?"

Halverson shook his head.

"Major Van Damm mentioned that you were friends with Colonel Adams."

"For a very long time. Very long. I—both my wife and myself, actually—we were very close with Frank Adams and his wife. Old friends. That made it very hard . . . writing her."

Harry meekly cleared his throat, feeling painfully intrusive. "I'm also told that Colonel Adams was good friends with Major Markham."

"Oh, yes, yes. Frank talked about the major a good deal. I think he'd taken quite a shine to him, in a sort of paternal way. And he considered Markham top-drawer material as a pilot and a commander. If you'd known Frank Adams, you'd know just how impressive a recommendation that was. As I said, I've met the major a number of times. He seems a nice enough fellow, very bright, very congenial without being sycophantic about it, which was refreshing. Markham wasn't the one that actually did the shooting, was he?"

"I won't know for sure who did the shooting until the ballistics analysis comes back from Scotland Yard."

Halverson shook his head. "I can't say that either Markham or Captain Anderson—what little I know of him—seemed the type to be involved in this sort of thing. Then again, I have a wife who doesn't think I'm the kind of man who sends boys out to die."

"I think that's an oversimplification, General. One that's a little unfair to yourself."

Halverson nodded appreciatively and took a long, slow sip from his glass. "That's what I do for a living, isn't it? I send men out to do a job, and part of that job is that some of them will die. If that becomes your chief concern, then you can't do your job effectively. You start holding back, which means targets aren't hit square, defenses are left intact. The consequent irony is you then lose more men by trying to save them. So, you strike some sort of balance, an unspoken agreement that your men will follow your orders because they believe you won't waste them; you balance getting the job done with giving these youngsters a fair chance of getting home. I didn't do that job too badly, Major. That's why they gave me this just a few weeks ago." He flicked a finger at the star on his collar tab. "I was going to be moved up to GHQ at the end of the month."

"And Colonel Adams was going to get the Wing?"

"Hm?" Halverson, his sense of propriety offended by his own self-flagellating lecture, had leveled an accusing stare at the brandy bottle.

"Colonel Adams was to be given command of the Wing?"

"You heard? No official announcement had been cut, but the paperwork on his full colonelcy was already in the pipe." Halverson smiled ruefully. "If the papers had moved a little faster, Frank Adams would've been here instead of at Donophan the night the Germans hit. He'd still be alive and you'd be here talking to him, while I'd be the one at GHQ siccing you on him."

"Nobody's siccing me on anybody, General. In fact, you initiated the investigation—so, for now, I'm working for you."

Halverson's smile turned cruel. "Of course. How so very forgetful of me." The smile faded. "Anyway, Frank was going to get the Wing, and we planned to give Markham the group for a probationary period."

"Probation? From what I've heard, Markham sounded capable enough."

"Frank had one reservation and, after he laid it out for me, I shared it with him. Markham is extraordinarily close to his men. There may be worse faults, and I'm sure there are those who'd say that's no fault at all, but it can be a problem—a big problem—in a line commander."

"Is it? A problem with Markham?"

"Markham has beefs—always on behalf of the men, mind you—and some of those beefs come to me. He can be pretty adamant about them, sometimes to the point of being an irritation, but nothing I thought was out of line. Even Frank said he saw no evidence it was interfering with Markham's across-the-board responsibilities. Frank worked closely with Markham, I deferred to his judgment, and that judgment was it was best to err on the side of caution. We planned a trial period. It never got to that."

"Because the Germans hit Donophan."

"Three days before we were going to make the announcements. Are you sure I can't persuade you to have a drink, Major?" Halverson didn't wait for a reply before he poured the last dregs into his glass. He looked mournfully at the empty bottle and set it aside.

"Major Van Damm seemed to have trouble seeing any justification for your authorizing the August fifteenth raids."

"He did."

"He seemed to think they were . . . ill-advised."

Halverson couldn't restrain a blurting laugh. He held his glass up in salute. "To your tact, Major. Van Damm was a touch more emphatic when he broached that particular point to me. In retrospect, I'd be an ass to take issue with him."

"You obviously had a different opinion beforehand."

"Obviously."

"Well, on what basis did you decide—"

"Major Markham decided. That's not to absolve myself, Major. I am Markham's commander. Markham may have persuaded me to go along with his decision, but, ultimately, it was my call. And, any day now, somebody—maybe you—from the JAG is going to come banging on my door and point that salient fact out to me. It's funny, but that's the same reason I agreed to the missions."

Harry shook his head, confused.

Halverson leaned forward with arch conspiratoriality. "The military, my dear Major, has a long, illustrious history of crucifixion. Kimmel couldn't've really done anything to save the Navy at Pearl, and there wasn't squat Fredendall could've done about Kasserine, but they both wound up on a cross. The night Donophan went up . . . that was my Kasserine. Markham made the point that the only way for me to mitigate the situation—if there was any way to mitigate the situation—was with some sort of a stunt. Something that would play very nicely in Life: 'The Fighting 351st: Broken But Unbowed.' Extremely inspirational. People do not crucify inspirations."

"And you believed Markham."

"Because I wanted to, I suppose." Halverson's voice was no longer that of conspirator, but the intimate, aching confessor. "Major, I've been in the Army all my adult life. I don't know anything else. I could try to make myself look a little less selfish, I suppose, and make the whole sick affair seem somewhat more noble by saying I did it for the men. And that'd at least be partly true.

"Do you know what the average age of the pilots in my command is? Twenty. I've got a son older than that flying Marine Corsairs in the Solomons. If something happened to my kid, I know I'd want somebody to—Let's just say I felt I owed the 351st something more than taking that kind of beating like a whipped dog. Those boys deserved better than that.

"Or maybe I could say I did it because Frank Adams was my friend, and when I see his wife I want to be able to say to her that we got something back for him, blood for blood."

Halverson stirred restlessly, finally pulling himself from his chair to return to the windows. The general lit a fresh cigarette, blowing the smoke out through an open pane of crimson glass. "You have more questions?"

"How badly was Donophan hit?"

"There's a folder on my desk. Take it with you if you like. It's the report on their losses. Donophan was caught flat-footed. The Germans knocked out the RAF radar station near Hawkinge, then came through the hole with the raid on the field. The station's comm links had been knocked out. By the time they got the word to RAF sector control, and they notified their superiors, then passed the word to their liaison to contact our liaison . . ." Halverson turned to Harry; he smiled sadly. "And so forth. I was told with sincere regret and condolences by the RAF that their people and our people have yet to work out a 'smoothly integrated communications structure.' The short of it is that by the time Donophan got the word, the German bombs were coming through their roof."

He turned back to the window and waved at someone Harry couldn't see. "Over thirty percent support personnel killed or wounded; nearly half of all facilities destroyed or damaged; all on-site fuel and ordnance supplies destroyed; almost two thirds of all aircraft damaged or destroyed. If the Germans had perfected that kind of operation during the Blitz, we'd be fighting them from Greenland by now." Halverson flicked his cigarette out the open pane. "Most of them were together in one shelter and the Germans pasted it square," he said. "That left them with only five duty-fit pilots."

"Markham, Anderson, O'Connell, Jacobs, and McLagen."

Halverson nodded.

"You didn't waste much time in deciding to go ahead with the operation. Van Damm says the request for targets came down—"

"The following morning, yes. August the ninth. I wouldn't say I'd made up my mind at that point, though. Actually, I never did. I was afraid not to go ahead with it, and once it began, I was afraid to stop it. The sin of omission as opposed to commission." Halverson sat in his chair, looked to his glass, but made no move toward it. "In any case, we felt we had to move quickly. There was a lot of work to do and we were operating under the impression that we didn't have much time to do it. The 351st didn't have the on-hand matériel to mount the raid. Fuel, ordnance, and so on had to be requisitioned and brought in. And, I wanted a target selection and mission plan from Markham that was going to bring everybody home safe. We needed all this before General DiGarre made a decision on the disposition of the group. The same morning I asked Van Damm for targets, the general was asking me for an assessment of the damage to the 351st, and a recommendation on either deactivating the group and replacing it with a fresh one from the States, or rebuilding it around the surviving core. In either case, he would've stood the 351st down until they were up to operational strength. By that time, we expected that I would be deactivated and replaced, too. . . . Funny how it worked out. The earliest we could get the mission together was Saturday morning: the thirteenth. I stalled on my report to DiGarre as long as I could, finally sent it up Friday, hoping it would take him a day or two to make a decision, which would still give us the mission."

"But it rained Saturday."

"Maybe that was somebody's way of telling me I should've just scrubbed the whole thing."

"You held off until Monday."

"We needed a day for things to dry out. The auxiliary fuel tanks for the planes are made of some sort of heavy resin-treated paper. That's what we're using until they start delivering metal tanks. You need a fairly dry field to operate without metal tanks. So, Monday."

"And General DiGarre didn't say anything in all that time?"

"If General DiGarre had so much as frowned, that would've been all it would've taken for me to scrub."

"I was looking over the different targets that Major Van Damm had selected. Why the depot at Helsvagen? How was that target chosen?"

"Simple pragmatics. We discounted the French targets because although they were closer, the fuel depots were easier targets. Touching off those fuel storage tanks isn't as tricky as getting bombs on the money with those other targets. Of the fuel depots, the one at Helsvagen was closest. And—" Halverson sighed "—God help me, we did think that when one of the depots went up, it would have a certain necessary . . .

'spectacle.' Bombing a bridge in the middle of a swamp hardly seems what the broken but unbowed do, does it, Major?"

Harry ignored the question. "One more thing, General. About the BDA flight over the target afterward. Or rather, why there wasn't one. Whose decision was that?"

"Like everything else, strictly speaking, it was mine. We had agreed, Al Markham and I, during the planning stages, that the mission was such a low priority, and the target so open, that it wouldn't require a BDA flight. He was pretty sure—and I agreed with him—that the gun films from the raid would suffice. But we also agreed that we'd wait and see. If there was a need afterward we'd send one out."

"And how was that need to be determined?"

"It was Markham's call; he was the man on the spot."

"So, when he returned, he contacted you and said it wouldn't be necessary."

"Right."

"Did you know the film magazine from Major Markham's gun camera was found empty?"

Halverson frowned. "No, I didn't."

They were done. As Harry packed his things Halverson got to his feet. "Major, I have no intention of disavowing any responsibility I have in this matter."

"Of course, sir."

"I don't know what your intentions or instructions are, other than those from Colonel Ryan and myself—"

"Sir, I have no—"

"—but let's go on the assumption that, as you said, for now you're working for me. Major Markham cost me three men yesterday I didn't have to lose." Halverson waited for a few seconds for the tacit writ to sink in. "Do you understand me?"

"Yes, sir," Harry said quietly.

"Whatever it takes, Major. If you need anything from me . . ."

Harry nodded. At the door, he stopped. The general had lowered himself back into his chair, cradling his glass in his hands.

"General? I'm . . . sorry for your troubles, sir."

Halverson nodded listlessly. "Have a safe drive back."

As Harry stood by his jeep in the car park he looked up at the windows of Halverson's office. The general's pale face was in one of the clear panes, lost in the mosaic of colored glass. Harry waved a farewell but Halverson made no sign that he'd seen him, his gaze locked on some point beyond the west horizon.

The charm which had served Joe Ryan so well for most of his life—the graceful bearing, the bright smile, the well-chosen bon mot—was also, in a way, his curse. Whenever his senior officers required one of their number to hobnob with the wing-collar-and-tiara set for purposes of diplomacy, or to entice an agreement for use of lands or other assets, or, simply—in a gesture of goodwill—to give a host and hostess an American officer to show off to their guests over cocktails, Ryan was the preferred tool. But even a born hobnobber like Ryan could grow tired of being displayed like the latest high-priced trinket from Harrods. Thus, his "invitation" to Harry to join him in such engagements. "If they turn out to be jerks," he'd told Harry on previous occasions, "at least I can talk to you."

Which is why Harry, clad in GI socks and GI underwear and a GI bathrobe, was standing before the mirror in his quarters practicing his bow. He tried a shallow, curt move, just a cock of his head, really, something he remembered from a Claude Rains film. "How pleased to meet you, my lord, and this must be your lovely wife?" But then he worried that it would be considered forward to declare a lord's wife "lovely."

He tried a deeper bow, something along the lines of Paul Henreid. "How do you do, my lord?" and offered his hand. Or perhaps he shouldn't offer his hand. Who was supposed to offer a hand first and to whom?

A sharp and formal bow this time: Conrad Veidt. No, it didn't feel right without a click of the heels, and he thought it quite inappropriate for the Allies to click heels. "A sincere pleasure to meet you, my lord."

"That's not how you do it." Nagel was suddenly in the doorway with Harry's cleaned Class A's on a hanger draped over his shoulder.

"You're ruining the crease," Harry snapped and grabbed the uniform away. "Don't you knock? Were you born in a barn or something?"

"I may not know when to knock, but I know how to do it."

"Do what? Nagel, are you sure these are my pants?" Harry was working up a sweat tugging on his trousers. "You're sure those clowns down there—"

"That is not how you greet royalty," Nagel interrupted, speaking with uncharacteristic conviction.

"Didn't I tell you to tell those clowns in the cleaning shop 1600 hours? Do you know what time it is? If I'm late, I'm going to skin—"

"I told them 1600 hours—"

"Damn!" Harry sucked in his belly and fastened the buckle. Had they done something to shrink his trousers? With a wheeze, he bent over to pull his shoes on. He managed only one before he had to come up for air. The air went right back out of him in a sigh when he saw Nagel still loitering in the doorway.

"OK, Nagel, if it'll make you happy. How do you greet royalty?"

Nagel's face broke into a satisfied smile. He bowed steeply, swept one arm across his middle and extended the other out behind him while one of his size twelves gingerly slid out in front of him. When he reached the farthest extremity of his dip, he lowered his voice and intoned, "Good evening, m'Luhd." He looked up and saw Harry staring at him in unhappy amazement. "That," Nagel announced, "is how it's done. Didn't you ever see *Robin Hood?*" He repeated the demonstration. "Good evening, m'Luhd."

"Good-bye, Nagel."

After chasing Nagel out, Harry pulled on his shirt and waddled into the bathroom to comb what there was of his hair. When he returned to the bedroom, Joe Ryan was perched on a corner of his dresser.

"Jeez, you scared me! You trying to give me a heart attack or something?"

"I don't need to," Ryan said, pointing at Harry's straining trouser buckle. "Looks like you're eating your way into one."

"It's the damned cleaners. They did something to these pants."

"Now, isn't that funny! That's the first thing I thought, too. Joe, I said to myself, I'll bet those guys in the laundry did something to poor Harry's pants. I mean it couldn't be that poor Harry is so god-almighty huge, could it? It must be those guys in the—"

"Why don't you knock? Doesn't anybody around here knock?"

"C'mon, Harry, shake a leg. Should I get you a crowbar?"

Harry's thumb was stuck in the knot he tried to make in his tie. "Don't give me any of this hurry-up stuff. You're five minutes early."

Ryan held up his wrist, pulled up his sleeve with a Houdini-like flourish, and pointed to the face of his watch. "See this, Harry? This is a *colonel's* watch. When I'm with a *major*, the major's watch is always wrong, and *this* watch is always *right*. *This* watch says I'm on time. The only time this watch is wrong is when a *general's* watch says different. Speaking of which, I had a very innnnteresting chat with a certain two-star general this morning."

Harry swallowed. "DiGarre?"

"I tried to get in touch with you about it this morning, but—"

"You know how full my hands have been—"

"I know, I know, and that's *exactly* what I told the general. But you have to understand, Harry; DiGarre's concerned. He's concerned because SHAEF's concerned. That's right, Harry. The word's gotten that high up. I warned you that a lot of bigwigs were going to take an interest—"

"What'd he want?"

"He wanted to know how things were going. How *are* things going, Harry?"

Harry sat on the edge of his bed. The general may have been a general but that didn't keep Harry from being annoyed with him. "How are things going? I've been on this thing all of a day and a half—"

"And in DiGarre's eyes, that's a day and a half too long. Don't bark at me, Harry, I'm with you. But I told you they'd get nervous. I guess the general just wants to know that everything's going along OK. Everything is going along OK, isn't it?"

Harry shrugged.

"Do you think you can be a little more specific?"

"The more I think about it, the more it doesn't make sense."

"The 'it' in question being? . . ."

"Something's come up."

"Something."

"I don't know if it makes a difference, but . . . did you know that Markham's gun film is missing?"

"No, I didn't know that."

"G-2 opened up the film magazines when they got them back to London. Markham's was empty."

Ryan processed Harry's nagging little item and found a reason to grin. "Missing means nobody knows what happened to the film. It's not missing, Harry. You know what happened to it. That little fink destroyed it."

Harry shrugged again.

Once more with peace of mind, Ryan interlaced his fingers and bent them backward until the knuckles gave up a relaxing crack. "If you ask me, that makes things even more clear-cut. Markham's the trigger man, making a pretty poor job of trying to cover his tracks."

"Maybe. But I keep running it over and over in my head and it doesn't quite all fit together. I mean, why would Markham destroy the film?"

"Harry, that better be a rhetorical question, or else I think I've grievously overestimated your abilities."

"Humor me. Why destroy the film?"

"To conceal his dastardly crimes, of course."

"But there's witnesses. Eyewitnesses. They saw him and he knows it."

"Which, no doubt, is why he tried to assassinate them."

"The Greshams were inside the house. He couldn't be sure he'd gotten them."

"And he couldn't be sure he hadn't. He had to play it safe, so he destroyed the film." Ryan slid his cap back and massaged his forehead. "Why do you have to aggravate me like this, Harry?"

"So, he destroys the film, thinks he's taken care of the witnesses, then leaves a ton of ballistics evidence at the scene of the crime."

Ryan stood, brusquely brushing off the seat of his trousers. "Don't you ever get anybody to dust in here?" he said tersely. He moved to the window and lit a cigarette, and considered. Then, "Markham's a pilot, Harry, not a policeman. Maybe he doesn't know as much about criminal ballistics analysis as you and me. Maybe it never occurred to him that the shells and slugs at the cottage could be traced to his guns."

"OK, let's grant that. But he knows he left a bucketful of cartridge casings on the Gresham lawn that have U.S. Army ordnance markings."

"So maybe in the heat of the moment—"

"No! Not him! Not this guy! You should read this guy's file some time. I've only had time to flip through his 66-1, but every page is high marks. Talk to some of the people who know him. Markham's top of the line, Joe. You don't get to be a combat officer with his ratings by losing your head when the heat gets hot." The room felt close just then, and Harry only now realized how his pursuit of the point was pressing Ryan. He changed his tone and smiled mockingly. "Or do you? How'd you get all that brass?"

Ryan welcomed the opportunity for a grin. "I live right. So . . . what're you getting at with all this?"

"I'm not sure. Maybe it's nothing."

"Oh, for crying out loud, Harry, don't run me through the wringer and wind up with *that*! You make it pretty damned hard to be sympathetic."

"If there is something going on here, Markham and Anderson are the only two who know what it is. I'd like to be on an even footing with them before I give them a chance to get their defense together."

Ryan pondered the point for a moment, then flicked his cigarette out the window and shook his head unhappily. "You can't hold somebody without probable cause, Harry. Not even in the Army. If this were any DA's office back home, we would've had to let these two go this morning."

"This isn't and we don't. Nobody's questioned them, nobody's tried to get them to incriminate themselves. They're merely confined to quarters pending—"

"Pending *what*, Harry?" Ryan's voice was harsh and demanding. "That's what I want to know! That's what *General DiGarre* wants to know! Give me something I can go to him with! I'm not going in there and say, 'We've got murder suspects concealing evidence and all my guy can do is look at that and go, Hmmmm, interesting.' I'm *not* going to do that!"

"There's something at work here, Joe. It's like when you know something's moving around in the shadows. You can't *see* it, but you *know* it's there."

"This Markham guy and Anderson, do they know each other?"

"Flew in the Eagle Squadron together, according to their records."

"Maybe . . ." Ryan was still hunting for the neat ribbon that would reseal all of the little Pandora beasties Harry seemed to be trying so diligently to stir out of their box. "Maybe Markham's covering for Anderson."

"But we've got Anderson's film. That clears him."

"Only if it is Anderson's film. Harry, the G-2 guys go out there to pick up these films, they don't know whose is whose; just what they're told. Maybe it's Markham's film we have, and Anderson is the one short of an alibi. Markham wants to bail his buddy out, so he says the film we have belongs to Anderson."

"I hadn't thought of that. That's a possibility."

"Either way, that's no reason to drag your feet," Ryan said with finality. "Scotland Yard should have at least the prelim ballistics and autopsy reports for you tomorrow. That'll decide who did what to who. But you have enough on hand not to have to wait that long. Unless there's something else . . ."

The business with the missing gun film still nagged at Harry. But he knew Ryan was right in saying that it represented no substantive reason not to move forward; at least none that would sit well with generals. Harry slid from the windowsill to his escritoire, picked up the telephone there, and dialed the Provost Marshal's office. "Major Posner? This is Major Voss at the JAG's office. . . . Yes, it's about those two men you have under guard out at Donophan. I'm issuing the order to place them under arrest. . . . Yes, bring them in. The charges are murder and attempted murder." He ticked off the necessary particulars, then hung up and turned to Ryan. "Happy now?"

"Very."

"I should be here when they bring them in. In case they want to make any kind of statement or—"

"It'll wait till tomorrow. They're not going anywhere. Now, fix your hair, Harry-boy. Tonight, we dine with the nobility."

I happened to have been on station at the Annex that evening, idling across the street from the Court gates from where I could see Harry's chuffy figure follow Ryan's across the cobbles to the butter-colored Rolls-Royce that had been sent for them. Ryan's head was jauntily cocked; his stride was a broad, aristocratic swagger. As he approached the aged chauffeur standing by the open passenger door, Ryan touched his finger to the brim of his cap, accompanying the gesture with a superior sniff and an unbelievably bad House of Lords accent as he called over his shoulder, "Do huddy along, Haddold." Then, to the chauffeur, "What am I to do with him?" The chauffeur, being a properly bred British servant, betrayed no more emotion than a slight flaring of his pinched nostrils. Harry's smiled apology on behalf of his commander was ignored with equal stoicism.

Then off they went to dine—as Ryan had said—with the nobility. I assumed the day's actions were probably over at that point, and headed home to a somewhat less soigné evening of my own: a tin of Spam warmed over a gas ring, a bracing dose of scotch, and a few hours of pondering.

I'd sit on my windowsill, watching the coming night, nurse my glass of harder-and-harder-to-find good scotch, and wonder about that unexplained cordon down in East Sussex, all the related fuss among the Allied senior ranks and Scotland Yard, about the waddling little man I'd followed to Grosvenor Square that morning.

And maybe by the second or third glass, I'd ponder that insulting little stump peeking out beneath my robe.

All I ever remember is a flash, a concussion, then blackness, until that moment days later when I could lift my head from the hospital pillow and see the ridge of blanket that was my right leg, and the flat expanse where my left should have been.

After another drink, I'd wonder how Cathryn made her nights pass.

When Harry told me the story of that evening, he told of how out of place he'd felt on the Roller's plush rear bench, the passenger compartment smelling of venerable leather, aged tobacco, and the brandy Joe Ryan had found tucked in the fold-out bar. Behind the thick window glass, the ride was smooth and the only sound that of the traditional Rolls purr. Below the rim of his window, Harry saw the swept lines of the automobile gleaming like freshly poured steel in the red of the late-day sun.

On the other side of the glass, pasty-faced women in faded dresses, squalling infants in their arms, waited in line for a ration of water from lorries stationed in neighborhoods where the water lines had been lost in some past bombing. Ragged children scampered about the debris of bombed-out buildings, shouting at the long, humming limousine as it passed. Constables, wrinkled and past the age of military service, touched the brim of their helmets, and workmen in threadbare trousers doffed their caps.

Harry was struck by the lack of rancor or jealousy afforded their way as the Rolls passed. Centuries of rank and order had done their job, and instead of anger and envy Harry saw eyes dipped in conditioned respect. He hoped the people outside could not see who it really was they were saluting.

Ryan suffered no such pang. His attention focused almost exclusively on the brandy nipperkin and neat little snifters in their velour-cushioned niches in the bar. He dipped into that bar more than once while he briefed Harry on the evening's program.

Sir Whosis—as Ryan enjoyed calling him—was one of those wealthy emeritus types who owned a stretch of land in the downs, south of London. The Grosvenor Square brass had decided that despite the acreage already at their disposal, this particular lot was indispensable for some upcoming maneuvers. Sir Whosis was not averse to granting use of the land, but felt, by virtue of his title, that a little fawning and groveling was due first. Ryan and Harry were to do the fawning and groveling.

The Rolls took them to a neighborhood in Bloomsbury scarred by a few sticks of bombs (strays, presumably, unless Jerry had gotten the idea that giving a few quaint restaurants the chop was the way to undermine British determination). The limo drew to a stop in front of a nondescript building on one of the quiet, narrow streets near the British Museum. The building's lower windows were filled with sandbags, and the upper story's were planked over. Chunks of plaster were chipped off the facade, and a tattered awning proclaimed the name of the restaurant in gold lettering too faded to decipher. The chauffeur held the limousine's door for them, and the restaurant door was tended by a stooped-over old gent dressed in ill-fitting livery as something vaguely akin to an eighteenth-century chasseur.

The deferential maître d' led them through the dark, heavily draped foyer into the high-ceilinged dining room. This, in surprising contrast to the scarred exterior, glittered: crystal chandeliers, golden sconces on the walls, brass serving carts, waiters in gold-braided dinner jackets, flashing silverware. All about were carts laden with marbled slabs of beef, dripping poultry, steaming vegetables, and squat pastries on engraved silver trays.

Harry was about to make some wry comment about what kind of coupon book was required for such sumptuous rations, but Ryan was already smiling and waving at a diminutive figure in evening dress. Sir Whosis had pink, watery eyes, very little hair, not all the best teeth, and a handshake that was scarcely a squeeze.

The gent's lady was a mousy, unprepossessing woman, coated in a veneer of silk and quite a few sparkling stones. She acknowledged the Americans with a tight-lipped smile, but held Harry's hand in a way that seemed—particularly after her husband's brief touch-and-go— improperly long and firm.

Sir Whosis proved to be an inveterate—and horrible—storyteller, with an inexhaustible fund of meaningless, humorless anecdotes. Harry listened to the knight's babble and Ryan's murmurs of interest the way he listened to the radio, just enough to provide an occasional nod when called upon.

As course after course of food piled on their table, and the wine steward ensured their glasses were always fueled, Harry felt a twinge, remembering his wife's letters and tales of waiting in long lines for her ration of beef. Here was enough meat, vegetables, sugar, butter, bread, fruit, and biscuits laid on to get Cynthia and the boys through a month.

His guilty reverie was broken by a grinning Sir Whosis, gesturing at him with his long-stemmed glass of Baccarat crystal, drunkenly saying, "The fox, yes? The fox?"

Harry looked helplessly at Ryan, who semaphored that Harry should respond with humor, and Harry mustered a "Ha ha!"

Perhaps it was the rich food, or the wine, or both, but Harry's stomach began to churn. He turned to excuse himself to Dame Whosis, but she had already vanished.

The restaurant was crowded, each table a replica of his own with a mix of swank evening clothes and uniforms of all sorts in attendance. A hallway took him off the main dining room. He padded down thick carpet and tried a few likely-looking doors, discovering an office and a broom closet. He turned round back the way he thought he'd come, pushed through a door he didn't remember passing, and found himself in another dining room, this one quiet, dark, and empty, apparently reserved for private affairs. A couple stood across the room in the shadows, embracing. The man was young, mustachioed, and striking in his RAF uniform. Most striking of all about him was that the woman in his arms was the much older Dame Whosis. Harry took an involuntary step backward and bumped into a table. Crystal and silver rattled, and the woman turned. Her jewels sparkled, even in the darkness, and her diadem swam loosely in her unraveling coif. She gave Harry a conspiratorial look, a smile that frightened him with its knowledge that he'd never tell.

He fumbled his way back through the door, hurrying until he finally collared a busboy who directed him to the nearest toilet, the staff loo in the basement. Harry relieved himself among mops and cans of disinfectant, then sat for a long while enjoying the cool of the little room. When the rebellious movements of his stomach ceased, he wound his way back to his table where Sir Whosis's wife was already seated, composed and smiling collegially at Harry.

In the Rolls, Dame Whosis clung to the arm of her husband, who had sunk into a wine-induced snooze, and chatted charmingly as if nothing were amiss. "Naturally, there will be no problem with your maneuvers," the lady said graciously as Harry and Ryan were dropped at the Annex gate. "Just ring first." She smiled, and her mousy features receded into the darkness of the passenger compartment as the Rolls purred off.

They were tired and sotted and their path past the gate sentries and across the Court wavered, taking them into several near-collisions with parked vehicles. They tossed off buoyant good-evenings to the men in the orderly room of their BOQ as they headed for the stairs. But one of the orderlies stopped them with news that the Provost Marshal had rung for Colonel Ryan and urgently needed the call returned. Repeat: urgently.

Ryan made the call from the orderly room and Harry, not sure he could make the stairs without Ryan's assistance, and certain Ryan could not make them without his assistance, parked himself on a nearby bench. At that late hour, filled with wine and heavy food, it was all he could do to keep an eye open. He wasn't even aware that the call had finished and Ryan was standing over him, weaving on his own unsteady legs, until Ryan poked him in the shoulder.

"Wake up, Harry. That was Posner."

Harry forced his eyes open.

"C'mon, Harry. Up! Get on the horn and tell those two beauties working for you to meet us over at the Provost. I'll see what I can do about scrounging up a steno."

"You mean now?" Harry's eyes were finally open, but he was hardly fully awake.

"Now."

"Why?"

Ryan dropped onto the bench next to him. Harry tried to force himself completely alert and to focus on Ryan's face and its mix of fatigue, puzzlement, and even a little pleasure.

"Major Markham has decided to make everybody's life a little simpler," Ryan said. "He told Major Posner he wants to confess."

CHAPTER FIVE

IN HOC SIGNO VINCES

HIMSELF—THE OLD BOSS, THE LORD and Master—had been the only familiar face waiting on the dock when my hospital ship pulled into Southampton. He was—as I'd fully expected— untouched by the sight of me hobbling down the gangway on my new crutches, the left trouser leg of my pajamas neatly pinned up behind what remained of my leg. He had spent thirty years chronicling the human race's catalog of incivilities. Next to famine, massacre, and the hangings of deranged sex criminals, a lost leg deserved little note. In fact, I was surprised—and even a bit touched—that Himself had seen it worthy enough to show up at all.

(Not long after, I called his attention to what I thought to be a rising tide of sentimentality in him. I twitted him then, wondering if perhaps his new softness was a product of advancing senility, bolstering my case by pointing to the touching little tribute he himself had penned for the paper, welcoming me home. With typical sangfroid, he shrugged me off and pointed to how the notice was buried near the end of the first section. "Hardly room for it at all, my son. Lucky we could fit it anywhere.")

Later, fitted with my contraption and back in the office, he sat across from me for "a bit of chat about your future, my son." He dipped into his bottom desk drawer for the bottle of twelve-year-old he saved for notable occasions and splashed some into a pair of chipped teacups he kept on hand (to this day I have no idea what pretense about his fairly regular nips the teacups were there to maintain).

"Eh, Ahab, if you think you're for being some old pensioner feeding the pigeons in Hyde Park, you've got it wrong," he informed me. "We're not done wi' you yet, my son. Soon's you're up to it, you buff up yer new pin and hop on back to work." The caustic insensitivity was calculated to confer a sense of business as usual. But both he and I were aware that the game had changed irrevocably for me. I knew, and he knew I knew, that he would look at me adjusting my squeaking new limb and decide my globe-trotting days were fini.

I was retained with all the honors and respect due my long tenure, and there was a form of work for me, though my new provenance was the local scene: the bores of Parliament, a coven of old biddies commemorating the Duchess of Bedford's inception of afternoon tea, and the like. I'm sure Himself considered it a favor that there was any work at all for me, but for me it was a form of slow suffocation.

On that morning when Dennis O'Connell was pulled dripping wet and dead from his aeroplane off the English coast—Monday, 15 August—I was, in fact, typing up just one of a series of airy-fairy pieces Himself had dubbed Stiff Upper Lips: items that showed English fortitude at its best. This particular piece concerned an elderly pub foursome in the South End who had kept blithely at their best-of-nine-frames snooker match during the last air raid. A stick of near misses served only to spark a debate among the geezers on whether movement of the balls by the nearby explosions constituted some sort of foul. (In the spirit of its being a Stiff Upper Lip piece, I discreetly neglected mentioning that at least part of the quartet's nerve in the face of enemy fire seemed to have come from the half-dozen or so pints of ale each had downed before the raid.)

Listlessly pecking out the prose, I overheard word buzzing about the office of the affair on the Sussex coast. I had lost my leg, but not my instinct for the hunt, so, along with the other Fleet Street hounds, I was quickly off to find out what I could. I was back at it the next day as well and had fully intended to go it again a third day, but on that day Himself saw fit to push another view.

I had meant to breeze through the office that morning, just long enough to check for messages and then be off.

"Could I trouble you?" he called from the doorway of his office. He had the gift of making requests sound like commands.

In his office he sat back in the cracked leather of his chair, his stubby fingers laced across the protruding crest of his substantial stomach, and smiled at me, his eyes crinkling behind his bottle-thick glasses. Though the clock had yet to strike nine, the twelve-year-old was already on the desk and the teacups had been dosed. He nodded for me to close the door behind me.

"Getting on all right then, my son? Been having fun stalking about, have you?"

"I've kept meself busy."

"All good things must come to an end."

"And I'm more than happy to let them come to their natural end," and I raised my cup in salute to the sentiment.

"I've got a box to fill and that snooker bit'd see it right."

"Won't take but a minute."

"And I've got another box for tomorrow—"

I held up a hand. "Shall we . . . ?" I made a twirling motion of my finger indicating an interest in leaping ahead.

He seemed genuinely pleased. "Oh, let's do."

"Something happened down at the coast on Monday."

"Old Rob the janitor knows as much."

"I checked with the locals, and the only human inhabitants in the area are an old spotter and his wife. Now, either this spotter saw something, or something happened to him, and it involves the Americans because within hours the Yanks were a-swarming out there. And whatever happened wasn't strictly within bounds, because they've put their legal apparatus into high gear, from the little snowdrops to dapper Joe Ryan."

He knew the name. He was, after all, The Old Boss, Lord and Master, etc.

"I'm not sure what's on over there, but all my usual snitches have locked the trap," I said. "At their press office, they all have this grim look, as if the family's found out Daddy's been buggering the neighbor's goats, but they won't say a word. Not even lies."

He let out a meditative, "Hmph," and sipped at his cup. "I have Brannagh on this, you know."

Brannagh was getting a lot of the assignments I'd gotten in my two-legged days. "Irish toff. He's never met a nauseatingly bright tie he didn't like."

"Quite."

"But very good."

"Thank you for saying. In Brannagh's view, the Yanks' attitude indicates some desperate damage control. Something quite dicky has happened and they've turned to slash-and-burn so's not to leave a trace."

"Sounds right."

"In which case, so Brannagh says, one could play fox-and-geese with the Yanks till Doomsday without turning a lead. You can't follow the clues, my son, unless they let you see the clues, and that doesn't look likely at this point. It would seem, then, that there are more productive things my personnel could be doing with themselves, don't you think? Such as those stories they've been *assigned*."

"The snooker match."

"Touché." He took another sip from his teacup, studying the whirling liquid as he tilted the cup this way and that. Finally, he gave up an assenting grunt. "I'll strike a bargain. You can play with this till close of business Friday. Then, old son, you go back to working for a living. And you'll be handing me that snooker piece before you're off, eh?"

He played the hard-arse, but I suppose he was turning into an old foof after all. His decision had little to do with serving the paper, or journalistic dedication, or any other practical or idealistic purpose. In fact, it was quite obvious he expected the story to go nowhere as, frankly, did I. For me, it was finding out if I'd left more than my leg in a bomb crater on the far side of the world. And Himself, bless him, was willing to let me.

Harry Voss pulled back the blackout curtains and pushed open the window. Big Ben was chiming five, and the morning breeze was cool and clean. Down in the Annex court, night still eddied so heavily he could barely make out Albert Markham and his Military Police escorts crossing the cobbles toward the gate.

Harry stretched and tried to soothe the tired muscles in his neck by rolling his head. His mouth carried the horrible taste of coffee and cigarettes mixed with food and liquor. The coffee, hastily brewed by the night orderlies, hadn't done much to settle the dicey situation in his stomach. A whistle from the courtyard focused his groggy vision on an MP below, signaling him to close the blackout drapes.

He pulled the thick shrouds shut and turned back to the conference room. The long table was littered with empty coffee cups, overflowing ashtrays, and scribble-covered notepads. The air carried the blue haze of dead cigarettes, and the lacy tendrils of live ones. The staff sergeant stenographer was still trying to pack up his machine while Ryan was shoving him out the door.

When he wasn't using his hands to push at the bewildered steno, Ryan was rubbing them together and bubbling like a winner of the Irish Sweepstakes. "I want a full transcript of that no later than 0900, you understand? Good!" he said, without waiting for a response, tearing the door open and shoving the sergeant clear. "And that's your-eyes-only! The original and the steno record go straight to me, and photostats hand-delivered to Major Voss, General Halverson, and General DiGarre. Got it?" Again, without waiting for a response, "And keep your lip buttoned on this!" he commanded and slammed the door closed. He turned his beaming face toward the room.

Grassi, in a uniform that looked like—and probably was—something he'd fallen asleep in, sat slouched at the table, looking over his notes, and shaking his head with pleased amazement. Peter Ricks was there as well, eerily composed and cleanly pressed for the hour, his face marked with grim resignation and finality.

Harry considered those contented and/or resigned faces. *Is it just me?* he wondered. *Am I the only one who feels it?*

Joe Ryan had called for the stenographer, stirred the orderlies after a coffee urn, had Harry call for Ricks and Grassi, all the time keeping Markham and his MP escort waiting in the JAG building's vestibule.

Harry had fretted about giving Markham enough time to change his mind.

"You haven't played in this league before," Ryan lectured Harry as he bustled about his preparations in the conference room. "Half the game is psychology. We let this joker cool his heels a while, give him time to sweat. When we finally let him in here, you want him to see that we're ready for him. You want him to know he's outgunned."

To which end Ryan had clustered his troops in a tight knot at one end of the table, Ricks and Grassi to his left, Harry at his right, giving himself the head chair. Markham's place was reserved at the far-off foot of the table, his only company to be the stenographer, whom Ryan had positioned to crowd the major.

But whatever intimidating effect all this was intended to have, Albert Markham entered the room under his MP escort no more impressed than a diner who has been informed that his table is now ready.

Other than the major's composure, remarkable in a man facing a hangable offense, Harry found himself surprisingly underwhelmed by the man. Having gleaned bits and pieces of Markham's daring aviation exploits, his list of—evidently—well-earned decorations, he'd expected a World War I–style knight-errant of the air: dashing good looks, a sparkling smile, trailing white scarf, and so on.

But the Albert Quincy Markham Harry met in those predawn hours of Wednesday, 17 August, was impressively unimpressive. A bit short, the twenty-seven-year-old's athletic days were long behind him, and his middle was a bit thick and a touch soft, his chin beginning to sag. His mousy hair was a short, efficient, unflattering bristle. Hours of sun glare through cockpit canopies had left squint lines round small, pale eyes, but the puffy face showed little else in the way of character.

He shuffled in between his guards, fingering his cap awkwardly. But at sight of Ryan and his cadre, he immediately straightened to attention and snapped out a crisp salute. For the moment, something in his bearing, in his—Harry searched for the word—conviction, showed him more matched to the uniform than any lantern-jawed, square-shouldered caricature on a recruiting poster.

Ryan tossed off an acknowledging salute, nodded Markham to the witness chair, and signaled the MP's to wait outside, closing the doors behind them.

Markham stood by his designated chair, still at attention. Ryan fixed him with a practiced glare, the objective being to start the accused trembling in his shoes. Ryan theatrically cleared his throat and Harry knew they were in for some prepared, prosecutorial speech, but before the colonel could open his mouth, Markham spoke.

"I want to apologize for disturbing all of you at this time of night," Markham said. His voice, marked by a Midwestern drone—was so soft that the four men at the other end of the table simultaneously leaned forward to hear better. "I know you don't owe me this kind of consideration. You don't owe me much of anything, I suppose, so I appreciate you meeting with me. I just figured the sooner we cleared this up the better for all of us."

He spoke haltingly, uncomfortable with occasions for oratory.

Ryan gave a harrumphing agreement, obviously irritated that Markham had undercut his momentum, but, again, before he could launch into his opening remarks, Markham—in his usual, deferential way—cut him off.

"Sorry, sir, but is it OK if I have some of this coffee? Anybody else want a cup? Oh, you've got some?" To the steno: "How about you, Sarge? No? I don't worry about it keeping me up. I haven't slept a peaceful hour since this whole thing started." His small mouth flicked in a sad, sheepish grin. "I guess that's guilt, huh?"

"As you say, Major," Ryan said, making a display of looking at his watch, "it is late."

Harry thought Ryan sounded surprisingly tentative. Poor guy, Harry thought, studying his friend. The colonel looked almost ready to break into a run, so eager was he to get Markham's confession down on paper before the flier could reconsider. And yet, Ryan wanted to be careful to do nothing to push Markham to that reconsideration.

"We should get started, huh?" Markham stood over the indicated seat, took a deep breath, then sat. He carefully arranged his cap to one side, his coffee to the other. "If I get the mumbles or you miss something," he said to the steno, "you let me know, Sarge."

The steno, surprised at being thought of as something other than hearing-room furniture, looked to the officers at the other end of the table, unsure of an appropriate response. "Um, sure, sir."

"So," the flier said with a tense clearing of his throat, "how do we do this?"

Ryan signaled the stenographer to begin recording, then made a rather stuffy introduction opening the proceedings and properly identifying those in attendance.

"Do I have to put my hand on a Bible or something like that?" Markham asked.

"Oh, hell," Ryan said. "I forgot all about that. Anybody see a Bible around?"

"Should I go look for one?" Ricks asked, rising in his chair. Harry signaled him back into his chair with a shake of his head.

"It's the Army," Grassi said wryly. "I don't think you'll find many just laying around."

"I don't think we need all the frou-frous," Ryan said to Markham, "do you, Major? You promise to tell the truth, don't you?"

Markham slowly raised his right hand. "I swear to tell the truth, the whole truth, and nothing but the truth." His right hand came down, the fingers tucked in except for his index digit, which made a small criss-cross on his chest. "Cross my heart—" he paused, seemed inwardly amused at the phrase "—and hope to die." To Ryan: "That should do it, shouldn't it, Colonel?" For a moment, Markham's self-conscious awkwardness had faded.

Ryan looked to Harry, obviously impressed with this sudden demonstration of Markham's coolness. "Now, Major Markham—"

"Um, Colonel?" It was Ricks.

"Yes, Captain?"

"I hate to interrupt . . ."

Ryan, who hated even more to be interrupted, frowned at yet another delay in getting on with the business of the occasion. He nodded at Ricks to proceed.

"I'm wondering if Major Markham has been cautioned as to the evidentiary status of any statement he might make—"

Ryan's frown deepened into a sharp glower. He turned to Harry.

"It might be better for the record," Harry said soothingly.

"For the record?"

Harry was offering more than a balm. It was typical Harry-esque diligence. He knew any irregularity or impropriety could turn the hoped-for case-settling confession into the basis for a future appeal.

Ryan took a breath. "All right, for the record. Major Markham: You are making a formal, sworn, and voluntary statement regarding charges of criminal action against you. This statement can be used against you as evidence in any future proceeding. Short and sweet, to make sure there's no misunderstanding: Whatever you say right now is gospel. There's not going to be any taking it back tomorrow." Ryan looked back to Ricks as if to ask, "Is that good enough for you?" Ricks sheepishly dropped his eyes to his lap.

"I understand, sir," Markham replied. "I appreciate you making the point clear to me."

He *is* something, Harry thought, studying the aviator. Neither impatient nor reluctant. Uncomfortable, but not nervous, nor at some icy remove. Perfect balance. Harry looked round his end of the table— Ryan, champing at the bit and fretting at the same time; Grassi, smelling blood, even more rabid than Ryan; Ricks, dutifully observing the proprieties. We're children next to him, he thought.

"Any other point of order I might have missed?" Ryan asked Ricks.

Red-faced as Ricks now was, he didn't hesitate. "Um, well, yes . . ."

Ryan groaned.

"Oh, brother," Grassi said.

Harry looked down the table at Markham. The flier was smiling, but there was a gallows-humor grimness to it. And something else.

"It was like him and me were outside it all," Harry told me. "You could see it in his eyes, him saying, 'Isn't it a shame we have to go through all this song-and-dance?' "

"All right, Captain," an annoyed Ryan continued. "What is it?"

"The major is entitled to legal counsel. He doesn't have to do this without having counsel present—"

Ryan's eyes darted round the table as if looking for something to hurl at Ricks. Grassi's fingers drummed impatiently on the table, freezing in mid-air when Ryan's angry eyes fixed on him. Again, Ryan turned to Harry.

"Well, he is," Harry said, almost smiling at Ryan's growing ire.

"What's a lawyer going to tell me?" Markham asked. "He's going to tell me to keep my mouth shut. And I think we'd all just like to get this over with. I know I would. Besides, there's enough lawyers in here already." His face took on a sad softness as he looked at Ricks. "I'm sure if things don't go quite according to the book, somebody'll let out a holler. I mean—" the grim smile again; that strange beyond-it-all connection to Harry again "—how much more trouble could I possibly get into?" To Ryan: "Why don't we just get down to this thing."

Ryan seemed momentarily puzzled to find his strongest ally sitting at the opposite end of the table. He quickly composed himself. "Why not, Major? You're being charged with the murder of Lieutenant O'Connell—"

"Second Lieutenant Dennis F. O'Connell," Markham interjected. "It's for the record, right? His whole name should be there."

"Fine, Second Lieutenant Dennis F. O'Connell," Ryan continued. "You are also charged with the attempted murder of two British civilians—Mr. and Mrs. Charles Gresham—both incidents arising from an operation you conducted on August fifteenth. You admit that—"

"Um," Markham said, holding up a finger to call a pause.

Ryan sighed. "Yes, Major?"

"I thought this was *his* case." The upraised finger fell toward Harry. "I don't know if it makes a difference. I just wondered . . ."

Ryan closed his eyes a moment to rein in his temper. He opened them and drew up a coolly polite smile. "Good point, Major Markham. Major Voss, why don't you take over?"

"All right, Major," Harry began, "we'll just go through this thing ABC to make sure everything goes down as clear as possible, OK? Good. You were in command of the 351st on the date in question? On August fifteenth?"

"*Acting* command," Markham corrected. "I was air exec for the 351st. When Colonel Adams was killed, command fell to me, but I was never formally given the group."

"You were the one who organized and led the mission on the fifteenth?"

Markham frowned and his eyes dropped to the tabletop. He nodded gravely.

"Your answers need to be verbal," Ryan said, nodding at the steno.

"I know," Markham said. "It's just . . ." He took a deep breath, looked up and into Harry's eyes. "On top of everything else, that's another thing I should be held accountable for."

"I'm not sure I understand," Harry said.

"That mission should never have gone off. I don't know what word you want to use: ill-advised, misjudged, a *mistake*. The plain fact is, it was wrong."

Ricks started to open his mouth but a glare from Ryan silenced him.

Markham hadn't missed it. "I know what you're going to say, Captain. 'Hold up, talk to a lawyer'; all that. But what you don't understand is all of this has been burning a hole in my gut since it started. I haven't been able to—" Markham cut himself off, shaking his head in self-admonishment. "I don't want anybody's sympathy here. I just want this out and done. The mission shouldn't've happened, and it wasn't General Halverson's fault that it did. The way I got him to agree was what I guess you'd call 'emotional blackmail,' the way I told him this was the only way to save his command. I've never been a book officer; I don't know if that's a crime. But if it is, it's my crime. All I know is three men are dead that wouldn't be if I hadn't led them out that morning."

He had spoken quietly, almost sheepishly, as if afraid that any aspect of the confession might reflect well upon him. He fell quiet for a long moment, staring back down at the tabletop. The four officers at the other end of the table looked confusedly at one another. Accused murderers taking on additional guilt was not a commonplace occurrence.

Harry led Markham through an account of the action on the fifteenth. Markham described the mission, in the main, much as Van Damm had imparted to Harry earlier with Angel Blue and Angel Red having reached Helsvagen without incident; O'Connell's P-47 subsequently being struck by debris on the first attack by Angel Blue; O'Connell's request for permission to abort the remainder of the mission, then exiting the target area at full speed without awaiting a response.

It was readily apparent to Markham that Angel Blue had effectively destroyed the depot on its first pass. That being the case, Markham's priority became O'Connell's vulnerability flying alone in a crippled aeroplane. Markham ordered Jacobs and McLagen to jettison their rockets, and, joined by Anderson, they all flew off to locate and cover O'Connell on the return trip. En route, they were attacked by German fighters.

At that point in his narrative, Markham paused. He drained his coffee, then held up the cup and nodded at the urn. "May I? . . ."

Harry nodded and Markham poured himself a fresh cup. "I trained Ray Jacobs," Markham said, eyes downcast into his cup, his back to the table.

"I'm sorry, sir," the steno said. "I didn't get that."

Markham turned, smiled apologetically to the steno. "Sorry, Sarge. I said I trained Ray Jacobs. And Andy McLagen . . . I remember when Andy got his silver bar . . ." Markham frowned in a way that made Harry wonder if the flier was trying to remember, or trying harder to forget. When he spoke, his voice sounded distant. "I didn't even know we'd been bounced until I saw Ray Jacobs's ship cross under me. Everything from the nose past the cockpit was burning. I could see him in there. Then I heard Andy on the radio calling them out, bandits, bandits on our six and high, coming out of the sun. I banked around, Andy was already up after them. But you don't win an uphill fight like that, not against FW's, not that many of them. There were three or four all over him. I didn't see him go down. But . . ." Then, to himself, "Oh, Andy . . ." Markham spent a moment on the reverie, only slowly reawakening to the presence of the other men in the room. Again, the apologetic smile that was becoming more familiar to Harry, and just as predictable. "I'm sorry, gentlemen."

Markham returned to his seat. He described how he and Anderson evaded the German fighters, then cautiously "cloud-skipped" out of the battle area, occasionally dropping into the clear to look for O'Connell. They finally spotted his aircraft trailing thick smoke, as they crossed the French coast, and did not close with him until near landfall England.

Markham paused again. Several times he made as if to continue his story, but the words didn't come. The smile, again. "This is harder than I thought it was going to be. Could I impose on somebody for a smoke?"

Harry rose and walked to the other end of the table. He shook a cigarette out of his pack of Camels, then extended a match and lit the end for Markham.

"Thank you, Major Voss. I don't know where mine got to. I can't believe I went through a whole—" The smile. "Well, thanks."

Harry nodded. He returned to his seat.

Markham took a deep breath. "Where was I? We were at the Channel. It took a good part of the Channel transit for us to close with O'Connell. His ship was going flat out, which was probably why she was making so much smoke. Hit like she was, she probably couldn't handle those kind of revs. By the time we caught up with him I figured we were far enough away from the mainland that I could break radio silence. I ordered him—ordered him several times—to ditch once we were close to landfall. I couldn't tell how bad off his ship was, but it looked bad. I didn't think he'd make Donophan and, well, frankly, I didn't think he was a good enough flier that he'd be able to keep his head when the time came. You lose your engine and very quickly—" Markham snapped his fingers several times in rapid succession "—you have to find yourself a good spot, if there is one, set her down dead stick—no power—and maybe you even have to go in wheel up and let her down on her belly. That's hard enough for a pilot who knows what he's doing, but for O'Connell . . . I thought maybe it'd just be easier for him to put down in the water."

Markham bowed his head, massaging a temple as if he was suffering a pain. "You've got to understand I had promised General Halverson that if he gave me this mission, there'd be no losses. And here I was already leaving Ray Jacobs and Andy McLagen behind. If O'Connell didn't put down in the water I was sure I was going to have to report another loss to the general. But I never got an answer from O'Connell over the radio. I pulled up and tried to hand signal him. Maybe he didn't see me because of the smoke from his engine. I couldn't tell. So . . ."

A long pause, so long that Harry felt compelled to nudge Markham along with a soft, "And so, Major?"

Markham nodded. He shook his head as if even he couldn't quite believe what had transpired and was replaying now before his mind's eye. "I thought . . . I thought maybe if I could put a burst across his nose, maybe that would drive him down. Or maybe that's what I've been telling myself I was thinking."

He turned to Harry, his face and tone seeming to say, "You explain it! You make me understand it! Because I can't!"

"The way I was feeling right then," Markham went on, "the way I'd been feeling about O'Connell ever since the krauts hit us . . ."

"And how was that?" Harry asked. "How did you feel about O'Connell?"

Markham's face turned contemplative. "Nobody wants to go up there. Most of the boys forced themselves. O'Connell couldn't. After the German raid . . . a lot of those other boys were dead."

"But not O'Connell."

"I guess I hated him for living through it. That wasn't right of me. But that's what it was." He straightened a little in his seat. "I can't say that none of that didn't affect my aim, not and be honest about this. Does that sound crazy? Maybe I've just been going crazy trying to figure it out.

"Then, he was down, in the water. I could see he was still alive. I saw him fighting with the canopy, trying to get it open. There were two people standing on the cliff, civilians. It was going through my head, the minute I saw O'Connell's ship going down, it hit me I was going to have to tell the general that this loss, this last man down, *that* was my responsibility. They *all* were, I know that, but this one, O'Connell . . . that was blood on my hands." Markham licked dry lips. He looked to his coffee cup but it was empty. He took a last drag on the cigarette then dropped it in his cup.

"After," he went on, "I could understand how they must've felt. Scared. Scared, hell; terrified. But at the time all I saw was two people standing there instead of helping. I have to make them move, I was thinking. *I have to make them move!*" Markham closed his eyes. He sat silently.

"So you fired on them," Harry finally said.

Markham, still with his eyes closed. "So, I fired on them." His eyes opened. "Of course they ran. I would've run if I'd been in their place. But at the time all I could see— . . . I fired on the house to drive them out. Stupid. *Stupid!* I wasn't even thinking; that's just what came. Maybe I was so mad at them for not helping . . . maybe I was just so damned *mad!* At the way it was all turning out! At *me!*"

Markham looked down at his palms, rubbed them together as if cleaning them. "Look, I'm not trying to make this sound like I was out of my head so I can take a walk on this. I was in command. I made the bad choices. I failed General Halverson. I failed my men. Poor J. J.— Captain Anderson—he's just been trying to be a good friend covering for me. He had no hand in any of this. Whatever failures there were that day are completely mine. My men—none of them—deserve the way I've dirtied them like this."

When Markham had finished, he sat at his end of the table, slump-shouldered, seemingly drained.

At the other end of the table, Harry and the others sat, surprised to find that Markham had left them with nothing more to ask.

"Um," Ricks began, and Markham tiredly raised his head.

"Yes, Captain?"

"Can Captain Anderson corroborate any of your statement?"

Which earned Ricks another of those baleful glares from Ryan. Markham had delivered himself up in toto and beribboned; Ryan saw no reason to tempt complications.

"Do you really need him to?" Markham asked, looking pained. "I know this isn't going to make you fellas happy, but I've advised him to keep his mouth shut." Markham took one of his head-bowing pauses before continuing. "J. J.'s a good friend. He's already got himself in trouble trying to protect me. He'd probably do it again, even if I told him not to. I'll confess to whatever you need me to confess to. I'll sign whatever you want me to sign. But I'm not going to let any more of my people put themselves on the line for me. I think they've been through enough."

Harry would show me the typed deposition. The document concludes: "Freely given and signed to this date August 17, 1943 by Maj. A. Q. Markham 0152793, 351st Fighter Group, Donophan Airfield," followed by Markham's precise signature, and those of the witnesses: Col. J. P. Ryan, Maj. H. J. Voss, Capt. P. L. Ricks, and Lt. A. G. Grassi.

It was a masterful performance, and Harry had no doubt it was a performance, otherwise all those niggling bits of the case that told him all was not what it seemed to be were meaningless. "He never let the seams show," Harry told me. "He signed his copy of the deposition as soon as the messenger brought it to him."

Peter Ricks, however, viewed Markham's confessional somewhat differently. "I have to believe part of it was true," he told me.

"Which part?"

"The pain."

"OK, OK, OK!" Ryan percolated, striding up and down the room with a happy bounce. "Let's take some time to clean up, catch a few winks, then we meet back here at 1000. I'll have some breakfast brought up, we'll go over the regs, see which articles apply, and see if we can't get a presentation together for Halverson and DiGarre by this evening.

Hell, there's no reason we can't have this whole mess wrapped up by the weekend."

"Um," Harry said.

Ryan's enthusiastic pacing ceased abruptly. "Um?"

"Nothing."

"Nothing?"

"It's just that, well, I have some things I still wanted to follow up on."

"Some follow-up things?"

"I should be done in time to make the presentation to Halverson and DiGarre, but I'd just like to, um—"

"Follow up on a few things?"

"Right."

Ryan looked to Grassi and Ricks, but Ricks's puzzlement and Grassi's exasperation confirmed for Ryan that Harry was a lone madman. "What things, Harry? Haven't you been listening? It's over, understand? The man confessed! What is it? You've got that puss on again, the same puss you had on when you were fussing about that gun film. You going to start up on that again?"

"It's just that, well, I'm sitting here watching this guy. He hasn't seen the evidence we have, he doesn't know what we've got on him. For a guy who doesn't even know if we've got a case he seems awfully eager to get himself hung."

Grassi slouched still further, and made a peevish noise with his mouth. "Markham's nailed and he knows it! He's just tryin' to make himself look as good as he can. You know—doin' the honorable thing and all that crap, hoping it'll be appreciated enough where maybe he'll only have to do twenty years in Leavenworth instead of ten minutes on the gallows."

"A four-oh guy like Markham scratches a foul-up like O'Connell; they won't hang him and he knows it," Ryan declared. "This is a smart guy, Harry. He may sit there giving up that I-wanna-come-clean-fellas song, but he knows what he's doing."

It had troubled Harry like a barely heard off-note from the orchestra, but only now had Ryan clarified it for him. "He is a smart guy, isn't he?" he mused aloud.

"They'll bust him, tag him for murder two, then plop him in Leavenworth at least for the duration. That," Ryan continued, "will just about satisfy all parties concerned: our brass, the limeys, everybody."

But Harry retained the "puss" Ryan found so objectionable. The colonel sighed heavily and dropped into a chair. "OK, Harry. Shoot. You got a case to make? Make it."

"First-year law school. Professor Dunlap, remember? The three components to establish the basis for a criminal case."

Grassi groaned. "Oh, gee, I didn't know there was gonna be a pop quiz!"

"Shuddup," Ryan told him.

Harry continued. "Number One: means—"

"I would call eight fifty-caliber machine guns ample means," Ryan contributed.

"—opportunity—"

"His own confession corroborated by two eyeball witnesses—whom he also took a shot at—place him at the scene."

"—and motive."

"You've got his confession—"

"Which does not provide motive."

"He says he lost his head and—"

"No! Not him! Not this guy!"

"Why not this guy?" Ryan was barking now.

"Joe, you've seen Markham's record. He's got a chest full of ribbons, he's been a combat leader for seven years—"

"Seven years is a long time," Ricks offered. "Maybe too long."

"Yeah!" Grassi chimed in. "C'mon, Major, one night this guy sees all his bestest buddies get blown into itsy-bitsy bits, and then he's got this washout O'Connell left. He's already predisposed against this guy. You look at it all and you say, Who wouldn't've taken a shot at O'Connell? Then you throw in those seven years, maybe the guy's flak-happy on top of everything else."

"Believe me, Harry, I can see where a commanding officer might just get fed up." Ryan said it pointedly enough to make Harry wince. "Look, we've got a confession. We've got physical evidence. Frankly, I don't give a damn why he killed the little bastard. He did it and we've got him. Closed case."

"OK," Harry said, then took a moment to get it clear in his head before he continued. "Let's say he can't stand O'Connell anymore. The sight of him makes him sick. Joe, you said it yourself: This is a smart guy. He'd have to be. You don't get to be a line commander with Markham's ratings without having something upstairs. So, put everything else aside—the means, opportunity, and motive thing, the gun film, all of that—and ask yourself why a guy *that* smart commits murder in front of two witnesses."

"Maybe he didn't know the Greshams were going to be—"

"Never mind the Greshams. Why not put O'Connell down across the Channel where *nobody's* ever going to know? Unless you want to say Albert Markham, with his experience and ratings, went completely out of his skull for a single morning—that for one brief moment, everything that this guy *is* went out the window. Unless you say *that*, none of it adds up."

The others went very quiet and very still.

But Grassi was desperate to maintain his belief in Santa Claus. "Look, Major, with all due respect and all that, when a guy goes off his nut enough to start shooting people, he's capable—"

Ryan waved listlessly at Grassi to silence him. "OK, Harry." His tone had altered now, to one of reasoned argument. "We've still got his confession and the evidence."

"You've got his confession until he recants."

Ryan grimaced. "You'll jinx this thing, you talk like that."

Ricks was nodding gravely. "If a man confesses for no apparent reason, it's not an unreasonable concern that he could withdraw the confession for no reason."

"He could tell us moon men knocked O'Connell down, for all anybody cares," Grassi rebutted. "That won't change the evidence. The only thing the confession gets us is we don't have to go through all the fuss of a trial."

Ricks pursed his lips. "Considering the major's point that Markham's confession seems premature, that raises the possibility he's confessed as a kind of smoke screen. Giving us what he thinks we want, he'd expect us to truncate the investigation. That'd buy him time."

"Now I've got two of them to deal with," Ryan said, frowning at Ricks. Ricks flushed and looked down into his lap. "Buy time for what?"

Ricks shrugged. "A better story."

"Or maybe Anderson's complicity." Harry's confidence was building. Hearing Ricks voice qualms made him feel less lonely.

"You back to that damned film, Harry?"

Harry walked round the table and pulled up a chair by Ryan. "I don't know what Markham's up to, Joe. But I don't like him preempting us by shutting Anderson up. That smells awfully funny for a guy putting on a big show about coming clean. Maybe you're right; maybe I'm worried about nothing. But if he is up to something, I don't want to get caught flat-footed. I'd like another day or two—"

Ryan closed his eyes painfully. "Two *days*?"

"Let me finish my interviews, let the boys here finish their ground-work. That way, if Markham pulls some last-minute moves, we're ready. If nothing else, maybe him knowing we're ready to jump on him the minute he tries to pull back from his deposition will keep him from recanting."

With a finger, Ryan traced the rings on the table left by the coffee cups. He was going over Harry's reasoning, evaluating his options, no doubt looking for the avenue that would cover him best.

"C'mon, Joe," Harry persisted. "Even if this runs into next week it's still going to be a land-speed record. If we go *too* fast we can run right by a hole that Markham can crawl through. Then how'll we look?"

The point hit its mark. After a moment, Ryan let out a massive yawn and stretched his arms so far he almost—and possibly deliberately— punched Harry on the cheek. Ryan stood. "I'm setting up a meeting with the generals for tomorrow evening. I'm going to tell them what the disposition on this thing is going to be and give them a schedule. I want to know what you've got before then, by 1700 hours today. Seventeen hundred's your deadline, Harry. I've got killers walking around here with smoking guns; you're lucky I'm giving you that much. You've got a perfect setup here, Harry. Don't screw it up."

The door closed behind Ryan. Ricks and Grassi looked at each other, then to Harry.

"How do we proceed, Major?" Ricks asked.

"Keep doing what you've been doing. Only do it faster." Harry looked at his watch and moaned. "Meaning that if either of you were thinking of catching any sack time, forget about it." And he left.

• • •

Harry barely remembered stumbling across the Annex yard to his office. Even with the blackout curtains open, the small room was dark and shadowy. He called down to the orderly room for a breakfast of toast and coffee, then sat back in his chair, facing the window, watching the sky lighten from predawn gray. He fished in his pocket and found a last cigarette. It was not until the back of his chair thunked against the rim of his desk, jarring him awake, that he knew he'd been asleep. He stood, rubbed his eyes, and lit his cigarette. He welcomed the appearance of the orderly with his pot of coffee and toast, didn't bother with the toast, but downed two cups of coffee as fast as the hot liquid would permit.

He brought out all the files and notes on the case. Years ago, in his law school days, Harry had developed a technique to help him in his case studies. He took each relevant fact of the case, boiled it down to a few words he wrote in bold, block letters on an index card. Once done, he set all the cards down on the floor. The cards were pieces of a puzzle, and Harry believed that if he could study them in such a fashion— moving this one here, that one there—he could at least begin to deduce the finished picture.

He was still notating the cards when the stenographer who had taken Markham's statement knocked on the door. Harry sent the sergeant back to a warm bed after relieving him of the sealed envelope containing his copy of Markham's confession.

Harry went down the hall to the latrine, the envelope tucked securely under his arm, threw water on his face, then returned to his office and propped himself against one of his file cabinets, the open documents on top of the cabinet before him, a fresh cup of coffee nearby. He did not want to risk sitting and possibly lapsing into another doze.

Now, that quiet, deferential Midwestern voice came back to Harry as he read over the deposition, freckled with erasures and typos, evidence of the steno's own fatigue and Ryan's command for haste. It was a remarkable document in which Markham—to use Harry's wry exaggeration— "confessed to everything but the Chicago Fire and Teapot Dome."

Harry was still mulling over the deposition when there came a knock at the outer door. It was one of the mail clerks with a sealed manila envelope from Scotland Yard. Harry signed for the envelope, shooed the messenger out, and closed the door behind him.

Harry sat at his desk with his coffee, Markham's confession, and the Scotland Yard documents in front of him. He rang the Annex switchboard and had them put him through to Van Damm's BOQ, where he was told that Major Van Damm had—unsurprisingly—spent the night in the G-2 complex. Harry rang him there. While he waited for the G-2 staff to find Van Damm, Harry opened the envelope from the Yard. Inside were two smaller, sealed envelopes. Harry opened the first, saw autopsy sketches, and set it aside. He was opening the second when Van Damm came on the line.

"Hey, Voss, what's up?"

"Did I wake you up?"

"Up? I haven't been to bed yet. What can I do you for?"

"When I was talking to your Captain Dell, he said something yesterday about a radio monitoring station on the coast."

"We've got a chain of 'em up and down our side of the Ditch. You want to know if we got something on the Monday raid, right? Gimme an hour and meet me in the officers' mess. I've been living on doughnuts and Hershey bars for days. I gotta have me some real food."

Harry rang off and opened the second envelope. It contained a preliminary ballistics report. According to the Yard, investigators had retrieved over a hundred spent bullets from the exterior, interior, and grounds of the Gresham cottage. They had also recovered a similar number of ejected shell casings. Another seven bullets had been extracted from O'Connell's ship.

SUMMARY:

Casings—Preliminary comparison between random sample of twelve recovered casings and casings from test firings show marked similarity in ejector markings. Indicates casings came from one or another of the eight .50-caliber automatic weapons mounted on Ship #1 (Markham's). Gresham Residence—Preliminary comparison between random sample of 12 identifiable bullets recovered from structure interior, 12 from structure exterior, 12 from vicinity, and bullets from test firings show several points of similarity in rifling indicating bullets fired from one or another guns #1–8 on Ship #1.

Victim Ship—Four of the seven bullets recovered malformed on impact preventing effective identification comparisons. Bullet recovered from fuselage bears rifling marks consistent with Ship #1 Gun #4. Bullet recovered from engine area bears rifling marks consistent with Ship #1 Gun #5. . . .

All of which eliminated the possibility that any of Markham's actions were some sort of cover for Anderson.

Reluctantly, Harry turned to the autopsy report. He skimmed through the neat block paragraphs and the anatomical sketches: "*. . . Victim received five bullet wounds from a point above and behind to the right at a descending angle of between 30 and 40 degrees with a similar transverse . . . signs of having been inflicted by a large-bore, high-powered weapon at close range . . . pierced body armor at back, completely transiting body and exiting body armor at front . . . severe tangential tissue damage along each projectile path indicating high velocity and malformation caused by impact on body armor . . . cause of death attributed to grievous gunshot wounds . . .*"

The text was cold and inanimate, the diagrams a poor cartoon, but as Harry's eyes flicked from one square of text to the next, his mind's eye saw the pale young man on the Gresham bed, still damp with blood and seawater.

He tossed the autopsy report aside, tossed his reading glasses after it, leaned back in his chair and rubbed his burning eyes, then absently flicked the stub of his cigarette out the window. Down in the court, a pair of PFC's were watering the sunflower planters in front of his building. The cigarette floated by. "Hey!" one of the men shouted angrily, and Harry leaned away from the window so they wouldn't see him.

He forced himself ahead, continuing to fill out his little index cards as he worked his way through the materials on his desk. After a bit, the outside office door rattled. He assumed it was Nagel, shouted at him— or whoever it was—to come back in an hour, and answered the puzzled mumbling that followed with another demand to go away, all without looking up from his cards.

When the cards were done he spread them out on the floor, then propped his elbows on his knees, and let his eyes ramble about the splayed cards. He bent over, wheezing, and moved them about, rearranging them, hoping that—as in the past—the connections would emerge, slowly and vaguely at first, then with growing clarity.

This time, however, the magic didn't happen. The cards sat there obstinately separate, like pieces from a half-dozen different puzzles tossed randomly together.

Albert Markham's killing of Dennis O'Connell bespoke a man acting out of pique, but what Harry knew of Markham suggested a man who didn't act out of pique. It was a rash and desperate act by a man who, from what Harry had thus far learned, didn't act rashly, or desperately. In the wake of the German raid on Donophan, presumably distraught over the loss of dozens of comrades—including his friend Frank Adams—Markham was capable of putting together an attack marked—in Van Damm's words—by "a nice, simple elegance." Even his confession came across as well thought-out, well reasoned, carefully addressing every point and question that had arisen over the course of the investigation thus far.

But it was just that last point that so troubled Harry: The confession was *too* well thought-out, *too* well reasoned, and too carefully answered *every* question.

Whatever piece would bring all the rest together into a picture that made sense, Harry didn't have it. Or, he considered, maybe it *was* there, sitting plainly in front of him, but he was just too tired to see it. Where—and at what—*hadn't* he looked?

Before Markham had been brought in for his deposition, Harry had had a few minutes with Ricks and Grassi in which they'd given him a quick catch-up on what they'd compiled that day on the men involved.

Harry picked up his phone and had the Annex exchange first ring Grassi's office, and failing to get an answer there, his quarters. While the phone rang—and it rang a long time before a groggy Grassi picked up his end—Harry parked the receiver on his shoulder, scooped up his cards from the floor and tucked them inside his jacket, then locked the two Scotland Yard reports and Markham's deposition in his file cabinet.

"Would it kill you to let me get even five minutes of shut-eye?" Grassi grumbled when Harry identified himself. "Can't this case spare me those five lousy minutes?"

"No," Harry answered. "Earlier tonight, you told me—"

"This morning, Boss. That was this morning, when all good lawyers should've been snug in their—"

"You said something about O'Connell. Something about a girl-friend . . ."

Still half asleep, Grassi spoke through a yawn: "I did?"

"I said," Major Van Damm repeated, trying to speak through a mouth filled with an oversized bit of fried egg sandwich, "you look like you could use a shave."

Harry self-consciously rubbed his stubble-roughened chin. "I can imagine."

Van Damm hadn't swallowed before he began on the second of the two sandwiches on his plate. " 'S just nice to see somebody in worse shape than me."

"Anything I can do."

They had found a quiet corner of the officers' mess. Remembering Van Damm's cigars and unshowered scent, Harry had picked a table by the window.

"Those radio intercepts," Harry began.

"What radio intercepts? There were no intercepts. Not from the An-gel flights. 'Course, that's no big surprise. First order of business for them would've been maintaining radio silence."

Harry flipped through his note cards. "Markham says that O'Connell radioed him—while they were over the target, over this fuel dump at Helsvagen—and requested permission to abort."

Before Harry had finished his sentence, Van Damm was shaking his head. "We didn't pick it up. That doesn't mean he did, that doesn't mean he didn't. It just means we didn't pick it up. They were a hundred and forty miles away, deep in the grass. Routine jamming, atmospherics—"

"Markham also says he radioed O'Connell to ditch just off the coast—"

Van Damm washed the last of his sandwich down with a slurp of coffee. "It's not just a matter of range. It was hot, it was humid. All in all, a pretty lousy day for radio transmission. It's not like we have this sponge that soaks up everything that's in the air. You get some, you lose some, OK? The only traffic we picked up was out of Helsvagen and that was pretty blotchy."

"Out of Helsvagen? You mean from the Germans?"

Van Damm nodded. " 'Bout what you'd expect. Reports they'd been hit, requests for help. Sounded like they'd been hit as hard as we thought. They were asking for everything: field hospitals, kitchens, tents, clothes, blankets, fire-fighting equipment, the whole shopping list, soup to nuts. And they weren't quiet about it, either. The calls went out un-coded. They don't usually like us picking up on bad news, so for them to put out a call like that in the clear, they must've been *really* hurting. Things quieted down by night; probably re-established hard-line communications they lost in the raid. One thing I could kick myself for, though."

"What's that?"

Van Damm slumped back in his chair, licking streaks of yolk from his fingers. He sighed contentedly. "Damn, I needed that. You got a smoke? I left my cigars back at the office. I could really use a smoke right now."

Remembering the noxious episode in Van Damm's office, Harry would've lied if he'd had one. "You were saying?"

"Oh, yeah. Remember me saying we'd originally pegged the kraut personnel count at about two hundred, right? And my Spy Brigade guess was that it was probably less by now?"

"Right."

"Well, spank me, I missed that one by the proverbial country mile. From what we could pick up, the Germans at Helsvagen were reporting casualties in the neighborhood of four hundred plus."

Thanks to Harry's shortcomings in map-reading, his drive from London to Lewes was longer and more winding than it need have been. Six times, he pulled his jeep to the side of the road, grappled with his map, and looked vainly for landmarks along the tree-lined lanes that crossed the downs, each frustratingly like another. Then, reminiscing mournfully over the precision-engineered Rolls-Royce of the night before, he arm-wrestled the rebellious stick shift into gear and off he rambled.

Still, the ride was not altogether unpleasant. The day was bright, the colors of the fields and trees, and the cows and sheep, quite vivid, the terrals that gently rocked the jeep were filled with the sweet smells of earth and pasture. There was something liberating about being far

from the gray stoneworks of London and the even more drab uniform-
filled corridors and court of the Annex.

Close to noon Harry finally drew up in front of a millinery shop on
one of Chillingham's side streets. He tapped on the dusty shop glass and
a woman's face hove into view: a porcelain-white orb marred by the
black slash of an eye patch. Grassi's quick brief hadn't mentioned an injury and, for a moment, Harry was not sure how to react. He produced a
well-meaning smile and spoke slowly and loudly, moving his lips in exaggerated fashion so even if she couldn't hear him through the glass, she
could read his lips. He pointed at her and asked, "Elisabeth McAnn?"

She nodded with a smile—it surprised him that a young girl's face
marred by that square of black cloth could smile—glanced at her watch,
then held up five fingers.

He nodded and toddled off, found himself a news kiosk, bought a
pack of Players for lack of anything American, then staked himself out a
lamppost and lit himself a cigarette. When Elisabeth McAnn touched his
elbow, he was nearly asleep.

"I think you're on fire," she said.

Harry batted at the smoldering cigarette caught in the folds of his
jacket. He refrained from cursing in front of her and forced a smile.
"Just mildly scorched," he said, frowning at a burnt smudge. As his eyes
came up from his jacket he saw that she was leaning heavily on a cane.

"Miss McAnn, I want to thank you for seeing me on such short notice. I know this isn't the best time. I mean, please accept my condolences about Lieutenant—"

She smiled tolerantly, and interrupted him. "Major Voss, is it? How
did you get here? Did you drive? You must've been on the road for hours.
I'm sure you could do with something to eat. There's a fair little tea shop
round the corner if that's all right?"

"I'm not too sure anything's going to sit well on my stomach.
Rough night."

She noted his haggard appearance with a nod and her smile turned
sympathetic. "Frankly, I've been feeling a bit off myself, but I should
have something. Do you mind . . . ?" She raised her arm, and Harry
thought she was offering it to him as some ladylike gesture, but when
he took it, she leaned heavily against him, limping as she walked, hanging the cane in the crook of her arm.

The tea shop was small and quiet, just a few tables, each decked with a fresh daisy in a water glass. The matronly little woman behind the counter came over to their table, nodding a familiar maternal smile at the girl.

"Early lunch today, dear?"

"Just some tea and dry toast, please."

"And the gentleman? We have a plate of dainties you might like."

"Just tea, please."

"We only have saccharine, I'm afraid."

"That's fine, thanks."

The woman waddled off behind the counter. The girl pulled an empty chair close, hung her cane on the back, and propped her bad leg up on the seat, rucking her skirt up a few inches. Harry took care not to let his eyes wander to the exposed knee.

"On the phone you said you were from the Judge something-or-another," she said. "I'm afraid I didn't take it all in."

"It sounded like I woke you up. Sorry."

She nodded it away as a trifle.

She was young, he thought, but he wasn't quite sure how much so. He'd take in the smooth skin, the slight cushion of baby fat in her cheeks, and think she wasn't yet twenty, but then focus on that black square over a missing eye and think she was years older . . . or should have been. She had a pleasant face made striking by the contrast between its whiteness and the jet hair that fell straight round her face to her shoulders, the sharp slash of matching eyebrows, and the one eye, brown but so dark as to look black. There was a lilt to her voice, a subtle un-English cadence.

"I'm with the Judge Advocate's Bureau."

"That sounds threateningly legal."

"I'm a lawyer with the Army."

"Oh," she said, raising her eyebrows slightly.

Elisabeth McAnn had a knack, Harry told me, of seeming, at first, as ingenuous as one would think natural for such a young girl. But in that eye was a sharpness, a shrewdness, a knowing. And, just beneath any other feeling, easy to tap . . . a sadness.

"And you're looking into his death, is that it? I was told he was killed in a crash. I didn't know there was anything . . ."—a flicker of a mocking smile here—". . . requiring the attention of, well, of you."

"There's just been some questions over the crash—"

"Nothing you can discuss, of course."

Harry blushed.

"Security and all that," she said.

He looked to her for any sign of rancor, but she merely seemed amused at his discomfiture. "I wish I could tell you more—" he began.

Again, that dismissive nod, that it wasn't important. Or maybe just not unexpected.

Harry sat awkwardly silent for a moment, hesitant to push on.

She took the lead. "Since I obviously know so little, Major, I don't see how I can help you."

"I'm just trying to learn a little more about Lieutenant O'Connell. I understand you two were, well . . ."

She nodded, amused again, smiling, again.

"I'm kind of surprised to see you back at work so soon. I thought you'd take a few days . . ."

"To mourn? Life marches on."

"So they say."

"Stiff upper lip and all that. Head up, give out with a verse or two of 'There'll Be Bluebirds Over the White Cliffs of Dover,' and press on, eh?" She said it casually, but Harry saw a cold flash in that one dark eye. "Well, that's the English way, they say. That must be my problem. Not quite English through and through."

"Irish, right? I could hear it."

"My Da," and the word touched that easy-to-reach sadness. She passed it off with a quick sigh. "Mum was from over here. We came over before the war. Da was a collier at one of the mines, then the mine closed. Mum had a brother who said he could get Da a job in a shoe factory. In Coventry. Now, there is no more Coventry."

Which, Harry took to mean, there was also no longer a shoe factory, a Mum, or a Da. All gone, he guessed, under the same rain of bombs that had taken Elisabeth McAnn's eye and maimed her leg.

"How well did you know Lieutenant O'Connell?"

"I loved him."

It was a bit more forthright than Harry had been prepared for. He nodded, clumsily trying to maintain a sense of savoir faire. "You, um, couldn't have known him very long. I believe he'd only just come over—"

"They arrived in May. I met him in late June."

"Well, that's, um, that isn't very long, is it?" he asked tentatively.

That amused smile, again, and that sadness, again: "How long did it take you to know you were in love with your wife?"

Harry reflexively moved his ring hand under the table.

"I didn't need to see the ring. There's a look about you."

"What kind of look?"

"A married look."

He laughed.

Their tea came. Harry stirred in some milk and saccharine. She took one bite of her toast, then set the bread down on the little serving plate.

"Major, where is he?" she asked. "Now?"

"Um, well, Scotland Yard. They have a . . . facility." He didn't want to use the word "morgue."

"Would it be possible for me to see him?"

Harry assumed he could arrange such a visit, but he had no wish for her to see the clinical butchery of a police postmortem. "I'm afraid that's not possible, Miss McAnn. Just next of kin. I'm sorry."

"I see. Perhaps that's best. 'Remember him as he was,' isn't that what they always say? I saw him just before, you know. Yes, it would've been the day before. Sunday. Because of the rain. They had postponed the mission and given him an overnight pass. We spent it together." She stared off through the tea shop window, off somewhere, nowhere, as musing people do, missing Harry's red-faced reaction to her revelation. Her eye regained its focus and turned back to Harry. "What will happen to him?"

"I imagine they'll ship him home. To his family so they can—"

"They won't want him."

"Oh. In that case, the Army will arrange something."

"I wouldn't think he'd like that. Then again, I suppose he would be the first to appreciate the irony of it; the people he liked least taking care of his afterlife and such."

The conversation drifted after that, and Harry was reluctant to steer it back to business. She queried him about home, his wife and children. Harry produced the cracked photos tucked in his billfold. He almost asked about her family, but then remembered the look on her face, the tone in her voice when she had mentioned Coventry.

There was a pause in the chitchat and Harry thought perhaps this was the time to get back to the matter at hand, but then she asked how he had traveled to Chillingham.

"I have a jeep."

"Would you mind a short ride? I'm inside all day."

"How much longer do you have for lunch?"

"Bernice—she's the girl I work with—she went to great pains to make it clear I owe myself an indulgence or two."

"Then let's go," Harry said and paid the bill.

They did not drive far. Still, she seemed to enjoy the ride. She slouched in the seat, her head back, heedless of the wind whipping her dark hair into a tangle, turning her face toward the sun, where it met the warm rays with a closed eye and feline smile. She asked Harry to pull to the side of the road just outside of town. She kicked off her shoes and held out her arm. "Can I borrow you, again? I hate that thing," and she nodded at the cane she'd tossed in the back of the jeep.

Harry held out his arm, she took a firm and practiced grip and, leaning against him, they started through the thick grass, kicking up flurries of small, pale butterflies as they went. She directed them up a low knoll overlooking the road that wound south. They paused at the top and she sagged against him to catch her breath. Feeling the curve of her breast against him, Harry held his supporting arm away from his body, inserting some prudent space between them.

"Are you all right?" he asked.

She nodded and stepped away, on her own, favoring the scarred leg. She lowered herself onto the grass facing away from the road, not bothering to tuck her hems properly about her. She scratched at where the grass had licked at her shins and Harry, for the first time, noticed that her legs were bare, starkly white except for the purplish parenthetical scars about the one knee. "It is beautiful, isn't it?" she said.

Harry took in the expanse of open country, the hillocks sheathed in waving heather, the casual splay of an orchard, the flat mirror of a pond, the shadows of clouds slipping across the grasslands.

"Do you see that? Down there?" She pointed to a pile of brown stones below, almost invisible beneath tall weeds and shrubs. "It goes back to the time of William the Conqueror. At least, that's what they say. Someone's home, they say. I imagine all this must've looked much the same back then, don't you? Do you see the pond down there? On the other side of the orchard? Sometimes this is where we'd come. We liked it out here so much that even when I wasn't working he'd hire a bicycle, a tandem, and we'd come out here with a basket of food. And after, we'd go down and nick a few apples from the orchard, and we'd swim in the pond. From the road, no one can see you."

The sun slipped into its next orbital degree and the little pond suddenly lit up like a flare, the sun dancing in a thousand glistening fragments on the minute wavelets stirred up by the wind. Harry considered her reference to its privacy and wondered if that implied that the trysts in the water were more intimate than simple swimming. He looked to see if she'd noticed his discomfort, but she seemed lost in memory.

They sat quietly for a few moments. Harry heard the distant buzz of an aeroplane engine. He thought the noise drew a moan from the girl, but then he saw the lowing cows, their legs folded under them as they nestled under the apple trees, their tails flipping idly at flies as their jaws ground at their cuds. He turned to her to make some droll comment about the hard life of cows, but stopped himself when he saw her face. Perhaps it had been her he'd heard after all.

She asked for a cigarette and Harry offered her one of his Players.

"I was hoping they'd be American," she said.

He apologized, but she took it anyway and he lit it for her. He didn't like the way the cigarette sat naturally between her little-girl fingers, adding a sullen maturity to her.

"You said you wanted to ask me about him?"

"Whatever you can tell me. Was there any . . . friction between him and any of the other men in his outfit?"

"Well, if you mean did anybody hate him, yes."

"Who?"

"All of them." She smiled at the uncomprehending look on his face. "He wasn't like them, Major. He was no soldier. He didn't belong here."

"I thought all pilots were volunteers."

She shrugged, offering no explanation.

"You said something about his family, about them not wanting him back. Was there a problem in the family?"

"He never said directly, but I gathered . . ." The same shrug.

"He doesn't seem to have volunteered much about himself."

"I didn't ask." She turned that one eye on Harry, and it grew dark and hard. "Look at me, Major. And tell me what you see."

Taken aback, Harry cleared his throat, smiled in a puzzled sort of way, but she didn't allow him to fumble his way to an answer.

"Eventually," she said, "you'll say something along the lines of, 'I see a very pretty, very brave young girl.' Someone like you would probably be overly polite and say 'young *lady*.' But you wouldn't say 'scarred.' You wouldn't say 'crippled.' But that's the truth of it, eh? And if you're crippled and scarred . . . The polite young men ignore me. The softhearted ones pity me. And the not-so-polite, well, some have a sick idea of sport."

"Dennis O'Connell was different."

"He was different. He took me as I was. And I took him as he was."

"Meaning no questions."

"Meaning no questions." She closed her eye. A hand came up to massage the broad, white forehead as if she were in pain.

"Are you all right?" Harry asked her.

Her head came up and she smiled, a bit forced. "Fine, thank you." She turned, looking back down at the lazing cows below. "The first time I saw him . . . I let a bedsit above a pub here in town. I was just home from the shop and some of your lads from the field were in the bar. He was alone in a crowded room, if that makes any sense to you. You could see he wasn't one of them. They were all on about this and that, flying, playing darts, so on, playing at the war being quite the game, working very hard at not letting on how afraid they really all are. . . . There's an old piano in the pub. I don't know why; no one ever plays it. I don't remember that anyone ever had. He was sitting at it. The poor old thing is so out of tune, but he could play it well enough that you didn't hear it. Nice music. Not the popular things his mates wanted to hear. Classical, eh? And to them, that was just a reason to mock him. 'Hey, Mozart, how about something that doesn't put people to sleep!' You understand? Then, later . . ."

"After the Germans hit Donophan?"

She looked off, to someplace west of the small town behind them, to where, Harry guessed, the aerodrome sat. Almost lost among the distant trees and tall grass he could see a broad, open expanse, a scattering of low buildings marked by a military dullness, a crisscross of wide tarmac paths.

"We all knew," she said. "Everyone in Chillingham. We could all see it that night. The explosions. The flames. Sometimes, when the wind is right, you can still smell it. . . . All the next day, until he could get me word, I wondered . . . I tried to prepare myself . . ." She seemed to drift for a moment, then remembered Harry and the cigarette in her fingers. She took a last puff then stubbed it out on the ground. "Even before that. They thought he was a coward. They said it to his face."

"Was he?"

The amused smile flashed. "How eagerly do you want to die, Major?"

He shrugged, conceding the point.

"I tried to talk him into deserting, you know. I still have family in Ireland. They'd've taken us in. But he'd have none of it."

"Why?"

"Obligation?" She considered that a moment, then shook her head, the question still unanswered. "He kept putting in for a transfer, but they wouldn't let him go. I had the feeling they were going to keep him there until they turned him into what they wanted, or until the war ate them all up." The sadness was back in her face. "I suppose I'd been waiting for this. I knew one day he wouldn't come back. That was just . . . the way for him." Her eye closed, squeezed hard, as if whatever pain had been prodding at her now gave her a sharp, deep stab. "How much can they take from you . . ." It was whispered, not intended to be spoken aloud. She looked up, then held out her arm for his assistance. "I should get back."

He drove her back to the shop and walked her to the door. "Thank you for taking the time."

"It didn't seem like so much."

"It was a help, though. Believe me."

"A coward would've run, wouldn't he, Major? Every day he looked the other men in the eye and said, 'I don't want to do this.' That's a courage of a sort, isn't it?"

Harry made a helpless gesture; it was a question too far outside his provenance.

"You'll let me know how things are going? When there's something you can tell me?"

"Of course," he said.

"Then," and she surprised him by rising on the toes of her good leg and giving him a little peck on the cheek, "good luck and good hunting."

He could feel his cheeks grow warm. "Tallyho."

She gave him a last farewell grin and limped into the shop, the little bell over the door tinkling behind her. It was only then he realized she'd never spoken Dennis O'Connell's name.

The 351st had arrived on station in the sylvan fields outside of Chilling-ham, about thirty kilometers south of London, in late spring of 1943, and was operational by June. They christened their aerodrome after the first of their number to lose his life in service of the cause: a flame-haired twenty-two-year-old from Decatur, Illinois, named Wayne L. Donophan.

Ironically, Donophan had not died in combat, but in a training flight gone wrong a few weeks before the 351st had shipped out from America. Naming the field after him was the close-knit unit's way of keeping alive a man who had trained and flown by their side since the 351st was formed. Few in the group had the experience to know that within a month of becoming operational, there would be more appropriate candidates for canonization. In fact, depleted by combat losses, and rotations home of the grievously wounded and the blessed few who survived a full duty tour, by August first, few on the 351st's roster re-membered, or had even known, young Donophan.

The fields around Donophan no longer smelled sweetly of heather and wildflowers. Now the acrid smell of defeat was there, oily on Harry's skin even before his jeep reached the Chillingham crossing sometime that mid-afternoon: that nose-wrinkling stench of burnt petrol and scorched wood. As he drew closer to the aerodrome, the smell of a past burning grew stingingly strong.

Harry girded himself for a scene of carnage, but as he drew up to the aerodrome gate he was surprised to see little beyond the perimeter fence. To one side was the flat expanse of the field, empty of aircraft and people, the strips of tarmac hidden by tall grass. To the other side, hap-hazard earthworks just inside the fence blocked his view. He jerked the jeep to a halt at the gate. Over the idle of its engine he heard the sounds of construction—hammers and saws—and above the earthworks could see the flexing arm of some sort of earth-moving machine.

The sun was painfully bright on the white helmets of the gate

MP's. One detached himself from the cluster by the sentry box and approached Harry's jeep. Passing clouds dulled the sun long enough for Harry to catch a quick glimpse of the figure beneath the helmet: a crisp, clean, razor-creased uniform, neat coils of gold braid hanging from a right-angled shoulder, buck sergeant's stripes creased cleanly through the apex of the chevrons, a holster of burnished white leather, boots that glowed as brightly as the helmet, and the bold black-and-white MP brassard. The MP studied Harry's AGO card for a long time before handing it back and snapping out a precise salute.

Harry flapped a salute back, then started arm-wrestling with the jeep's gear stick, trying to coax the vehicle through the gate. After a half-minute of gear grinding that set the teeth of the gate MP's on edge, Harry mercifully jiggled the stick into gear. The jeep lurched forward a meter and stalled.

"Tell you what, sir," the MP sergeant said. "Just leave it here. One of the boys'll park it for you. It's not a very long walk. You can find Major Korczukowski in the Headquarters building right over there."

Harry mumbled a flustered thanks, grabbed his briefcase, and clambered out. A few steps through the gate and past the mounds of earth blocking his view, and Harry's pace faltered. The MP's posted at the gate were the polished machines of the Provost Marshal's office, he now realized. Nothing that spit-and-polish could be native to Donophan Airfield.

And it was not the sounds of construction that Harry had heard, but deconstruction. Beyond the piles of earth, few solid structures still stood, and those only barely. The sounds of hammers and saws, the groaning of crowbars were the work of labor crews stripping their remains, vultures picking among broken bones for scraps.

A new smell arose from the mounds where the earthmover was working, a sickening rot that went immediately to his stomach. Amidst the piles of dirt a Negro soldier sat atop a backhoe clawing at the ground. A squad of other workers clustered round, some carrying picks and shovels. All had rags wrapped round their faces, covering their noses and mouths. A corpse, its wrapping of white canvas streaming dirt, rose from a hole in the earth. The wrapping was still bright; interment had been recent. The workers standing round the rim carried the body to where two dozen other bundles lay neatly arranged side by side. The soldiers set the corpse down among its fellows and returned to where the backhoe was opening a fresh hole.

Harry held a handkerchief over his mouth and nose and nodded one of the soldiers over. "What's going on?"

" 'Ey's goin' home," the soldier replied.

Headquarters was an ugly, one-story clapboard building. From somewhere inside, above the sound of hammers and crowbars at work, Harry could hear the faint crackling of a wireless newscast. He stepped inside the screen door to stand before an empty reception desk. There was a bulletin board behind the desk with the usual layer of yellowed sheets tacked to it: memoranda, scores from the intersquadron softball league, notes of items for sale or purchase. A poster warned pilots to "Avoid performing aerobatics at low altitudes—Hitler laughs every time we crash." The main hall of the building was cut short by a tarpaulin hung from the ceiling. There were doors on either side of the hall, some barred by planks nailed across them. The door marked "Adjutant" was unobstructed. The hammering seemed to be coming from just the other side. Harry stepped up to the door and knocked.

When there was no answer he swung the door open and found himself staring into blue sky and emerald fields. The rear half of the building had been blown away. Fresh dirt had been poured to fill the bomb crater. A labor crew was dismantling the building one plank at a time, saving the nails in coffee cans and putting the wood in neat piles.

"Where's Major Korczukowski?" Harry asked.

The crew shrugged. "Maybe inside?" one ventured.

"Yeah?"

Harry turned at the voice behind him to find a broad figure propped in the door stenciled "Commanding Officer."

"Major Korczukowski?"

"You must be Voss." Leo Korczukowski nodded Harry into the office. "I've been using the CO's office while mine's being . . . redecorated. Grab a seat while I turn this off." There was a small wireless set in a corner of the office. Harry couldn't quite make out what the excited newscaster was going on about, drowned out as he was by the sounds of cheering and marching bands in the background.

"Sounds like good news."

Korczukowski switched off the wireless. He eased himself into the squeaking swivel chair behind the wooden desk. "Patton marched into Messina this morning. Sicily's ours."

"That is good news."

Korczukowski shrugged with little apparent concern. From across the hall, Harry had thought the adjutant's rugger build intimidating, but, up close, the major was not unlike the buildings Harry could see through the screened windows behind the desk: still standing but battered, scarred. Despite the natural way his uniform hung on his broad shoulders, the admirably erect bearing, and the piercing dark eyes, Leo Korczukowski was no soldier. Like so many of his countrymen, he had only taken up the uniform in the wake of Pearl Harbor. Before that, he'd run a family business making and selling furniture, and at the time Harry met with him, more than any other time in his military service, he hungrily ached for home.

The adjutant nodded Harry toward a chair across the desk. Harry took a few steps into the office but did not sit.

He felt every bit as intrusive as he had at Halverson's office, with that same sense of stumbling upon a mourner. He fidgeted on his feet by the proffered chair and let his eyes wander round the office, avoiding those weary, annoyed eyes across from him.

It was a small room with bare wooden walls marked by dark-colored squares where framed items had once hung. The top of the large, scuffed desk was clear but for a pack of Camels and a Zippo lighter. Behind Harry a large, framed map of Europe hung on the wall. Red ribbon marked paths Harry recognized as the approach and return courses of the Monday raid. But the major attraction was behind Korczukowski, framed by three screened windows in a hellish triptych: Donophan Airfield.

In every direction the field was pocked with the earthen blotches of filled-in bomb craters. Vehicles, blown to pieces, had been dragged into tidy rows to be stripped of usable parts. Other debris—splintered and burnt lumber, twisted metal lockers, shredded bedding, the broken eggshells of blasted Quonset huts—had been bulldozed together into tangled piles. Fire, shrapnel, and concussion had tainted everything, even those buildings still standing. And beyond that, the backhoe heaved and flexed and lifted another canvas-wrapped bundle from the dirt.

"If you're staying," Korczukowski said dryly, "you might as well have a seat."

Harry lowered himself into the chair.

Korczukowski nodded at the now silent radio. "That's all you get these days. The good news."

Harry made a vague gesture toward the nonexistent rear of the building. "You mean—"

"This?" Harry found Korczukowski's lazy chuckle disquieting. "This is pin money." The adjutant drew a cigarette from the pack of Camels, flipped open the Zippo, lit the cigarette, and took a deep draught. He did not offer Harry one. "Eighth Air Force bombed the ball-bearing plants at Schweinfurt and the Messerschmitt factories at Regensburg this morning. Just about the same time Patton started his parade." Korczukowski blew a lazy stream of smoke toward the ceiling. "Air Marshal Dowding calls them 'panacea targets.' You know: 'Knock this one out, boys, and it'll shorten the war by six months.' That kind of thing. Every other week somebody's coming up with another way to shorten the war by six months. The Air Marshal has a very low opinion of panacea targets. I'm coming to share that opinion."

"It was bad?"

"If you think sixty Forts is bad." It was a breach of security to bring the subject up: both the raid and the losses. Korczukowski knew this, but he was drawing a line. On one side were fighting men, with the men of the 351st direct kin to the men who flew—and died—on the Schweinfurt raids. On the other side was poor old Harry: a desk jockey, a paper-pusher.

And, sitting in what looked to be the only intact piece of carpentry on that tortured piece of earth, that's how poor old Harry felt: an outsider. He took his cap off and rubbed at the itching line it had left on his forehead.

"It looks like they're going back," Korczukowski continued. "To Schweinfurt, anyway. And take another beating. So you see," and Korczukowski smiled sickly, "this really is small change."

"I appreciate your seeing me, Major. I know this isn't easy."

"You're right. It's not."

"I'll try not to take too much of your time."

"It's a little late to be worried about the niceties, Major. I've got your MP's out there sealing us in, Hans and Fritz poking around—"

"Hans and Fritz?"

"Those two Katzenjammer Kids who work for you. I liked them better in the funny papers than hanging around here. And then last night, those storm troopers from the Provost's came rolling in to haul Al and J. J. away."

Harry cleared his throat. "I apologize for the way they were brought in. You should have been alerted beforehand. That was my fault."

"No kidding. Did they ever get chow?"

"Excuse me?"

"You had them shanghaied right in the middle of evening mess."

"I assume they're being looked after properly."

"Yeah. Just what are you charging them with, anyway?"

For the first time, Harry did not feel defensive. He may not have had a right to be there, but he did have an obligation. "The murder of Dennis O'Connell, and the attempted murder of two British civilians."

"I . . . I didn't know about that."

"You're not supposed to."

"I see." Korczukowski's face sagged, and the condescending air dissipated. "I didn't know about that," he said again. Neither said anything for a moment, Harry leaving the other officer to his thoughts. Finally, Korczukowski sighed resignedly and drew himself up in his chair. Now, he too recognized Harry's obligation, and his own as well. Leo Korczukowski was a man who placed great stock in those obligations. "What is it you want to know, Major?"

Before Harry could ask his first question, the wall behind Harry, the one with the map, heaved and with a loud crackling flew to one side. Harry and Korczukowski found themselves staring into the bright outdoors. The face of a soldier, hanging onto a crowbar, hung down from above. "Oops," the soldier said. "We didn't know anyone was in here."

"I think we better take a walk," Korczukowski told Harry. He collected his cigarettes and lighter and calmly led the way through the place formerly occupied by the office's fourth wall.

A steady breeze moved across the flats of the airfield, kicking up spindrifts of dust, perhaps from the fresh earth used to fill the bomb craters, perhaps from across the field where the backhoe labored.

Korczukowski lit a fresh cigarette and looked out over the airfield grounds. There weren't many men in sight, just a desultory few picking over the debris, or dismantling the buildings. "They're not sure what they're going to do with us. Save the pieces and build it up again, or just wrap it up and send it home."

He said "home" and Harry heard the sputter of the backhoe.

Korczukowski bent his head, a debate going on within himself, then he held out the pack of Camels to Harry. Harry drew one, Korczukowski lit it for him, and they started walking again.

"What do you want to know?" the adjutant repeated.

"Tell me about Colonel Adams and Major Markham. They were good friends, I understand."

"From the start. Not just friends. They respected each other. Frank Adams was a good commander. Fair. Not one of those brass hats likes to bark just to see you jump. But he knew he was green, that he didn't know much more about actual combat flying than the boys under his command. Al had been logging combat time since Spain, all the way back to the beginning, I think, in '36. Frank wasn't going to act like a hotshot just because he had brass on his shoulder. That's not how he was. When he didn't know something, he turned to Al and said, 'I don't know; teach me.' You could tell Al hadn't met too many officers like that.

"You know, they actually met each other—Al and Frank—long before the group was formed up. When Al and J. J.— Captain Anderson— dropped out of the Eagle Squadron to join up with our air, they were assigned to teach fighter tactics in Oklahoma. Frank was there to learn, and that's where he bumped into Al for the first time. That would've been in '41, even before Pearl. Then, they transfer Frank here, move him there—you know the way the Army does—and then they send him to Texas to head up a new group. This would've been last summer. Frank found out that Al had been transferred to the fighter school in San Antonio. He couldn't think of anybody better to help him bring the group up, so he wangled a transfer for Al. He brought him on as a squadron commander. A month after we activated here he was air exec, the number two man."

"And Anderson?"

"J. J. was Al's idea. I think Frank thought he might be a bit much, you know? J. J.'s all right, don't get me wrong. A little wild, upstairs and on the ground, but you get pilots like that. Feel if they're not raising hell, why bother to get up in the morning? Al could keep him from getting in too much trouble, so Frank went along with it when he asked that J. J.

come in with him. Tolerated him, I guess is the best way to put it." Korczukowski shook his head in amusement. "Great combat flier, J. J. Lousy
officer." He paused and sighed wistfully. "This group," he nodded at the
field around them, "no matter what the roster said about who was
the CO and who was the exec, Frank and Al commanded it together." He
spat out a flake of tobacco. "Not that you haven't heard this already, but
for the record: They didn't come much better than Frank Adams, except
maybe for Al Markham. I'll tell you something else you probably already
know: If there's a better pilot than Al, you and me don't know him. Not
Bong, not Gabreski, not Boyington. *Nobody's* better."

"That's pretty much what I've heard."

"Then you heard right."

"In fact, I've only heard one major criticism of Markham—"

Korczukowski stopped and faced Harry. "All that crap about Al being
too close to the men? Yeah, I know about that. I'm the adjutant here,
Voss. I see all the paper that goes in and out of here. Officer Fitness reports, Officer Evaluation sheets, memos, letters . . . You want the poop
on that? Al squawked about defective tracers, gun stoppages, props running wild on takeoff . . . When what we had worked, he squawked about
what we *didn't* have: self-sealing fuel tanks, metal drop tanks, whole milk,
chow that didn't look like dog food, indoor plumbing . . . Sure, if you're
sitting up at Wing you start thinking, Boy, this guy Markham's a royal
pain in the can, ain't he? He's always up here with some beef! But *we*
weren't up at HQ. It didn't look like he was being a pain to *us*, and it
sure as hell didn't look that way to the kids that had to go upstairs."

The words had come in a heated burst. Belatedly, Korczukowski realized that Harry had merely made a statement, not an accusation. He began walking again.

"If it was such a big, happy family here," Harry posed, "what about
Dennis O'Connell?"

A dark cloud passed over Korczukowski's face; he'd apparently spent
much time brooding over that same subject himself. "That poor kid was
a disaster waiting to happen. It didn't take long to see it coming."

"O'Connell wanted out of the group?"

"Toward the end seemed like week in, week out he was in my office
with a new request for a transfer."

"But Markham kept him here."

The superior twist of Korczukowski's lips was that of someone who knows what the interrogator fails to understand. "For one thing, Al wasn't going to dump his problems on another outfit. You must've done enough nosing around to know that he wasn't that kind of guy. For another, he didn't think Dennis O'Connell was the foul-up everybody else figured he was. Frank Adams did. Frank went one better: he thought O'Connell was a gutless wonder, pure and simple. Wanted to bust him, tag him for Leavenworth. A lot of the other guys picked up on that, gave O'Connell a rough time. Can't say I blame them. You go up and damned near get your tail shot off, then come home to find out this guy aborted before he even got to the Channel because some wire in his radio jiggled itself loose . . . or one morning he sticks his finger down his throat, pukes, and puts himself on sick call so he doesn't have to fly. Your temper's going to wear a little thin, right? Voss, nobody particularly gives a damn what your problems are up there. They go and you don't, and that's all that counts. They try and you don't. That keeps up and one day somebody's going to throw a punch."

"But that's not how Markham felt?"

"First mission, Dennis O'Connell was textbook. He scored the group's first kill. Didn't know that, did you? Then . . . something happened. Jekyll and Hyde. The kid who flew that first sortie was not the kid who flew that last one."

"He got scared?"

Korczukowski looked surprised, then smiled his superior smile again. "Nobody wants to die, Voss. You're fighting the cold, the g's, the krauts, you mix it up a mile in the air and in a few minutes either you're coming home a hero or you're not coming home at all. Only the psycho cases aren't scared. You'd have to be crazy not to crap in your pants up there." Korczukowski tilted his head back and watched a flight of sparrows dart low across the field. "Sometimes they just wear out. The medics call it 'combat fatigue.' Or maybe O'Connell did just get scared. One day, a guy wakes up and it occurs to him if he goes out enough times the odds say he won't come back. Whatever it is you have to put on the shelf so you can keep doing what these kids have to do, well, he couldn't put it on the shelf; not and keep it there. He was a sensitive kid, Voss. And what makes you a good poet makes you a lousy soldier." Korczukowski gave an embarrassed smile, self-conscious over his brief attack of lyricism.

"Al tried to turn him around. He looked at how the kid started and tried to get him back to that."

"Teach him to be a good soldier for his own good, right?"

Korczukowski studied Harry closely for a sign of skepticism. "Voss, Al tried to be there for all his men. All of them. You know, once he made air exec, his kill rate went straight down the toilet. He wasn't up there chasing bandits anymore. He didn't care about running up a score, not that he ever did. He was all over the sky, watching after his boys, keeping their tails clear, babying the hurt ones home. And he was up there every day he could go, more than Frank Adams wanted, more than the medics said was safe."

"Maybe *too* much."

"Maybe. Maybe Frank Adams and the medics and the brass hats at Wing were right. Maybe Al's way wasn't the best way to run the show. I don't know. But that's the way it was run here and it worked. You never get over being afraid of dying unless, like I said, you're some kind of Section Eight. But they were never afraid to go up with him. They didn't go up for God or the United States or FDR or the flag or their mothers. They went up for him, Voss, because *he* was the one who'd watch their asses."

"So, for whatever reason, Markham wanted O'Connell kept here. And Adams let him have his way."

"Well, they fought about it. A lot. Especially as time went by and it looked like O'Connell was getting worse. But this was Frank's first combat command and, like I said, Al had been at this for a lot of years. I think Frank gave in to that." Korczukowski's face twisted.

"Something else?" Harry nudged.

"I knew that kid, Voss. I was the one he came to with his transfer requests. Whatever was eating at him, you could see he wasn't cutting it. Sometimes he'd come in, he was practically in tears. And it was getting to the other pilots. Nobody wanted to fly with him. If O'Connell was on your wing you couldn't trust him to keep your tail clear. Forget what it was doing to morale: Upstairs, he risked getting somebody killed. I'd think—like you—let's just get rid of him. You don't want to bust him, fine, let's send him to ATC, let him fly cargo for the duration. It didn't look like keeping him here was doing anybody any good. Including himself. I wonder about it, and I think, maybe, what it was . . ."

Harry waited patiently while Korczukowski sought the right words.

"Those things O'Connell couldn't put on the shelf?" the adjutant continued. "Al's been putting them there a long time. Maybe convincing O'Connell was a way of keeping himself convinced."

They were by the cemetery now, watching the work gang. The rank of shrouded corpses had grown quite long, a corduroy road leading home.

"You know what I think hurt Al most?" Korczukowski nodded at the white bundles laid elbow to elbow. "That he couldn't do anything to help them that night. This was a guy, when someone in his outfit went down, he wrote the letter home himself. But this . . . After that night, he couldn't even look over here."

Harry turned away from the graves. Across the field the sun touched two aluminum bodies and a pair of P-47 Thunderbolts lit up like flame.

"Those their ships?" he asked.

Korczukowski turned, saw where Harry was looking, and nodded. Without being asked, the adjutant led the way across the grass, past the blackened, roofless ribs of the hangars and the scorched revetments. Two open-backed trucks were parked by a tangled mountain of debris piled on the charred and patched grounds of the apron. Harry could see the mound was made up of what had been the aircraft of the 351st Fighter Group. Each craft had been surgically stripped of all usable parts: spinners, propellers, exhaust pipes, landing wheels, canopy stripping. The hulks themselves were being loaded piecemeal onto the trucks. They would be carted away to foundries, stripped even further, and then melted down. The aluminium would go into new aircraft bodies; the Plexiglas into new cockpits and gun blisters; the rubber into oxygen masks, truck tires, periscope eye cups; the steel into trucks, tanks, bomb casings, perhaps to wind up another burned-out hulk, to be stripped and sent through the cycle again.

Harry reached into his jacket for his note cards. He leafed through them as he and Korczukowski walked, checking to see if any points remained to be covered with the adjutant. Again, he had that sense of puzzle pieces all there but refusing to come together. He flipped to the cards based on his interview with General Halverson.

"There's some chronology I'd like to get straight," Harry said.

"Shoot."

"The raid on Helsvagen was initially set for Saturday morning."

"It rained Saturday, then we needed a day for the field to dry."

"I know. General Halverson told me he sent his report—an assessment General DiGarre wanted on the group—Halverson sent that up to DiGarre on Friday."

Korczukowski shrugged. "I guess."

"You didn't know about that?"

"I knew about the report. I helped Al put the info together for it, then sent it up to Wing. That would've been Wednesday, Wednesday night. I dragged my feet on it. We all did. We were figuring once DiGarre had the numbers in front of him he'd do something to make us scrub."

Harry flipped through his note cards. "Did you ever hear from Di-Garre's office? Did anybody from GHQ ever contact Donophan?"

"Not that I know of. Something like that, especially if it had to do with the shape we were in, if it didn't go through me I would've at least been party to it."

"Did all the dealings with DiGarre go through Halverson?"

"That's the normal chain of command. From us to Wing, Wing to Division. I don't know why that's bothering you."

"I would think, considering how badly you were hit, just because of the extent of, well . . ." Harry held up his hand and offered the devastated aerodrome. "The general might've taken a more, oh, personal interest."

"I do not pretend to be able to understand the minds of generals."

Fair enough, Harry thought, but . . . "Halverson dragged his feet on that report, too. He saw things the way you did; that once DiGarre saw the report, he'd stand-down the 351st. Halverson didn't send his report up to DiGarre until Friday, assuming that it would still be too late for Di-Garre to do anything to interfere with the Saturday mission. But the mission didn't go off until *Monday*. That seems like an awful long time for DiGarre to be sitting with that report."

It was Korczukowski's turn to frown. "It does." He shrugged again. "Generals," he said, as if that could explain anything.

They stopped before the two P-47's parked wingtip to wingtip in a remote corner of the apron, their black-painted muzzles turned slightly toward each other. A half-dozen of the spit-shined Provost MP's were picketed round the aeroplanes. Harry's ID got him past the MP's but the adjutant chose not to follow. Harry stood between the uplifted black noses of the Thunderbolts. Their cockpit canopies were peeled back, and the inspection ports in the wings were still open from when Scotland Yard's ballistics personnel had extracted their guns. Harry stepped closer, standing beneath the two great propellers.

"Were all the ships in the group the same?"

"What?" Korczukowski hadn't heard him; Harry had been unable to turn away from the cyclopean stare of the air intakes.

"Were all the ships in the group the same?" he asked again.

"We were phasing out the D-25's with E's," Korczukowski replied. "There were still a few—"

Perhaps it was the psychological effect of looking up at the two craft looming over him high on their landing gear, solid and thick with muscle, but when Harry thought back to the broken-backed wreck of O'Connell's plane it came to him twisted and dwarfish.

"I saw O'Connell's ship. It looked smaller."

"Shouldn't be."

Harry moved closer. He could see the open ports in the wings where the guns had been set, and next to them where the ponderous metal-link ammunition belts had been neatly laid, fold upon fold. And there, under the wings, were the extraction slots where the empty casings tumbled out.

From a distance, the sun had given the ships a pristine glow, as if they'd come freshly poured from the foundry, but now Harry could see each ship's battle wear. The shining aluminum showed scuffs, and around the exhausts were smoke and oil stains. The once smooth, ovoid bodies were blemished with dents. Patches of metal were bolted here and there on the wings and fuselages, and there was a scattering of small holes—bullet holes, he guessed—too fresh to have been patched. But even marred, unmanned, and unarmed as the planes were, Harry felt puny and vulnerable before them.

I've stood before a Thunderbolt and I've felt the same way. The P-47 looks as if nothing will get it off the ground. Its elliptical wings look too frail and short to generate enough lift to push the thick body into the air; it waddles about taxiways like a lost farmyard orphan. There was so much difficulty seeing over the bulbous nose that ground-crew men were required to stand to the side where they could be seen from the cockpit in order to guide the pilots along the tarmac. The men who flew her and the ground crews who cared for her had nicknamed her "the Jug" and despite an evolving series of modifications since Number One had rolled off the production line two years before; in August of 1941, the Thunderbolt was still the largest, heaviest, and most heavily armored single-seat, single-engine fighter anywhere in the world.

She was also the ugliest. She'd been built a brute to do a brutish job, but if that made her stagger along on the ground like a wounded bird, she became a different animal in the air. The model in use by the 351st was powered by a 2000-hp Pratt & Whitney Double Wasp radial engine giving her a top-rated speed, in level flight, of over 540 kph, meaning that in those days the fattest, ugliest fighter in the world also happened to be one of the swiftest. The great weight that so bogged her down on the ground also meant that no other aircraft, with the possible exception of the twin-boomed Lockheed P-38 Lightning, could match her in a dive. (I'd heard that the "hotshot" pilots who'd first tested her had, off the record, pushed her diving speed close to 1000 kph.) She could cover over 1000 kilometers on the petrol she carried on board, and had wing and belly stations for either auxiliary tanks to stretch that range, or for bombs or rockets.

The truly brutish part of her job was to provide a platform for the battery of guns set in her wings: eight M2 .50-caliber machine guns sighted on convergent lines of fire and fed by 2400 rounds of ammunition. The manual will tell you that each of those weapons can fire a variety of steel-jacketed ammunition up to a maximum range of almost 7000 meters at a rate of 450 rounds per minute.

Smiling young men who a few months before were chasing ponytailed bobby soxers told me that with as much pressure as it takes to flick a fly from your tea cake, a touch of the firing button, held for a three-second burst, will produce approximately forty kilos of lead. They will tell you that when forty kilos of steel-jacketed lead traveling at high velocity meets a German aircraft at the point where the eight lines of fire converge, a target disintegrates.

Harry had seen O'Connell's body, the holes punched in his ship, through his seat and body armor. He had seen the Gresham household. He knew the capacity of the napping guard dogs looking down on him.

"We had more planes than pilots after the krauts hit us," Korc-zukowski said. "A stick of bombs went right through the barracks quad where the pilots slept. That's how we lost so many of them. The extras, the other planes, they've already been flown off as replacements to the other groups. Anderson flew that one. It wasn't his, his was lost in the kraut raid. But Al flew his own ship."

Harry edged toward the aeroplane with "Markham" stenciled be-low the rim of the cockpit. His kills had been laid out just underneath, canted swastikas arranged below the flags under which he'd earned them: one under the flag of the Spanish king, two under the French tricolor, twenty-one under the British jack, and six under the Stars and Stripes. Toward the nose, The Cleveland Indian had been painted in fire-engine red. Below was pictured a hawk-faced caricature of an Ameri-can Indian in a Cleveland baseball uniform, a brave's feather stuck in his cap. The Indian was grinning feverishly, his mouth full of massive white teeth, as he cocked his bat and sighted on an oncoming base-ball. The ball wore a swastika on its rear; on its front was a Hitler face full of horrified anticipation.

Korczukowski gestured at the artwork on the ship's nose. "Some of these kids blew a month's pay to get somebody to do a good job like that. But that was Al's ground crew's idea. Even the name. They were proud they were his crew, Voss. If you asked him, I'll bet he couldn't even tell you how many kills he has. I don't think he wants to know."

Harry pulled himself up on the low trailing edge of the wing. He walked along the root of the wing, his fingers tracing along the sun-warmed aluminum of the fuselage. The cockpit smelled of leather, oil, and sweat. The seat was faded and cracked by the sun, the leather indeli-bly imprinted with a human form impressed by hours of piloted flight. Peering into Dennis O'Connell's cockpit two days earlier, Harry had been too distracted by other matters to notice the cramped quarters, but now, in Markham's ship, he shuddered claustrophobically. He reached into the cockpit and his index finger rested on the firing button of the con-trol stick. He looked over his shoulder to the open gun ports, assuring himself that there was nothing there, then pushed the button. It didn't take much pressure at all. Even a child . . .

Korczukowski went for his Camels but the package was empty. He crumpled the package, prepared to toss it, but then thought better of it and tucked the crackling ball of cellophane into a trouser pocket. "Would you like to stop in and say hello to Fritz? We set him up in the mess tent."

Harry climbed down from the wing. It took him a moment to recall the Katzenjammer reference. "Which one's Fritz?"

"The nice one."

"Ah. Captain Ricks. Where'd you put Hans Grassi?"

"Nowhere. He didn't come in today. You didn't know that?"

"No."

"Maybe the little fella's playing hooky."

"If he is, the little fella's going to get a good talking-to."

They ended at Harry's jeep, parked not far from the gate by the sentry MP's. Harry proffered his own package of cigarettes. "They're Players, I'm afraid."

Korczukowski smiled appreciatively and drew one. "They'll do. Thanks." He lit the cigarette, then turned to where the backhoe was still at work. "I keep meaning to write to their folks. But forty-seven letters is a lot of letters to write. The way the Army does it . . . 'The Secretary of War regrets to inform you . . .' " The adjutant was referring to the little Western Union scooter that would put-put down a street, people growing quiet as they stood by their curtains to see if it would stop or go by. Then the put-put would cease and it was like counting until thunder came after the lightning, those few seconds needed to read the Army's terse form of sympathy, then would come that high, pained wail. "Anybody deserves better than that. Even O'Connell. I don't know what to tell them. Especially O'Connell's folks."

"I'd prefer you didn't tell them anything. Any of the families. At least until this is cleared up."

"Is that an order?"

With a call to Halverson's office, Harry could've seen that it was. "A request," he said, sliding behind the wheel of his jeep.

Korczukowski looked from Harry to the cemetery, then back to Harry. "OK, Voss. A request. Granted."

Then Korczukowski was heading back toward the Headquarters building. Harry's foot went for the starter but stopped.

His exhaustion rose up in him, and that and his exchange with the sad figure of the adjutant left him drained. He glanced at his watch; it was after three. He had less than two hours before Joe Ryan's deadline for closing his investigation, and he was no closer to the key he had sought than he had been in the conference room seven hours earlier.

Were Harry an experienced criminal solicitor, the case might well have ended that afternoon, for Ryan was right: with means, opportunity, and even a serviceable—if arguable—motive, Harry had all he needed for a court-martial panel to put the accused promptly on the gallows.

But Harry was not an experienced criminal solicitor. His livelihood had been deeds and documents, legal swot work. Harry had lived by his ability to see every t crossed and each i neatly dotted. Sitting there in his jeep, contemplating his case, he kept coming across t's that adamantly refused to be crossed, and i's that would not dot.

Once again he pulled his note cards from his jacket. He would have preferred to lay them out on the grass of the aerodrome but images of himself chasing wind-tossed cards across the field to the amusement of the gate MP's discouraged the impulse. He slipped on his reading glasses and flipped through the deck of cards.

Al Markham had murdered O'Connell; the physical evidence was clear. But everything Harry had learned about Markham indicated the flier would have been more likely to throw himself in the way of guns aimed at the luckless lieutenant than to be the man behind them. Harry could not accept the contention that a man who had fought courageously in two wars, survived nearly seven years of combat by his superb flying skill, had been cited by four air forces for his valor and leadership, and was a wizard pilot rated Double First as a commander by his peers, could have suddenly—and briefly—gone completely potty and downed O'Connell and attacked the Greshams.

Let's dispense with the Markham-goes-berserk-for-two-minutes theory, he thought. He closed his eyes, and tried to send his tired mind back through his mental files. The shootings on the coast had seemed desperate. Anyone can be desperate: even a Markham. Desperation is simply the last act left to someone who considers all reasonable actions exhausted. But desperate to accomplish what? There was that troublesome question of motive again.

Back to basics, he thought. Why do people murder?

Rage. Anger. Revenge. Jealousy. Gain. Self-defense.

Doesn't apply here. Why else?

Fear. To silence someone. To conceal something. A secret.

What would make Markham desperate enough to kill O'Connell so rashly when, where, and how he did would be to keep O'Connell from revealing something that had occurred earlier in the mission. That, in turn, meant the thing that required concealing—the *motive*—lay somewhere on the other side of the Channel.

"Excuse me, Major."

The delicate poke at his shoulder snapped Harry's eyes open. He turned and saw the concerned face of the MP sergeant from the gate.

"You all right, sir? You having a problem with the jeep again? I saw you—"

"Fine, fine. Did you see which way Major Korczukowski went?" Then Harry was off to find the adjutant to ask him for use of a telephone.

Korczukowski escorted him to the field tent serving as communications center, then discreetly ushered the comm personnel out, leaving Harry alone with a telephone and his call to General Halverson.

"General, remember you said that whatever I needed to—"

"I know what I said, Major. What do you need?"

"Well, it's a pretty big request."

"Go ahead."

"I need an aerial photo reconnaissance flight, maybe more than one. Maybe a single flight can cover it all."

"Cover *what* all?" The general's voice was irritated. Harry couldn't tell if it was the size of the request or its vagueness that was the cause.

"I need them to cover Markham's return route from the Helsvagen fuel dump. At least the area where Markham says they were jumped by the Germans. And, I suppose, they should get pictures of Helsvagen, too."

"You *suppose?*"

"They should."

Thereafter, there were those who would say that Harry had acted recklessly, that his obsession to make a bigger case overrode any other consideration. But in truth, he had no real idea what he was after. He was just being his usual conscientious, diligent self. Despite his uniform, Harry was no soldier, and so had not even the experience to contemplate the eventual truth.

So, when General Halverson objected that such a recon was unnecessary because Jon-Jacob Anderson's gun film plainly showed the attack on the fuel depot, Harry persisted that photos should still be taken of Helsvagen. He pushed not out of suspicion, but out of the very Harry-like desire to be comprehensive. "The gun films only cover the fuel dump," he explained to Halverson. "I need pictures of the area around the town."

Consequently, no one was more surprised than Harry when the recon photos came back later that day to show that the Belgian village of Helsvagen was burning.

PART TWO:
THE FALL

CHAPTER SIX

ULTIMA RATIO REGUM

THEY WERE ALL GATHERED IN THE briefing amphitheater of the G-2 complex beneath Grosvenor Square. Voices rebounded harshly off the raw walls still awaiting a coat of acoustic tiles. Scuffed and cramped school writing desks were filling in for the planned padded seats, and raked desks with little attached reading lamps. The portals for the unfinished projection room were boarded over, and Major Christian Van Damm stood at the front of the room trying to make do with a small motion picture screen whose tripod tottered on the bare floor. Rough-hewn as it was, however, the briefing theater, off in a freshly dug but as yet uninhabited part of the subterranean sprawl, provided a measure of desired privacy.

Van Damm's audience was sunk in darkness, betrayed only by curls of cigarette smoke snaking through the projector's beam, and the clearing of throats irritated by the cement dust shedding from the walls whenever the muffled drills were at work elsewhere in the complex. Grassi was there, co-opted by Van Damm to operate the projectors set on a rolling cart, and so was Ricks, alone in a far corner of the room. Harry sat with Joe Ryan, close to the projectors. Harry's attention was on the screen but he could hear the tap-tap-tap of the legs of Ryan's chair as the colonel nervously rocked back and forth on the uneven floor. And General Halverson was there, sitting alone near the room's center, above and behind them all, his only visible sign the glowing tip of his cigarette, pulsing like a stuttering heart.

Van Damm's pointer floated into the ray of light and toward the screen as Grassi fed the first photo into an opaque projector.

"These were taken just about three hours ago," Van Damm began. "They're of the general vicinity where Markham claims he was bounced by kraut fighters. The photo passes were made at about five thousand feet, which allowed us to cover a good amount of area in the least amount of time. That seemed the best way to handle the run since we didn't know how long the krauts were going to let us dawdle out there.

"That we didn't find anything doesn't prove much either way. Markham's not sure where the intercept took place. We're working on a best-guess and that means we could've missed the actual crash site by miles. We've got the added problem that we're not looking for much: wreckage from two burned-out fighters. Two days after the fact those Thunderbolts could've already been carted off for scrap, so, even if we *were* in the right spot, there might not be anything there left to see." Van Damm signaled to Grassi with the pointer and the lieutenant ran several aerial photographs through the projector, each showing an unblemished checkerboard of cultivated fields and irrigation ditches, each accompanied by his announcement: "See? Nothing . . . Nothing . . . Nothing . . ."

Van Damm had Grassi turn off the opaque projector, and the film projector sitting next to it flickered to life. "What you're going to see now, gentlemen, is Captain Anderson's gun film from the mission on August fifteenth, two days ago."

The grainy film image was disorienting, fields and trees moving closely beneath the camera so swiftly as to be only slightly more than a blur.

"Here's his first pass," Van Damm told them. "The approach is low, under a hundred feet maybe, as down in the grass as you can go without wheels, and he's coming in flat out, maybe four hundred per or more. Chances are they never heard or saw him coming. He's coming up out of the southwest. You can't see the village, it's too low, on the other side of the fuel dump. All you're going to be able to make out are the tanks. You'll just have a second—"

Van Damm's pointer darted at some gray smudges and then the image shuddered, the picture flashed and white columns streaked from both sides of the screen, converging on the image's vanishing point.

"OK," Van Damm said, speaking urgently now. "These are the trails from Anderson's rockets and these here, up in the corner, those are from O'Connell's—And boom, there go the fuel tanks!"

The image shook again: The gray smudges vanished in two enormous, swelling mushrooms of fire.

Ryan's chair stopped rocking. Grassi whistled appreciatively. Ricks's voice was a prayerful, "Good God . . ." Harry looked back into the dark toward where Halverson was sitting, but there was no sound; just the sporadic pulsing of the general's cigarette tip.

Harry turned back to the screen. The camera angle was shifting sharply skyward, clouds darting by, capturing Anderson's extreme maneuvering to avoid the fireballs that were still rising, spreading, licking at the edge of the frame.

"Now he comes around, steadies himself, and this is his second and final pass. According to Anderson's debriefing statement, at this point O'Connell's already on his way home. Now here, he's working over this line of buildings across from where the tanks used to be. There's not much left. You can see they're already burning, but he hits them anyway, first with the rest of his rockets and then with strafing. You can see his tracers working them over: headquarters, comm shack, barracks, motor pool, so on."

The image quivered from the recoil of Anderson's wing guns. Harry saw little balls of light, the tracers, floating earthward to disappear into the maelstrom of smoke and flames and fresh explosions that now completely obscured the ground. In a gap in the smoke he caught a fleeting glimpse of a human figure, the only one he'd seen, then the tracers kicked up a line of dust enveloping the man. The figure's knees began to buckle, but before he could hit the ground the camera had moved on.

"Lieutenant? Can you freeze it? Yeah, that knob there. Run it back a bit, then hold it. See these? All these little blobs? Here, here, and here? Tracers from the ground. AA fire is sporadic and uncoordinated. These little bitty ones, that's machine-gun fire. These bigger ones, I would guess twenty-millimeter. There's nothing heavier coming up. Probably wasn't much left to shoot back with after those tanks went up, but—you should remember for later—they still had working guns down there.

"OK, Lieutenant, roll it ahead but stop when I tell you. Right there! Freeze it! Take a good look. This is the tail end of Anderson's pass. The run along the building line is a diagonal, southeast to northwest. You can see he's climbing after the run and banking hard over to his right. That points him toward the town. Look up here in the corner. You can just see a piece of the village. Lieutenant, kill it and turn the opaque back on. Take the top picture out of that next file. OK, good. This is a blowup of that last frame you saw from Anderson's gun film."

Grassi turned the photo on end: Now the village was sitting properly on the horizontal. The enlarged grain of the 16-mm motion-picture film broke the image into dissoluble bits of light and dark. Only Van Damm's guiding pointer tip held shapes together, outlining cottages, walk-ups, the dark finger of a church steeple truncated just before the pinnacle by the frame's edge.

"What is it you *don't* see here?" Van Damm asked. No one offered an answer.

"Remember Markham and Anderson's debriefing. O'Connell's already gone. Anderson makes his last run, then heads out after O'Connell. What happens to Markham and Angel Red? Markham says they abort the rest of the attack. Angel Red dumps their rockets and takes off after Anderson and O'Connell. That's what they *say.*"

The pointer tapped the screen. "Now take a good look at that town. What you *don't* see is smoke, fire, any perceptible damage. That place is *intact.*" Van Damm gave them a moment to make the required study. Then, "Lieutenant, next folder please. Start with the top picture. Gentlemen, this is Helsvagen less than three hours ago."

Van Damm went silent. Any comment or analyses would have been redundant. Even a novice like Harry could decipher the image now on the screen. In the lower left-hand corner of the picture, where Harry guessed the burning fuel depot was, smoke poured diagonally up and across the frame, devouring space like a rampant cancer. Thick and invasive as it was, there were still gaps. Through them Harry could see that the neat grid of streets that had comprised the village had been violently disrupted. Streets ended in jumble, as if the loosely knit grain of the enlarged film had disintegrated. Building facades abruptly broke off. The smoke hovering over the village did not all come from the burning depot. Several pyres pointed downward inside the perimeter of Helsvagen.

Twenty years earlier, in the sun-baked square of a Mexican village, I stood looking up at the bloated bodies of six Villa sympathizers hanging from a cottonwood tree, left there the week before by Huerta's men under the order that the corpses hang until they rotted. That was the first time I looked into the animal eye of Man. One doesn't react at first; there's no shock, no pity, no revulsion. There's not even anger. One can't react until one can comprehend, and those first moments of that first encounter defy comprehension—there is no answer to *Why this?*

And so Harry sat curiously impassive to what was presented on that wobbling screen. In fact, he seemed more affected relating this all to me later on.

Harry looked about to see how the others were responding. Van Damm's pointer dropped, like the dipping of the colors at a passing funeral cortege. In the light spill from the projector Grassi was for once—astoundingly—speechless. Ryan remained a cipher, the darkness in the room so complete as to conceal his face even though he sat at Harry's shoulder. Harry heard him sag into his seat with a wheezing sigh akin to that of a collapsing balloon.

Van Damm took a breath, and his pointer returned to the screen. "This is from about five thousand feet—"

"*Jesus Christ on a crutch!*" Halverson's oath was almost lost in the explosive sound of one chair violently colliding with another, and then both splintering on the hard floor.

A startled silence followed. Harry looked in Halverson's direction. The glow of the cigarette was gone. Presently, a match flared, bright and alone, and Harry had a brief glance of painfully narrowed eyes, a jerky nod of the head to Van Damm to proceed.

Van Damm cleared his throat and resumed. "Here's the depot down here in the lower left-hand corner. The tanks must've been at or close to full capacity for them to still be burning after all this time. The wind is out of the southeast, blowing the smoke toward the town, and that makes it hard to get a clear picture. Here, we're just starting to lose the sun, but through these holes in the smoke you can see fires *inside* the town. And through here what appears to be battle damage. Next picture, please.

"This is lower, somewhere around three thousand. Through these gaps you can see better. This isn't a collapsed building; look at the way the debris sprays across the street. That indicates explosive impact. Here, more fires.

"This last picture is down around fifteen hundred feet. These are the fields northwest of town, out from under the smoke. Field hospital here, though by this time most of the wounded have probably been evacuated to Brussels. Tent city here, this looks like a field kitchen, water trucks here. Now this blotchy-looking area looks to be freshly turned earth. If I had to guess, under these circumstances, I'd say a mass grave. Look by this bulldozer. See this ditch? Lined up here, nearby, these are bodies, apparently under blankets. Next picture, Lieutenant."

"How do you know—" General Halverson began, then stopped, as if uncertain he wanted to hear the answer. Then, "How do you know that those 'bodies' aren't wounded men?"

"You don't cover a wounded man's face and leave him out in the open for two days." Van Damm said it emotionlessly. "Look closely here. See these men working down in the ditch? They're spreading something around, something light-colored. Quicklime would be my guess." Van Damm paused again.

After a moment, the general tiredly asked, "Anything else?"

"The first radio intercepts we had of calls for assistance to Helsvagen were disproportionate to the number of military personnel we esti-mated on-station, but they would seem consistent with the apparent damage to the town. Those transmissions went out in the clear. I guess they were pretty desperate that first day."

"Any follow-up to that?" the general asked.

"No, sir. They probably restored hard-line communications within hours."

"What about civilian radio? Nothing on the propaganda broadcasts? Goebbels would have a field day with something like this."

"That was my first thought, too, sir, but it's not going to do Joe Goebbels and Fat Hermann and the other boys any good for their peo-ple to know that American fighters are roaming free and clear and hitting civilian targets at will. In the last year the krauts have lost North Africa and Sicily, and we'll be in Italy in a month—which I'm sure they expect—and the Russkies have been kicking their collective ass pretty steadily since Stalingrad. Goebbels is having enough problems explaining to Mrs. Shickelgruber what Allied bombers are doing over Germany, let alone fighters roaming around Belgium. And he's got Hamburg to account for."

At the mention, Harry heard Halverson stir in his seat. "That's not for here, Major."

"Yes, sir."

"Do we still need that?"

Van Damm knew what he meant. He had Grassi kill the projector while he found the room lights. The cold fluorescents flickered on.

As Harry's eyes adjusted he could see all the players now. Ricks was leaning forward, his forearms propped on the writing arm of his chair, his eyes lost to some point on the walls. Grassi, too, was remarkably introspective, but Harry saw his eyes (one still framed by a bruise from his unsuccessful boxing stint) darting here and there, his predatory instinct already working at the double-quick. Van Damm stood by the blank screen rolling his pointer idly between his fingers. He began to reach for one of the cellophane-wrapped cigars in his breast pocket, but with his fingers hovering over his pocket he thought better of it.

Halverson was slumped in his seat, cigarette smoldering in one hand, his other slowly massaging his forehead. On the tier below him two broken chairs lay where they had tangled after the blow from his foot.

"The point is," Van Damm continued, "the krauts might figure that what they gain in outrage they lose in panic. And, you've got the embarrassment factor here. The air-defense commanders for this area have to explain how our guys flew halfway across Belgium unmolested and took this place out. It's even possible that Berlin doesn't know about this. An air commander who lets this happen, and lets that news get back to the brass . . . that guy could definitely find himself trying to improve his work skills against the Russians. It wouldn't be hard to localize this: a place out in the middle of nowhere, not on any of their major supply routes, and since the dump is a storage facility, not a fueling station, it's rarely used. Other than the dump, Helsvagen has no real military value. As rigidly controlled as the information flow is over there, public and military, if they don't tell anybody, chances are nobody outside the immediate area is going to know about it."

A long minute went by before Halverson spoke. "How do you account for the two missing pilots?"

"Jacobs and McLagen? That gets a bit more problematic. There's no sign of them in these pictures, but if they went down in the town, well, they might just be lost in all the mess. Remember: Even after the fuel tanks went up, there was still working double-A fire coming up from the dump."

"Enough to bring two planes down?"

Van Damm shrugged.

"Or maybe they're not there at all," Halverson said.

"Maybe. Maybe they really did get bounced on the way home; maybe they're down somewhere else. On that point, there's nothing we can find to corroborate or refute Markham's story."

"What about this Anderson fella?" Halverson asked Harry. "He must have something to say."

Harry shrugged. "If he does, he's keeping it to himself. Since his initial debriefing, he's clammed up. At this point, knowing anything he says is probably going to be self-incriminating, I doubt he's going to supply us with anything useful."

Halverson nodded grimly. To Van Damm: "Tell me about the recon flight."

"We used a three-plane flight out of Manston. Mosquitos. One camera ship, two flying cover." Van Damm turned to Harry and Ryan. "We use the Mosquitos on a lot of BDA runs because they're long on range, fast, maneuverable, and primarily made of plywood, which means a low radar return. Poststrike, the krauts are usually looking for a recon flight, so if you can get in and out without provoking them—"

"Mosquitos," Halverson mulled uncomfortably. "Does that mean an RAF involvement?"

"The Mosquitos are on loan. It was our people in the cockpits."

"Can they keep their mouths shut? The crews?"

"They're my people, General. They keep their mouths shut *all* the time."

"How much do they know?"

"To them, this was a routine BDA flight consequent to a routine attack mission on a legitimate target."

"I don't want them to think otherwise."

"Yes, sir."

"Where are the crews now?"

"The crews from the camera ship and one of the cover planes are waiting for debriefing."

"The third crew?"

"Well, like I said, the krauts are looking for a poststrike evaluation. Our boys saw FW's coming up from the fighter field outside Ghent, made their last fly-by—we're lucky they got the pictures they did—and lit out. They had to mix it up before they could duck into the clouds. One of the cover ships got chopped up a little bit. They made it back, but both those boys are in the hospital."

"They'll be all right?" the general asked, his voice strained.

Van Damm paused, weighing how much to say. "They'll be laid up for a while," he said, trying to make his voice casual, "but they'll be OK."

Halverson nodded, relieved. He cleared his throat and sat erect in his chair. When he spoke, his voice had regained the hard burnish of command. "Major, are these pictures everything you have?"

"These are the best from the run."

"Are the rest secure?"

"In my safe, sir."

"I want you to take all of the pictures, the gun film, the negatives and all prints, everything you've got on this, and I want them in that safe, too."

"Yes—"

"Nobody—and I mean *nobody*—gets access without a written and confirmed order from me."

Before Van Damm could answer, Grassi's hand was up. "General." Grassi drew himself up to what there was of his height. "We're going to need those pictures."

Harry winced. It was a legitimate point, but it was delivered with the tone of a flat and discourteous demand. Harry wasn't sure, but later he'd swear to me he heard Ryan whisper, "Oh-oh."

Halverson slid his long legs out from under the writing arm of the desk and stood. He walked casually down the center aisle of the auditorium, absently tugging at the hem of his tunic, pulling the wrinkles out of the fabric. He walked directly past Grassi, making no sign he was even aware of the lieutenant's presence. The general stepped into the speaker's area, dropped his cigarette on the floor, and gently snuffed it out with the toe of his polished shoe. Pulling a fresh smoke from the pack in his breast pocket, he spoke quietly to Van Damm. "I'm going to need your room for a few minutes, Major, if you don't mind."

"Of course, sir." As Van Damm scooped up the pictures and film from the projector stand, Harry thought the major seemed relieved at the dismissal. From the look on Grassi's face Harry thought, for a moment, that the little lieutenant was going to say—or worse, do—something to stop Van Damm from removing the material. He almost sighed audibly in relief when the briefing-room door closed behind the major without incident.

Halverson faced the room, his feet slightly apart, casual but firm, one hand slipped into his trouser pocket, the other a home for his cigarette. "I believe you had something to say, Lieutenant?"

"We're going to need those pictures, General," Grassi declared. "Those pictures are *evidence*. It's customary to have *access* to *evidence* to prepare a *case!*"

"Is that a fact?"

Harry shrank back in his seat, awaiting the explosion.

"We have the legal *authority to demand*—"

"Demand?"

Grassi stopped himself. Even he knows he's overstepped, Harry thought.

But the explosion never came. Instead, Halverson smiled slightly, coldly. "Lieutenant, you have as much authority as the Army lets you have. So, if I were you, I'd learn to get by without those pictures for now."

"General—"

"None of those pictures are going to see the light of day until they have to. The day you need them in court is the day they come out of the safe and not before."

Grassi looked to Harry for support. It was a rare occasion: Harry sympathized with the lieutenant. They *should* have access to the photographs. But it was painfully obvious to Harry that General Halverson's mind was as closed to the idea as Major Van Damm's safe. Now, what Harry was trying to signal to the lieutenant with frantic looks was not to annoy the general any further. The case had suddenly grown wildly beyond his expectations and Harry felt that, more than ever before, he was going to need Halverson's goodwill on his side.

Grassi looked from Harry to the general, then back to Harry. Finally, he smiled, gave a barely perceptible nod, and parked against the wall.

Halverson acknowledged the surrender with a tight smile of his own. He turned to Harry and the smile was gone. "Major, I take it, then, that your supposition is this O'Connell kid was killed to conceal all this," and he nodded at the blank projection screen.

Harry stood. "Uh, yes, sir, that does bring the pieces together."

"What about a motive, Major? Why this?" and he nodded at the screen again.

Harry's mouth opened reflexively but he had nothing to say.

"Um, sir?" Ricks came to his feet. "A motive is always a useful element of prosecution, but it's not a prerequisite."

"I know that, Captain." Halverson turned to the empty screen. Was he, too, looking for nonexistent answers? "I was just curious."

Ryan cleared his throat. He did not stand. For the first time since the lights had come up, Harry had time to regard his friend. He found the sight unnerving. Joe Ryan was slumped in his seat, his face slack and pale, his eyes shining with a shocked, unfocused glaze. A cigarette burned forgotten between his fingers.

"Something to say, Colonel?" Halverson asked.

Ryan cleared his throat again. "The captain's right." His voice was faint, his tone tentative.

"I can't hear you, Colonel."

"If you've got the evidence to make the case, the captain's right. I mean, what he said about motive. But we don't have the evidence."

"You don't."

"When the time comes to introduce them, we've got these photographs," Ryan said. "That's not proof positive. There's no precedent for using this kind of material as evidence of—"

"Set one," Halverson decreed.

"Sir?"

"Set a precedent. That's how you get a precedent, right? Somebody does it first? Be the first."

It was obvious to Ryan—to all of them—that Halverson was not looking to debate the point. Ryan sank back into his chair.

Halverson turned to Harry. "Major, how long to trial?"

"We haven't even drawn up an indictment—"

"I didn't ask you about an indictment, Major!" The general was growing peevish. "If you told me you could be in court by tomorrow morning, I'd say, 'Do it!' Can you be in court tomorrow?"

"With all due respect," Ryan interjected, "normally, what with all the paperwork, if we could pull it together in four weeks—"

"Half of that's protocol, waiting for signatures, that kind of stuff," Grassi interrupted, ignoring Ryan's glare. "We can get off the dime and cut that down by a week. Maybe two without a problem."

"Tomorrow," Halverson counteroffered grimly, still focused on Harry.

"General," Harry pleaded, "I can understand the urgency here, but—"

"No, you can't. Saturday."

"General," Ricks put in, "the faster we go, the greater our chances of leaving some opening for an appeal so that even if we get a conviction—"

"Let someone else worry about the damned appeal, Captain!" The rebuff exploded so curtly that Ricks's head snapped back, his eyes blinking, as if he'd suffered a physical blow. Halverson was back to Harry again. "OK, here's how it's going to be: I want this thing in court bright and early Monday morning. I don't care how many hours you work or what you have to do. Whatever you need to get it done, call me, but *get it done!* In court on Monday! If you don't think you can handle that, tell me now and I'll find someone who can."

Harry exchanged a quick look with Grassi and Ricks but knew before their eyes locked what he'd find. Grassi's face was wide-eyed with adrenaline; if Halverson had told them to be in court the following morning, Grassi would've been happy for the early debut. Ricks, on the other hand, wore a hangdog look that seemed to be hanging lower with each passing moment. Harry's feeling may have been more aesthetic than moral (as Ricks had said, such speed almost guaranteed a host of procedural errors that could turn a conviction into a nightmare of appeals) but he agreed with the captain that this was not the way the law—even Army law—was supposed to be.

Yet Halverson had been quite clear on their options.

"Monday morning, sir." Harry glumly nodded an assent.

"Colonel Ryan, you'll naturally do whatever you can to expedite the matter. I'll look to you to see that the accused are secured counsel and whatever else they need to be in court Monday A.M."

"Yessir," Ryan murmured.

Halverson stood with his hand on the doorknob. He turned and smiled at the four officers among the school chairs. All looked a bit lost. It was an odd smile, sad, as if he alone knew a sad truth. "Believe me, Major Voss, if you don't get this to court by Monday, you may never get it to court at all." And he left.

Harry looked back to Ricks. The captain's look was part indictment, part resignation, and the rest represented by a silent sigh and small shake of the head that made Harry want to say, out loud, "I'm sorry. It's not my fault, but I'm sorry."

They were silent for a long while, and then Grassi spoke, swaggering down to the front of the room, an annoying, cocky smile on his lips. He opened his mouth, no doubt prepared to say something acidic.

"Shuddup!" Ryan snarled. "I swear to Christ, Lieutenant, unless the next words out of your mouth are 'Good-bye,' you don't want to say them!"

Grassi's mouth closed, slowly, and his smile evaporated.

Ryan turned to Harry, his face a fiery red, looking ready to tear into his friend next. "Harry—"

The briefing-room door squeaked open; Van Damm leaned in. "I saw the general leave. You gentlemen going to be much longer? I need this room."

"We've got to talk," Ryan hissed. He gave Harry enough time to tell Grassi and Ricks to wait in his quarters, then dragged Harry out the door by his arm and through the G-2 darkness. Harry wasn't quite sure where they were going, or even if they were going anywhere, but he eventually realized that Ryan's frantic zigs and zags were a search for privacy that finally ended with them bursting through the door of a glaringly lit latrine.

A second lieutenant stood at a urinal. He looked over his shoulder and saw Harry and Ryan glaring at each other, waiting. With all the expertise of his Intelligence-staffer status, the lieutenant deftly interpreted the situation, forced an abrupt halt to operations, and scooted past them.

As soon as the latrine door clicked shut behind the lieutenant, Ryan detonated. *"What the hell is going on?"* The words reverberated off the concrete walls of the loo like artillery rounds.

Harry stood dazed and blinking, partly from the shock of the noise, partly in earnest confusion. "What do you mean—"

"You waltz me around with all this 'Just a few more days' crap! 'Oh, Joe, pretty please, oh, I need just a little more time—' "

Harry bristled. "You wouldn't mind telling me what this is all about, would you?"

It occurred to Ryan that he had not adequately secured the premises; now he began to look under the doors of the stalls. "That's my question, Harry! You should've come to me first, you really should've, before you went flapping your gums to Halverson—"

"Come to you first about what?"

"Don't play games with me, Harry!"

It was Harry's turn to shout. *"I'm not playing any games! I don't know what you're—"*

"How long have you been sitting on this thing?"

"Sitting on <u>what</u>*?"*

"Dammit, Harry—" Ryan's voice dropped to a comparatively discreet hiss. "That butcher's orgy we just saw!"

"Joe, I knew about it when *you* did; when Van Damm put those pictures on—"

"You've been stretching me out all along, telling me you had questions—"

"That's right! *Questions!* And I got the answers a few minutes ago, right along with you! I didn't know where they were going. That's why they were *questions.* You think I was holding back—"

The latrine door opened; Harry cut himself off. This time, it was a young captain. As quick-witted as his colleague the lieutenant, he took an instant to analyze the situation, then about-faced and exited.

Harry understood now—or thought he did. In the beginning, two days ago, Ryan had been bestowing a gift. But Ryan had not expected the gift to turn into a coup. "I get it!" Harry said. "Joe, I know this is a lot bigger than how it started. You think I don't know who I owe? If you want a piece of this, all you—"

"A piece of this? Harry, I wouldn't go near this thing in an asbestos suit! You really have no idea what you've gotten yourself into. Let me clear it up for you: You're in the shit, my friend, right up to your eyeballs!"

"Instead of browbeating me," Harry persisted, "why don't you try explaining—"

"Don't do anything!" Ryan bellowed, driving the point home with a painful jab of his index finger to Harry's chest. "Not until you hear from me."

"What do you mean, don't do—"

"I mean don't make a move, don't do a goddamned thing on this case, don't talk to anybody—"

"What about Halverson? If he asks how it's going, do I just say, 'Well, General, I've just been sitting around twiddling my thumbs because Colonel Ryan—' "

The possibility of such an attribution struck a responding chord in Ryan. He sprang back to Harry. "All right, all right, you go ahead and keep moving the paperwork along, but before you make any big moves you talk to me. Understand? Before you get us in this mess any deeper, let me see if I can get us out."

"I still don't understand what you're—"

Ryan wasn't waiting; he was already at the door. "You're putting yourself in a corner where I can't help you, Harry. I won't!"

Then Ryan was gone and Harry was standing alone in the loo, more at sea than when he'd entered. He was still standing there when the patient but anxious captain, the one who'd bounced in and immediately backed out, stuck his head inside.

"All clear, sir? We're developing a line out here."

He held the door respectfully as Harry passed stonily through.

I had just emptied a tin of kippers into the small skillet atop my little gas ring and had left the door open to help dissipate the consequent smell, when Himself was suddenly there in my doorway. He scarcely waited for my nodded welcome before he stepped inside, the door sighing shut behind him as if closed by his immortal will. He fleetingly smiled a greeting and set himself in my most comfortable chair, resting an ankle across a knee, and parking his trilby on the upraised toe of his shoe. He nodded at the kippers sizzling malodorously in what should have been sweet butter but, in its rationed absence, was margarine.

"That'd be dinner?" Himself asked.

"Afraid so." I prodded the kippers with a fork. "Care to partake?"

"Oh, I think not."

I looked down at the kippers curling in the crackling margarine and saw his point.

He felt an obligation not to be deprecating in my home, however, and justified his refusal with, "The missus has one of her usual culinary monstrosities waiting for me. She was never what you'd call your gourmet, but I think all the rationing has completely done her in. The nice thing about me being late home is it gives her an alibi for damage done. 'Of course it tastes off, ya silly clod!' " he said à la his wife. I'd seen her in the office once or twice and his mimicry of her voice—the trilling shrillness and barbed declaratives—was more impressionistic than accurate. " 'It always tastes off when it's been sitting about cold half the night!' Ah, well," he sighed, then his eyes darted about hopefully. "Um, there wouldn't be a taste about, eh? Something to numb the palate for what's to come?"

It seemed a good idea for both of us. I turned off the gas ring but the kippers continued to crackle and smoke, throwing off a dockside smell thickening inside the closed blackout curtains. I produced a pair of glasses and a fair bottle of scotch, not as good as the one he kept in his desk drawer, but then again an editor's purse stood a bit thicker than mine. I poured the drinks and dragged a chair close by. We raised our glasses, nodded solemnly, and sipped with equal devotion.

"Ahhh," he said and I agreed. "You see Cathryn?" he asked.

"Since the divorce?"

"I'd like to think you'd seen a bit of her before, you silly git."

"Permit me to amplify: since the divorce, or since my triumphal return?"

"Either or."

"Yes, no, respectively."

He set his glass down on the lamp table by the chair and absently drew a triskelion in the dust there. Perhaps it was the thick coat of dust, something one would never have seen in Cathryn's house, that prompted him to say, "I miss that one. Good lass, her."

"They're all good lasses after they're gone."

"I'll toast that, my son. How about another? Mine seems to have evaporated. Ah, thanks. She were a good one, though, Cathryn. Any chance at that? A resurrection, I mean? You're on the list, you know, my preferred list when one of the editorial desks opens. Old Glatley's practically at death's door. Don't know why the old duffer doesn't just take his pension and race his damned pigeons. Be that as it may, it's yours come the time. No more gadding round the world then, eh? She'd like that, I fancy. Maybe not you, not at first, all that sitting'd be quite a change, eh? But you're good enough for the desk, my son, always thought so, you being right for the desk once you got the gallivants out of yourself. Any chance with her, then? Or is that all tick, eh?"

"One of the things I admired most about Cathryn was her good sense."

"Ah, then she won't be back."

"I think not."

"Well, as you say, she were always a sensible girl, wot?"

"Aye. Not to be rude, or to suspect your goodwill, but was there some business? Or is this just a friendly chat?"

"There are no friendly chats in business, my son, particularly in this line of country." He sighed. "It's off. The story. Close the book." He finished his drink in a gulp and set the glass down on the dusty tabletop with a rap of finality.

"You said I had until—"

"Two drinks does not interfere with my recall, my son. It's not you, if that's your concern. In fact, I've been quite happy to see you running with the hounds again. Put a bit of color back in your cheeks, it has. No, no, not you at all. Not my decision, so you know. It's just the word."

"From?"

"From the people that give one the word. 'National interest' and all that, a call from the general-list blokes, waving the flag and the Official Secrets Act, vital military information and all that rot. You know the program. Off-limits and such."

The tactic itself didn't disturb me. One bounded into it rather regularly covering the war. What took me aback was that I could see nothing in this particular story to merit such severe treatment.

Himself pretended a tone of polite, disinterested conversation when he asked his next question, but it was still the good reporter at work. "Had you come across anything of note?"

"I thought the story was over."

"Academic interest, my son."

I smiled and poured another pair of fresh drinks. "Since last we joined our heroes, it seems we have one American aeroplane—a Thunderbolt, a wreck—sitting in a Scotland Yard warehouse aswarm with the Yard's ballistics boffins. They've been whiling away the hours digging through it for bullets. I've also found out that the Yard has brought in the guns from some other Yank aeroplanes to do ballistic comparisons."

He tried not to express interest. He was a good editor: Let the reporter work to convince that there is a worthy story here. "What else?"

"You remember that spotter I told you about? Name's Gresham. He and his wife, they lived down on the coast where whatever happened happened. The bogies spirited the Greshams away somewhere, where they're being kept under lock and key. And there's a dead Yank in the Yard morgue been put through a postmortem. And—this is the plum part—two American pilots were taken by their Provost Marshal and tossed in the clink. They're from the 351st Group, down by Chillingham."

"Where the blazes is Chillingham?"

"East Sussex, a few hours south of here. They were the unit that took such a drubbing about a week or so ago."

He nodded. He wasn't bothering with feigned disinterest now; the story had been sold. "Who's the poor bloke on the P.M. table?"

"I don't know yet. Quite honestly, I'm surprised I've gotten this much. It's been like trying to infiltrate the 33rd Degree of Masons. This isn't just people not talking. It's been *tightening*. The press officers have gone from keeping a secret to building walls."

"As if they've come across something they didn't know they had at first."

I nodded.

"Any idea who's running this show for the Yanks?"

"There's a JAG major named Voss. He has a couple of legmen: a captain named Ricks and a Lieutenant Grassi. I've heard Grassi's name before and not by favorable mention. Bolshie, anarchist, Bluebeard—"

"Not well loved, then, eh?"

"Hardly. But the indications are that all the big movements—the lip-tightening, the new walls—are not coming from this Voss bloke."

"That JAG dandy? Ryan?"

"Perhaps even higher. Earlier this evening they were all at that nest they have under Grosvenor Square."

"Intelligence?" He frowned. "What would Intelligence have to do with . . . well, with anything criminal?"

"My question exactly. And when they came out, they were all looking quite off. I got the distinct feeling something had rattled their cages. But to your point about who's directing the show; immediately afterward, Ryan made expeditiously for a very tête-à-tête meeting at General DiGarre's digs after which, within an hour, the new silent curtain fell."

"When was this?"

"As I said; early this evening. About seven."

"Hm. That was when Fleet Street started getting the calls from the War Office to be on best behavior. Quite queer, eh? One wants to think a murder, all the elements seem there. That could be a sensitive bit, but it hardly seems dodgy enough to justify all this, eh? All this business with Intelligence, and caballing with DiGarre."

"You think there's something else about?"

"I'm inclined to think there'd almost *have* to be."

"Seems worth carrying on, eh? Just out of 'academic curiosity'?"

Himself smiled briefly, sympathetic to the notion, but then the smile vanished, and he grunted to his feet. "Afraid not, my son. The 'request' has been made by those on high, and as dutiful Englishmen, we have agreed."

I stood with him. "Need I remind you, I'm not English."

"You're still a citizen of The Empire. Leave it be, my son. You've done a good job. Shame to turn it off, but . . . Jump in the kip, sleep late. You owe yourself a reward. Then back to work. I think you've covered your last snooker championship." He smiled, then, and began to leave, but stopped in the doorway, well understanding the dramatic effect of the pause. He cast a condemnatory eye round my hovel, settling it at last upon the now-still skillet of kippers. "Do try to get the old girl back, my son. The bachelor life isn't for you." And he left.

The kippers looked rather less appetizing after lying half-cooked in the skillet than they had in their tin. I hesitated before I relit the flame. I turned out the lights so I could cook with the heavy curtains pulled back. Another drink helped dampen the dissuading effects of the kippers' smell and shriveled appearance.

I was not happy the story had been killed, but I was reconciled. It was not the first time; it would not be the last. In fact, I gave more thought to Himself's acknowledgment that I now rated better than royal teas and flower shows. By the time my head hit the pillow that night, I was giving the matter of the killed story very little thought at all.

CHAPTER SEVEN

THE VARANGIANS

ABOUT THE TIME I WAS HAVING my little confabulation with The Boss, Harry Voss was arriving back at the Annex, his head still awhirl with his latrine face-to-face with Ryan. He made the long trudge up the stairs contemplating the splendor of falling face forward onto his bed without the bother of disrobing or washup, but the door to his quarters swung open and there he unhappily saw Ricks and Grassi.

Ricks sat in the room's one chair—the one at Harry's escritoire—and had moved it a few inches away from the desk, turning it respectfully away from the writing surface to show he had no interest in Harry's personal affairs. Grassi, on the other hand, was sprawled across Harry's bed as if it were his own, atop the pile of mail left there by the orderlies, leafing through Harry's newly delivered copy of Life.

Ricks saw the befuddlement on Harry's wan face as he groped through the cobwebs of fatigue for some reason for them to be there. "You told us to wait for you here, sir?" he offered. "Back there at the briefing room?"

Harry remembered with a moan.

"Would you like us to come back?"

Harry shook his head, then went to the loo to splash some water on his face.

"Whaddaya think, Boss?" a leering Grassi asked when he returned to the room. "You think she's really naked under there?" Grassi had the magazine turned to a double-page spread of Hollywood showgirls and his blackened eye narrowed in a particularly lewd squint. There was Gene Tierney who, according to the caption, servicemen considered "The Girl We'd Most Like to Guard on a Lonely Pacific Isle." Veronica Lake was "The Girl We'd Most Like to Make Our Objective." Grassi's attention was devoted to Maureen O'Sullivan: "The Girl We'd Most Like to Ride with on a Bumpy African Road." In Miss O'Sullivan's photo, she was bare-shouldered, looking down into a mirrored tabletop that obscured the rest of her body from view. Grassi's thumb was caressing the naked shoulders. "How 'bout it, Boss? Hey, Cap'n, whaddayou think?"

"Of course not."

"Are you *sure*? How do you *know*?" Grassi brought the magazine closer to his face. "She *could* be naked under there. You see that little thing she wore in those Tarzan pictures? She's the type; I wouldn't put it past her. She *should* be bare-ass naked under there!"

Ricks shook his head. "You are a sick individual, Lieutenant. Sick."

Grassi responded with wagging eyebrows and "whoo-hoo"'s co-opted from Daffy Duck cartoons.

Harry ended the performance with a backhanded slap across the lieutenant's thighs. "*Get off my mail!*" Grassi popped off the bed and Harry angrily snatched his *Life* back. "Get your own damned magazine!"

"My, my, don't we get grumpy when we've missed our nap," Grassi said, but found himself a perch on the windowsill.

Harry took a seat on the bed. "And now," he said, kicking off his shoes, "if it's not *too* much trouble, do you think we could get to work?"

Notebooks flipped open, throats were cleared, and then Ricks and Grassi briefed Harry on what they'd learned of the five young men who'd flown against Helsvagen on August 15.

Name: First Lieutenant Raymond Daniel Jacobs
Born: October 11, 1917
Place of Birth: Quincy, Washington

Not shy, but deliberately quiet and reserved, the man from the Washington forests never allowed an address more informal than "Raymond." His nominal birthplace was a spot found only on the best and most detailed map, but Quincy was listed more for the convenience of record-keepers than for accuracy. Jacobs had been born and spent his early years some miles away, actually, amid the tall trees and crags of the Cascades.

His mother, of whom little was known, had died with his birth, and his father was a flinty, spare man who eked out a living hunting, skinning, and occasionally scouting for logging companies. While Jacobs never explained what drew him out of the mountains, one could guess at a typical adolescent restlessness fueling a desire to see if there were more to the world than the monastic life he shared with an uncommunicative father in a rustic cabin walled in by timber and steep cliffs, and capped by the dark, tumultuous skies of the American Northwest. In any case, at the age of fifteen he came down out of the mountains to Quincy and never looked back. At the time of his enlistment nine years later, in 1941, Jacobs could not even answer as to whether or not his father was still alive.

While there are no records of formal education, Jacobs was, evidently, sufficiently self-taught so that when he appeared in Seattle in the early 1930's he was competently equipped with the abilities of reading, writing, and math. And, perhaps from his association with the lumbermen with whom his father sometimes worked, and from toying with the various machines that served their trade, he also evidenced by that time a fair ability with things mechanical. It is a measure of those skills that, young as he was, and at a time when lines of men looking for work were more common than work, he soon found positions as an apprentice engineer among the coastal steamers plodding up and down the West Coast from Alaska to Panama.

Another gap in his sketchy record leaves unanswered the question of what moved him from steamers to aeroplanes, but by late 1936, Jacobs was no longer signing on with any further crews. After another blank in his chronology, he surfaced as an aeroplane maintenance engineer at Los Angeles Airport in 1938. Soon after, he signed on with Chennault when the flamboyant general began enlisting personnel to fight for the Chinese as the American Volunteer Group, known more colorfully as "The Flying Tigers."

Jacobs served in China until Pearl Harbor, when America formally entered the war and most of the AVG personnel gravitated back to the States to serve in the American military. Jacobs's performance, according to Chennault's staff, was commendable. The AVG fields were always undermanned, ill equipped, and badly supplied, but Jacobs proved a wizard at scavenging—or forging—the parts to repair what most mechanics considered irreparable. On returning to the States he, like many of his fellow AVG alumni, enlisted with the Air Corps and put in for fighter pilot training. Despite his lack of formal schooling, his service with Chennault stood him in good stead and he was accepted. He struggled a bit with the bookwork, but proved himself able enough in the air and completed training at the fighter pilot school in San Antonio in mid-1942, in time to be assigned to the then-forming 351st Fighter Group.

Jacobs's record with the 351st showed an unexceptional but reliable pilot, a bit more unflappable and less reckless than most, a product of his natural reserve one would guess, or perhaps due to his comparative maturity, there being an average difference of five years between him and the scrappy Young Turks filling most of the group's cockpits.

There was an earnest, if lighthearted, respect among the younger men for his ability and a service record that extended back to the legendary AVG. They called him "Pappy" and "Methuselah," and subjected him to his fair share of pranks. And, while he did not join his comrades on their excursions to pubs and whorehouses, nor indulge in their rabid pranksterism, keeping to himself much of the time, he did overcome his natural reserve to tolerate the jibes and tricks with good nature.

After all, he had come from the hot flats of Texas with them, fought their first battles with them, and despite any difference in personality or background, any gap in age and experience, they had been bloodied together. It would not have bothered his solitude, one might think, to know that he had come to rest with many of them as well.

Name: Second Lieutenant Andrew Paul McLagen, Jr.
Born: May 19, 1924
Place of Birth: Boydton, Virginia

Even after his facing German fighters (and downing two of them), soaring tracers, and ugly blotches of flak in eleven sorties over the Continent, even after his drunken, giggling mates had trundled him down to a Brighton brothel to celebrate his nineteenth birthday with the end of his virginity, "Andy" McLagen still retained enough of his native shyness that, in conversation even with his closest acquaintances, he would still avert his eyes, shuffle his feet, mumble his drawling responses.

He was second born—first to survive—of six children delivered of God-fearing Baptists, his father being a tenant farmer on a stretch of tobacco land not far from the North Carolina border. Mother and Father McLagen taught their children to pray before every meal, and at night before climbing into the straw-filled pallets the young ones shared, and when they woke every morning, especially on Sunday when they hiked en masse down the red clay road to a sun-baked clapboard church where they sweated through hours of sermonizing by a flushed-faced, button-straining minister. If they forgot to pray, or did not pray with accepted sincerity, they were ordered to bend over a rail fence and spirituality was branded on their bottoms with a whipping cane.

As the eldest, it was Andy's responsibility to shepherd his siblings down that same road every day, rain or shine, hot or cold, in mud and dust, to the one-room schoolhouse standing across from the church, and shepherd them home in the afternoon, after which he took his place by his father in the fields. At night, by the light of a kerosene lantern (electricity was a luxury held only by the most affluent Boydton towns-people) he did his lessons and practiced his reading on passages of the Bible until Mother McLagen was satisfied and ushered him off to evening prayers and bed.

He showed a flair for machines as a young boy. His father and the other tenants would squat on their haunches, scratching in the dust with twigs as they stared dumbly at the inert tractor they shared, but young Andy could puzzle out a function, remove and dissect its pieces, and replace them healthy and whole.

Out in the fields, he looked across the sprouting tobacco leaves and saw crop dusters seaming the fields with their sprays, rising in and sliding out of the sky with the ease of the angels cited from the pulpit every Sunday. As he had puzzled out the tractor's engine, so he puzzled out that his mechanical talents could take him beyond the world of a share-cropper's tin-roofed shack.

A likable and deferential sort, and quick to learn what he didn't

already know, it was easy for young Andy to find work with the itinerant
fliers. It was not long before he knew his way round the engine of a
Curtis Jenny as well as that of a John Deere tractor. To his parents' dismay, however, the boy was all too willing to exchange his work not for
badly needed cash, but for a ride in the forward cockpit with the control stick in his adolescent hand for a brief minute or so. Such derelic-
tion earned him a caning or two, but he considered that a fair price
for an exhilarating, if stomach-churning, trip through a high, ascend-
ing loop from whose peak he could see that the few square miles of Virginia he knew were just a small corner of the world; not the whole of it.

On December 7, 1941, men on horseback rode through the countryside round Boydton to spread the word received through the few wireless sets in town: The U.S. was at war. Andy, along with nearly every
other male in the county, including his fifteen-year-old brother and forty-
five-year-old slope-backed father, gathered at the church that night to
pray and await the Army enlistment clerk who arrived the following
morning.

Father McLagen took his rejection with stoic resignation, compensat-
ing himself with the unbounded pride of his eldest boy's enlistment. He
and Mother McLagen prayed for their boy's safe return, escorted him to
the Boydton train station, thrust the family Bible in his hands, warned
him against fancy women and liquor, then wished him well and reminded him not to forget his daily prayers.

Though Andy McLagen had not completed his formal schooling, his
mechanical skills were plain and his experience valued. His battery tests
placed him in aircraft mechanic school, and by the end of 1942 he was
proudly writing his parents in his simple, block lettering that he had
earned his sergeant's stripes. The following year, the "Flying Sergeants"
program was instituted to cull flight-worthy noncoms from the ranks to
replace the growing losses in the expanding air offensive against Hitler's
Festung Europa. Andy McLagen was accepted into the program, earned his
wings, and by spring 1943 was transferred to a fighter pilot replace-
ment pool in London. Just a few weeks before the 351st began combat
operations, he was assigned to the group to replace a lost wingman (the
ill-fated Wayne Donophan, ironically enough).

He quickly proved his mettle, gaining a reputation as one of the
steadiest of the new pilots. On his third mission, his element leader's

aeroplane was struck in the engine. The leader ordered McLagen to stay with the group while he tried for home. Albert Markham, who was leading the mission, issued the same order, taking on the responsibility of escorting the crippled ship home. But Andy McLagen didn't go, and when a gaggle of FW-190's pounced he didn't flinch, fighting them off alongside Markham.

A few days later, Markham and Colonel Adams called the youngster into the CO's office. "The kid was so nervous I thought he was going to pee in his pants," Korczukowski chuckled, as he relived the story for listeners some time after. "I guess he thought Al and the old man were going to prang him for disobeying orders. And they knew he was sweating, too. They let him sit out in my office and stew, and when they finally called him in they were sitting there stone-faced. Like the Inquisition."

When finally McLagen was admitted, Adams cowed him immediately, declaring, "I've got the best boys in the world flying for me! They're too good to have some low-rent striper flying on their wing!"

"I swear," Korczukowski told me, grinning, "you could see that kid's arms flinch, like those sergeant's stripes were biting him."

Then Al Markham, without so much as the flicker of a smile, handed Andy the gold bars of a second lieutenant. "There," he said. "That takes care of that."

The battlefield commission was a long way to come for somebody from a family that had yet to produce a member who had finished his schooling or seen much beyond a few miles of Virginia and North Carolina. Andy's mates were just as proud of him as he was of himself. He became something of a mascot to them, being the youngest in his squadron, and, arguably, the most naive. For all the miles he'd logged he'd seen precious little: mostly military installations and a few tentative, excitingly sinful forays into saloons with his comrades. The story went that even on the excursion to the Brighton brothel, wherein his squadron fellows conspired with a prostitute to finally deflower the lad, Andy remained a gentleman behind the closed door of the lady's boudoir, exchanging nothing more than conversation with her. When affectionately badgered about the encounter, he blushed and dissembled for, whatever the truth of the matter was, he still remained too much the good child of his parents to divulge details of his personal affairs.

Six weeks later he was gone, and those of his mates who had survived the bombing of Donophan thought back to the blushing youngster from tobacco country, and wondered if he'd died still the virgin boy.

Name: Second Lieutenant Dennis Francis O'Connell
Born: September 23, 1920
Place of Birth: Boston, Massachusetts

Dennis O'Connell's father was a stonecutter who had left Ireland during the Easter Rebellion for Boston, where he regularly gathered with other expatriates and descendants of expatriates in corner bars and argued adamantly for the cause they'd left. Of his father O'Connell had little to say, other than vague complaints of oppression and ignorance. Of his mother, another Irish émigré, he said even less; she might very well have disappeared for as much as he mentioned her. It was not a dismissal but rather, it seemed, a memory he savored privately and quietly, as one might worship one's private saint.

His father enrolled him in Boston College but O'Connell chafed under the Jesuits and, against his father's wishes, enrolled in the Massachusetts Institute of Technology; if his father wished to push him toward Catholic divinity, then O'Connell would strike back with heartless science. When his father came to accept the change, and even boast of his boy's progress, O'Connell left school to pick up work as a day laborer here and there while roaming up and down the East Coast. His occasional visits home lasted only long enough to antagonize his father with his apparent shiftlessness.

A year of roaming in those hard Depression days was enough for O'Connell, and in 1939 he turned to the same avenue as that of many other rootless young men of the time: the military. His smattering of university and the results of his battery tests landed him in flight training. He emerged an adequate pilot assigned to the Air Transport Command, where he was quite content to enjoy the myriad sights of the country as he shuttled men and matériel about the States. As the war in Europe grew more ravenous, threatening to draw in America, he betrayed no sign of anxiety in his visits home, but privately he began counting the days until the end of his enlistment.

Like certain Irish constituencies, O'Connell's father saw the war as an opportunity for Ireland to break the bonds of English fiefdom. So reflexively opposed to his father was O'Connell that he could not resist touting English resilience in the war, and boasted that America would soon be rallying to the Royal Family's side to roll back Ireland's potential liberators. It was then that Dennis O'Connell's father finally and permanently closed his door on his son.

The war did come and O'Connell, along with every other man in uniform, whether he had two years or two hours left on his term of service, was now in uniform for the duration. His enthusiasm for the war against the Hun in Europe (or any other for that matter), with which O'Connell had tweaked his father, waned abruptly.

Although the American Air Corps was the first military arm extended overseas, with their bombers flying out of England by the summer of 1942, O'Connell continued to play the role of aerial lorry driver safely back in the States. However, the considerable pilot losses of those early days of the American bomber offensive sparked a search through the service's ranks for qualified fliers with multiengine aircraft experience. A number of ATC pilots fit the bill, including O'Connell, but he sidestepped reassignment by putting in for a transfer to fighter pilot training, a move misinterpreted by his seniors as evidence of an admirable ambition. Eventually, the bottomless manpower needs overseas expanded to include fighter pilots as well.

He received transfer orders late in '42 to a unit already operating in England. O'Connell claimed hardship, saying his family's poverty and mother's ill health required him stateside. Without his father's knowledge, he obtained a corroborating letter from his mother, and the transfer was canceled. Early in '43 he was ordered to San Antonio to replace a 351st Fighter Group pilot injured in a ground mishap. Again, O'Connell claimed hardship, but this time his father intercepted his son's request to his mother for a second corroboration, and supplied his own document to the Air Corps in which he frankly claimed his son's only hardship was an inability to find a family member to lie for him.

At San Antonio, O'Connell was assigned to Al Markham's squadron just as a transfer to combat operations in England was in the offing. O'Connell's ambition to avoid combat remained unabated. He investigated conscientious objection; he pleaded to the base psychiatrist that he was mentally unfit; he put in for transfer back to his ATC unit.

According to Leo Korczukowski, O'Connell's frantic maneuvering to avoid combat duty hardly went unnoticed. One hot April afternoon, Al Markham took him under his arm and walked him off to a far corner of the field. What transpired between them neither Markham nor O'Connell ever shared with anyone else. Whatever it was, O'Connell's attempts to leave the 351st ceased immediately. His conduct on the ground and in the air improved. He fulfilled his responsibilities unenthusiastically but reliably, and continued to do so through his first combat sortie. Thereafter, whatever equilibrium Markham had given the boy rapidly evaporated; this time no walk to a quiet corner of the field would put things right.

Some thought they could see O'Connell deteriorate with every sortie. Though Markham had continued to try to turn the boy round, Adams, with his promotion to Wing in sight, declared that the O'Connell situation had to be resolved before his departure. Markham agreed. That discussion, to which Korczukowski, Markham, and Adams were party, took place at evening mess on August 8. The group had been alerted for a mission the following day, and Markham suggested that further discussion of the matter be put off to the following morning so they could dedicate their evening to the usual preoperation activities. Adams assented.

Approximately six hours later, the Germans bombed Donophan and Colonel Adams was dead. Seven days later, so was Lieutenant Dennis O'Connell.

Name: Captain Jon-Jacob Anderson
Born: May 12, 1920
Place of Birth: Matson, Kansas

There were seven children on the Anderson farm—five boys, two girls— all with the same azure eyes and cornsilk hair. J. J., as they called him, was the runt, and as such was determined to prove himself the equal—or better—of his littermates. Meaning: If the other children were jumping from the barn loft into the straw, J. J. would leap from the rafters, flashing his consequent broken arm like a Medal of Honor; if his older, taller brothers made the school basketball team, then basketball became a sport for nancy boys, and J. J. threw his undersized body into the grinding gears of football.

With a boy so adventurous and impulsive, it was unsurprising for him to be attracted to the air circus that drifted across Kansas during the summer season of county fairs. Once J. J. tasted the scent of seat leather and gasoline fumes, and felt the rush of air past an open cockpit, the farm lost him forever. His parents managed to hold on to his leash long enough for him to finish his schooling, but thereafter, he was with a troupe of barnstormers crisscrossing the farm country.

But for someone like J. J., the derring-do of flying loops over county fairs could not compare with the tests of aerial combat. One summer morning in 1940, J. J.'s mates awoke to find one of their pilots missing, along with one of the show's aeroplanes. The craft was located a week later, abandoned in a fallow field outside Toronto.

Toronto was his gateway to the RAF's Ferry Command, flying Hudson bombers to England. J. J.'s interest surpassed being a mere "airplane cabbie" (his disparaging self-description); it was simply a vehicle to get him across the Atlantic. That done, he soon after appeared in RAF uniform, where his story intertwines with that of Al Markham.

Name: Major Albert Quincy Markham
Born: November 11, 1915
Place of Birth: Euclid, Ohio

Al Markham was the middle child—bookended by sisters—of the owner of a small hardware shop. His father worked hard, his mother alongside him, and, as the children grew old enough and capable, each took a place behind the counter. The shop had always struggled, then struggled still more come the Crash of '29. The Markhams did without, worked longer hours, and did not complain. Their mother died the following year. (This event Markham related stoically to acquaintances thusly: "She just worked herself out for us.")

Despite the demands of keeping house with his siblings, and shop-keeping with his father, Markham managed to maintain respectable marks in his schooling, and made a name as a running back on the school football team. His grades and athletic skills earned him a partial scholarship from Ohio State University. But Markham's interests had already been waylaid by an odd bloke identified in Markham's tales only by the colorful sobriquet "Skipjack Bailey."

Mr. Bailey, it seems, was a one-man aviation industry who encamped at a small aerodrome outside Euclid every spring. Throughout the season and into summer and fall, Mr. Bailey secured a living with his patched, creaking Curtis Jenny, performing aerial displays on festive occasions, aerial sightseeing tours, and crop-dusting. Markham never said what first attracted him to Bailey and his patchwork flying machine. What attracts a young man to any first love? It happens.

When Markham could cadge time away from the shop and the schooling and the athletic field, he was with Bailey, learning to make aeroplanes run, to make broken aeroplanes run again, and eventually to fly them. However taken Markham was with Bailey and his shopworn Jenny, so Mr. Bailey was taken with his young disciple. By the time Markham was seventeen, he was Bailey's partner during the flying season, sharing flying time and profits. To atone for his increasing absence from the family shop, Markham unhesitatingly turned over most of his earnings to his father, putting aside for himself only a small cache for upcoming university expenses.

But the university could not compete with flying. Markham left OSU early in his second term, on the eve of the spring flying season, to join Bailey full-time. But just a few months after the lad returned to the aerodrome outside Euclid, Skipjack Bailey—with as much irony as one could want—was struck down by a bus.

Bailey's death took the pleasure out of the little business, and for a bit Markham was all at sixes and sevens as to what to do with himself. His father offered him a place at his shop, but Markham still felt drawn to the air. With his extensive experience it was not difficult for him to secure a position with one of the many birthing airlines that made most of their money flying the mails while experimenting with the concept of air passenger travel on the side.

Markham's particular route was among the cities of the Great Lakes region, and he quickly attained a reputation as a welcome crewman in the copilot seat where all newcomers served their apprenticeship. With many new pilots coming from the likes of barnstormers and crop dusters, pilot trainers always anticipated investing a certain measure of time disciplining the air-circus lone-wolf tendencies out of their pupils, but Markham, from the outset, showed a welcome ease at taking the subordinate seat. If Markham served with a pilot who considered his control of the aeroplane God-given and as such not to be shared with any other human being (including his second), Markham did not complain, and diligently applied himself to his logbook and control checks. And, when flying with a generous captain who would benevolently turn to him and say, "OK, kid, take 'er for a while," he took the control yoke like a veteran.

He had an admirable and remarkable cool about him. Bad weather left him unflustered; bad airfields with bad winds and bad runways he met with thought and calculation instead of anguish and worry; a peculiar vibration in an aeroplane was a puzzle to deduce, not a reason to fret. The airline was sorry to lose him to a competing offer.

Hitler's was a name that made little impression across the oceans in those days, and the events in China were tragic, yes, but it was only yellow men killing yellow men, and the bloodshed had been going on for so long that it had become as unexceptional a part of the news reports as sports scores. And as for the Italian excursion in Abyssinia, well, the cribbage chat ran along the lines that the idea of the fuzzies and Eye-ties chasing each other round the bush seemed downright comical. But in 1936, all that kindling finally birthed the first licks of flame as Spain fell into civil war.

On the other side of the Pond, young men in the doldrums of the Depression became caught up in the classic American adventure tale: overbearing bad guys (the "Insurgents," comprised of rather nasty Fascists) besieging outgunned good guys (the Loyalists) to whose rescue the stouthearted cavalry could ride. Three thousand American idealists read Hemingway's reports of blood, regarded Capa's stunned Spanish foot soldier—an explosion of splayed arms and legs—dropping to the ground, but saw only the glamour of a grand cause and pretty nurses with lilting Spanish accents, soothing "a mere flesh wound" with soft, loving hands. Brave, foolhardy, and naive, they gave themselves over to the illegal recruitment that violated America's neutrality policy, and were smuggled across the Franco/Spanish border. Twenty-one-year-old Al Markham was one of them.

To any young flier, aerobatics, dusting fields, the routine of domestic air routes—all paled at the idea of combat in the air à la Rickenbacker and von Richthofen. Even the normally cool and responsible Al Markham could not resist that allure. But aerobatics are not the same as air combat tactics. Markham was new to the game and discovered—with the first thunk-thunk-thunk of German 7.9-mm machine-gun bullets into the fuselage of his I-16 fighter—that what went on in the Spanish skies was not a game or the chivalric jousting of von Richthofen's day. Markham grappled with the same epiphany that finds every new warrior: Across from him, men he did not know, and would probably never see, were as blindly committed as a thunderstorm to depriving him of his life.

A person's world changes in that moment; the moral compass he has been raised and lived with goes madly spinning. Understanding that there are those who wish to kill one, one now needs to set oneself seriously to developing the skills to kill them first.

The German Condor Legion providing air support for the Insurgents had the Loyalists out-trained and out-equipped. The plucky little I-16's fell regularly to the guns of the German Messerschmitts. Markham was game, and he had a raw ability, enough to gain a kill ("More luck than skill," he often related humbly), but he had yet to perfect that ability. Consequently, in April of 1937, his I-16 plowed a long furrow in the dry Spanish earth, though he managed to turn what should have been a crash into a crash-landing. He hobbled away from his burning ship with a horrendous gash in his right leg, a wound that would still give him a twinge in bad weather. (Markham's fellows would often remark of the invitingly casual air he exuded when one entered his office and saw him leaning back in his chair, one leg propped on an open desk drawer; but that devil-may-care pose had less to do with ease than easing the pain in his old wound.)

A few weeks later, on April 26, Markham was still recovering in a small hospital in a Basque village thirty kilometers from the combat lines. It was Monday, a market day, and Markham first thought the church bells he heard late that afternoon had something to do with the festive air of the crowd milling among the costermongers in the square. A few minutes later he was tragically corrected by a flight of Condor He-111 bombers which, after they emptied their bomb bays, turned round to strafe. After the Heinkels were gone, Ju-52's arrived with loads of incendiaries, and then it was their turn to strafe as well. When the Germans were done three hours later, nearly one-third of the seven thousand Basques who lived in Guernica were dead or wounded.

The war had changed, and so had Al Markham. Still limping, he took up a rifle and returned to the battle line.

He finished the Spanish Civil War in '39 with a letter of commendation from the deposed Díaz government, a recurring pain in his leg, and the fervent belief that the Germans were far from finished. It had been too easy for them; they would come for more. He looked at the map, calculated the possibilities, and settled in France.

He applied to and was accepted by the *Armée de l'Air*, who, while sharing the prevailing French thinking that the *Boche* would never attempt to penetrate the impenetrable Maginot Line, were nonetheless happy to have Markham's experience against the Germans on their rolls.

The French were correct in one assumption: Jerry didn't come through the Maginot. Instead, von Rundstedt's forty-four divisions blazed through the Belgian Ardennes and, with Guderian's panzers in the spearhead, punched through at Sedan, flanked the Maginot, and opened northern France like a tin of kippers. As the French collapsed less than four weeks after the German breakthrough, Markham, along with a number of his dispossessed French colleagues and a mixed bag of refugee combatants from Belgium, the Netherlands, Poland, and the rest of the Reich's shopping list, escaped through Cherbourg a step ahead of the Germans and made the short journey across the Channel with an aim toward—as the saying goes—fighting again another day.

He joined the RAF and was assigned to the 501st Hurricane squadron at Gravesend, directly in the path of the Luftwaffe strikes on London. Not long after Markham started flying with the 501st he received a new wingman, also an expatriate American: Jon-Jacob Anderson.

At first, one would have thought them as likely to shoot at each other as at the Germans. Anderson was a loud braggart, bridling at his junior status on someone's wing. More than once, he went off chasing German aeroplanes instead of holding the confining but necessary confines of the wingman's slot keeping his element leader's tail clear. Quiet, well reasoned, Markham often seemed more concerned about his compatriots than his score. At first, the mix of the two was decidedly volatile.

In a little-known incident the RAF preferred to keep tactfully quiet— and which Anderson saw no reason to resurrect, and Markham was too discreet to reveal—Markham taught Anderson a lesson in responsibility the second time he found his wingman off hunting down a kill and leaving him vulnerable. Taking off after Anderson, Markham sent a short burst through Anderson's tail. "Now," Markham supposedly told him, "you know how it feels."

That took care of the obedience issue. It did not take Anderson long, flying on Markham's wing during those exhausting, countless sorties that made up the Battle of Britain, to develop respect. And, finally, as Anderson began to curb his more erratic and extreme tendencies—in the air, at least—the respect became mutual. From there it evolved into friendship. When the first of the RAF's three all-American Eagle Squadrons was formed in September 1940, Markham and Anderson transferred together.

During his RAF days, Markham came of age. His flying had always been capable, but over the months of combat his instinctive talents became honed. His actions in the air, even when appearing rash and desperate, were always based on calm consideration of the capabilities of his machine and skills, and those of his adversary. More than one RAF colleague described Markham's removal of enemy aircraft from the sky as "surgery."

It was not only Markham's expertise that was maturing. Flying with the Spanish, and later the French, had been different from his RAF service. The separations of culture and language did not allow anything more than a superficial fraternity between him and his fellow pilots. But with the RAF, and especially in his days with the Eagles, Markham experienced that iron bond that occurs between men who fight and face death together. If that brotherhood was fueled on the one hand by the spirit of adventure that brought so many young men across the sea, and on the other by their repugnance for the indiscriminate devastation inflicted during the Blitz, then Markham could add, in his own case, what he'd lived through at Guernica and in France.

The rhetoric tossed about by political and military leaders on all sides was just background static in his ears. While Markham was too truly humble to think of himself as in the service of the Forces of Good, he had seen too much to think of the enemy as anything less than truly evil. That belief strengthened not only the conviction of his fight, but the bond between him and his comrades, for that belief positioned them as the thin, defensive line between what—with all its foibles and frailties—still passed for decency and what was certainly obscene.

Anderson learned at Markham's elbow and became not a perfect officer but an inspiring leader. In the air, his rabid energy compensated for his deficiencies at the stick. He still gloried in his reputation as a reckless madman with no concept of mortality, but from his mentor he took on a semblance of discipline and teamwork. Perhaps it was precisely those peculiarities of his nature, including his earthbound peccadilloes, that were part of his attraction to the more staid Markham. One was the free spirit the other envied; the other the all-American hero one aspired to be.

Perhaps their most defining difference came in their relationship to fear. Fearlessness is the product of romantic fable-tellers more interested in box-office receipts and book sales than truth. Only certified nutters are without fear. Markham understood fear. When the 351st became operational, he took the mechanics aside and quietly told them that after a mission there would always be some red-faced pilots who climbed out of their cockpits and left some mess behind. Perhaps they'd been sick, or their bowels had shuddered loose when they felt Luftwaffe bullets punching through the thin aluminum skin of their ships. The mechanics were to clean the mess and be silent. "One wisecrack," Markham warned, "and the guy who says it spends the duration shoveling snow in the Aleutians."

Anderson, like so many other young and eager types with a head full of myths gleaned from the flickers and pulp novels, denied his fear. The camouflage was the rows in pubs, the constant run-ins with the military and civilian constabulary, the female conquests, the Apache yell over his wireless in combat (issued even as his cockpit filled with the bodily smells of fear).

One wag, describing their differences, said, "Watchin' those two was like watchin' your grandpa walking his grandkid's new puppy. There's this little pooch strainin' at the leash, and Grandpa's doin' his best to get it to heel."

After Pearl Harbor, Markham, Anderson, and the other Eagles were absorbed into the U.S. Air Corps as part of the Fourth Fighter Group. However, by dint of their collective experience, they were singled out and transferred to teach aerial combat tactics in Oklahoma. There they had their premier encounter with Frank Adams.

"You think I made it through all that just to wind up a wet-nurse?" Anderson would gripe, his standing lament concerning his removal from the war. But Markham took the posting with no misgiving. Combat was also Markham's preference, but he understood the importance of blooded pilots mentoring new fliers. Markham was always the good soldier, and the good soldier looks after his fellows.

Some months later, they found themselves instructors in San Antonio where the 351st was being formed up. Adams had no trouble remembering the coolheaded, adept and likable Markham from Oklahoma. Had he been more forgetful, Markham and Anderson might've remained in Texas, and there this story could have ended much to the satisfaction of all concerned.

"I don't think he heard half of what we told him that night," Ricks related to me. "The poor old fella was nodding off right in front of us."

Harry didn't remember when the briefing had ended, or when Ricks and Grassi left. All he knew was that when the harsh alarm of his telephone woke him a little after eight, he found himself still wearing his wrinkled and stale uniform, and his shoulders and neck were achingly stiff. It did little for his waking irritability to find that the voice on the other end of the wire belonged to Corporal Nagel.

The corporal began with a long litany of apologies and excuses, which only vexed Harry further. "Just tell me what in hell you want!"

"It's late, sir. I just wanted to know if you're coming in today."

"Of course I'm coming in today. I just overslept a—"

"Because you got a message from General DiGarre's office and I didn't know what to tell—"

"General DiGarre? What'd he want?"

"I don't know what *he* wants, but his office said for you to come in."

Harry sat up in his bed, swinging his feet to the floor and smoothing out the wayward strands of his sleep-tangled hair. "General DiGarre wants to see *me?*"

"It was his office, so I guess—"

"Where and when, Nagel?"

"In his office, they said. At 1400, they said. When you didn't come in, I didn't know what to tell them so—"

Oh, God, Harry thought. "What did you tell them, Nagel? Never mind. I don't want to know. Just call them now—and confirm I'll be there."

"So that means you're coming in?"

"Why don't I just surprise you, Nagel," and Harry rang off.

He could think of no good reason for such a summons, but Ryan's ranting in the G-2 latrine had demonstrated the possibility for bad ones. He lay back down on the bed, and for a half hour he forced his eyes closed and tried to clear his mind, but his thoughts kept racing ahead to the meeting. So, like a nervous student preparing to sit exams, he gave up the bed, sat at his escritoire and began going through his case notes, studying.

Around noon he shaved, showered, polished his shoes, then dressed himself carefully in a fresh set of Class A's. He neatly packed his briefcase, then sat quietly by the window, smoking and listening to the radio until 1:30. His nervousness did not even allow him to think about lunch.

As soon as Harry's shoes touched the cobbles of the Annex court, a gust of wind took his cap and sent it skidding across the car park. Harry lumbered after his cap, chasing it about the parked machines, and, in just a few seconds, the neat—if portly—image of professional deportment he'd taken so much time to compose had blown away as well.

The Ganymede Club was one of the many private clubs that had sprung up during the Victorian era like churches of a fevered religion, a shrine to The Empire. Within its carved cornices and gargoyles and colonnaded entryways was the evidence of British global hegemony: marble tabletops from the quarries of the Middle East; handwoven rugs from Egypt spread across parquet floors; mahogany wainscoting from the East Indies; lion's-paw chairs of Malaysian teak; finishings of African ivory; embroidered napkins of Indian silk; engraved brass servants' bells from the Middle East; and at the bar, thickly sweet rum from the Caribbean.

When Air Vice Marshal Dowding's office requested the club members "contribute" their building to the war effort, the gray-templed ranks, too old to carry weapons themselves, were proud to do their bit. They set down their briar pipes, poured themselves a round of B & S's, and toasted the health of the King, the Union Jack, and a quick end to the war. Then they solemnly folded up the club colors and sent a telegram to Dowding's office, a verse of typical lordly brio: "She's all yours, sir; have at it."

But "Stuffy" Dowding had not requested the club for the home team. The old club members huddled together across Park Lane under the shade trees of Hyde Park, and nipped at toddy-filled thermoses for sorely needed comfort as they watched the pagans invade their venerable shrine.

Blasphemous gum-snapping Yanks clomped about on the hand-woven rugs, scraping the parquet floors with metal file cabinets, piling the marble-topped chess tables in the cellar to make room for government-issue desks, taking down the wall hangings and life-sized portraits of venerable past Ganymedians to make way for situation maps and Status of Operations charts. The aroma of pipe tobacco and Havana cigars was replaced by the sting of American cigarettes, the civilized shuffle of whist made way for paper-pushing bother, and the soft click of billiards was exchanged for clacking typewriters, teletype alert bells, and jangling telephones.

Harry threaded his way through the clerical warren that now wound through the high-ceilinged salons. On his way up the wide, sweeping stairs to DiGarre's top-floor office, he passed General Halverson on his way down. Halverson didn't notice, not until Harry called after him. The general stopped and turned, presenting Harry with a face even more ashen and haunted than when Harry had seen it last in the briefing theater. The general's eyes appeared weak and empty until they focused on Harry, then they grew hard.

"Hello, Major," Halverson said tonelessly. "Being called before the bar?"

Harry shrugged.

"Keep this in your head," the general said, looking up from his position several steps below. "Remember what your job is. And do it." Then, without bothering with further explanation, Halverson headed down the stairs.

With a wave, the captain at the desk outside DiGarre's office stopped Harry from sitting on the anteroom divan and nodded him straight through the tall double doors. Harry passed his hand a last time over his scant hair, tugged at his jacket, and entered the office. The captain closed the doors behind him.

The room within looked to have been some sort of grand salon or study at one time; high-ceilinged, thickly carpeted, the walls dark with wood paneling. There was a long conference table to one side of the room under low-slung billiard lamps, a chattering teleprinter nearby; along the other side ran tall windows overlooking Hyde Park, their panes marked by a lattice of masking tape. At the head of the room, facing Harry, was a wall map of Europe with the German-occupied territories—running from a wavering line through the Russian steppes to the English Channel; Norway to Italy—shaded in gray.

Beneath the mural-like map sat a massive desk of mirror-finished oak, a goodly portion of its vast surface covered with papers and file folders. Joe Ryan, looking humbled before the monolithic desk, was seated before it, his head turned awkwardly away from Harry. Harry could see another man sitting, against the wall under the map, in the cross-hatching formed by shadow and sun coming through the latticed windows at a sharp oblique that left half the room dark. Harry could only dimly make out an RAF captain's uniform.

Harry stood at attention in front of the desk, but DiGarre, without rising from his studded leather chair, waved Harry to an empty seat directly before him and said, with a slight drawl, "Take it easy, Major, or we'll never get anything done."

Throughout his tenure in Europe, Lieutenant General Thomas Quinton DiGarre remained quite the enigma. He regularly absented himself from the usual ambassadorial activities and even the most major press briefings, socialized little, and only did so quietly among the closed circles of the upper echelons. At times, he was so rarely seen one could easily wonder the general existed at all. His official biography—three neatly typed paragraphs consigning twenty-five years' military service to a single page—gave little clue to the man. He was ". . . a native of Versailles, Kentucky," and ". . . a graduate of significant standing in the Virginia Military Institute's Class of '16." His military career properly began with his service as a pilot with Rickenbacker's "Hat in the Circle" squadron in the First War, but the following twenty-two years, from the Armistice to DiGarre's promotion to brigadier in 1940, were, in that same bio, described thusly: "He was thereafter promoted regularly as he ably fulfilled his responsibilities in a variety of posts." A woeful understatement that did not account for the military and political skills that brought a man up so steadily through the ranks in peacetime (particularly in a service, as the crucifixion of Billy Mitchell illustrated, still striving for legitimacy) and landed him an appointment to the U.S. military attaché in London during the Blitz.

Of his attaché service, my London colleagues were able to amplify the official record. DiGarre's role at the time was to closely study RAF operations both in fighter defense and, later, in its first bomber forays against the Germans. He became a regular nuisance to Fighter Command, poking about the entire strata of the organization, from individual aerodromes to old Stuffy's offices; from sector station operations hutments to the Cabinet War Rooms under Parliament Square. There is an unsubstantiated but oft-told tale of DiGarre nearly instigating a diplomatic flap—the Americans then still being officially neutral—by contriving his presence aboard a Wellington to on-hand observe one of the first RAF offensive raids against German industrial targets in the Ruhr in the fall of 1940.

Summer the following year, DiGarre was using that acquired expertise to help plan the Eighth Air Force's first tentative B-17 strikes against the European mainland. By February '43 he was back in the States, given his second star and command of his own air division, which began operations in England that spring. "Ably fulfilled" indeed!

On the rare occasions I had glimpsed the man I felt— as Harry did on that first meeting—that Thomas DiGarre was something of a physical disappointment. Short, pudgy, practically bald, he had small, colorless eyes squinting behind steel-rimmed spectacles. He had a stubby nose and feral canines visible only during his rare, quick-flash smiles. But, also like Harry, I sensed a man well aware that he had found his place in the commander's seat. This was not a Joe Ryan who had worked his way up on a winning way, or a Patton or Montgomery driven by an addiction to the limelight. Command came as naturally to DiGarre as breathing, and he needed no acknowledgment of his abilities—no medals, no headlines or parades—to confirm it. That ease with power made his attempt at cordiality feel feigned and unnatural to Harry.

"Nice of you to come." The general's voice was raspy from whiskey and cigars, thick with the sound of Kentucky.

"I wasn't aware I had a choice, sir."

DiGarre's smile made its momentary flash, so fleeting as to almost seem a tic. He tapped the stars on his collar. "One of the benefits of these. I never have to worry about my invites being refused. Drinks, anybody? I know it's a bit early in the day, but if anyone's so inclined, feel free."

"Scotch and water," Ryan said.

"I'll pass, sir." Harry pointed to his stomach and made uneasy motions with his hand by way of explanation.

DiGarre nodded understandingly. "Let me have that, Captain; I'll freshen 'er up for you," and he took a glass from the RAF officer to a brass-and-glass liquor stand in a corner. "Captain, this is the infamous Major Voss you've been hearing so much about. Major, Captain Leighton-Dunne, my RAF liaison."

The British captain nodded from his seat and Harry nodded back, his eyes narrowing as he tried to piece together the figure of the RAF man, separated into slices of light and dark by the shadow of the tape on the windows. It was clear to Harry from the soft shape he could see inside the man's blue uniform that his flying days—if there ever had been any—were long past. Harry saw the glint of wildly uneven eyes, the shadow of a skewed nose.

"Voss," the RAF man said. "German, isn't it?"

"Russian, actually," Harry replied. "My family changed it when—"

"Russian," the RAF captain interrupted. "Yes."

The general set a glass down in front of Harry. "In case you change your mind." He distributed the other drinks then returned to his chair, cupping a tumbler of whiskey and water. He took a sip. "Good, but it's not bourbon. I'm a bourbon man myself. Was raised on that good bonded stuff with a little branch water thrown in. Doesn't get any better than that, but to each his own. Right, Captain?"

The RAF captain shrugged.

Harry cleared his throat. "I noticed General Halverson—"

"He have anything to say?"

"Not much. But he didn't look very happy."

DiGarre pushed his glasses up on his nose. "General Halverson is not a very happy man. Can't say I am, either. Of late, we're not operating under very happy circumstances. Cigar?" No one accepted the invitation. DiGarre drew one from the embroidered humidor on his desk, snipped the end with a silver clipper, and was soon enjoying a rising cloud of bluish smoke, a lush fragrance quite a few notches above that produced by Major Van Damm's Tampa Nuggets. The general nodded at the humidor. "Maybe in a few hundred years we'll have that kind of—" He looked questioningly at the RAF captain.

"Panache?" the captain offered.

DiGarre smiled and nodded again. "Panache."

"About General Halverson—"

"You mind if I call you Harry? Harry, a lot of the other air commanders think I'm pretty lucky. They're jealous because my Wings are situated so as to make London the best location for my headquarters, while they're all stuck out there in the boondocks. This puts me nice and close to all the goodies London's got to offer. Also puts me in a good position to get the inside dope on what's going on over at SHAEF. I may be close to SHAEF, but that also means SHAEF is close to me. Understand?"

"I think so."

"When I lose a whole group, Harry—a third of one of my Wings— on the ground in one fell swoop no less, well, my bosses down the street find out about it pretty damned quick. They want an accounting from me. That means I'm going to want an accounting of my own."

"From General Halverson."

"The 351st was one of his groups." DiGarre twirled his glass, looking down into his drink. "You a friend of the general?"

"No, sir."

"But you have sympathy for him. Laudable. But whether he just had a case of the bad breaks or no, Halverson's got a responsibility to me and to the men I entrust to him. There are things that have happened subsequently—the things you've been poking into—for which he is accountable. That, I imagine, is why he's so unhappy these days." The general flashed his quick, lupine smile again. "But that's not really your concern, is it, Harry? So let's discuss something that is. I think we'll be more comfortable over there, gentlemen. Bring your drinks."

A stack of files in one hand, his drink in the other, DiGarre led them to a collection of lion's-paw furniture nestled round a marble-topped coffee table under the windows. Harry hesitated, taking an opportunity for a better look at the RAF captain as he passed into the mote-filled columns of light from the windows. Early thirties, Harry guessed. Moving stiffly as if each movement pained. The face was truly misshapen, each of his features unnaturally uneven, and made to look more so by an odd paleness. Harry thought back to his attempt at reassembling the broken porcelain sheep in the shattered front room of the Gresham cottage, and that thought cued his eyes to the barely perceptible lines in the captain's face—like seams—that might have been scars, and which the captain had tried to dampen with face powder (Harry could see the residue on the man's collar).

Harry and Ryan shared a settee while the general and the RAF captain took cushioned chairs across from them. DiGarre set his files down on the table and nodded at a crumbly cake on a silver salver. "Piece of cake, Harry? My wife sent it. It's very good, and you don't have to agree with me just because I'm your boss."

"Thank you, sir, but I don't feel all that hungry."

"Well, you feel the urge, you help yourself." DiGarre slipped off his glasses and set them carefully on the table, then took a pair of half-moon reading spectacles from his pocket. He flipped open one of the folders, reading as he enjoyed a few puffs on his cigar and another sip of his drink. Harry took the moment to look over at Ryan for a clue as to the nature of the proceedings, but Ryan's face was slack and colorless, the usually glinting eyes now flat and lost in the swirls of the Persian rug.

"Yes, well . . ." DiGarre said. He sat back in his chair and eyed Harry over the rims of his reading spectacles. "I've been reviewing your case, along with Colonel Ryan and Captain Leighton-Dunne here. I want to go over it with you to make sure we're all on the same trail, so to speak. If there's something you don't think I have down right, you let out a holler."

"All right, sir."

DiGarre leaned forward again, running a finger along the typed sheets in the folder. "Let's see. . . . The way it looks, seems there was some kind of bad blood all along between this Lieutenant O'Connell and Major Markham. But, uh, as I understand your premise—you correct me, now, if I don't have this right—you don't think that's why he was killed, or because Markham was a little het up that this O'Connell fella lived through the kraut raid while a lot of his other boys didn't. What was it? Something like forty-odd dead? And then there's the wounded. . . . But you think it was because of this, um, supposed 'business' out at Helsvagen."

"It was forty-seven dead, sir. And yes, that's the way the facts—"

"We'll get to the facts in a bit, Major. That's essentially your case?"

"Yes, sir."

"And then you go on that Markham destroyed his gun film not to hide the attacks on O'Connell and these other two folks, this Gresham fella and his wife, but to hide this Helsvagen thing. I'm supposed to say 'alleged,' right, Colonel? 'Allegedly' destroyed his gun film?"

Ryan forced a weak smile in response.

Harry looked over at Ryan but Ryan's eyes were still swimming among the dark colors of the rug. There was something about the dry, quiet way DiGarre ticked off each element of the case that made them sound suddenly fragile. He looked back to DiGarre, his eyes darting between the general and the RAF captain, both of them barely more than silhouettes against the sun-filled windows.

"And your evidence of this 'alleged' Helsvagen thing—" DiGarre pulled a folder out of the pile and opened it. Harry recognized Van Damm's reconnaissance photos. "—is based on these recon photos taken yesterday afternoon, and Major Van Damm's interpretation of same."

"Yes, sir."

"The way I get it, even Major Van Damm doesn't think these pictures are exactly Grade-A quality."

"We always have the option of another recon fly-by."

DiGarre nodded, not looking up from the open files. "Van Damm says that at this late date it's doubtful they'd show anything conclusive." The general poked the top several photos out of the file, spreading them out on the marble table. Harry recognized them as the photos of the field representing Markham's approximate position at the time he claimed Angel Red had been attacked by German fighters. "We have these, but Van Damm doesn't consider them indicative, for a number of reasons that I understand he laid out to you, not the least of which is Markham isn't sure where he was jumped. And then there's these . . ." Now he fanned out the smoke-blotted pictures of the burning village. "Know what these show, Harry? They show a town on fire, a few hundred yards downwind of forty thousand gallons of exploding gasoline," Harry felt his evidence go from fragile to brittle as old biscuits.

"Those pictures also show collapsed buildings," Harry said. "Fire doesn't knock a building down."

DiGarre sat back in his chair. "No, it doesn't. It *can* weaken one till it can't hold itself up anymore. Or, it *can* get knocked down by somebody trying to create a firebreak. And this is an old place, Van Damm tells me. He says a lot of the buildings there are maybe a couple hundred years old. The concussion of forty thousand gallons of gas going up just next door might could blow some of them right over. At least that's what Captain Leighton-Dunne here tells me. He saw enough of the Blitz close up to be an expert."

Harry scratched at an itch over his brow. His fingertips came away damp. "There's the radio traffic that came out of Helsvagen—"

"And Major Van Damm's *interpretation* of it, which, to my mind, is another way of saying informed speculation. As somebody who has to deal with his hits *and* misses, I ought to know. Van Damm's taking guesses here based on a three-year-old RAF file on this place; that and kraut tendencies. I think it's worth noting, Harry, that despite Major Van Damm's 'feeling' that Helsvagen has been stripped over the last few years, these pictures—and Captain Anderson's gun film—show antiaircraft guns that weren't there three years ago. The major does have his misses."

DiGarre slid the photographs back into their file and closed it. He took a sip of his drink and let the liquor sit on his tongue a few seconds before he swallowed. "And there's this." He pulled out still another folder and nudged it toward Harry. "You're pretty thorough, I hear; you would've come across this eventually, but let me save you some time and trouble. When Mr. Gresham spotted the incoming flight, he routinely contacted his sector Air Traffic Controller. The ATC alerted Air/Sea Rescue, then contacted O'Connell. What you have there is a photostat of the official log of the ATC station covering that sector."

Harry flipped open the folder and slipped on his own reading glasses to study the white-on-black image:

0824: Station 3-B-3 confirm visual 3 US P47 course
       270 range/speed unreptd. 1 ship trailing smoke.
0827: Alert ASR possble splash Sector 3-B.
0830: Contact 47, self-ID radio desig Angel Blue Baker (confrm—
       elmnt 351 grp Don). Reprt no injury, minor engine damage;
       safe ETA Don 5 mins.
0832: Attmpt contact other craft—N/R
0834: Attmpt contact Angel Blue Baker—N/R
0835: Attmpt contact Station 3-B-3—N/R
0838: Alert RA 133rd Inf. Regmnt, request investigate.
0842: Infrmed by 351 grp HQ Angel Blue Baker splash Sector 3-B.

Harry closed the folder. He pushed it back toward DiGarre.

The general let loose a thin stream of cigar smoke before speaking. "So, you say Markham splashes O'Connell because of what O'Connell saw at Helsvagen. According to that log, the RAF was in voice contact with O'Connell, but he didn't say anything about it to them. O'Connell was in range of every radio receiver in the south of England, in fact, and didn't say squat. Why do you think that was, Harry? It leads a fella to entertain the notion that maybe O'Connell didn't say anything because O'Connell didn't have anything to say."

The general paused, but Harry said nothing.

"I'm no lawyer," the general continued, "and I don't pretend to be. I'm just a civilian—in that regard—and that's how I'm looking at this. But I've been going over this with Colonel Ryan and, for my money, I'd have to say an awful lot of what you've got here, Harry, is, oh, I believe the proper term is 'circumstantial.' "

Harry reached for his drink, concentrating on making the move look smooth and relaxed. "Is that Colonel Ryan's opinion, too?" Again, he looked over at Ryan, only to find the colonel's eyes fixed on the floor.

DiGarre's response was a shrug. "I didn't ask him."

Harry shifted in his chair, trying to portray an image of confidence he no longer felt. "A preponderance of circumstantial evidence in a criminal case is hardly rare, General. I'm sure if you'd asked, the colonel would've told you as much. And, talking the case out like this isn't the same thing as a proper presentation in front of a jury—"

"Oh, did I overlook something?" DiGarre went through a show of concerned alarm as he riffled through the files. "Is there some material I don't have here? No? Then I can only go on what I see, Harry. And I can tell you that the officers in my command—the officers who'll probably find themselves sitting in judgment on this thing—are no more lawyers than I am. I'd be inclined to think they'd look at all this the same way I do."

Harry took another sip of his drink, a slow one. Where the general was going was now clear, however obscure his motive remained. Harry mustered what he thought was a savvy smile. "If you don't mind my saying so, General, you're taking the long way around to tell me to back off."

DiGarre seemed neither offended nor surprised at Harry's presumption. "Oh?"

"In which case I have to ask: If that's what you want, why don't you just order me to back off? Better yet: Have me relieved from the case."

The RAF captain let out an audible and impatient sigh.

DiGarre ignored the captain, and presented Harry with his furtive little smile. "Truthfully, I considered it. Problem is a lot of people've got to where they know about this thing. Oh, not all of it, especially this end of it, but a lot of people know something's cooking. We're not looking to pull something that's going to make those people even more curious. So, we're looking for a way to bring this whole mess to a close. Quickly—"

"And cleanly," Harry said. "Right?"

"Hit the nail right on the head, Harry. Can't close this in a way that leaves more questions than it answers."

"Which means you remain on the case." The RAF captain's voice was cold, passionless, the ferretlike teeth in his mouth showing the lifeless gleam of porcelain. "It also means that you must be the one to decide its disposition. Willingly."

"Willingly," Harry said, nodding. He set his glass down on the table and smiled. "A silent Harry is a happy Harry, right? And this subtle piece of extortion is supposed to make me 'willing'?" Harry was frankly astonished at his own effrontery. Perhaps he'd taken one sip too many of his drink.

If his abruptness troubled DiGarre, the general didn't show it. "Extortion? Harry, we're just taking the time to lay out the situation the way we see it. I'm not sure you appreciate the predicament you're in."

DiGarre fingered out and opened another folder. Harry could see his own ID photo in a corner of the typed cover form. "I hear from Colonel Ryan you're pretty good at what you do. But you're no Tom Dewey, and Ryan also tells me this'd be a tricky case even for an old hand. No offense, Harry, but I see you haven't had much heavy criminal trial experience, in or out of the service. We're all worried that you—what's the phrase? That your reach might be exceeding your grasp?"

It was at that point, so Harry told me later, when the scotch might've gotten the better of him, and his anger flared. "You're asking me— 'nicely'—to close up shop and let Markham and Anderson walk, right? Is that it?"

DiGarre's look of shock and dismay seemed no more sincere than his earlier warm welcome. "No, no, no, of course not! Sorry to give you that impression, Harry. I guess we hadn't gotten to that yet. Colonel Ryan, I believe we're in your territory now."

Ryan cleared his throat. He tried to face Harry, but his eyes kept wandering back to the rug. "We'd still like you to prosecute the case."

"That's practically a precondition, Harry," said DiGarre.

Harry shook his head, thoroughly confused. "Prosecute what case?"

Ryan cleared his throat again. "The O'Connell murder. The attack on the Greshams. Both are more substantive cases. Airtight, actually. The general, he's, um, sure that any jury panel would convict."

DiGarre nodded in agreement. "I'd be willing to bet they'd convict that Anderson character in the bargain, too. Accessory, complicity, whatever it is. You boys know the right legal term."

"It's a solution which would see the situation right all round," the RAF captain said. "Even for you, I'd imagine."

DiGarre nodded again, quite pleased with the offered tertium quid. "The Army enforces discipline, our Allies are assured of our good intentions, and you . . . Suffice to say that such a conviction would be appreciated top to bottom. That's what you're worried about, isn't it, Harry? Making sure you get that conviction?"

"C'mon, Harry, don't play the virgin." Ryan smiled weakly, a pitiful ghost of his usual style. "It's no different from a plea bargain, and you know as well as I do how many times we plea 'em down just to clear the docket. And it's not like they'll come out of this with just a rap on the wrist. A conviction on O'Connell and the Gresham attack . . . They go all the way on that."

"After all, Major," the RAF captain sniffed, "you can only hang them once."

Harry sat for a long moment, taking in the presentation. "You don't care if they're guilty or not. You'd hang these guys for something they didn't do just to hush this up? Why? *Why?*"

The large room went quiet. There was Ryan, slumped and weak in his chair. DiGarre sat studying him with careful calculation. And there was the RAF captain.

"It's not a matter of caring," the RAF captain said finally.

"I can see that," Harry said.

"It's a question of priorities," the RAF captain said. "At this particular juncture, their guilt or innocence is, at best, of only secondary importance."

"Captain's right, Harry," DiGarre said. "It *doesn't* matter what they did. The issue is that they would even be charged with this; that they would even be *suspect* in this kind of action."

"I can't say you gentlemen have persuaded me," Harry said, "but you sure as hell have me bamboozled."

DiGarre nodded in genuine sympathy. "We have, at this moment, two central priorities, Harry. One is the preservation of the Alliance. You know, people back home look at us as one great army making war on the Hun. The sad truth is that destroying the Germans is just about the only thing we agree on. On its best days, this grand alliance is nothing more than a very shaky coalition."

"Colonel Ryan explained the diplomatic problems to me."

"No, Harry. Ryan explained *some* diplomatic problems to you. We've got DeGaulle and his Free French making more trouble for us than Vichy. There's Czech units, Polish units, and God knows who else jammed on this island, and they've all got something to say about what we do, when we do it, how, where, and every other damned thing. We've got the Bolshies and they've been rabid paranoid since 1917. It doesn't matter that a lot of their predicament is their own damned fault. They figure the ten or fifteen million people they've lost in this war so far is atonement enough. Hitler's throwing almost eighty percent of his war effort at the East right now, and the Reds aren't too subtle about accusing us of letting them wear the krauts down with Russian blood. There's a lot of people looking for us to make a misstep and use it as proof that we don't know what the hell we're doing."

DiGarre paused to allow Harry to absorb that much. He tilted his head back, took a puff on his cigar, and let the smoke out to gather over his head like a luminous cloud. "Harry, there's military targets in every one of the occupied countries. Some have civilian laborers, some use slave labor. Some are close to residential areas and historical landmarks. Our allies accept the fact that hitting those targets means hitting things we wish we didn't have to, even in their home countries. It means people who shouldn't suffer are going to suffer, and they accept that, too. Even the people on the ground—the poor slobs drafted into building the sub pens at Calais, the dock workers at Antwerp, the guys just doing their jobs in the stockyards at Rouen—they all know they're going to take a beating right along with the krauts. They take it because they figure we wouldn't do it if we didn't have to; that's the implied contract. The question is, would they take it if they thought we were just laying our eggs anywhere we damned well pleased? Would they take it if they thought we'd broken the faith?"

"If we become suspect in that regard," the RAF captain broke in, "we risk balkanizing the alliance still further. And there's the question of certain strategic neutrals, such as Spain and Turkey. If the Germans make the claim against us, in all probability it will be dismissed as typical Nazi folderol. But if we indict, we substantiate the German claim and give over a propaganda weapon possibly strong enough to move the neutrals further from us and closer to the Axis. It could be just the tool someone like Mr. De Valera, for example, and his cronies in Dublin could get no end of use from to further their separatist movement at our expense."

"What's the reaction of the Belgians?" Harry asked. "The target is in their country."

"That's all we'd need," DiGarre sighed. "Another country heard from."

The RAF captain twitched in his seat, prodded by those deep aches Harry had glimpsed in him earlier. He took a small pillbox from his breast pocket, a cue for DiGarre, who crossed back to the liquor stand and returned with a glass of water. "There is no official Belgian government-inexile," the RAF captain's flat voice stated. "As for King Leopold, our information is that he may be—and the Germans suspect as much—some sort of component in the Belgian resistance despite claiming otherwise. That being the case, and if the Germans have informed him of the incident, and even if he believes them, it's doubtful that he'd make any statement that would compromise us. The King wants the Germans out of Belgium as much as we do." The RAF captain placed two small white tablets from the pillbox on his tongue and washed them down with the water.

DiGarre's cigar had grown short. He stubbed it out, walked to his desk, and drew another from the humidor. "I wish you'd try a piece of that cake, Harry." He took a moment to light his fresh Havana, then asked, "You think we'll win the war? I'm asking you straight. I don't want all that *Why We Fight* stuff about Mom and apple pie or God being on our side and all. Practical, strategic point of view—we going to win?"

The question seemed so irrelevant that Harry was at a loss for an answer. DiGarre waited patiently. "I'm not a strategist, sir, but I'd say so. We seem to have the industry, the manpower—"

"The leadership?" DiGarre smiled wryly. "Yes, we'll win. Eventually. Maybe in three years, maybe five. That's a long time. I really wish you'd try that cake, Harry."

It was obviously more than a casual suggestion, so Harry cut himself a sliver and took a bite. "You were right. Your wife is a good cook."

"Thank you, Harry. Tastes different, doesn't it?"

"Different?"

"From the way that cake would've tasted a year and a half ago. It should taste different. No eggs, no butter, no milk. They gave that up, Harry. They give us their old pots and pans and steel wool. They have meatless days and grow vegetables in their backyards. Women wait in line for hours for one pair of rationed nylons so we can have silk for parachutes. Women are building airplanes and tanks; they get together in clubs and roll bandages. I was just reading about someplace up in Oregon where the ladies stick their kids in twenty-four-hour playrooms so they can work three shifts building Liberty ships. They give us their sons, Harry. They give up a lot. You see this map behind me? Take a good look. We had a good year this year. The pendulum is finally swinging our way. In the Pacific, Guadalcanal's ours and Yamamoto's dead. On this side of the world the krauts have lost so many subs that Doenitz has pulled his U-boats out of the North Atlantic." He raised the red tip of his cigar toward the map. "The Germans have been backing out of Russia since they lost Stalingrad and the Reds broke the siege at Leningrad. We took back North Africa and Sicily, and I'm not giving away any big military secret when I tell you we'll be on the Italian boot inside a month. But see all this, Harry? This shaded area? All this in gray?" Emphatically, then: "Do you see it?"

"I see it, sir."

"That's the territory that's still occupied, dominated, or allied with the krauts. That's what the German Reich is today. Most of continental Europe, in fact. Quite a piece of grazing land, wouldn't you say? A lot of fighting left."

"Yes, sir."

"They sacrifice because we're on a sacred crusade, Harry. To them, it's Good versus Evil and nothing less. It doesn't register with them that the Reds were no friends of ours before the war and they probably won't be after, or that nobody elected DeGaulle, or that we may just be fighting to save our own hides. They sacrifice because they *believe* in what we're doing, Harry. *That's* our other priority: making them believers. Taint the crusade, and you create doubt. Doubt begets hesitation. You know the old ditty about for want of a nail the shoe was lost?"

"Are you telling me," Harry said incredulously, "that you think the whole Allied war effort is going to grind to a halt because of—"

"Hell, no, Harry! Hell, no!" DiGarre chuckled. "Tell you the truth, nobody has the vaguest idea of what would happen. Could be that whole Murrow bunch beats a big drum for this and it wouldn't bring sweat on a cow's brow."

"You just think it's an unacceptable risk."

DiGarre wandered to the conference table and scanned the piled yellow paper spewing out of the teleprinter, then resumed his seat at the marble table, his face now quite cold. "I think if the possibility exists that this could cause just *one* American boy in a foxhole to so much as nick his finger—that this war could go on for one *second* longer than it needs to—then it's an unacceptable risk."

"As we told you, Major Voss," the RAF captain said, "we're discussing priorities."

"I'm well aware of what we're discussing," Harry said.

"See here, Major," the RAF captain went on "Jerry has been doing this sort of thing since Spain, and the Eye-ties since Ethiopia, and the Nips of course—"

"I wasn't aware that the actions of the Axis powers constituted a mitigating factor," Harry snapped.

The captain's small, lopsided mouth twisted in a caustic smile. He made no pretense at concealing his disdain. "The Royal Air Force has been engaged in nighttime area bombing over German population centers since we began our air counteroffensive in 1940."

"We're not talking about the RAF," Harry responded.

The RAF captain's smile twisted a little tighter. "Ever since your people mounted the first American air raid little more than a year ago they've been trying to prove the efficacy of daylight precision bombing. You may've heard of the results at Ploesti and Schweinfurt. Quite cost-ineffective, to say the least."

DiGarre's shoulders heaved in begrudgingly agreement. "I'm afraid we're going to have to start taking another tack."

"Shall I tell him?" the RAF captain asked, almost eagerly.

The general took a moment to weigh the strategic value of proceeding. He nodded as he inhaled from his cigar, then said, through a cloud of acrid blue smoke, "Harry, what you're about to hear is classified. Any breach of security means the next court-martial you work on will be your own."

The RAF captain shifted in his seat, trying to make himself more comfortable. "Approximately three weeks ago, beginning the night of 24 July, the RAF was joined by elements of the American Eighth Air Force in bombing the German city of Hamburg. They bombed the city that night, then again on the following day and the day after, and then again on the night of 27-28. The newsreels have depicted the event as yet another successful air attack against the Reich with no further details. As for those omitted details: Reports from our agents in Germany are still rather sketchy, but what we know thus far is that the initial destruction from the sustained bombing was devastating. There were also some unanticipated secondary effects. Apparently, some manner of freak weather condition was at work in the target area, something to do with odd winds or some such. In any case, coupled with the enormous destructive force of the bombings and resultant fires, some sort of blast-furnace effect was created. Our Intelligence people have been using the word 'firestorm.' This 'storm' generated heat to one thousand degrees centigrade. People were incinerated in their shelters. The updraft was great enough to pull trees from the ground. One report cited that even the river running through the city was afire. Our assumption is that the oil spillage from the ships at the docks combusted from the heat. Reconnaissance photos show half the city of Hamburg is gone. Approximately eight hundred thousand Germans have lost their homes, between thirty and fifty thousand inhabitants are probably dead, which means the Germans suffered more dead in four days than we did during any one month of the Blitz. While the participation of your Air Force in such actions is singular to date, we feel they will now be seriously considering their enormous impact on the enemy in light of their comparatively light cost."

Harry looked to DiGarre.

"It has to be considered," the general said. "If the people back home have to choose between their sons and kraut civilians, the hausfrau is going to lose."

"I think you'll find," the RAF captain continued, "that to the public at large—at least here, where the bombs fall—the Germans are the enemy. Not the German Luftwaffe, not the German Wehrmacht, but the *Germans*."

"We're not talking about Germans here," Harry said through clenched jaws.

"Yes," the RAF captain mused. "That does bring up the point as to whether you would press this case as you have if we were. And if not, then it's apparently not the act itself that troubles you, eh, Major? I suppose that hypocrisy is like influenza; even the doctor gets it."

Harry's mouth began to open and he could feel his vocal chords tighten in preparation for something shrill and nasty, but DiGarre stepped in first.

"What we're talking about is easing the American public into a frame of mind that'll tolerate the deliberate infliction of massive civilian casualties and equally massive collateral damage. Now, obviously, the boys who flew those planes are the ones going eyeball-to-eyeball with the krauts and frankly, Harry, the boys are not squawking. They'd rather fly another Hamburg milk run than go through the meat grinder again over Schweinfurt." DiGarre left Harry to his thoughts for a moment as he finished his drink, studying him over the tops of his spectacles. "Well, Harry?"

"That's a hell of an agenda you have, General."

"That's what they pay me for," the general said grimly.

They had shown Harry how calculating they could be and in doing so, he'd begun to appreciate how extensive those calculations were. The thought that came to him so stunned him that he wasn't, at first, aware that he'd spoken aloud. "You set Halverson up."

"What do you mean," said DiGarre, his voice soothingly inquisitive, "by 'set him up'?"

"Harry," Ryan cautioned.

But Harry didn't hear Ryan's warning. "You asked General Halverson for an assessment on the 351st after the Germans hit them. He stalled to buy time for the raid. He didn't send the report up until the day before the raid was scheduled, thinking it'd be too late for you to scrub the mission. But they had to postpone. You had an extra two days—"

"Major," the general said heavily, "I'll bet enough paper crosses my desk each day to give every man, woman, and child in my grand home state of Kentucky something new to read each week."

"No," Harry said. "You would've been looking for this. Like you said; you have accounting to do. I can't believe you wouldn't've read the report as soon as Halverson's messenger showed up. If the raid had come off, everybody would've been a hero. The guys on the raid'd get a medal or something, the heat would've been off Halverson. And you would've been in the clear, too. But if the raid went sour, you could just say you didn't know anything about it. It would all fall on Halverson's head."

Harry braced himself for the retaliatory fusillade. The sun moved another degree in the sky and a painfully bright glare swept across the windows behind the general. The rows of taped crosses dissolved in the glare.

"Harry," DiGarre said, "we've hit you with an awful lot here. Why don't you think over everything we've talked about. Talk it over with your two associates. They have a stake in this too, you know. This could be very beneficial for all of you. Then, come by sometime tomorrow and let me know your thinking on the matter. Fair enough? Thank you for coming."

It was a dismissal. Harry stood. There wasn't much room between the settee and the table and he barked his shins on the sharp, stone edge. With his hand on the gnarled brass knob of one of the double doors, he hesitated, then faced back toward them. Ryan was at the liquor stand, and the RAF captain was standing by the windows, massaging the small of his back. DiGarre sat like some divinely appointed king, sunk deep in his chair, an ankle carelessly tossed across the opposite knee, his fingers knitted across his chest, his smoldering cigar rolling slowly from one corner of his mouth to the other.

Harry left.

If Harry seems naive, a bit oblivious to what we might condescendingly point out to him was painfully obvious—"War is hell, old boy!"—he merely shared what remains a prevailing schizophrenia regarding some of combat's more unsavory truths.

At the time a benumbed Harry was leaving General DiGarre's office, millions back in his home country paid their two bits to sit riveted by the film *Destination Tokyo*. They huddled in darkened cinemas and cheered Cary Grant and his submarine crew of fresh-faced lads as they slunk about under the sea. They cheered their torpedo ambush of defenseless Japanese cargo ships. Sorry, Tojo, but war is hell, you know!

Afterward, they crossed the way to another cinema, set down another two bits for *Action in the North Atlantic* (from the very same studio, no less), where this time the fresh-faced young Americans manned a cargo ship, and were fighting off skulking *German* submarines. Curiously, cinema fans did not accept the actions of the U-boats and their sneery-faced *Kapitäns* as more war is hell. They booed and hissed what they considered to be Teutonic villainy.

A year earlier I'd been sharing drinks with a colleague from the American photo magazine *Life*, and he told me of a complaint they had received concerning a particular photograph they had run. The picture was of a British tank officer in hospital, wounded during the North

African campaign. The young captain's arm and eye were swathed in bandages, and he lay between two other gauze-draped men. After publication, there came a letter objecting to the running of such material for the sake of other young soldiers. "Must they," wrote the correspondent, a woman from Rochester, New York, "go to fight with a horrible ending in their minds?"

So, don't condescend to poor old Harry. If any number of us truly believed that war is hell, how could we ever have permitted another war after the first one? On that score, we are hypocrites and liars all.

As he left the Ganymede, Harry was barely aware of the salutes of the guards at the wrought-iron gates. Without conscious direction, he passed through Brook Gate into Hyde Park, wandering until he found himself on the esplanade along the Serpentine. Sticky, hot, and very, very tired, he found an isolated bench by the water and sat himself down.

The warm afternoon made his eyes heavy. A breeze stirred the lake, nudging the water into the bank with quiet, licking noises. Across the lake, Harry could see a nanny feeding the swans with her two preschool charges. The children squealed nervously, thrilled and terrified at the closeness of the large white birds.

Above, marring the pastel blue sky, were the brooding gray shapes of barrage balloons staggered out over London in a swaying phalanx. But if Harry dropped his gaze just a few degrees, the city vanished. Brompton, Belgravia, Mayfair and General DiGarre's headquarters, the looming balloons . . . all disappeared behind the thick branches of the trees about the park, and the only noises he could hear were the lapping water, the chiming laughter of the children, the trumpeting of the swans.

A tune, a faint whistle, came to him on the breeze. It took Harry's fogbound mind a moment to remember the words:

> In Dublin's fair city
> Where girls are so pretty
> I first set my eyes on sweet Molly Malone . . .

Harry turned, following the whistling, and saw a man on the esplanade. He was perhaps Harry's age, though the face showed a good

deal more weathering (no doubt as much a product of scotch and cigarettes as wind and rain). He wore a shapeless dark suit that had been
out of style even before wartime rationing had made matters of style
academic, and a fraying Panama hat. He walked with an odd, rolling
gait, almost a limp.

I whistled the next verse:

> *As she wheeled her wheelbarrow*
> *Through streets broad and narrow*
> *Crying cockles, and mussels*
> *Alive, alive-o . . .*

CHAPTER EIGHT

FIDEI DEFENSOR

HIMSELF AND HIS MENTION OF CATHRYN had touched a chord of loneliness in me that evening, and it had resonated through a restless sleep. Eventually, I slid out of bed, not bothering to strap on the apparatus. I hopped to the table where I'd left the bottle Himself and I had shared, then hopped over to the window where the blackout curtains were open and London lay outside dark and quiet.

I sat on the sill and poured myself a small dose and lit an American cigarette. The street below was empty but for a couple, young I assumed by their cooing and smothered giggles. He was in uniform, though what kind I couldn't tell in the darkness. They circled each other, pretending a chase. He would grab her about the ribs in a thinly disguised attempt to touch her up, and she'd laugh, then he'd allow her to wriggle free. She'd run along the cobbles, her tam hanging oddly from her hair, held in place by a hatpin, mocking and teasing him to spur him to chase her again.

From the other end of the street, out of sight from my flat window, came the slow, steady rhythm of heavy boots. I saw the boy and girl recompose themselves like errant children hoping to throw off any suspicion of naughtiness, and then, trying to restrain giggles, they toddled off hand in hand.

The owner of the boots wore a cocked helmet, held an unlit torch in his hand, and had a gas mask satchel on his hip. His tread bespoke an older man. Home Guard, I thought. He stopped on the walk below me, glanced up and down the street, then upward. He must've seen the glow from my fag. He raised his torch to the brim of his helmet. I waved the amber tip of the cigarette back in returned salute, then he trudged off.

Thereafter I had more of the scotch than I should have.

I fobbed off, appearing at the office that morning with a vague tale of a lead on a new story, and returned to my observer's station across from the Annex. It soon became obvious to me from the lack of the bustle and urgency that had marked the courtyard in recent days that whatever story had been a-brewing seemed to be finished. Still, I stayed until Harry Voss appeared as nattily put together as I'd seen him since the case began. The reason for his attentiveness to appearance became clear as I followed him to General DiGarre's headquarters. I was still there when he exited a short time later looking very much a man adrift.

None of it—the lying in wait, the surreptitious following of Harry to DiGarre's offices and then, afterward, into the park—had anything to do with the story. If asked I would've said otherwise, something to the effect of these simply being the actions of a damned dogged journalist and if there were a story about, by heaven, no warning from Himself, Whitehall, or the Almighty would hold me off. But it was none of that.

Harry was different from those bubbly cohorts of his who looked at their stationing in England as some grand holiday adventure. Nor did he have the swagger of those who considered themselves the heirs presumptive to a fading Empire. From the first day I saw him—and even more so since I'd seen him emerge from the Grosvenor Square complex after seeing the photographs of a burning Helsvagen—he looked like a man who would rather be at home. And more and more, I was feeling like a man who longed for one.

Sitting by the Serpentine, sunk within himself, he seemed painfully alone. Without really being conscious of the act, out came my whistling: a contact. He looked over to where I was on the esplanade. I nodded and smiled, and he smiled back. And then—again not even really considering it—I made over to him and tipped my head toward the empty side of his bench. He shrugged in return and scooted over, and I sat.

Across the water, the children were running at the swans, only to run off shrieking, terrified by the flapping of large, warning wings.

"They'll get themselves in a bit of trouble," I said.

"Excuse me?" Harry said.

"The wee tykes there. Those birds are under protection of the Crown. All the swans in England, actually. Property of the King. Foul-tempered beasts, too. Odd what a person'll care to protect. That's the sort of queer business I suppose a visitor would describe as 'quaint.' And you do appear to be a visitor."

He looked down and seemed surprised to find himself in uniform. "Oh, yes."

"They'll be all over the park soon, I imagine."

"Who? The swans?"

I laughed. "The wee ones. They plopped most of 'em down in the countryside in the early days. Blitz Babies, they called 'em. Some went overseas. Australia. Canada. Some even to the States, so thank you for that. Oddly, the ones who stayed seem to have thought the whole affair a jolly pink tea. Enjoyed themselves immensely, climbing about the rubble, scavenging, dodging school, the whole lot of it quite fun. Too young to know any better, I suppose."

Harry squinted across the lake. The nanny had grabbed the children by their hands, scolding them for abusing the birds as she led them off. "Do you think they ever grow out of it?"

"Some do." I held out a hand. "Eddy," I said in introduction. He took the hand. I nodded at the insignia on his shoulder. "Major, is it?" I asked, affecting a certain naive earnestness.

"Harry. You're . . . Scottish? I hear the brogue."

"Burr. It's a Scottish burr. The Irish have a brogue, the Scots a burr. And you have a good ear, Harry." I looked after the receding nanny and her charges. "Aye, they'll all be coming back. Already started, it has. Bombs'll be a lullaby to that lot running amuck. You have kids?"

"Two."

"Then you know I'm spot on about the rumpus."

"They do get noisy." He smiled wistfully.

"Pictures?"

He hesitated, not wanting to appear another boringly boastful parent, then he drew out his billfold, opening it to the transparent sleeves that housed his family. There were the boys, then the wife, then the boys and wife.

"Nice lot, that," I said. "Prettier than you, I dare say."

It was his turn to laugh. "I agree. I wonder if I'll recognize them when I get home. It's been so long."

"Oh, you will."

He nodded, still doubtful, then took another glance at the pictures before he tucked the billfold safely away.

I thought of Cathryn and mishandled welcome-home's. "There's always an awkward bit at first."

"It passes?"

His eyes were still across the lake and that gave me a chance to study his soft face. I could see it there: I should never have come home, and he should never have left.

"For you," I told him, "it'll pass rather quickly, I should think."

We sat a few minutes more, exchanging bits of inane conversation, but the chat seemed to please him. I offered him something from the tea stall at the end of the lake, but he glanced at his watch, then shook his head.

"Things to do," he explained sadly. "Too many."

I rose with him. "Ach, I know the feeling. A day like today you could almost forget it was on, eh? The war, I mean. You should come back, Harry. When it's over. It's like this all the time, then." I pointed at the quiet, green park.

He grinned. "Except for the kids."

"Well, aye, except for that."

We wished each other a pleasant day and he moved on. When I thought a discreet distance had appeared between us, I followed. Again, I told myself it was only business.

At the Annex, Harry put in calls to Ricks and Grassi to meet him in his quarters immediately. While he waited for them he went back over the case material for the nth time.

He was looking for two things:

Paramount was the answer to DiGarre's riddle concerning Dennis O'Connell's wireless silence on the return trip from Helsvagen. A mechanic's report on O'Connell's aircraft stated that the damage to O'Connell's wireless equipment had been inflicted both by the burst of gunfire that downed the aeroplane, and by the final crash into the sea. Ergo, O'Connell had had a working wireless on his way home. So, DiGarre's question gnawed at him: Why was O'Connell silent?

Beyond that, he was hoping that by going through the material again he could find the solidarity it'd had before DiGarre had pummeled it into bread pudding with his subtly deprecating voice and dissecting gaze.

Finding neither, Harry was left looking for a third thing: What to do next.

When Ricks and Grassi arrived, Harry made sure the door was closed firmly behind them before outlining their current position. DiGarre's warning in mind, he avoided any mention of Hamburg. But he did state, in vague but forceful terms, Headquarters' objection to pursuing the Helsvagen matter, and DiGarre's offer of a quick conviction on O'Connell's murder and the attack on the Greshams in exchange for not charging Markham and Anderson with an attack on the village of Helsvagen. So there'd be no illusions as to the risk involved, Harry also presented his own view that—win or lose—there existed a strong possibility of punitive measures against them afterward, official and otherwise, if they prosecuted Helsvagen-related charges.

Harry's warning of the danger of prosecuting the Helsvagen case only roiled Grassi. "You know what that is?" he declared heatedly, pacing about Harry's room. "You know what all that crap is? That crap is obstructing justice is what that crap is!"

"It doesn't matter," Ricks said tiredly, but before he could continue, Grassi was waving a finger in his face.

"What the hell do you mean 'it doesn't matter'? We should slap these sons of bitches with a restraining order and have the whole bunch of them yanked clear of this case!"

"A restraining order." Ricks rolled his eyes. "A restraining order."

"Or something!" Grassi declared. "File for conflict of interest, get Ryan recused . . ." Grassi was fueling his anger to the point where he almost couldn't speak. He took a deep breath. "We're holding onto a case bigger than Scopes, Leopold and Loeb, and Baby Lindbergh all rolled into one, and maybe you don't care if these bozos want to pull it out from under us—" Grassi stopped, struck by a thought. His tone turned accusing. "You *don't* care! You've been gun-shy on this thing from the beginning—"

"And where are you going to go to get your restraining order?" Ricks snapped back. "Where are you going to find the referee to slap them down?" The unprecedented burst of anger from the usually reserved captain set Grassi back on his heels. Ricks recomposed himself, speaking quietly, but firmly: "Think a minute, Armando! This is Army law! You can't protect this case without the cooperation of the same people who are trying to suppress it! *They* run the game. They *are* the referees."

Ricks turned to Harry, curious as to his senior's silence. He marked it strange that Harry had made none of his usual attempts to quiet Grassi down.

"If you two are done with the free-for-all," Harry said impassively, "I want us all to have a clear picture of where we're at right now, and then maybe we can figure out where we go from here. I want to hear everybody's thoughts. What about you, Pete?"

Ricks remembered it as the first instance of Harry addressing him by his Christian name. "Maybe I'm just imagining it," he told me, "but it almost felt like he was asking me . . . asking *anybody* what the right thing was to do."

With a certain degree of embarrassment Ricks told me he could only muster a confused shrug. Harry continued to stand over him, not pressing, but hoping.

Ricks cleared his throat and stood. He began to pace; a convenient vehicle for getting out from under Harry's beseeching eyes.

"First," he began, his voice somewhat strained, "we have to decide on our priorities." Armando Grassi was already rolling his eyes impatiently. "If our first priority is a conviction, then, obviously, the strategic thing to do is to accept the general's— "

"And just forget everything else?" Grassi exploded, shooting to his feet.

"Armando—"

"Don't 'Armando' me!"

"You know as well as I do that what someone did, and what is viably prosecutable, are not the same thing. You look at what you have and try the best case—"

"And that's what you want to do? Let them off—"

"This has got nothing to do with what anybody wants to do!" Ricks tried unsuccessfully to keep his voice from rising. "If we're interested in a felony conviction and appropriate sentencing, the most practical course—"

"Meaning the *safest.*"

"In terms of—"

"In terms of saving your own ass!"

"Enough!" Harry snapped, stepping between them. "I think we've got enough to worry about without having to worry about each other. Agreed?"

Like schoolboys caught fighting, they shamefacedly nodded, then nodded apologies in each other's direction. Grassi backed away, and Ricks returned to his chair.

Harry walked to a far corner of the room to gather himself. They were three men squabbling in a small boat and if the fighting didn't stop, the boat would capsize and drown them all. *Think,* he told himself. *It's just another case. Study it, think it through, and look at it like just another case.* He lit himself a cigarette.

"All right, then," he said quietly. Then more firmly: "You're right, Peter, about setting priorities. Number one is let's get our house in order. I don't have to give an answer to DiGarre until tomorrow. We'll meet here at 1200 tomorrow and when we do, I don't want to hear moral indignation, or right makes might. I want to hear *practical courtroom strategy.* I want to hear *solid trial argument.* I want to hear the charge, the defense's counter, our rebuttal. How do we handle a prosecution on O'Connell? On Helsvagen? What are the possible combinations? Is there another avenue we haven't yet considered?

"Both of you can start by addressing yourselves to this little hole in our case the general sprang on me. Go see that sector ATC," he commanded. "Get a look at the original air traffic log if you can. See if the controller's got anything to add. Go back to the mechanic who drafted that report on O'Connell's plane. Is it possible there was something—*anything*—wrong with O'Connell's radio *before* his ship was hit? Get me some radio expert; is it possible O'Connell *did* transmit something before he went down but nobody picked it up? Go back to old man Gresham. Is *he* sure O'Connell didn't say anything before he died? Maybe he mumbled something and the old man didn't think it meant anything, but it might mean something to us. Failing all that, craft me a good reason why the man we say was killed because he witnessed a massacre didn't see fit to make a peep about it!"

They had been scribbling notes furiously, Grassi on a piece of paper cribbed from Ricks and with a pencil fished out of Harry's escritoire. When he looked up, he was startled to find Harry's hard face a few inches from his.

"You win a case, Lieutenant," Harry said, "not because you're right, but because you make a better case than the other guy. Make me a better case."

"You got it, Boss."

"We'll see. I also want you both to seriously consider possible repercussions to yourselves. If we get involved in a Helsvagen case in any way, there's going to be hell to pay. You better start thinking about how high a price you'll be willing to pay. Now go to work."

As they started to leave, Harry made a slight motion of his head to Ricks. Ricks told Grassi he needed to use Harry's loo; he'd meet up with him in a minute. After Grassi was gone, Harry nodded Ricks into a chair and pulled another close by. He offered the captain a cigarette and lit one for each of them.

"Grassi's not hard to understand," Harry said, waving out his match. "Grassi's—Well, Grassi's Grassi. If he'd said anything even remotely reasonable a few minutes ago I would've fallen over dead from shock." Harry smiled but Ricks didn't see the joke. "I don't agree with him that you're just concerned with saving your own tail."

Ricks nodded appreciatively, but he looked past Harry, trying not to meet his eyes.

"Come on, Pete. What is it?"

Ricks stood to pace again, feeling hemmed in by Harry sitting so close. "I've always thought if we could just present this case in front of an impartial jury without having to concern ourselves with everybody else's agenda, then everything'd work out the way it's supposed to."

"If that was an option, it'd be my first choice."

The captain's face reddened. "You asked us to consider what price we would pay. If I end up directing traffic on the Burma Road, I suppose I could live with that. Permanent latrine officer in Benghazi, Eskimo liaison in the Aleutians—"

"It seems like you've given this a lot of thought." Harry smiled

But again Ricks didn't see the humor. "I've done nothing but think about what could happen to us . . . since Major Van Damm showed us those photos yesterday. Major, you've got more time in than I do. Grassi may not understand, but I shouldn't have to tell *you*."

"Tell me what?"

"How much are *you* willing to pay?" Ricks shook his head, embarrassed by his own boldness. "I don't mean any disrespect, Major—but if you work for a law firm, and they don't like what you're doing, you either leave or they fire you. Then, you go to another firm, or set up your own shop. But this is the Army, Major. The *Army*! For the duration, they own us! One day you forget to shine your shoes for inspection, and by the time the Army's done with it, it's insubordination and a court-martial offense. Don't laugh, Major! You know they can do it! Look at how some of this case has been handled! You can end up home, dishonorably discharged, maybe even looking at disbarment."

Ricks stopped his pacing, his eyes to the floor, running his cap round and round through his fingers so hard Harry thought he would crush the wire grommet "cheater" in its crown. "If I lost the law, Major . . . I wouldn't know what else to do." Slowly, he raised his head and asked, hungrily curious, "Would you? If that's the price . . . I don't know if I can afford it."

It was Harry's turn to flush. He was angry. Not with Ricks; with himself. The captain was right: Ricks should not have had to spell out the obvious for Harry. Harry may have made a proper speech about understanding the risks of pressing this case, but now he sharply realized that he'd never really understood how great those risks could be. He'd spent most of his time in service under Ryan's sheltering wing, forgetting what life in the Army universe could be like out from under that wing.

He was angry with himself for having forgotten. And angry for now being as fearful as Ricks.

"When the major asked me what to do," Peter Ricks said to me later, still filled with self-recrimination, "all I could think was, Don't look at me, old man! You got us into this; you get us out!" Harry had asked for help and the young man had been afraid to offer it. Looking back on that day, Ricks felt he'd failed not only Harry, but himself. "Armando was right about me," he said, his voice thick with self-disgust.

It had been a very human stumble in an otherwise fine young man and it disturbed me to see him flog himself so. So I asked him what, with the benefit of hindsight, he could have done differently that, considering the course events came to follow, could possibly have made any difference?

He shrugged. "But I might've felt better."

After Ricks left, Harry returned to the case files. Just three days earlier there had been no file; only a few scribbles in his pocket notebook. Now there were personnel files, diagrams, annotated maps, photostats, reports from Scotland Yard, Markham's deposition, and page after page of notes. He sifted through the pile of paper looking for the answers to the questions he'd posed for Ricks and Grassi. But there was something less concrete he was after as well.

"Somewhere in here," and he tapped his head as he related this to me later, "I was telling myself I was just trying to make sure I had a case against Markham and Anderson so damning I *couldn't* turn away from it. But I don't think that was it, not now." He hung his head, shaking it. "I was hoping—no, I was *looking* for the flaws that'd tell me I had to be out of my mind to push that case. When Peter Ricks walked out of there that day, I was looking for something, a reason—an *excuse*—to drop it, so I could say *that's* why. And not because I was a coward."

Which was typically Harry, ruthlessly—and unnecessarily—castigating himself. He was wrong to do so: Cowardice is about self-preservation, and it was not himself Harry was so fearful of preserving.

As the afternoon wound on, and the scribbled notes and typed words began to dance in front of his eyes, he pushed the paperwork aside. He reached into his trouser pocket for his billfold and extracted two photographs, which he laid on the desktop.

They were two of the photos he'd shown me as we sat by the Serpentine earlier that day, products of the family Brownie box, cracked from years riding on Harry's hip. One was taken the winter before Harry's enlistment, in early '42. There's two small boys in the photo. The smaller, perhaps four years of age, sits on a sled on a field of snow, and his brother, a year or so older, is tugging on the tow ropes. Both are grinning and waving at the camera. They are so bundled in winter garb—coats, hats, scarves, mittens—that they are barely distinguishable from each other, and the faces, tiny in the small frame, are a blurred grouping of eyes and smiles.

The other photo is Cynthia Voss. It is an older picture, taken at some sort of festive occasion. The photo shows a woman in her mid-thirties, the line of her jaw going soft, her fair hair pulled back with a ribbon in a style one would expect in a younger woman. A shrewd eye would estimate that the features of her broad face, while not unpleasant, would generally be described as plain, but it would take a shrewd eye because her smile transformed her face into something light and gracious and warm.

I'll always remember that last glance Harry gave the photos as we sat by the Serpentine, before he tucked the billfold back in his pocket. He looked at that slightly plump woman and his two tykes, and despite the many years of marriage, and the many months of separation, he wore, for a moment, the face of a school lad gazing at a picture of his first love.

Peter Ricks had fretted about what future he'd have if the Army took the law away from him. But Peter Ricks was still a young man with most of his life before him. For Harry, the answer to that same question was decidedly bleaker. Most of Harry's years were behind him. There would be no time to start afresh.

Ironically, the stakes for Harry that were highest were also the most banal. The issue was no longer one of a career-making case, or a deft exercise in jurisprudence, or even one of moral argument. The issue was rent and groceries.

He turned to the 66-1 files on each of the four pilots involved in the attack on Helsvagen. He withdrew their identification photos and laid them out in a squared quartet on the escritoire. He set down Markham alongside Anderson, a handsome fellow with loose blond hair that almost glowed. Even in the ID photo, Anderson couldn't repress a cocky smirk. Below them he set Jacobs and McLagen. Jacobs was a lean-looking sort, sunken-cheeked and hollow-eyed, his long face topped by a tuft of bristly hair that looked as if he'd cut it himself. McLagen was victim of either an inept photographer or his own small stature, for his photo showed an inordinate amount of headroom. The round face lost at the bottom of the frame was dappled with freckles and a few pimples, and his smile was that of a boy posed for a school photograph.

On the right-hand side of his desk Harry imagined the recon photos Christian Van Damm had splashed on the projection screen in the G-2 briefing amphitheater: the crosshatched village streets interrupted by collapsed walls, blanketed by the malignant smoke of the burning depot.

He looked again and again from the four young fliers to that empty square of desktop where he imagined the burning village. As a group— despite their individual distinctions—the four were wholly unexceptional. Harry could have reached into any military unit in any theater of the war and, at random, drawn out a similar handful of men. But there had to be one unique note, he was convinced, some quality that made the connection possible between those four faces and the pyre at Helsvagen.

But he couldn't see it.

He slipped Cynthia and the boys carefully back into their cellophane sleeves and returned them to his wallet.

He gathered up the 66-1's and reached for his cap. For his unanswered questions, Harry could only go to the source.

There was a knock at the conference room door, then an MP stepped inside, ushering Albert Markham into the room. Harry nodded the MP out and the guard closed the door behind him. Markham stood at attention, his cap tucked under his arm.

"Relax, Major," Harry said. He was standing by one end of the table, the four 66-1's open in front of him. "No reason we have to be so formal." Emphasizing the point, Harry slid a package of cigarettes across the polished wood toward Markham. Markham nodded a thanks, set his cap down on the table, lit himself a cigarette, and slid the package back.

"Just us today," Markham said without looking round the empty conference room. He nodded at the chair at the far end of the table. "Do I take my usual seat?"

"Wherever you're comfortable, Major."

Evidently, Markham was, for the moment, comfortable where he was. "The way Colonel Ryan was acting in here the other day, you'd think this was his baby. He's the boss, but you're really the guy who'll get credit for the kill, right?" There was no bitterness in the way he said it. No sarcasm. It was simply a flat statement of fact. It was the choice of words that stung Harry.

"I don't know that I'd put it like that, but it's my case, yes."

"Mind if I ask you a question, Major?"

Harry nodded.

"Is that what this is? You trying to run up a score? Or is it serious for you?"

Harry weighed an answer. "At this point, something in between."

Markham nodded appreciatively. "That's honest."

Markham found an ashtray and carried it with him as he walked to the end of the table. "My little friend isn't here today." He mimed an industrious stenographer.

"This is more of an informal little chat."

Markham nodded. "Does that mean I don't need a lawyer? Your boss sent J. J. and me word that we should start thinking about that. He said if we didn't have anybody in mind to represent us, that he could appoint somebody. Can I trust your Colonel Ryan to look after us like that?"

"Do you have any reason not to trust him?"

"I don't know. Should I?"

They both smiled.

"If you want a lawyer," Harry began to offer, but Markham shook his head.

"I may come back to you on that, but not today."

Markham's head cocked and, at first, Harry didn't hear the sound, but then, through the open windows, a faint, lazy drone. Markham, still carrying his ashtray, careful not to dribble any ash from his cigarette, moved to the windows.

"An L-1. Some general going fishing."

"You could see that?" Harry asked, his eyes roaming the skies until he found the far-off dot poking about over the London roofs.

"You get to know the sounds. Do you mind . . . ?" He gestured that he'd like to lean against the conference table. Harry nodded that it was all right. Markham parked a haunch on the table and reached down to massage his right leg. Harry remembered the six-year-old injury from the war in Spain. "You know what a soldier's job is, Major?" Markham asked. "His job is to kill, and sometimes to die. An officer's job is to tell a soldier when to kill, and when to die. I've had both jobs and I didn't much care for either of 'em. This is a vacation for me."

"Vacation? You've got a hell of a sense of understatement, Major. Or is this that vaunted Al Markham courage everybody keeps telling me about? Keeps his cool, cracks wise even when the heat's on."

Markham flushed. "Nothing like that, Major. But, even looking at a gallows, any day off the flight line is a vacation to me." Markham sighed, tiredly, looked up again to follow the progress of the small plane in the distance. He noticed his cigarette was growing short, stubbed it out in the ashtray. He pointed questioningly at the pack sitting in front of Harry and Harry slid it over to him.

"You believe I used to play ball when I was a kid?" Markham said as he lit another cigarette. Markham took a draught on the cigarette and poked at his thick middle with a finger. "Look at that. All soft. And my wind's shot. Too many of these, I guess," and he indicated the cigarette. "I really should lay off these things. Now, Major Voss, what can I do for you?"

Harry glanced down at the open files. He noticed Markham's face growing soft as he recognized the identification photos.

"We know what happened out there, Major." Markham looked up at him, confused. "Recon photos of Helsvagen," Harry explained.

Markham smiled. Harry noticed that a Markham smile always seemed to have a touch of resignation to it. It was as if he'd already anticipated every word out of Harry's mouth, every maneuver, and pitied him for it. "You don't know. You think you do, but you don't."

"Believe what you want. The fact is, however much trouble you thought you were in before, you're in a whole lot more now. When you finally get around to getting a lawyer, if he's any good he'll tell you not to count on your glowing record to get you through this."

"The record is yesterday. Today's a new day, right?"

"That's right. Don't have any illusions of you somehow coming through this thing OK. It's in your interest to help me get a better picture of this whole . . ." Harry sought for the word.

"Mess?" There was that Markham smile, again.

"I'm not going to ask you anything incriminatory, Major, but maybe you can help me with this." Harry gestured at the files. "All I really want is you to tell me a little about these men."

"Tell you what? You guys've been pretty thorough poking around on all of us."

"You're an officer, Major, a commander. You know as well as I do—"

"That you can't boil somebody down to his personnel file."

"Yes."

Markham looked back out the window and shook his head. "I don't know what I could tell you. J. J.'s my friend. Maybe his loyalty's a little misplaced, but he's the best friend I got. He's a good joe. They were all good joes. That's all you need to know."

"Even O'Connell?"

Markham's face clouded. "In his way, yeah. I know it doesn't mean anything, not in a legal way, and you may not even believe me, but I'm sorry he's dead. And not just because I may get hung for it." He smiled ruefully. "I'm sorry about a lot of things."

"Major—"

"I haven't told my father about any of this. If I do get hung, does the Army tell him? I mean . . . how do they do that?"

"I don't know."

"That part of it isn't your job?"

"I've never tried a capital case before."

"This is a first for both of us, then. I've never been tried in a capital case before."

It was Harry's turn to sigh. "You're not going to help me, are you?"

Markham stubbed his cigarette out in the ashtray. "Major, you already know everything you need to know. What you want has got nothing to do with those files. You want to understand what happened out there." Markham shook his head. "You just think you do. Believe me; you don't." Markham stood, straightened his jacket, and turned from the window. "I could talk to you about what really happened out there, I could talk to you about each of those men day in and day out until you walk me up the gallows, and you're not going to understand anything any better then than you do now." If there was any emotion to his voice at all, it was sympathy.

"But I'll make you an offer," Markham continued. "You pick up a weapon. Spill some blood. Then, you come find me if I'm still around. Then we'll have something to talk about." Markham picked up his cap and knocked on the conference room door. The MP appeared in the doorway.

"All done, sir?" the MP asked Harry.

Markham turned to Harry, his look asking the same question.

Glumly, Harry nodded.

Markham cast a last look out the window, at the pastel August sky. "You know, all I ever wanted to do was fly."

After the door closed behind Markham, Harry looked down at the open files on the table and closed them, one by one.

Back in his quarters, Harry went over the case files again, and kept at it until the orderlies made their dusk rounds warning that it was time to draw the blackout curtains.

He considered a walk to the canteen for a light supper but balked at the possibility of bumping into Ryan. He took up his tie, jacket, and cap and left the Annex. Outside the court his steps felt lighter, his mood less fatigued. The moon was rising, sharply articulated stars appearing early, uneclipsed by blacked-out streetlamps and city lights. Harry considered an ale and a meal at The Old Eagle but again, the specter of Ryan pushed him elsewhere.

He felt compelled to put some distance between himself and Mayfair. He wandered the dark streets until he came to an Underground station; Oxford Circus, I imagine, as the line took him to Embankment Station. He remembered this put him near the Strand and he climbed back to the street and made his way up Charing Cross. Only an occasional cat's-eyed cab and horse-drawn tram traveled the road, and the sidewalks carried only a thin sprinkling of couples moving like shadows through the gloom.

Harry felt uncomfortable alone on the dark street and nosed into the first cinema he came across, catching the last half of a British production about hijinks between competing fire crews during the Blitz, and then Mrs. Miniver. At that moment, however, he was not particularly receptive to confronting the war with a stoic attitude and stiff upper lip, and Greer Garson's upper-crust diction reminded him awfully of Sir Whosis.

What made the film palatable at all to him was knowing it was something Cynthia would have liked. He knew where she would have sniffled with emotion, slipped her fingers in his, and held her breath, moved during the climax when a minister stands over the graves of civilians lost in the bombing declaring, "This is the people's war! Fight it with all that is in us—and may God defend the right!"

After, Harry treated himself to dinner at a small restaurant admirably lacking any of the pretentious airs of Sir Whosis's dining palace. He had just begun digging into a rather desiccated fruit compote when sirens began their low moan far off across the City. They rose into a mourner's keening. The lights in the restaurant went out as the waiters glided familiarly through the darkness to light candles at each table.

There was another sound, a high tinkle, like a persistent alarm. Harry looked down and in the flicker of candlelight saw his hand shaking, the spoon in his fingers vibrating against the rim of the dessert cup. He dropped the spoon and stood abruptly, letting his napkin fall from his lap. His waiter, an old Cockney, emerged from the dark and took him by the elbow, lowering him back into his seat.

" 'Ere. Not to worry, sar. Sounds like 'ey's off a ways, 'ey are. Give St. Paul's a knock again, sounds like. I'll get ya a clean spoon, sar, 'n' ya just relax 'n' enjoy yer meal."

The thudding of the antiaircraft batteries started, throwing up a flak umbrella over the far end of the City. Then, in harmony with the sirens, came the overhead thrum of aircraft engines.

In the candlelight Harry saw shapes bent over their tables, sipping their drinks, dining without pause, dispassionately discussing the night's possible targets. A few diners gathered at one of the restaurant's tall windows, dabbing their lips with napkins and peeping round the blackout curtains through the starburst pattern of tape on the glass. The first bombs whistled down and the explosions sent lurid red and yellow flashes across the City that lit up the faces at the window.

Harry felt sweat breaking out all over his body.

"Ya ha'n't finished yer meal, sar." The waiter was back at his elbow.

"No, no," Harry stammered, making a poor pretense at simulating the calm of the other diners. "I'm, uh, I have to go. I'm late, see—"

"O' course, sar."

"I need my check, please."

"Well, then, I'll be right along wi' it." The waiter took a few steps, then turned back, dropping his voice confidentially. "If ya feel the need, sar, there's an Underground just down the way."

Sirens started going off closer. A bomb—a stray, Harry hoped—fell close; windows, dishes, and silverware rattled.

"Might' near nicked us 'at time!" someone in the dark chuckled.

Harry threw some pound notes on the table and left.

Out on the street, a few brazen individuals and couples, some giddily giggling at their own daring, stood, looking at the sky show: beacons rolling crazily back and forth; dissipating ack-ack bursts glowing with moonlight; an orange glow showing along the skyline toward the river.

The waiter had said something about a shelter but Harry couldn't recall it. Seeing the steeple of a small church silhouetted against the fire glow, he headed for it.

The church was a dark, granite pile, its steeple a blunt, glowering pyramid. Harry took the church steps two at a time, then gripped the wrought-iron handles of the massive doors and pulled. The doors did not open. He looked helplessly up at the steeple and tugged again. Now, sirens were sounding all round him. He looked about and saw the streets were empty.

An Underground; that was what the waiter had said! He ran, past a 90-mm antiaircraft gun in its sandbagged pit, the crew frantically swiveling the tall, graceful barrel of their piece into place in response to the commands of the "talker" taking his instructions over his headset from the RDF controllers. Beyond the gun he saw the sandbagged entrance of Embankment Station. He stumbled through the entryway and down the steps to the platform below.

Candle flames dotted the platform, fragile circles of amber glow, and he saw a match flare to light up a cigarette, and over there a covered torch, but for the most part the platform was dark. Harry could sense the people crowded on the platform, the air stale with body odor and sweat. Just a few steps from the stairway his shoes began nudging bodies.

" 'Ave a care there, mate!"

"Sorry," Harry mumbled and went back to the bottom of the stairs. Leaning against the wall he could feel the pulsing of the earth on the other side of the tile as the antiaircraft guns nearby began pumping fire into the night; first the high-shooting 90-mm guns, then the thud-thud-thud of the Bofors guns, then the clatter of the Oerlikons and quad .50's as the bombers pressed in.

"Ruddy great racket, eh?" There was something familiar about the voice. In the blackness across from him, Harry could not make out anything more than a shadow. "Ruddy great waste, too," the voice added cheerfully.

"A waste?" another voice asked from somewhere on the platform.

"I hear they don't really expect to hit anything with all this," the first voice replied. "Morale, you understand. Makes us all feel a bit better hearing the guns bang away on our behalf. So they say."

"I know I feel a 'elluva lot better wif it," the second voice said.

"Oh-oh," a third voice warned.

There was a second chorus of humming engines now, detached from the heavy main droning south of the river, sounding deeper, closer.

"They're lost," the first voice said.

"That's for us," said the second voice.

"Here it comes!"

The bombs began whistling down close by and these weren't odd strays. They came down in a close-knit stick. The pulses of the AA guns were washed out by the quaking of bomb explosions. Harry pressed himself against the wall and fought to keep a tight rein on his bowels. Men came running down the Underground stairs, silhouetted against the flashes of bombs landing nearby. Harry heard a child cry. It sounded like a little girl.

"Here, lass." Harry heard the first voice, and now he identified the Scottish burr. "Lose your mum, eh?"

He saw the shadowy figure across from him stoop, then rise, a small bundle in its arms. He could see the cradled child heaving with sobs.

"Your mum'll be along, girl, so for now you just stay with me. You sing a song with me and you won't even be hearing all this fuss, eh? It's not worse than a thunderstorm. Sing with me, girl." And they sang:

> In Dublin's fair city
> Where girls are so pretty
> I first set my eyes on sweet Molly Malone . . .

A bomb crashed, so close that Harry felt the tiles against his back crack and buckle. The crowd hiding in the dark murmured and shuffled. He heard the droning of prayers.

The crying little girl hugged the Scot tightly, but calmly he sang on:

> Crying cockles, and mussels,
> Alive, alive-o.

Fifteen minutes later, Harry was standing on the sidewalk near the Underground entrance, mopping at the sweat lying thick on his hatband. Behind him people filed out of the station—those who weren't among the bombed-out souls forced to take up permanent residence there—and headed back to homes they hoped were still standing.

As close as the crashing bombs had felt, Harry saw little damage on the street. Concussions had shaken a good deal of window glass onto the sidewalks, and far down the block, beyond the 90-mm gun crew openly praising God for their good fortune, a smoking crater reached curb to curb, arcing geysers of water spurting from a ruptured water line. Wherever the bombs had come down was already the target for the sounds of fire engine and ambulance bells.

Harry put his cap on and walked round the station to the Embankment. Across the river, toward Southwark, tall flames rose from among the buildings there, and alarm bells clanged. The spray of the hoses shone in the firelight.

"After the docklands is my guess," came the Scottish burr.

The moonlight helped Harry pick out the features of the man from Hyde Park. The Scot held out a pack of cigarettes.

"Not that awful Brit stuff, if that's your worry," the Scot promised.

Harry nodded and took one. His hand was shaking so much he almost dropped the cigarette. The Scot drew one for himself. Harry extracted his own matches from his breast pocket. He had trouble keeping his hands steady enough to strike the match. He felt a strong, callused hand come round his and hold the match steady, then the Scot bent down to the flame. Harry tried to get a glimpse of the man's face by the match light, but the wide brim of the frayed Panama hat blocked Harry's view. The Scot pulled the match from Harry's fingers before he burned himself, then took the book of matches and struck a fresh light, holding it out for Harry.

"You look like a man who could use a drink," I said.

He nodded.

I found us an outside table at a pleasant little *osteria* I knew just a block away. Harry said nothing until I had the waiter set a second sherry in front of him, then, plainly embarrassed, he said, "I'm afraid I've forgotten your name."

"Eddy."

He nodded. "Sorry. I feel like an idiot."

"This can all be a wee distracting. This can't have been your first. How long have you been here?"

"I came over in January. I've been through them before, but . . ." He turned toward the gentle rumble of flames and the clanging alarms across the river. "Never this close. I don't care how long I'm here, I don't think I'll ever get used to them."

"Some never do. Then there's those—Ach, you'd be surprised what some get used to. During the Blitz they were coming over every night, Jerry was, every night all night it seemed. After a bit, I knew people who couldn't sleep without it."

"You almost sound like you miss it."

I shook my head. "But it *was* history, eh?"

"I'm still not sorry I missed it."

"Typical American. No sense of history."

Harry was silent. By his third sherry he had finally stopped shaking. "Do you live around here?"

I laughed. "Aye, that'd be the ticket, eh? Me in this neighborhood? Picture me ensconced at the old Savoy, eh? I'd like that, I would."

"I'll take that as a no."

I thought of offering some sort of fat tale about who I was and how I'd come to be there, but I saw that despite his having stopped shaking he still held his wineglass hard and close to him. I'd followed him all the evening, seeing how alone he was, and now seeing how afraid he was. He didn't need a lie or two added to his burden.

"Let's just say it's a small world," I told him.

We chatted; nothing important or intrusive. He spoke of Cynthia and his children; I told him of my disaster with Cathryn. I told him of Scotland, and how the small gravel beach where, as a boy, I'd skipped stones, was now behind the perimeter fence of an Air/Sea Rescue base; he told me how grand hotels in the coast towns of his youth—places like Atlantic City—were now massive hospitals for wounded GI's returned from Europe. It was the first time in a long time I could remember sitting at a table in conversation having nothing to do with my work. We were just two old duffers alone and far from home, keeping each other company.

After a bit, we felt the need to stir the blood and took to our feet. For the first time he noticed my gait.

"Are you all right?"

I rapped on the limb and the sound of wood made him flinch. "Don't let it worry you, Harry. Rare's the good Scots pubster not born with a hollow leg as standard kit."

We made our way down to the Embankment. There were few people down there; the hour had grown late and the sight of flames was no longer the novel attraction it would have been three years earlier. At the sound of another fire engine clanging along behind us, streaking toward the small conflagration on our side of the Thames, Harry jumped.

"Chap I know in Whitehall says the whole bloody mess started as accidents," I said. He looked at me quizzically, so I explained: "Back in the beginning, during the Blitz, Jerry would come over and there'd be strays. Then, we'd go give it 'em back and there'd be more strays. Then chaps on both sides got a bit wrought up over all these noisemakers going astray, so they started dropping them all about with what you might describe as concerted effort and determination."

He leaned on the wall over the river and repeated what he'd said earlier, about never growing used to it. He said it with his gaze fixed across the river, the flames a sorrowful glow in his eyes. He asked if I was used to it.

"You get used to the fact that it's done, and that it's going to be done. You don't get over being terrified of someone dropping a bomb on your bean."

"You didn't seem terrified down in the Underground tonight."

"You don't have to look afraid to be afraid, Harry. They start going off right over your noggin and it sounds like Death himself stomping round up there looking for you, you'd have to be a bit of a loon not to be afraid. 'Death plucks my ear,' said the old poet, 'and says, Live—I am coming.' I always remember that afterward."

Harry yawned. "It's late," he said apologetically, squinting at his watch face in the moonlight.

"The full name's Eddy Owen." I held out my hand in reintroduction.

"Harry Voss," he said and took my hand, then we bid each other good night.

The Annex court was dark but not empty. Two men on one of the stoops quietly debated the respective merits of Glen Miller's version of "In the Mood" versus Tex Beneke's. Another of the Annex's occupants reclined in the passenger seat of one of the parked jeeps, smoking a cigarette, his head tilted musingly toward the moon. Behind blacked-out windows Harry heard a laugh, the clatter of poker chips, orchestral strains from a wireless.

The two duty PFC's in the orderly room of his BOQ were being re-galed by a third man Harry vaguely recognized as a captain quartered there. The captain's dressing gown was splotched with dampness and there were little patches of drying soapsuds in the captain's hair. He wore slippers.

"Y'all believe these sumbitches?" he demanded of the giggling or-derlies. "Ah mean, do y'all be-leeve 'em?" He was a youngish sort, loud, with a crawling Oklahoma drawl. "Ah'm waitin' thu-ree weeks for 'em to run the wateh lawng 'nuff to take a damn bath—How do they say it ovah heah?" The captain stuck his nose up in the air and held it even higher with the tip of his index finger. "Draw me a bahth, Reginahld!" The two PFC's howled. "So Ah'm sittin' there soapin' my best parts 'n' that's when the sumbitches start to get all military! Ah damn neah didn't make the shelteh 'cause 'o all that damn soap in mah eyes!" The captain finally noticed Harry in the orderly room door. "Ten-hut!" he called out and all three snapped to.

Harry nodded at the robe. "You out of uniform?"

The captain grinned. "Not really, suh. It's government issue."

Harry grinned back and went up to his room.

He left the lights out and pulled back the blackout curtains. The courtyard slowly emptied and went quiet except for soft music from a wireless somewhere. He heard a cry above him, sounding like a child. He looked up and saw a hawk, aglow with the moon, carrying off a small wren.

From the wireless, Ted Lewis finished his song and asked, "Is everybody happy?"

A breeze whiffled the mustaches of the elderly Home Guardsman standing in front of Harry's jeep, carrying toward Harry the sting of smoke and the taste of cinders. Harry had sampled that same taste all night, and it had been there when he had awakened from his fitful sleep.

He had not bothered with breakfast or a morning brushup, but had clambered unwashed into yesterday's clothes. He was sure that any distraction—even something as trivial as a cup of coffee—would lead to some reason for him to abort his journey. I asked him what he thought he'd find there.

"I wanted to *see*," he explained simply. So, within twenty minutes of waking he was driving across Westminster Bridge and heading east toward the docklands, driving until he'd been stopped by a Guardsman at a line of barricades hung with warning signs.

"Can't get through here," said the old man from under his oversized white helmet. "Jerry paid a visit last night, 'e did. Lot o' cleanin' up to do, 'n' the UXB chaps is all at it, too, 'n' 'ere's the casualties ya see, 'n' all that. Won't be able to get in for quite a bit, I'd say." The man leaned close. "If it's important, try goin' round t'over side; down by the river. It's all open down there."

Harry nodded a thanks, shifted the jeep into reverse, and turned the vehicle round as the old man waved him on his way.

Cobblestones paved the narrow streets that led down to the river, which glared with a sheen of oil and grease. Skeletal dogs trotted furtively alongside the houses, ducking into alleys as Harry drove past. Adolescents stared. Between houses lines of laundry hung like tattered flags, threadbare shirts and knickers and dresses waving wearily. Here, the smell of the breeze mingled with coal smoke, septic refuse, slum cooking. The closer Harry drew to the river, the narrower the streets became, the fewer the people, the danker the stones, the more oppressive the shabby buildings pressing in on him from either side. The gloomy, twisting streets brought back a memory from university days: something about the Minoan labyrinth and the beast preying within.

Harry stopped his jeep, stood up on the seat, and looked about. Behind him rose dark blocks of dingy flats. To one side were abandoned houses; plain, brick hovels with grass tangled round their facades. To the other were old maritime warehouses with rusting hoists and lopsided shutters. Beyond their dull, brick silhouettes, shining in the interstices, was a golden plain, stretching off under a sky of lowering clouds to a horizon of dust dancing in the wind, and gleaming like a revelation.

Harry slid back behind the wheel and turned the jeep toward the glittering expanse. Was it a few hundred yards to those low, blue-shadow buildings poking through the dust clouds on the other side of the clearing? Or a few thousand? Except for an occasional patch of scrappy brush and wildflowers his view was of a vast, unbroken stretch of emptiness carpeted with cracked bricks and splinters and twinkling bits of broken glass.

There had been warehouses there, some from the time when they had housed goods from the American colonies. Harry pondered the years, the money, the material and blood, the expenditure of human genius required to erase so completely a few centuries of history. He turned round to look back across the river, at familiar London. There was the dome of St. Paul's, and the spires of Parliament framed by Victoria Tower and Big Ben. Turning round again he saw emptiness, the dirt and clay and shattered glass underlying it all. Here, the City had been rubbed raw.

Harry set off toward where columns of dirty black smoke boiled up from a line of buildings. His jeep lurched out of the dust and into a world of cobblestones and shadows, fire and brick, and human faces streaked with soot and sweat.

Firemen stood by the smoking ruins. Rooster tails of shimmering water hung high in the air and thundered down on the smoldering wreckage of a house, a garage, a shop, the hulking shell of a warehouse. Men in white helmets walked solemnly up the inclines of broken walls, or picked their way through mounds of plaster and lathing. With hands cupped about their mouths they looked down at their feet and shouted, "Hoy! Hoy!" and listened for an answering call from under the debris.

Others followed the sniffing noses of dogs hunting human scent. Still others, with hooks and joists, peeled back crumbling floors to reveal dusty sacks of cloth and hair; corpses that flailed awkward limbs when hauled from their burrows. Hitched to a horse lazily twitching its tail at a cloud of flies, a wagon stood nearby. The corpses were piled neatly in the wagon. Civilians, returning to what remained of their homes, shuffled past Harry's jeep, ignoring his uniform, and delicately picked through the wreckage, salvaging a framed photo here, a box or brooch there.

The reedy exhalation of bagpipes sailed eerily over the sound of falling water and grumbling flame, the shifting of debris and the shouting of orders. Spinning the steering wheel, Harry followed the music. It was a song he'd often heard after a bombing, a dirge—"Flowers of the Forest."

The piper led a small procession of men in ill-fitting, working-class suits, and women in dark, old dresses. Some of the women held handkerchiefs to their eyes. Two of the men pulled a dogcart with rubber automobile tires, which bounced over the bricks and timbers in the road. On the cart were three bundles wrapped tightly in winding sheets. The diminutive size of one of the wrapped bundles revealed a child. Harry turned away.

A church bell sounded, merrily it seemed, in incongruous contrast to the fading bagpipes. Harry followed the chiming down a dead end and a blocked street before coming upon a small chapel standing between two ruined walls. Its bell hung from jerry-rigged timbers atop the shaky stump of a steeple. A little crowd was gathered round the cockeyed doors. From beneath a sign reading, "Dangerous: Unstable Structure—Do Not Enter," a bride and groom appeared, she cloaked in yellowing lace and he in the uniform of a Royal Army private. Both smiled shyly under the cheers and confetti of their well-wishers.

Harry quietly moved the jeep off, down one after another of the strange, desolate, half-inhabited streets until he came upon a lone fireman sitting on a crate before an empty lot.

"I'm lost," Harry said.

For a moment, the old fireman's sooty features seemed intent on the scarred hands folded over his knees. Then, the firefighter lifted his head and his exhausted face rolled into a cordial smile. "You look lost, Yank."

• • •

Harry had imagined himself an image of brazen defiance, standing before General DiGarre's massive desk in his rumpled uniform still smudged with the dust and soot of the fires of the South End. But, when the time came to actually stand in front of the general's polished wooden altar in his rough clothes, Harry felt only pathetic.

Again, Harry had been ushered in without waiting. DiGarre was waiting for him at his desk. The general was not alone. Round the long conference table a collection of senior officers (Harry noted oak leaves, eagles, and five-pointed stars winking at him from the host of collar tabs) huddled under a haze of cigarette smoke. The harsh light of the billiard lamps drained their faces of color and sank their features into bottomless black shadow. They looked up at him only briefly, fixing him for the shortest of moments with the dark chasms that had replaced their eyes before turning back to the paperwork that whispered back and forth among them across the table.

DiGarre was slouched deep in his desk chair, the stub of a cigar in one hand, a whiskey tumbler in the other. The sleeves of his wrinkled shirt were rolled up past his sinewy, hirsute forearms, and his tie hung low and loose. Harry noted the red-rimmed eyes, the stubble on the general's chin, the before-breakfast drink, and concluded the general'd not been to sleep. Perhaps none of the men in the room had been to sleep; the air in the office was stale and ripe, and despite the morning hour, the blackout curtains remained drawn.

Harry stood at attention, his arm raised in salute, before the general's desk. The general smiled without humor. "Sit yourself on down, Major." Not "Harry" this time. The lilting, coddling tones of yesterday's genial host were gone.

Harry remained standing.

DiGarre nodded. He pulled himself up in his seat, removed his spectacles, and tiredly massaged the bridge of his nose. "You're here to tell me you're going to be a pain in my old ass, right?"

The general's prescience left Harry with nothing to say. He heard the flutter of birds against the windows on the other side of the curtains, hunkering down on the sills for the storm. The first tumbling roll of thunder sounded distantly.

"That's what I thought," the general said. He replaced his spectacles, snuffed out the stub of his cigar, and drew a fresh one from his humidor.

"I'm not doing this to be trouble, General, but—"

DiGarre chuckled. "Your friend Colonel Ryan's got a lot of faults, Major, but I figured him for a better judge of character. He was sure you'd bite at our offer. Said you'd be worried about your career and taking care of your family and all that."

Harry wished he'd taken the general's invitation to sit.

"Well, I'm going to have to take another look at the colonel's ratings, because I knew the minute we all sat down you were going to be a pain in my old ass. I don't know how long Joe Ryan's known you, but the first time you opened your yap I said to myself, 'This fella's going to be a real tick about this thing; he's not going to let go.' I probably knew it before you did. You've got integrity, Major." The general's lips twitched. "You stink of it. More integrity than good sense." The general took several starter puffs on his fresh cigar. "Bet you don't think much of mine."

"General, I'll leave that to you and your conscience."

DiGarre's head lolled as he laughed. The laugh became a cough. The general stood and walked to his liquor stand. He poured himself a glass of water and took a sip to soothe his throat. He went to the windows and pulled one of the curtains aside. The windowpanes rattled as the first drops of rain slapped against the glass.

"Know something, Harry? There's no second-place over here; no consolation prize. I for one will get no satisfaction from posterity proclaiming, 'Well, they lost, but by God they fought fair!' My conscience'll rest easy, Major." The general looked back up at the dark clouds, then sighed and let the curtain fall back across the window. "All right, Major, you said your piece." The general joined the other officers around the conference table. It took Harry a moment to realize he'd been dismissed.

There was a message waiting for Harry with the BOQ orderlies that General Halverson had called twice during his absence. Harry called the general's office from his room.

"He's gone, sir," replied the callow voice on the phone.

"Oh. Well, can I reach him at his quarters?"

"The general's not there, sir. Didn't you hear?"

"I know he was relieved."

"Relieved and transferred, sir. Cut his orders late last night. We were up till all hours packing his stuff. They had him on a plane for Iceland about an hour ago."

"Iceland? Is that where he's been transferred?"

"That's just a stopover, sir. General Halverson's on his way home."

"I see." Harry lowered himself into a chair and reached for his cigarettes. "He tried to call me this morning, but—"

"You said your name was Voss? The Judge Advocate's, right? Yes, sir, General Halverson left a message for you, Major Voss. Uh, it just says, 'Good luck,' sir. That's all. That's funny, isn't it, sir? The general saying 'good luck' to you? Seems like that's the kind of thing you say to the person what's leaving."

CHAPTER NINE

DROIT DU SEIGNEUR

SUMMONED AT MIDDAY, RICKS AND GRASSI found Harry waiting for them in the conference room. Shaved, showered, and attired in a clean, pressed uniform, Harry was moving deliberately along the conference table slapping down files and sheaves of paper. There on the table went the mechanic's report on O'Connell's aeroplane; here went the postmortem; over here, the ballistics report; here, the analysis of Anderson's gun film . . . The decisive flavor of his movements indicated there was a carefully conceived plan at work, one he was keeping to himself. Harry made no acknowledgment of the presence of his two juniors.

The fog that had clouded and oppressed him just the day before as he had sat in Hyde Park was gone. Now, his mind was possessed of a remarkable clarity. Like a man jumped, pushed, or fallen off a cliff, for good or ill he realized he was now committed. His only chance to survive was to manage the fall as best he could. He was, at the table, applying the same method for formulating a trial strategy as he'd used a few days earlier when he'd spread index cards on the floor before him, trying to formulate his case. He had his case now. Now he was looking for the picture that would win it for him.

Both young men were startled when Harry said: "In reflecting on

our little predicament, it occurs to me that while your respective opinions are always appreciated, whatever we do and however we do it is, ultimately, my decision. I have reached that decision. We're going ahead
with a Helsvagen prosecution."

Ricks was nonplussed, and wondered if in Harry's statement there
was some subtle rebuke to the captain's conduct the day before. As for
Grassi, the lieutenant harbored no doubts about his own feelings or
Harry's decision.

"Now that calls for a celebration!" the lieutenant said. He breezed to
the sideboard and held up half of a bologna sandwich in salute.

"Before you get yourself all a-quiver, Lieutenant," admonished Harry,
"let me repeat what I said yesterday. Win or lose, we go into the Army's
crapper on this. If anybody wants out, just say the word. No hard feelings. I don't want anybody getting burned that didn't want to go into
the kitchen in the first place."

"In for a penny, in for a pound," Grassi said through a mouthful of
sandwich. "That's what makes the world go round. Right, Cap'n?"

Harry ignored Grassi; there'd been no question in his mind about
the lieutenant's inclinations. But toward Ricks there was no remon-
strance, no bitterness. *You were right,* the captain felt Harry was telling him
now. *It is my call. And if you want out, it's all right.*

"Anybody can pull out," Harry repeated. "At any time. Understood?"

"Understood," Ricks replied.

Harry nodded. He had finished arranging the documents on the
table. He touched a single sheet of paper covered with the notes he'd
made after his first visit with DiGarre. "What about that sector ATC? The
one who picked up O'Connell?"

"Checks out with the general's story," Grassi said.

Harry touched Charlie Gresham's deposition. "And Gresham?"

"O'Connell was dead by the time he got him to the beach," said
Ricks. "If he said anything, the old man didn't hear it."

"The mechanic's report?"

Grassi again: "O'Connell's radio should've been working 5x5, right
up until Major Markham punched some .50-caliber holes in it."

Harry propped himself against the edge of the table. "That brings us
to the problem of O'Connell's silence. Something, Captain? A theory?"

"Just a thought. Nothing for the courtroom."

"We're not in the courtroom."

"You said this girlfriend of O'Connell's offered him a chance to go over the hill. He didn't go."

"He was too yellow to fly and too yellow to run," Grassi said dismissively. He reached for a second half-sandwich.

"Maybe," mused Ricks. "I just wonder if maybe he still felt some kind of obligation to the men he served with. That's why he kept going up. Maybe that's why he didn't say anything. Maybe he even understood why they did what they did."

"I wish he was around to explain it to me," Harry said. "OK, so we've still got to come up with something to fill that hole. We'll come back to it. The way I see it, there's a way we can pull this thing off and still maybe come out of it with our hides. To do that we've got to accomplish two things, the most obvious of which is to make as tight a legal case as we can. To do that with the jury panel DiGarre's probably going to stick us with means we won't be able to rely on circumstantial evidence. These guys are going to be looking for holes to let Markham and Anderson squirm through. That also means keeping conclusions to a minimum. Anything we can't substantiate with at least one half-decent piece of direct evidence we have to drop. If Van Damm can only point with certitude to twenty bodies on his recon photos, then we only go with twenty murder counts. If he says he can only—"

Grassi tossed his sandwich down with a disgusted flop. "You've got a whole damned town on fire—"

"That's how it's going to be!" Harry spoke with a quiet firmness that carried enough of an edge to silence the lieutenant. "And before we even go that far we're going back to Van Damm and ask, 'How do you know those're civilian bodies? Why can't they be military bodies?' I want answers from him and every other so-called expert we can grab that won't flap around in the wind. We only go with what's sound and sure.

"That's the legal end. The other side is this: Forget the law, right, wrong, and check the moral issues at the door. The brass are looking at this case from a point of military practicality, and right now they have a compelling military reason not to convict. So, the game is for us to advance a compelling military argument for conviction. So forget about making a big song and dance about Al Markham being the greatest mass murderer since Jack the Ripper. We don't care. He could've butchered puppy dogs and eaten children. That's not the Army's concern; it's not our concern. The main thrust of our prosecution will be that Al Markham exceeded his authority; that he was derelict in his duty; that his willful neglect cost the U.S. Army Air Corps Jacobs and McLagen, two good pilots who represented a substantial investment of government resources, as well as two very expensive aircraft.

"Is there enough to push for manslaughter charges on Jacobs and McLagen? If not, what can we get? Wrongful death? Negligence? Destruction of government property? Any damned thing, I don't care, but that's where the heart of our case is now. From now on, there is only one moral question in this case: whether or not Al Markham acted as a competent commander. Anything else, if it isn't irrelevant, is secondary."

It was a major adjustment for them to make, and Harry gave them time to absorb it. Ricks considered, but Grassi had made his appraisal even before Harry was finished. It was plainly evident on Grassi's face that the lieutenant's verdict was negative.

Harry ignored him. "Our one ace to play is that the jury panel has to convict on O'Connell. Between the evidence and Markham's confession, that's a given. That gives us a strong base to build on. We have to establish O'Connell as the climax of a pattern of abrogated responsibility. The Army may not have a conscience, but it does have a soul, and gentlemen, that soul is discipline. Disobedience will always be the military's mortal sin."

It was a perfectly logical strategy, but Grassi—as Harry anticipated—was not responding to logic. He saw only the largest prize slipping away. "You take that route," he said glumly, "and you might just get a conviction on everything but Helsvagen. By the time you're done hammering all this home, they might not give half a damn about what really happened out there!"

"I've considered that," Harry said coolly.

"Then what in Christ's name is the point?" Grassi demanded.

"As I said, anytime anybody's not happy with the way things are going . . ." He concluded by pointing to the door, which was enough to bring Grassi's hands up in surrender. Harry nodded, then gestured to the documentation spread across the table. "Our case is there, gentlemen. You two start assembling it. I'm going to try to get us another ace to play. No matter what a court-martial panel wants to do, they can't contravene a confession."

"Anderson?" Ricks guessed.

"Jesus!" Grassi stormed, flopping his sandwich down again. "You're not going to offer that flak-happy cowboy a deal, are you?"

Harry was unfazed by the outburst. "It's a gambit. I have to figure what we could gain against what we lose."

"He's an accomplice," Ricks said. "His testimony—"

"Isn't enough to convict, but with the recon photos as corroboration, I think Markham's nailed. I'm willing to trade Anderson's conviction for Markham's, because if we can turn Anderson, Markham has no defense. That's worth a deal."

"To you, maybe," Grassi said sourly.

"That's right. To me. Remember, Lieutenant, my opinion's the only one that counts."

Later, reminiscing about that moment, Ricks told me that in those few minutes in the conference room Harry Voss was no longer the slightly comic picture of a pudgy, middle-aged codger squeezed into a uniform. "For that moment," Ricks said reverentially, "he was the kind of lawyer I'd always hoped to be."

The Provost Marshal was housed in a former police station unobtrusively situated on a side street just fifteen minutes' walk from the Annex, a cottagelike structure of red brick wrapped in ivy. Inside the station Harry stopped at the front desk, shaking water from his brolly much to the disapproval of the young MP private at the counter, who scowled at the puddle Harry made on the wooden floor. Beyond the counter was a barred door leading to the cellar stairs. From below, Harry heard a faint and thin voice with only the most tentative hold on a melody, singing a few bars from "Someone's Rocking My Dreamboat."

Major Posner, the Provost, was on an inspection tour but in his stead the counter MP offered a smooth-faced lieutenant wearing an Officer of the Day brassard.

"Lieutenant Mathias," the officer introduced himself, trying to drop his reedy adolescent voice an octave or so.

"Major Voss, JAG," Harry replied and displayed his ID. "You're holding a Captain Anderson for us. I'd like to talk to him. If you'll check your records you'll see he's part of a case of mine."

Mathias went to one of the desks behind the counter and flipped through a leather-bound ledger. "So he is," he said finally. "We were just about to start serving the prisoners lunch."

"It is important." Harry tried not to sound dismissive of the lieutenant's priorities.

"I'll have to ask him if he wants to see you." Mathias took note of Harry's irritation. "Sorry, Major. It's your case and my jail, but it's his right."

The lieutenant headed for the barred cellar stairs. Harry called to him: "Lieutenant! If he says yes . . . someplace with a little privacy?"

Harry passed the wait shifting from one foot to the other. The rain had soaked through his shoes and his feet were cold and uncomfortable. He glanced about the foyer but there was no place to sit.

The phone rang. The desk private grunted a few acknowledgments into the receiver, rang off, and turned to Harry. "Follow me, Major? Oh, and um, why don't you leave the umbrella here?"

The private left him in a small interior room Harry guessed was used for interrogations. The four walls were blank, and there was scarcely room for the scuffed wooden table and two equally scuffed chairs. On the table was a C-ration can crammed with a half-dozen extinguished cigarettes. Harry lit himself a cigarette and left the package and matches on the table. He sat in one of the chairs and squeezed the cuff of one of his trouser legs. Water dripped steadily from the cloth.

He stirred at the sound of the door opening behind him. When it shut, there was Captain Jon-Jacob Anderson, his shirt, untucked and unbuttoned, advertising his muscled chest, his hands thrust into his pockets, leaning against the door as casually as a man waiting for a tram.

If Markham had offered a disappointing portrait of an air ace, Anderson seemed to have walked off the cinema screen. He was small-bodied but muscular, blessed with silky yellow hair, sparkling cornflower eyes, and a wide, cocky smile of bright, ruler-straight teeth. Hours of sun under a cockpit canopy had been gentle on his still-boyish looks, and afforded him a lustrous tan and a few lines of character about his eyes, the corners of his mouth, and across his forehead. When he smiled, the lines deepened in a pattern bespeaking good cheer rather than erosion.

"My guess," he said in his flat Kansas twang, "is y'ain't the Fuller Brush man."

Harry smiled politely. He nodded at the chair across the table. "Nothing says we can't be comfortable."

"I consider spendin' time in the calaboose a real big obstacle to bein' comfortable." Anderson reached across himself to scratch his left arm, which Harry noted hung at an unnaturally akimbo angle. He remembered the story of the Anderson youngster vaulting out of a Kansas hayloft, earning a compound fracture of the arm in the process.

Anderson shuffled by the table to the open chair. As he passed, Harry noted that the shuffling and pocketed hands had less to do with affecting an unconcerned air than they had practical application; his trouser belt and shoelaces had been confiscated. "Just a precaution," the Provost would tell Harry later. "He seemed a little hinky down there in the cells. Made me nervous just to watch him."

Anderson's face lit up at the sight of the package of cigarettes. One of his arms shot out, scooped up the package with the exclamation, "Fenhunks!" and he was soon puffing on one. He tossed the package back to Harry's side of the table. "That's somethin' I learned from ya Jersey boys. I hear that's where ya from, right? Jersey? Had a Jersey boy in the outfit way back when."

"Don't believe I'm acquainted with the ritual."

Anderson chuckled. " 'Acquainted with the ritual'. Jesus, ya even talk like a lawyer, lemme tell ya. He told me it was like callin' dibs on somethin'. Means ya gotta share."

Harry shrugged. "I was going to offer you one."

"Welll, in that case . . ." Anderson tipped a few extra cigarettes out. He dropped them into his breast pocket.

"Help yourself."

" 'Preciate it. Hey, it still rainin' outside?"

"Still."

"Good. Give the fellows a chance to stand down for a day or so. Cool things off, too. Not that we need to in here. Where we're at downstairs, it don't ever really get all that warm, lemme tell ya. I guess bein' in the jug worked out awright for me, huh? Down there where it's all nice 'n' cool, let all the rest o' ya poor bastards suffer through the summer."

"I'm glad this is working out so well for you," Harry said. He let a moment pass in which he held himself still.

Anderson shifted in his seat, and he scratched at his crooked arm. "So, at long last, huh?"

"At long last. I should remind you that you don't have to speak to me without—"

Anderson waved his cigarette dismissively about. "A lawyer's what ya need when ya got trouble."

"You don't think you're in trouble?"

Anderson's grin widened. He lapsed into a fair imitation of Curly of The Three Stooges: "I'm a victim of coicumstance!" The grin faded a bit. "Heard the news 'bout takin' Sicily coupla days ago. Guess it won't be too long 'fore we're on the mainland, hm? So, whatcha think? Think the war'll be over by the time I get outta here?"

Harry shrugged.

" 'At could mean a short stay or a looong war."

"It could mean it's up to you."

Anderson's grin turned wary. "Ah." One hand reached out and toyed with the book of matches on the table; Harry noticed the fingernails, bitten to the quick. "Now we're gettin' to it, huh? I figgered on this."

"You're a pretty smart guy, then."

"I thought so," he chuckled as he brushed at the cigarette ashes dribbling onto the table, "till I got myself put up in here. For nothin'! How smart can a guy be to wind up in the can for nothin'?"

"You hoping that if you say that often enough it'll come true?"

Anderson laughed, but there was an edge to it. "Ya just don't give up, do ya, Major? Lemme tell ya, I admire 'at! I wish ya'd use it on somebody a little more deservin', but I still admire 'at." He leaned forward, studying Harry with earnest curiosity. "Lemme ask ya; why ya got it in for us so bad? I heard 'bout ya, how back home ya was on yer uppers 'n' all. So's, I figger, OK, this guy wants to make himself a name or somethin', I understand 'at. I don't like it, but I understand it. But now I'm sittin' here lookin' at ya 'n' I don't see it. You don't look the shark type, so what is it?"

"They call you J. J.?"

"Used to be 'Jon-Jacob!' when my daddy got all steamed. 'Jon-Jacob, ya get yer bee-hind in this house right now, boy!' But to be friendly, make it J. J."

"Let's keep it friendly then. J. J., I'm not in this to see how many scalps I can put on my belt. I don't want to hang somebody that shouldn't be hung."

"Oh, ya think somebody's gonna hang? 'Cause a' what? I know what you think you got. I heard ya got yerself some pitchers from that whiz kid Van Damm got you thinkin' you got somethin'." The captain stood. He wanted to pace but there were just a few steps to any wall. Instead, he propped himself in a corner away from Harry, caressing his arm again as if to disperse a chill. "Lemme tell ya, Major, I *seen* those pitchers! Lemme tell ya somethin' else: I was *there*! Boy, oh boy, ya guys . . ."

"What guys?"

"*All* ya guys! Ya fly a desk 'n' ya think ya know somethin'! I was *there* when 'em tanks went up! Nothin' happened out there 'at wan' *suppose*' to happen 'n' lemme tell ya; when I saw those pitchers? I was surprised the place looked that goddamn *good*! 'At happens to be what the war looks like, Major."

Harry's cigarette began to taste flat and acrid. He dropped it into the C-ration can. "Sorry, J. J., I don't buy it. You're right: I don't know what happened out there. I've just got the evidence to go on. But don't tell me what I saw and Major Van Damm saw in those pictures is the way things are *supposed* to look out there. Make it make sense to me. Look, maybe it was a few strays. Maybe somebody got a head of steam up and couldn't stop. I don't know. You tell me."

"Al and me *been* tellin' ya! But y'ain't gonna hear what ya don't wanna hear!" Anderson shook his head as if he hadn't expected anything else. He sat back at the table, pulled two fresh cigarettes from Harry's pack, slipping one behind his right ear and lighting the second with the stub of the one he'd been smoking. "Lemme tell ya, Major, I ain't afraid of ya. They always say if yer innocent ya got nothin' to worry 'bout 'n' I-am-in-no-cent! Ya can't hang a fella for what he *didn't* do." Anderson spat out a fleck of tobacco. His grin turned malevolent. "Lemme tell ya who in this room is scared. You, Major. 'At's why yer here."

"J. J., you get an earful of one of the cracker-barrel jailhouse lawyers that hang around a place like this and you think he sounds like he knows what he's talking about so you listen to him. Let me clear up a point or two for you upon which your legal advisor of the moment may have failed to enlighten you. The *least* I have Markham for is killing Dennis O'Connell. I've got that locked up with ballistics evidence and testimony from two eyewitnesses—whom your friend also tried to take out!"

Harry leaned forward in his chair, crossing his arms in front of him on the table. "Here's the part you really need to listen to, J. J. You were there. You watched it, you didn't do a damned thing to stop it, you didn't even do a damned thing to report it. That's conspiracy, complicity, aiding and abetting, compounding a felony, accessory after the fact, concealing evidence, making false reports, conduct unbecoming, and I can probably make it into a few other things, too. Forget everything else: On just O'Connell's murder, if by some miracle you don't hang, you won't see daylight until you're old enough to try out Mr. Roosevelt's Social Security program." He leaned back and softened his tone. "You made some bad choices, but I understand; Al is your buddy. You served together, you fought together. That doesn't mean you have to go to the gallows together."

For the first time Anderson's grin disappeared.

Harry continued. "I've got more than O'Connell's death. General DiGarre doesn't seem to think my case is as shaky as you do. In fact, he's so afraid it'll stick he's willing to promise me that you *and* Markham'll go to the gallows if I *don't* bring up Helsvagen. That solves an awful lot of messy problems for them, J. J. So that's it. No matter how I prosecute, Al Markham's a dead man. I don't lift a finger and he hangs on O'Connell. The only question for you is, Do you want to hang with him?"

They sat for a long while, Harry watching Anderson, Anderson watching the cigarette in his fingers burn down. Then the captain flicked the long ash onto the table and reached across to scratch at his misaligned elbow. "What it is is ya want me to sell him out."

"I want you to testify for the Judge Advocate."

"I finger 'im for ya 'n' ya go easy on me."

"I want you to tell the truth."

"Truth is," and Anderson looked up, his blue eyes wide and fixed on Harry's, "I don't know what happened out there."

Harry blinked, confused. "Come again?"

"I don't know what happened, Major. I testify for ya, 'at's gonna be a lie. I testify for Al, 'n' 'at'll be a lie, too."

"Captain, your debriefing report states that after you made your runs on Helsvagen, you flew top cover for Angel Red—Markham's section—and then withdrew with Markham. What're you saying now?"

"I *wanted* to stay with Al, but he ordered me to light out after O'Connell. He knew O'Connell's ship was hurt 'n' he wanted me to fly cover for 'im. Me? I coulda given less a damn 'bout O'Connell. Little turd goes down? Fuck 'im. But lemme tell ya, Al wouldn't have it, no sir. Ordered me out after 'im. I didn't tell nobody 'cause 'at meant Al's section went in on their runs with their ass wide open. It was stupid for 'im to go in open like 'at, 'n' I figgered he was in deep enough trouble, so I said I was there. Truth is, Major, I don't have the goddamnedest idea what went on at Helsvagen after I left."

Had Anderson punched Harry square on the nose, it wouldn't've left him any more flummoxed. It was a perfectly logical, perfectly plausible, perfectly inarguable story, and it left Harry absolutely no maneuvering room. Harry could see Anderson's eyes narrowing in study. *Don't show him he rocked you,* he told himself. He settled in his chair, relaxed, smiled as he shook his head appreciatively. "That's a hell of a story, Captain. A hell of a story! But get this through that plowboy head of yours: Even if a jury panel buys it, that doesn't get you off the hook for O'Connell. Your only way out on that one is *me.*"

Anderson's face turned sad. He stood and shuffled to the door and knocked. The door opened, revealing the escorting turnkey outside. Anderson sniffed at a heavy aroma of hash and potatoes in the air and his grin returned. "Ahh. Luncheon is served. Would you like me to ask 'em to set another plate, Major?"

Harry stood and tossed the package of cigarettes to Anderson. "For dessert."

"Obliged."

The turnkey stood at Anderson's elbow and followed him down the hall, Harry tailing behind. At the counter, the turnkey led Anderson to the barred door leading to the cells downstairs.

"Hey, Major," Anderson called, "let's say you win this thing, 'n' me 'n' Al . . . well, you know . . ." He smiled as he drew his index finger across his throat. "Whatcha gonna do when you find out you was wrong? You sleep on 'at tonight, Major." Anderson made a pistol of his throat-slashing hand, aimed it at Harry, and fired.

Harry watched the heavy door clang shut behind them and heard the captain's tenor on the stairwell: singing about someone rocking his dreamboat.

"It's simple," Grassi declared. "He's cutting Markham loose. He knows it's time to save his own ass."

Harry had found Grassi and Ricks still hard at work in the conference room. He sat on the windowsill, enjoying the breezes that had come with the rain, and recounted his conversation with Jon-Jacob Anderson. Ricks had taken the story with his usual quiet contemplation, but Grassi had a ready opinion.

"That was my first thought," Harry responded. "But you want to hear something funny? After they took Anderson back to his cell I sent word to Markham that I wanted to talk to him. Thought I'd bounce all this off him and see what happened, maybe shake him up a bit. Markham wouldn't see me. So, I sent down a note with the gist of Anderson's story. He still wouldn't see me."

"He didn't believe it," Grassi explained, untroubled.

"Maybe," Harry said. "I asked the guards down there to keep an eye on the two of them, let me know if they talked to each other. Not the content of the conversation," he added in deference to the perturbed look on Ricks's face. "We wouldn't want to intrude on a private conversation, would we? Just if they talked." Harry glanced at his watch. "It's almost an hour and I haven't gotten a call. If I was sitting where Markham is, and I got word that my codefendant—and my only defense corroboration— was throwing me to the wolves, I'd want to ask him about it. These two have been flying buddies for four years. You'd think one of them would at least say, 'How'd it go?' when the other one comes back from a meeting with the prosecutor. But not even a hello."

"Look, Boss, you're the one that's always going on about what a cool cookie Markham is," said Grassi. "Maybe he just doesn't want us to know he's spooked."

"There's another possibility," Ricks said. "Markham's been taking us through series of fallback positions, only giving ground when he has to. He comes back from the August fifteenth raid, MP's show up to hold him, but he doesn't open his mouth. We press harder, and he cops to

O'Connell's murder, hoping that's where we'll stop. But we get beyond that. So now he has to retrench again. It's possible he and Anderson rigged this story together about Anderson cutting out."

"Why?" Grassi demanded.

"There's no direct evidence putting Anderson in the air at Helsvagen during Markham's attack," Ricks replied. "There's not even a circumstantial tie. His debriefing says he was there and saw nothing, now he says he *wasn't* there, that he was already on his way home when Markham's section attacked. Threatening him with filing a false report is hardly going to shake him up, not when the alternative is a charge of accessory to multiple murder counts. If Anderson holds to this story that he wasn't there, and we can't crack it, it removes him as a defense witness *and* as a possible prosecution tool."

Grassi was shaking his head, not wanting to accept an unpalatable possibility. "You said that was only part of it."

Ricks and Harry exchanged a look of understanding. Harry took up the thread now. "Anderson's Markham's friend. It's not Anderson cutting Markham loose. It's the other way around. Markham's trying to save Anderson."

"And there's always this, Harry," Ricks said. "We have to consider the possibility—unpleasant as it may be for you—that Anderson's telling the truth."

"Truth? Never heard of it. Not in this case." Grassi turned to Harry. "So the trip to Anderson is a scratch."

"Not quite." The rain had tapered to a sporadic dappling, and great seams of warm light were beginning to lance through the cloud cover. Harry slid from the windowsill. "Damn." Dampness had seeped along the sill, leaving a wet stripe across the seat of his trousers.

"You were saying," Grassi prodded, unconcerned with Harry's predicament.

"No matter what Markham wants and Anderson says, Anderson is in the crosshairs on O'Connell." Harry thought back to the captain's sun-lined but youthful face. It was not unflappable, he was certain of it. "Let him stew for a while. It might take him a bit to see how far in the frying pan he's sitting. Now, why don't you boys show me what you've put together for me so far?"

•   •   •

I found myself spending the better part of the day watching the rain sluice through the soot on the windowpanes of our Fleet Street offices. I would look at my familiar desk and all the other familiar desks about me in the newsroom manned by familiar faces doing familiar tasks and I thought how nice it would be, even for a moment, not to be so familiar with it all.

"You seem to be taking an inordinate interest in the weather," Himself noted, drawing a chair up to my desk. "Thinking of writing the meteorological column?"

Normally such lackadaisical conduct would have earned me a frown from The Boss, along with a growling ha-rumph and possibly some drollery about how perhaps he could grant me more time to pursue this new climatological interest of mine by relieving me of the burdens of a job. But instead came a dark, concerned look under the heavy brow. He'd never seen me behave this way and, frankly, it was new—and equally unsettling—to me as well. He sat quietly for the moment, not looking to probe, waiting for me to volunteer, but all I could offer was a shrug. "You haven't had a proper holiday since you've been back," he finally said. "Perhaps it's due."

I began to say something along the lines of how unnecessary the offer was, that it was, oh, just the effect of the weather, my leg, the weather on my leg, too much scotch, a coming illness, whatever, but he spoke over me.

"No need to play good soldier, my son. I'm sure a few days holiday'll see you right. Do something new with the time; try to enjoy yourself." Then he grunted out of his seat and began to walk past, back to his sanctum. I felt him stop behind me, saw his hand out of the corner of my eye hover over my shoulder, unsure, then it came down in a fleeting, awkward pat. "Maybe see some old friends," he mumbled and left.

He meant one old acquaintance, really. I headed home. But the thought of another evening of kippers and whiskey stopped me and turned me round toward Mayfair. I reached the Annex gate not long after the rain had lifted. I sent word through the sentries to Harry, and soon he was carefully stepping across the rain-glistened cobbles. As soon as he was close enough to recognize me, his jowled face broke into a welcoming smile.

"I thought since it's turning into an absolutely wizard evening you might care to dine alfresco tonight."

"Al-who?"

"Out-of-doors."

He seemed enthused at the prospect and left me for a moment while he ran back inside for his hat and jacket. As I watched him skirt the puddles in the Annex yard and try not to slip on the court's stones, Mr. Dodgson's verse came discomfortingly to me:

> "*The time has come,*" *the Walrus said,*
> "*To talk of many things . . .*"

We took the Underground to Baker Street and, returning to the street, found the evening brightening and fresh after the rain. I treated us to newspaper funnels of fish and chips and two bottles of ale from the shops. We strolled along Marylebone Road, munching on the greasy bits of fish, enjoying the buskers. Here was a young flautist, and a bit beyond him some ancient duffer with a banjo affecting a bad American Southern accent. One of us would toss a few pence into the upturned hat at their feet and on we'd go. I navigated us into Regent's Park, past the marshy patches left by the rains, across York Bridge and into Queen Mary's Gardens. We found a bench and sat, finishing our food, sipping our ale, enjoying the scents of the garden's blooms. From the other side of the Inner Circle, beyond the hedges, we could hear a recitation of some sort at the open-air theater. The sun dipped below the horizon, and the sky's rich mauve began to slip into the blue of early night. We wiped the grease from our hands with our handkerchiefs, disposed of the wrappings in a nearby bin, then reclined on our bench to savor the remains of our ale and an occasionally well-delivered phrase of the Bard from the theater. I lit us cigarettes.

"That was a nice change of pace," Harry said through a satisfied sigh, sucking at a bit of food caught between his teeth.

"Aye, I'm for that as well," I said. "Rarely have the time, I'm afraid. I'm sure you know the feeling."

He shrugged.

"I mean," I continued, "you have been a busy sort of late, eh?"

It began to register with him that this was not just a point of idle conversation. "What makes you say that?"

It was my turn to shrug.

He frowned. "Are you some kind of spy?"

"Not quite." And then I told him what I was. I knew it would sting but the honesty leavened, for the first time, the mood I'd felt all day.

His face had gone oddly blank. I'm not sure he knew how to take it. After a bit, he slowly set his ale down on the bench, then looked upward to the first stars poking through the darkening canopy. "You've been following me all along," he said softly. "Even before the other day in the park."

"I'm caught then."

He lowered his head and cleared his throat, and assumed a rather diffident cordiality. "And your interest in me would be . . . ?"

"What would you think?" It was the old familiar journalistic game, and I was sorry to see us become players. I wished I'd found another way to broach the subject, but the habits of the profession were hard to break. He said nothing and so it was my move again: "Perhaps the Greshams. Perhaps that dead flier of yours who's on the postmortem table at the Yard. Or perhaps something else. Something that would cause a frightful lot of running between Rosewood Court and General DiGarre's HQ and the Provost Marshal and G-2 . . ."

It may not have been much—just bits and pieces, really—but he was clearly surprised at how much someone knew outside the Annex cloister. For a moment I thought he'd tell all. It was in his eyes: He wanted it out, cleansingly exposed, as I had with my own nasty secret. But the moment passed and he stood, straightening his uniform jacket. He snuffed his cigarette out. "Any questions about possible Judge Advocate General investigations should be addressed to the Press Office—"

"Sit down, Harry. Please."

Instead, he took a few slow, backward steps, as if afraid to turn his back on me, the way one would back away from a growling dog.

"Harry, I'm not your enemy. I'm not here to hurt you. We've been talking as mates. I'd like that to stay the case. Please, sit."

After a hesitation he did. I handed him his bottle of ale.

"Drink your drink," I said, raising my own bottle.

"How much do you really know?" he asked, not taking his.

"You know the stories about the monster at Loch Ness? I don't know that there is any such beastie but I know there's something big afoot round the loch because *something's* been leaving bloody great tracks. That's what I see in your neighborhood, my friend. I don't know what you're all on about over there, not entirely, but there is definitely *something* big afoot. I don't know how well acquainted you are with big things afoot, Harry, so I wanted to tell you, to *advise* you; walk carefully round them. It's times like this when you discover too many of your colleagues—people like your friend Colonel Ryan—have a bit of the Vicar of Bray about them."

He cocked his head in question.

I smiled. "There's an old English verse about Symon Symonds who managed to keep his church office under Henry VIII, Edward VI, Bloody Mary, and Elizabeth. Symonds was Catholic when he needed to be Catholic, and Protestant when he needed to be Protestant. 'If I changed my religion'—this is how the verse goes—'I am sure I kept true to my principle, which is to live and die the Vicar of Bray.' Understand?"

He nodded glumly.

"If you need me, Harry . . . even just to talk," and I told him how to reach me. We finished our ales and I walked with him, back to the Underground and then to the Annex gate. After he showed his identification, the sentries opened the gate for him but he didn't pass through immediately. "Can I trust you?" he asked.

"You can trust me to tell you when you can't."

He nodded a good night and was off, the heavy iron gate clanging shut behind him.

Harry slept fitfully, no doubt a result of our conversation that evening. Consequently, he was so fagged out the following morning that he slept through reveille, the orderlies' morning wake-up rounds, and his own alarm clock. He would've slept through the ringing of his telephone except that the ringing went on so insistently long. Groggy and irritable, he fumbled the receiver out of its cradle and then fell back on his pillow with it nestled near his ear.

"Are you coming to work today?" came a churlishly abrupt voice.

"Nagel?"

"I shouldn't have to keep calling you to ask you this every—"

"What time is it?"

"Oh nine hundred. Nine A.M."

"I know what time 0900 is," Harry growled. "Yeah, I'll be in."

"There's a messenger on his way to you. He was over here with a sealed YEO envelope. He wouldn't let me—"

"YEO?"

"Your Eyes Only. He wouldn't let me sign for it so he's on his way over to you now. He thought you'd be in your office since it's already—"

"If you tell me the time again, Nagel, I'll hurt you. I'll be there as soon as—" There was a knock at his door. "Bye, Nagel."

Nagel began to say something more but Harry had already dropped the receiver into its cradle.

The knock was, indeed, the messenger Nagel had mentioned. Harry signed a chit for a thin manila envelope sealed with red security tape and marked TO: MAJOR HAROLD J. VOSS, JAG, EYES ONLY.

Far later, Harry was charging across the Annex toward "Judge Advocate General—Building A" in clothes hastily drawn on, the sheaf of flimsies from the envelope clutched in an angry fist. He pushed through the door stenciled "Col. J. P. Ryan, Judge Advocate." In the outer office, a razor-creased corporal sat outside Ryan's door. The corporal rose, waving halting hands at Harry, but Harry brushed him aside and stormed into Ryan's sanctum. Sitting with Ryan in his spacious, airy office were a captain and a lieutenant Harry recognized from the JAG staff. Harry held up his fistful of flimsies. "What the hell is this?"

Ryan raised himself slowly from behind his desk, his face hard with anger and annoyance. "This—" and he waved his hand at the captain and the lieutenant, "—is a conference, Major."

"Now you're in conference with me!" Harry declared.

Harry's uncharacteristic assertiveness took Ryan aback and it was a moment before he recovered. He weighed his options, then nodded the other two officers outside.

Harry waited for the door to close behind them, then started jabbing the wad of flimsies at Ryan. "Now what is—"

"Before you even get started, be quiet and listen!" Ryan snapped. He parried Harry's thrusting fist of paper with his own jabbing index finger. "At General DiGarre's perfectly legitimate request, I rendered a perfectly legitimate opinion."

"I should've been consulted! This is *my* case, and I—"

"I apologize for the lapse in protocol, Major, but maybe you didn't notice the sign on my door: I'm the Judge Advocate here. Let me put that in plainer terms: I'm the *boss!*" Ryan dabbed at the spittle gathering at the corners of his mouth. He forced control on his voice. "Nothing's changed on this case. You're still free to pursue your investigation and file whatever charges you see fit. But right now, you could tell me those two were planning to assassinate Eisenhower and I wouldn't have the authority to detain them, not with DiGarre having authorized their release."

"You could make a case that—"

"As long as they make their appearances, I'm not going to make word one!"

"You could make a case to continue their detention here."

"I could. But I've got no cause to get into another fight I can't win."

"All right," Harry steamed. "All *right!* Just so I know what kind of *crap* I'm dealing with!"

Ryan's eyes came up now, locking unflinchingly with Harry's. "Major," he said icily, "this kind of crap is exactly the *same* kind of crap that's been going on since this thing started! Don't play the bleeding virgin with me just because you've got yourself on the wrong side of it now!"

"You interfere with my case, and after I nail these guys—and I *will*— I swear to God, Joe, I'll come after *you*—with contempt, abuse of authority, a baseball bat! I *will* come after you!"

Harry slammed the door so hard behind him he was surprised it didn't shatter.

He later showed me those flimsies. I render copies herewith:

MEMORANDUM

TO:	Colonel Joseph P. Ryan	cc: Maj. H.J. Voss, JAG
	Judge Advocate	
FROM:	Lt. Gen. T. Q. DiGarre	
DATE:	8/19/43	
RE:	Markham/Anderson Investigation	

Since the combat operations of my division must naturally take precedence over all other administrative matters, the continued effective management of my combat forces requires I get from you ASAP a rendering on this matter. Reply forthwith.

MEMORANDUM

TO:	Lt. Gen. T. Q. DiGarre
	Divisional HQ
FROM:	Col. Joseph P. Ryan, JAG
DATE:	8/19/43
RE:	Markham/Anderson Investigation

cc: Maj. H.J. Voss, JAG

Under separate cover you will be receiving a formal filing by the JAG requesting and granting a motion for dismissal without prejudice concerning charges thus far raised against Markham/Anderson.

So you may better understand the legal ramifications of this filing: This in no way dispenses the case against Markham/Anderson. This motion provides only a temporary dismissal and allows a revival of charges at a later date.

Since the scope of the initial JAG investigation has obviously expanded past the expectations of all concerned, this would permit the IO to more properly revisit evidence thus far uncovered for a more appropriate application of charges. I would estimate this renewed investigation to produce grounds for formal charges in 3–6 weeks.

MEMORANDUM

TO:	Colonel Joseph P. Ryan
	Judge Advocate
FROM:	Lt. Gen. T. Q. DiGarre
DATE:	8/20/43
RE:	Markham/Anderson Investigation

cc: Maj. H.J. Voss, JAG

Have received your formal rendering and concur.

In interim, as no charges are currently outstanding, there remains no justification for continued detention of Markham/Anderson. Consequently, I am authorizing their release. Pressing need for combat pilots mandates returning Markham/Anderson to active duty pending reapplication of charges, but they will remain at JAG disposal as required.

ORDER #16/8/20/43

TO: Lt. Col. James T. Eckhardt   cc: Maj. H.J. Voss, JAG
CO 52 Group
Elsworth Airfield
FROM: Lt. Gen. T. Q. DiGarre
DATE: 8/20/43
RE: Personnel Assignment

Be apprised that Maj. A. Q. Markham, Capt. J. J. Anderson herewith assigned your group.

Markham/Anderson are subjects in JAG proceeding. Decision not forthcoming before 3 weeks. Recognize your need for qualified combat pilots. Have taken liberty of assigning Markham/Anderson your unit pending decision on their case.

Markham/Anderson should not be subject to question re: case by field personnel, yourself included. Suggest you quarter together and assign as unit. Markham/Anderson to have functioning authority of 1st lt. Duty assignments to be made at your discretion, however Markham/Anderson shall make themselves available as required by JAG.

ORDER #17/8/20/43

TO: Maj. A. Q. Markham   bcc: Maj. H.J. Voss, JAG
Capt. J. J. Anderson
FROM: Lt. Gen. T. Q. DiGarre
DATE: 8/20/43
RE: Reassignment

JAG has rendered temporary repeat temporary dismissal of charges against you effective as of now. It is expected that formal charges will be refiled within several weeks with anticipated probability of court-martial proceedings soon to follow.

In interim you are hereby ordered to present yourselves ASAP for active duty assignment to CO 52 Group, Elsworth Afld. However, you will at all times hold yourselves at disposal of JAG pursuant to your case.

While your actions with the 52 cannot be admitted in your favor, poor performance and failure to meet JAG requirements cannot help but prejudice your case. Recommend you continue to conduct yourselves in manner that best reflects on yourselves, your unit, and your service.

CHAPTER TEN

THE CHILDREN'S CRUSADE

THE NEGRO MESS BOYS WERE BUSY with mops and rags, replenishing the sparkle of the canteen tables, floors, and counters in preparation for noon mess. Alone except for the mess boys, Harry, Ricks, and Grassi sat with their coffee and cigarettes in a corner of the canteen.

"What I got was the back-and-forth between Ryan and DiGarre happened late last night," said Grassi. Every word out of his mouth, point of information or no, was a snarling accusation. "Get this: They handed the release order to the Provost at 0430 this morning. Talk about sneaking them off in the dead of night! Do you *believe* these sons of bitches? They were dressed, packed, and on their way in ten minutes." Grassi glanced at his watch. "They should be nice and settled in by now. Charlie Paddock should move this fast. *Goddamn* these guys! They make pirates look respectable!"

The frowning Ricks nodded in glum agreement.

Throughout Grassi's fulminations and Ricks's brooding concern, Harry had sat blank-faced, staring out the canteen window. It was actually quite a nice day out there, fresh and vibrant from the rain the day before. He wanted to be as angry as Grassi, rant about Ryan and DiGarre and the whole HQ cabal and their sly maneuverings, but he knew—as he'd known the first time he had faced DiGarre—that anger, effrontery, righteous indignation, no matter how well warranted, wouldn't win him his case. *Think* ...

"What do we do now?" Grassi fumed. "Go back to DiGarre and his deal? Do you think that deal is even still on the table?"

"Probably," Harry said, with what Grassi no doubt interpreted as misplaced unconcern but what was really careful thoughtfulness. "It's in his interest to leave that option to us. It'll be there at least up to trial."

Grassi shook his head in disbelief. "*What* trial? Correct me if I'm wrong, Boss, but didn't the bogeymen sneak over to the Provost's in the wee dark hours and spirit off our defendants?"

"I don't know about you fellows, but I'm not that well acquainted with this 'dismissal without prejudice' business," Ricks said. "So I've been doing a little homework. As I understand it, it's only a temporary—"

"Temporary shmemporary!" Grassi blurted. "Hey, you know where this Elsworth Field is? I checked. All the way the hell up past Norwich, maybe a hundred and fifty miles north of here! Hold themselves at our disposal my ass! I can *see* how *this* is going to run. 'Excuse me, the JAG would like Major Markham and Captain Anderson to present themselves for a deposition. Could you *please* have them come down to London for us?' 'Oh, sorry, Bud, they're off beating back the filthy Hun today. I'll give them the message when they come in.' "

"Then *we* go up *there*," Ricks said. "They have to come back sometime from beating back the filthy Hun."

Grassi had a caustic rejoinder half out of his mouth, but Harry raised a hand for silence. He nodded toward Ricks. "You were saying about 'dismissal without prejudice.' "

"It's normally a bid to keep the prosecutor's hand in a case that hasn't jelled yet. The prosecutor's saying, 'All right, we made charges, we investigated, we haven't found enough to make the charges stick. But there's enough here for us to keep looking, and if we find something we'll be back.' "

Harry turned to Grassi. "Before you get yourself any further into a lather, have you asked yourself why Ryan didn't just quash this thing?"

Grassi's mouth opened but, as was often the case, he had done so without considering what he'd actually say. His mouth closed.

"Let's not take these memos at face value," Harry said. "Assume there's a conversation behind them. You can bet your GI shirt a flat-out dismissal was high on DiGarre's Christmas list, and you can also bet Ryan would've given his eyeteeth to give him one. But there's too much evidence on the table. My sense from DiGarre is there's a lot of parties interested in this case. Maybe that interest runs to SHAEF, maybe White-hall, maybe further. People want to know what went wrong when the 351st got pasted last week, what's gone wrong with it this week, and what's somebody going to do about it. DiGarre's no dummy, trust me, but he may have painted himself into a corner here. He precipitated when he sacked Halverson. Now he's got no fall guy; he's the one on the spot now. He can't just turn the investigation off. Think about it: Halver-son starts the investigation, DiGarre cans Halverson, then calls it off? That's a sequence that screams that the general's got something to hide. We can claim he squelched the investigation to cover his own butt, and that's how it'll look. DiGarre's got to let this go to trial and hope for an acquittal. He's got no choice; that's the only thing that permanently puts all questions to rest. If we lose, any complaints we make get written off as plain old sour grapes."

"If we lose?" Grassi mocked. "If I was the general I wouldn't sweat that too much."

"I don't think we're played out yet," Harry said.

"You still think that discipline argument has a chance?" Ricks asked him.

"It's not quite the blasphemy of murder and mayhem DiGarre's ex-pecting us to present."

Grassi, as most fervent men are, was reluctant to give up his fervor. "What about Markham and Anderson?"

"What about them?" Harry asked casually.

"We still don't have access, not unless you want to take the captain's advice and spend the next three weeks sitting on our duffs up at Els-worth trying to catch them."

"To hell with Markham and Anderson," Harry said. "Unless one of them confesses, which I'm sure you'll agree is unlikely, all you'll get from a trip up there is more b.s. All we really need to do over the next few weeks is show the flag up there, and that's primarily for Anderson's benefit. Right now, I'll bet that little cracker's thinking he's clear of this.

We need to let J. J. know we haven't forgotten him. Let him sweat a bit over the next couple of weeks. That's a long time to sweat."

Harry fell silent. Then he said, "They're desperate. This was just the first round. It was a good one for them, but all Ryan could do was provide DiGarre with some breathing space to try to figure a next move. As long as they're providing that kind of time, let's use it to our advantage.

"Pete, in the beginning you were worried we were moving too fast. Now we've got the time to go back over our evidence carefully, time to go back to our witnesses and talk to them again, a proper follow-up, now that we know what we're dealing with. Maybe Van Damm and those whiz kids of his have come up with something new for us. They can't close the door all the way on us fellas, so let's see if we can't push it back open a bit."

"As long as we have this kind of time, maybe we can take a little breather ourselves," Grassi said with a yawn. "The way we've been going, everything's starting to run together in my head."

"I'm surprised to hear myself admit it," Ricks said, "but I agree with Armando. If I might make a prudent suggestion—"

"Do you ever do anything but?" Grassi jibed.

Ricks ignored him. "—a little time off might not be a bad idea. Tired men make mistakes. Say we resume tomorrow after Sunday services?"

Grassi smiled mockingly. If he worshiped at all on Sunday mornings it was from his bunk.

Harry stood. "It *has* been a bear of a week. Why don't we make it Monday morning?"

"No argument there!" Grassi trumpeted.

Ricks turned to Grassi, feigning a look of being impressed. "No argument? What a welcome change of pace!"

"Hey, Boss, hear that?" Grassi hooted. "The captain made a funny!"

Harry allowed himself a small chuckle.

But Harry did not heed his own advice. He did not put the case away but sat in his quarters poking through his notes and files. He considered going down to the canteen for something to eat, or maybe even a stroll to The Old Eagle, but standing at his window he saw Ryan down in the yard crossing the cobbles for the gates, and decided instead to have the canteen bring food up.

After dining in his quarters he slid open one of his escritoire drawers and drew out a framed photograph of Cynthia and the children. In the photo all three were standing in a park against a field of blossoming cherry trees. Evidently they had come straight from church, Cynthia wearing a dark suit with a matching ribbon in her hair, and the boys flanking her with forced smiles as they chafed in their miniature suits. In the black-and-white photo, the slender streaks of gray in her hair had disappeared. He had made a practice of not displaying the photo as the other married men did, keeping it something private. Leaving the photo out, he drew a sheet of V-mail paper from the escritoire and began to write:

Cyn—

I miss you.

Nothing else came. He thought of crumpling it up, but then thought the better of it, signed it, and sealed the fragile little message in an envelope. He called for an orderly and had the envelope placed with the outgoing post.

The fine day began to come to a premature close late in the afternoon as a fresh rank of storm clouds pushed in over the city. With the early dusk, Harry tuned the wireless to soft music, sat at his lamp table, drew on his reading spectacles, and turned to The Dain Curse, which he had set down five nights before. As he tried to pick up the thread of the story, struggling to recall what he'd already read, those five nights began to feel like an eon.

When he awoke, the book had toppled to the floor, the sky was black, and the breeze through the open window was damp with rain. Distant thunder rumbled like far-off artillery, and lightning presented a short-lived frieze of rooftops and cloudscapes framed by Harry's window. He was surprised that no one on the night watch had called to him to draw his blackout curtains or douse his lamplight. Perhaps in the rain such precautions were academic. He glanced at his watch but it had wound down, stilled just before midnight. He guessed it to be quite late since there was no music from the wireless, only a low hum broken by a crackle of static sparked by the flashes of lightning. He picked up his volume of Hammett, set it down on the lamp table and his spectacles alongside. He sat a moment, rubbing his tired eyes, then switched off the lamp.

At first he thought the rattle came from his fumbling for the lamp chain, but then he realized it came from elsewhere in the room: the door. The noise stopped and he sat still in his chair. Someone passing in the hall? Or, he thought only half facetiously, ghosts. But ghosts did not leave shadows and, in the dim light under his door, Harry could see a shadow.

It was too dark to see but Harry heard the doorknob turning, first one way, then another. Another thing ghosts did not do was fumble for keys, and now Harry heard them jangling as they stabbed at the lock.

He stood, telling himself there was no reason to be afraid, this was obviously a simple mistake on someone's part, nothing more. But his heart accelerated, beating a little harder, sounding a little louder in his ears.

Now he heard the sounds of someone trying to force the key into the lock.

Harry turned off the wireless, thinking this might help inform the keyholder that the room was already occupied. The scratching at the lock didn't stop.

"Yes?" Harry called out, his voice tight and high enough to embarrass him.

The noises stopped.

Curious now, Harry took a few steps toward the door, his hand reaching for the glass knob. As his fingers touched it, the knob jumped in his hand as something akin to a cannonball pounded the other side of the door. Harry jumped back. *Bang!* It came again, the door shuddering, and then again.

His mind was oddly clear. He was terrified, yet another part of his brain was scientifically analytical about what was being used on the door. What could the intruder have found in the hall to use? A chair? Yet still another part of his mind declared that only a complete loon would calmly stand by investing his time in such pointless observations.

He went to the window and tried calling across the courtyard to the gate MP's, but his voice was lost in the storm. He went to his telephone and dialed the orderly room. He held a hand over his heart, but it didn't deaden the pounding in his ears and he could barely hear the answering voice in the receiver.

"This is Major Voss in—" He blinked. Now, wasn't *that* funny? He couldn't remember his room number.

"Yes, Major?"

They'd know the number, he told himself. Of course. "There's someone trying to break into my room." He strained to keep his voice even.

"Now?"

"Yes, they're in the hall right now. Could you send someone up as soon as possible?"

"On the—"

Lightning flared, very close this time, and instead of a dull rumble, the thunder came as a sharp, startling *crack!* that rattled the windowpanes. The phone went dead. Harry set the receiver down. He turned to the door.

The pounding had continued but a new noise had been added: a cracking and splintering of wood. In the next flash of lightning Harry could see the door beginning to buckle down the middle. He found himself stepping backward until he was against the wall farthest from the door.

New sounds: footsteps. Then scuffling. Then silence.

A knock. "Major Voss?"

It took Harry a few seconds to find his voice. "Yes?"

"Corporal Yelavich, Major. Military Police."

Harry suddenly realized he was panting.

In the hall, beams of electric torches flashed about. In the swaths of light Harry could make out three MP's: the corporal at the door and two others standing over a figure slumped on the floor. Harry recognized him as the captain from Oklahoma he'd found sitting in his damp bathrobe in the orderly room the night of the air raid. The captain smelled heavily of whiskey and was mumbling drunkenly into his collar. Nearby, Harry could see a fire extinguisher on the floor, its bottom rim dented and scuffed.

"You all right, Major?" The MP corporal looked concerned.

Harry could feel the sheet of sweat across his forehead. "Sure. Fine. What happened to the—"

The lights flickered and resumed their liverish glow.

"Ah, here they come," the corporal said. "Musta been the storm. You sure you're OK, Major? He give you a scare, sir?"

Harry shrugged.

The corporal pointed to the captain. "Captain Bowman," and the corporal made some bottle-tipping motions. "Overdid it a bit, know what I mean? It happens. He's got the room right below yours. Got himself a little confused is all. We can haul 'im down to the Provost if you wanna press charges."

"No, no, that won't be necessary. Just get him to bed."

"By tomorrow, he may not even 'member he did this. I'll see he knows, make sure he apologizes."

"No need."

"I'll have someone come up about the door in the morning."

"All right. Thanks, Corporal."

"Have a good night, Major."

"Right. Thanks."

It was hours before Harry fell asleep. Though he didn't remember his dreams, they must have been nightmares; he was drenched with sweat when he awoke the next morning.

As a rule, Harry had not attended Sunday services since coming overseas earlier that year. In part, this was because of the difficulty of finding a practicing Russian Orthodox congregation in central London. But there was another more important reason. He had, on occasion, sat in a variety of churches, even attended a service at Westminster. But church service had reminded him of worship at home, his wife on one side, his older boy to the other, and his youngest son on his lap. The memory offered more heartache than solace.

This Sunday, he enjoyed breakfast at his window, drinking in the rain-burnished morning along with his somewhat less savory plate of Spam and powdered eggs, then tended to his morning toilet, pulled on a fresh uniform, and attended services at a small Anglican chapel a few blocks from the Annex. Heartache or no, it was still a touch of home and this day he found himself sorely needing it, for he had lost Joe Ryan.

Harry could never forgive Ryan's conduct over those last few days, but neither could he forget a lifelong friendship. They'd grown up together, and Ryan had been just about Harry's only friend since he'd come into the service, and particularly during their time in London. Though caustic and condescending, self-absorbed, self-indulgent, and self-seeking, Ryan had always been his guardian, getting him into the Army, helping him to his majority, feeding him choice cases including, ironically enough, this last one. To Harry, who had never been farther than a few hours' drive from his home, Ryan's companionship throughout these months overseas, and that bit of home he represented, had kept him from going half-mad with homesickness.

Now, Ryan was gone, aligned against Harry with what was beginning to seem like the entire rank of Allied military chiefs.

Harry had had, until then, little responsibility for the welfare of others. The only impact his actions normally had was on whatever defendant was sitting across from him. But now he had to consider more far-reaching impacts. Ryan had, all along, told him what the professional consequences of the affair could mean. Harry's concern had always been less what they could mean for himself than what they could mean for Cynthia and his sons.

There was also Ricks and Grassi. Harry's decision could very well blot their ledgers as well. Ricks had stepped back from sharing that responsibility with him, and Grassi, with his nearly sociopathic lack of empathy for the situation of others, could never be a true sharer.

And there was my contribution. A friendly hand extended from a cordial stranger had turned out to be the hand of a spy, a peeper.

All in all, Harry had never felt so woefully, vulnerably far from home.

He tried to chase the feeling away all that long, empty day with a trip to the cinema, with strolls in the park, with closeting himself in his quarters poring over the case information for the hundredth and hundred-and-first times. But as surely as the ghosts of Rosewood Court reasserted themselves in the shadows of the waning day, back came that haunting heartache, that emptiness, and with it . . . doubt.

There was no chorus of support for him, Ricks, and Grassi; no concession from any quarter that there was any merit to their arguments. As he had in those early-morning hours when he had first detected the discordant notes in Markham's confession, Harry wondered, *Is it just me?* He wondered if that's how madmen thought.

All of which was why dusk found him stretched out on his bed, his head bobbing to the music from the wireless, a half-empty bottle of Black & White on his nightstand, a glass of same sloshing in his hand. He closed his eyes and reached through a liquory haze for the memory of a place near a lodge on Lake Hopatcong in the New Jersey woodlands where he and Cynthia had sometimes gone. On the wireless was a tune from those days, Bunny Berrigan tooting his way through "I Can't Get Started."

Harry reached for the Black & White and freshened his drink. He took a sip, chased it with a drink from the water glass on the nightstand, then lay back on his bed until the liquor stopped churning in his stomach.

It wasn't true, he mused, no, no, no, that one could forget with booze. In fact, it was stirring up old memories—along with his treacherous stomach—and bringing them up quite clearly. He could smell the old varnished wood smell of his desk in third grade, the arid smell of chalk dust, the stale scent of Miss Friedlander's five-and-dime perfume as she stood at the head of the class and had them recite "I'm a Little Teapot." That was some teacher, that Miss Friedlander, Harry reflected. Sweater girl. Knockers like footballs.

The name of that place in the Jersey woods came back to him now: "Freddy 'Hi Ya!' Watha's Wahoo Palace." A place worth forgetting, perhaps, with its faded paper streamers and insect-filled Chinese lanterns, but worth recalling—especially now—for the balm of the lake licking at the beams of the dance floor that extended over the water, a whipped-cream moonglade floating on the waves. Across the lake they could hear the discordant mesh of ballroom orchestras from the first-class hotels along the lakeshore, the places visited by the likes of the Rockefellers and celebrities like stripper Sally Rand: the Bon Air, the Mt. Arlington, the Alamac and its gardens Cynthia naively likened to those of a French palace, the Westerley looking like a fairyland castle sprawling down one of the lakeshore hills to the water.

But Freddy's and its adequate but spirited band was palace enough for Cynthia and Harry. They swayed on the dance floor, over the lake, until the band went home, then drifted back to their room at the Sunny-side (a bit more within their means than the likes of the Westerley) to tumble together like bobby-soxers in a cinema balcony. Another drink of Black & White and he could recall the cold, mossy smell of the lake, the mustiness of the warped boards of the dance floor, Cynthia's scent of Ivory soap and talcum and rosewater, and the vaguely erotic air of summer perspiration.

Another drink and his head was spinning. He swung his feet to the floor, trying to anchor himself, closing his eyes until the shadows twirl-ing about him ceased moving. He opened his eyes to the darkness, to the ghosts fluttering the open curtain, to the dull, grinning glow of the wireless dials.

Open on the bed next to him was a letter that had come with the day's post. A photograph had been enclosed showing a stretch of Branch Brook Park not far from their four-room walk-up. In the background Harry could see furrows and support sticks for tomato plants and peo-ple working the ground with hoes and rakes. In the foreground stood Cynthia in smudged coveralls and dirty gardening gloves. Her hair was tied up in a kerchief. Harry thought of Rosie the Riveter posters. The boys flanked her, Ricky sporting an exaggerated Bugs Bunny grin and Jerry—always the shy one—trying to slip behind his mother. The letter read:

> There's so little open ground in this part of town the city is letting us use that part of the park up by Factory Street as a neighborhood Vic-tory Garden. Father DeStasio from St. Lucy's has been teaching us all one end of a hoe from another. Don't worry. I don't think he's trying to convert us—it's just none of the Orthodox priests seem to know much about farming.
> Don't forget to send something to Jerry for his birthday. I've been sav-ing up my red points and might have enough gas to take the boys down the shore before it gets too cold. . . .

For the tenth time since he'd opened the letter he peered closely at the picture, at the three faces squinting and smiling into the sun. He studied its background, picking out the playground where he'd taken the boys so many times. His mind's eye took him beyond to the field where he'd played softball with them in summer and football in the fall; he could see the old reservoir where all of them—Cynthia, too—skated in the winter; beyond that was the boathouse where they paddled in rented boats about the winding pond, looking over trees budding with spring to the spires of Sacred Heart Cathedral.

Tears came.

He heard a shuffling of feet in the hall and thought perhaps the Court ghosts—or an inebriated Captain Bowman—had presented themselves for a visit.

"It's Ricks, Major. May I . . . ?" The door creaked open and a blade of light from the hall cut across the dusky shadows of the room.

Harry groaned and closed his eyes.

"Major?" The room went dark and footsteps crossed to the window. Ricks reached for the blackout curtains.

"Whadderya doin'?"

"I was going to turn on the light."

"No."

"I tried calling."

"Something's wrong with the phone."

Through slitted eyes Harry saw Ricks's silhouette cross the windows, pick the telephone receiver off his nightstand, and set it quietly in its cradle. "Is this what you've been doing all day?"

Harry shrugged.

"You want to tell me what this is about?"

"I don't want to think anymore," Harry grumbled. "I'm tired of thinking. This seemed like a good way to make it stop."

"Is it working?"

"Not yet. I'm still conscious. Want a shot?"

"No, thank you."

"Then gimme that!" Ricks handed the bottle over and Harry splashed a fresh dose into his glass.

Ricks walked to the wireless. "Are you listening to this?"

"Leave it alone," Harry said.

Ricks found a chair by the open window and sat. He leaned his head back toward the window.

Harry fumbled about his nightstand. "I need a cigarette. I can't find my damned cigarettes."

Ricks found Harry's cigarettes on the escritoire. He stepped across the room, handed Harry one, and lit it for him.

Ricks picked up the whiskey bottle and filled Harry's glass half-way, then took the glass with him back to his chair by the window. "My father's been practicing law for thirty-five years. He says, over time you discover there's no such thing as right and wrong, just one side and the other side. Not long after I came over, I was out in the country just north of here. A German plane had gone down in one of the fields. I saw some of the people from the farms around there, people just like old Charlie Gresham, a whole crowd of them. They were marching through the village square with the head of the pilot stuck on a pitchfork. That won't make the newsreels back home. You can say they did a horrible thing, but we weren't here for the Blitz."

"So that makes them right?"

Ricks shrugged. He took another sip of his drink. "We can still take General DiGarre's deal. At least that'll finish it. Or play it out. But, whatever you decide, I'll ride this case out with you."

Ricks held up his glass, Harry his bottle, and they exchanged a salute and a smile.

"After that," Ricks said, his smile fading, his eyes drifting to the drink in his hands, "I'm putting in my papers. I'm transferring out of the JAG. I don't imagine Colonel Ryan'll put up much of a squawk."

"Transfer to where?"

"The 34th Infantry Division is slated for Italy. They'll need officers."

Harry shook his head and climbed off the bed. He scooped up an old lace antimacassar from the back of a chair and swiped at the sweat on his forehead. "It wouldn't be right for you to wind up pronged on some Hitler Jugend's bayonet, Pete. What would that solve?"

"Nothing."

"Then why?"

"Clarity."

The telephone rang.

Harry, slumped in his chair, barely heard it. Ricks crossed to the nightstand, picked up the phone, spoke briefly, and rang off. "Major?"

Harry had lolled his head toward the window, letting the cool breeze dry the dampness on his face.

"Major!"

"What?" Harry snapped irritably.

"That was the orderly room at my BOQ. They've been calling all over trying to find me. They have a message from Armando for me. He's at some hospital—"

"A hospital?" Harry asked hopefully. "Somebody catch 'im canoodling with his girl? Or did he just open that trap of his to the wrong person again?"

"It's the girl. Elisabeth McAnn."

The liquor in Harry's stomach coalesced into a cold lump. "What about her?"

"I don't know the whole—"

"What happened?"

"Looks like she tried to commit suicide."

Harry grabbed his stomach, clapped his other hand over his mouth, and ran for the loo.

Harry remembered little of the two-hour journey: Ricks riding heavily on the accelerator of the jeep, a blur of empty road in the hoarded slats of light from the car's eyes, pulling to the roadside several times so Harry could be sick. Chillingham had only a local doctor's surgery, so the girl had been taken to the nearest hospital at Lewes. The signposts had been removed back in 1940 in the hopes of confusing the spearhead of what had then seemed an imminent German invasion, and now the effort was unfortunately successful in sending Harry and Ricks first up one street, then down another, until they eventually stumbled across the hospital. The lights inside barely illuminated brown tile walls and long benches alongside the admitting desk where a solitary nurse sat flipping without interest through a magazine.

On one of the benches sat Armando Grassi, tapping his feet, drumming his fingers, and occasionally allowing his face to collapse into a silent howl like a figure from *The Last Judgment*. Grassi looked up at the sound of Harry's and Ricks's footsteps. While Ricks dealt with the admitting nurse, Harry looked over to Grassi, who squirmed in his seat as if looking for some way to submerge himself in the creaking woodwork. Harry started for him, but Ricks waved him to consult with the white-coated, silver-haired man in wire-rimmed glasses now standing with him.

"Major," said Ricks, "this is Doctor Pratt."

"How is she?" Harry asked. "Is she . . . ?"

"She's alive, Major. Are you all . . . friends of Miss McAnn?" There was something accusatory in the way he said "friends." "Was one of you the friend that gave her these?" The doctor held out a small pill bottle. "That's a U.S. Army Medical Corps prescription label, if I'm not mistaken."

Harry looked at the bottle. "There was a boy, a pilot. They were very close. He died a few days ago."

"Oh." From caustic to contrite in a single syllable.

"How is she?"

"She'll be all right. In a bit."

"Can I see her?"

"She's still unconscious. I would think she'll probably sleep on through tomorrow at least. Seems she's been taking these pills for a while. That worked in our favor: She has something of a tolerance for them, and there weren't very many left."

Harry grabbed a pencil and paper from the nurse's desk. "Look, Doctor—what is it? Pratt?—if she needs anything, I can be reached at this number in London. If she needs *anything*—"

"I'll be sure to call," the doctor said. "There's, um, one other thing, I'm afraid." Uncomfortable now.

"Yes?"

"Yes, well, I don't know how well you gentlemen know Miss McAnn . . . It's just, well, I don't know if *she* knew herself—"

"Didn't know what?"

"Miss McAnn was pregnant. Unfortunately, the incident instigated a spontaneous abortion. I was wondering if perhaps either of you knew she was pregnant?"

How much can they take from you . . . she'd asked, days ago, on the knoll that looked down on her trysting place with O'Connell. He reached out a hand to steady himself against the admitting desk.

"You see, it's possible," the doctor went on, "she may not have known herself. I'd say she probably hadn't been any further along than six weeks or so. Perhaps eight."

"Doctor, you know more about obstetrics than we do," Ricks said, "but wouldn't she have missed . . . you know . . ."

The doctor shrugged. "What with rationing, typical wartime stress, now you tell me about this fellow's death . . . An irregular menstrual cycle wouldn't've been anomalous. Actually, that's why I bring it up at all. I'm wondering if—"

"No," Harry said. "I don't think she knew. I can't think of any good reason why she should know now."

"Quite."

Harry faced Grassi. The little lieutenant was standing now, feet braced, face defensive yet defiant, waiting for him. Harry turned away, fought his way through the tangled blackout curtains and through the emergency entrance doors. He stood in the drive outside breathing greedily, tasting dew-dampened meadows in the dark. The night sky was clear and the fields surrounding the little clinic were bone-white under the moon.

Grassi's voice behind him: "You got something to say, Boss, say it."

"What did you do?"

"You were painting us into a corner, Boss. We needed—"

"*What did you do?*" Harry reeled and grabbed Grassi by his collar, stumbling as he backed the lieutenant against an empty ambulance.

Grassi shrank fearfully, but only at first. "I told her about DiGarre's deal. I told her how you passed on it, and how if we didn't take it we were screwed. It didn't look like anything *we* said to you was going to change your mind, so—"

"Why didn't you talk to me? *Why didn't you say something to me?*"

"Because I *read* you, Boss! Like I said, I could see once you got an idea in your hard head you weren't going to listen to—"

Harry didn't want to hear Grassi finish. "Then what happened?"

"I thought she'd come up to London, maybe bat that big eye at you, turn on the tears, and get you to . . . But she just went into the other room . . ." Grassi let out a low whistle. "Man, the last thing I thought she was going to do . . ."

Harry was seething to the point where he could barely see. He could feel his trembling hands closing into fists. "You . . . told . . . her—"

"Don't get pissed at me, Boss! We had a chance—one chance—to nail both those guys and you were losing it! We could've got them, and you were losing it!" Then, cruelly, "She deserved to know that! And I had a right to try to salvage us! Hell, Boss," and now Grassi's lips twisted into an ugly sneer, "it's not like she was ever going to get the straight dope from you, right?"

Grassi tried to brush past Harry, and Harry pushed him back against the ambulance and cocked a fist by his ear, sighting it on Grassi's nose.

Grassi's face had screwed up in painful expectation, but then it relaxed as he watched the fist, poised and quivering, finally lower to Harry's side.

"Come on, Harry," Ricks warned from the emergency doors.

"I should've known," Grassi sniffed. "You don't have the balls—"

Harry pulled Grassi round by his shoulder. Harry was not a skilled boxer so there was nothing pretty about the blow, but there was a great deal of heart behind it. There was a sickening crunch as his knuckles met Grassi's jaw, and the lieutenant went airborne for a second before falling back squarely on his arse. There was another nasty crack as Grassi continued to topple rearward and his head collided sharply with the pavement.

"Hmm," Ricks said in quiet, approving appraisal. He went to Harry, who was cradling his throbbing right hand. "Let me have a look at that."

"You better have a look at him, first."

"Only if you insist."

Harry insisted.

Ricks knelt over the figure sprawled in the dark. Harry heard a moan.

"Well, he'll live," Ricks said, returning to Harry, "but I'm not sure that's good news. Let me see that hand. Does it hurt badly?"

"Damn!"

"I think you've broken it. We better have the doctor look at it."

"Get him inside first," Harry said, nodding at Grassi.

Ricks shrugged, unconvinced, but went inside for help.

Grassi stirred. He tried to speak but his broken jaw allowed only a low moan.

Harry ignored him. He sat down on the curb of the drive, his hand carefully cradled in his lap. He took off his cap, hung it on his knee, and smoothed his hair with his good hand. He heard the rustle of the breeze through the hedgerows of the hospital gardens, the drone of a solitary aeroplane, a shifting of gears as a far-off lorry struggled uphill. Between these sounds was a long silence which, at that moment, he loved dearly.

•   •   •

I drew open the blackout curtains to vent the grim odors of intimate desperation: cigarette smoke, perspiration, liquor, tea I was surprised to see the eastern sky tattered with a rising orange. Sunday was gone, and perhaps God along with it, leaving us to our own resources for the new week. From my flat I could see down to the Thames. The riverfront was lost beyond the roofs along the way, but I saw the explosion of wrens that burst from Big Ben at the first tolling of the hour, saw them whirl about Parliament Square till the bell had tolled six times and they resettled amongst the spires of Parliament. I lit a fresh cigarette, turned back, and tossed the package onto the table in front of Harry.

He had appeared at my door at some godforsaken hour of the deep night, his face racked by more than the pain of his hand in its pristine cast. He shuffled in, apologizing for waking me, flushing with embarrassment at the sight of me in my dressing gown, eyes blank with sleep, balancing on one leg. He turned his back as I affixed the limb. I drew on trousers to save him the discomfort of watching the mechanism at work. Then, he spent the remainder of the night, me feeding him cigarettes and tea laced with my whiskey as he talked.

It was more than storytelling. It was a verbal purging of the weight he'd carried too long alone; of the haunting guilt of possible missteps and miscalculations; of a course that, as he regarded it at that moment, had produced nothing but a wake of collateral damage and a growing casualty list. Upon concluding his tale he seemed to collapse in exhausted relief at having the whole bloody mess in the open. His eyes closed and I thought the poor bugger would nod off at my table. But the chimes of Big Ben spurred a fleeting thought in him and his eyes opened slowly.

"Do you go to church, Eddy?" he asked.

The non sequitur took me by surprise. "Hm?"

"Church. Do you go to church?"

I shook my head. "Did you know that the first bombards were cast by the same men who cast church bells?"

"Bombards?"

A fresh kettle whistled on my gas ring. I poured us each another cup of tea with its required dose from the whiskey bottle, then sat across from him at the little table. "The first cannon," I explained. "The Chinese had used black powder to scare away evil spirits. Traders brought it to the West, where we had more temporal concerns. The old bombard was nothing more than a church bell put on its side and stuffed with powder and stone projectiles. One day you're building something to praise God, the next you turn it on end and make it something to send more of His worshipers into His company."

He was unamused by the historical footnote. His face twisted in pain and he held his cast to his chest. Whatever the good Doctor Pratt had given him for the ache of his broken hand was wearing off, and my whiskey offered a poor substitute. He looked up at me, awaiting my response to his story. I had yet to find a palatable way—palatable for me—to respond.

"You're an interesting man, Harry. You think the truth will set you free. But whatever it does, that's not it."

He continued to await my answer.

I took a sip of my tea and a puff of my cigarette, and then there was nothing for it but to tell him. "If I turn this story over to my editor, and if through some burst of journalistic altruism he were to actually run it, I would lose my job, he his, the publisher would suffer a blistering censure from Whitehall and quite probably be permanently excluded from military press pools. There could be a diplomatic flap between our respective governments. Have you considered, old man, how two old duffers like ourselves would fare in the dock at the Old Bailey? Violation of the Official Secrets Act and all that?"

"I thought you *wanted* this story!"

"Ach, I wanted *a* story. The one I had in mind had your flyboys trying to top each other off, then maybe trying to give the chop to a pair of citizens of the realm, the poor old Greshams. Scandalous, inflammatory, aye; but not seditious."

I had looked generals and princes in the eye before, and faced down their accusation of my being everything from a scandalmongering bedroom-peeper to the spawn of the Tawny Prince himself. I had grinned and retorted, "Sorry, laddie; simply doing my job." But I could not bear the eyes of the poor old sod across from me just then. I could find nothing to say of solace to either of us.

"You'd be surprised what you can live with, Harry," I said. "I've seen things you couldn't imagine in your worst dreams; things that make this—" I tapped my hollow leg "—look as trivial as a child tearing the wings off flies. It's an old war, Harry. There's no novelty left in it."

"I've already been lectured once this week Spain, China , , , I've heard it. I don't need to hear it again."

I smiled mirthlessly. "Oh, this is a much older war than that."

"How far back do you want to go?" he snapped. "Versailles? Bismarck?"

"You're thinking on the wrong scale, Harry. Charlemagne was only yesterday and so was Caesar. Go back before Cain coshed poor Abel, before Paradise, to the first war when the angels fought. That's a lot of blood over the dam since then. This isn't even a ripple in the flood. Let it go."

The truth of it withered him like a collapsing balloon.

"Can I ask you something? I've been doing my lessons, and as I understand your courts-martial, the officer who calls for the trial—"

"The Convening Authority."

"Yes, well, he's the chap that picks the officers for the jury. Originally, that would've been Halverson, but when DiGarre sacked him, that fell to DiGarre, so he would've been the man picking your jurors. Both counsel can challenge any juror, but DiGarre would pick the replacements, correct?"

"Yes."

"And all courts-martial verdicts automatically go to the Court of Military Review before being set, and the defendant can take his case further, to the Court of Military Appeal, and even all the way up to your Supreme Court. You couldn't possibly have expected a guilty verdict to stand up to all that, could you? Providing you could somehow coax, arm-twist, and/or beg a conviction out of a DiGarre jury? Well, did you honestly think you could get it to stand up? You couldn't actually have thought you'd win?"

He shook his head slowly. "It would have been on the record that no matter what else happens in this war, what happened at Helsvagen on August fifteenth, 1943, was not an act of war committed by soldiers. They murdered a town, Eddy! It would've been on the record that even in a war, you are accountable for your crimes."

"That would've been enough for you?"

He shrugged bleakly. "It would've been *something*."

It was all so painfully clear on his face: the frustration, the self-doubt, and the nearly complete lack of comprehension. That complicity of agonies elicited a pang of recognition and when he turned to me, surprised, I realized it was in response to my sigh. I had felt everything he felt, only it had been a long time ago.

"You're feeling like the sole rational voice among the insane," I said, and he nodded. "You wonder why you're the only one who can see the great wrong here. You wonder how such things can happen. What kind of men do such things? What moves them? I'll wager you've been over the biographies of these men a dozen times, thinking there must be some clue there, some taint of villainy, something that makes them different from you or me. But you're looking for order in a disordered universe. There is no 'us' and 'them.' Just us."

He began to shake his head, but I cut him off. "I told you, Harry: I've witnessed every malfeasance one human being can visit on another; experienced one or two—" I tapped my wooden leg in illustration "—close up. I've recorded it all and sent it home for the entertainment of my readers, this gallery of the grotesque we call 'news,' because that's my job. And from that vast, unpleasant experience I can tell you that if you're looking for that definitive insight that will let you sleep at night, you won't find it. You want to know why such things happen? They happen."

"It's not that simple."

I shrugged grimly. "It only *sounds* simple. Before this war is over, there'll be a million Major Markhams, maybe more. They'll all have done something they wish they hadn't, something they'll want to forget, something they'll never tell their children. They'll do those things because that's their job. And by that time, what may or may not have happened at Helsvagen will be just a raindrop in the flood.

"It may also very well be by that time—and I suppose this is a sad thing—you will come to stop wondering about these things. You grow . . . numb."

I reached out a comforting hand and laid it on his forearm. "Sorry, old man. If you want comfort, don't ask for the truth. Ask for this." I poured him another splash from the bottle.

We finished a last drink, and then he let me guide him to my bed, dumbly shuffling along as I pushed him down atop the bedclothes. By the time I'd loosened his tie and pulled off his shoes, he was asleep.

He did not sleep long, and when he awakened I invited him to join me for breakfast at a patisoorie I knew, but he declined. I suggested an afternoon at the pubs come opening time, sitting outside in the summer air sipping pints of Courage ale until we became silly and shrugged off the dark humors with a good binge. But he'd have none of it and I knew—knew even then—it would take more than a pint of Courage to clean out what gnawed at his vitals.

"I just want to go home," he said.

I promised to ring him on the morrow for lunch and he nodded agreeably.

Big Ben had come round to another hour as I watched him trudge off from my window, his slope-shouldered, stodgy form growing smaller down the street. He brought to mind a verse from Thomas Gray:

> The curfew tolls the knell of parting day,
> The lowing herd winds slowly o'er the lea,
> The ploughman homeward plods his weary way,
> And leaves the world to darkness and to me.

I crawled into my kip and was soon asleep, but found no rest in it. Toward late afternoon I roused myself, had some lunch and a pint at a nearby pub, and then afternoon became evening and I was still at the pub.

What had I used to do with myself? I wondered. Those days when there wasn't some story to chase, a column to write? There were colleagues I could join at the pub, us buying each other rounds and grousing about "the job," but colleagues weren't friends. Family? My parents rested under a moss-crusted marker in a Stonehaven graveyard I'd not laid eyes on in years. Except for Cathryn, it hardly seemed to have been much of a life.

Such grim musing kept the drinks going down until I stumbled home late that evening and dropped into bed in a blissfully blank liquored stupor. Only an urgent knocking at the door stirred me the following morning.

I answered the door snarling and growling, but froze at the sight of the messenger in the hall. I recognized him from Harry's narrative, this gawky figure in American uniform, corporal's chevrons, and confused demeanor: the infamous Corporal Nagel. He carried a sealed manila envelope marked with my name and the caution "Personal." The corporal offered no explanation other than to say that Major Voss had ordered him to see that the envelope was placed directly in my hands. It was the major's last instruction.

"They shipped him out," Nagel explained. "Orders came in yesterday. He just about grabbed the train for Liverpool. He went out last night on an OB convoy for the States."

I thanked him and he asked if I wanted him to wait. I couldn't imagine what he imagined I would want him to wait for, and I began to understand why Harry could not mention his corporal without wincing. Before I could shoo the young man away he begged my pardon and told me he couldn't stay.

"Got another fella coming in later this week, they tell me," he said. "Got to get the office ready for him," and off he went.

I closed the door, sat on my bed and opened the envelope. Inside was a file folder, and in the folder photostats of what seemed to be some sort of after-operations report. There was also a scribbled note:

> Eddy—
> Tried calling but no answer. No time to come by.
> The girl should know about this. Tell her for me.
> Take care.
>
> —Harry

Then, scribbled across the bottom of the page in what, compared to the measured script above, appeared to be a hasty afterthought:

> Do what you can for her.

At approximately five o'clock the morning before, during the very same time when Harry was spinning out his long and woeful story to me, an orderly at Elsworth Airfield, lighting his way with an electric torch, entered the dark, shared room of Major Albert Markham and Captain Jon-Jacob Anderson to nudge them awake for their first mission with their new unit. The orderly woke Markham first, and would remember that it took considerable shaking to rouse the major from his deep sleep. "There's few sleep that good before a mission," he'd recall. Then he turned to Anderson.

The captain was already awake, and it was the orderly's impression that the captain had been awake for some time. The orderly noted a faint glimmer in the gloom of the floor, and his light illuminated a piece of hammered tin by the captain's bunk that had been used as an ashtray. It was filled to the brim with butts. As the beam of the orderly's torch swept across the captain, Anderson's face glittered with beads of perspiration. Later that morning, when the orderly returned to make up the bunks, he would notice a human outline left on the captain's bedclothes, a silhouette imprinted by sweat.

After the orderly made his rounds of billets in the Quonset hut, he returned to each room to see if any of the pilots required assistance suiting up. Markham dismissed him with a polite and appreciative smile, assuring him they were just fine on their own as he and Anderson helped each other on with their burdensome flight kit: thermal underwear, flight overalls, .45 automatic pistol in a shoulder holster, heavy fleece-lined flight trousers, and boots. The rest of their kit they carried over their shoulders to morning mess.

Heeding the 52nd Fighter Group's CO's admonitions, contacts with Markham and Anderson had been friendly but reserved since the duo had arrived at the aerodrome two days earlier. Still, there had been discreet tokens of support from their fellow fliers: a round of drinks at the Officers Club, conspiratorial winks. The men of the unit didn't know the details of Markham's and Anderson's predicament, but knew all too well that it was two brother warriors on one side and "deskbound brass hats" on the other. They didn't need to know more than that to extend their support. Their squadron commander, a heavy-browed captain from Colorado named Matthew "Big Matt" Berger, told both with inordinate deference that if they required anything they should not hesitate to ask.

Markham, it would be remembered, was friendly, open, relaxed, made a point of wishing all who made greeting good luck on the day. Anderson made the same attempt, but there was a tinny quality to his jests and apparent enthusiasm for the day's action. Still, they thought he—like any of them—was entitled to deal with his stresses as he saw fit. So they played along, commenting appreciatively on his hearty appetite when he forced down a second helping of breakfast that day; the young flight lieutenant the captain hadn't noticed in a corner stall of the latrine would not mention to his fellows seeing Anderson vomit up that very same breakfast not long after.

After morning mess they all trekked to the briefing hall, where they took notes on the small pads clipped to their legs regarding the target (U-boat pens at Emden), weather conditions along the line of flight, course changes and escort assignments, altitudes, radio frequencies, code designations, flak and enemy fighter concentrations, time and point of rendezvous with the B-17's coming up from Bushy Park, notes on developing enemy tactics. Then it was on with the rest of their equipment—the heavy flight jacket, the dragging parachute, the bright yellow Mae West—after which jeeps ferried them to the flight line.

The sun was up now, the morning growing warm and humid, more so for the pilots encased in their fleece-lined flying clothes. The coveralls of the ground crews were already dappled with sweat from the fueling and gun-loading procedures. The ground crews had just finished the preflight cockpit checks as the pilots drove up.

Anderson, still playing the jaunty cavalier, called his crew to help his foreshortened figure—weighed down with his flight kit—onto the wing of his ship. He made some lighthearted remark that perhaps as the armor-drenched knights of old had been horsed, the ground crews should similarly use a winch to raise up the pilots and lower them into their cockpits. The ground crew laughed. "Good idea, Cap!" one called out.

Markham's ground crew chief was a weather-beaten mechanic from Idaho with a son half the age of his pilot. The crew chief greeted his new charge with a proper salute, which Markham returned, but then he broke the formalities by taking the chief's hand in a warm handshake. "Always like to stay friendly with the people who make sure it flies." Markham smiled and nodded at his P-47.

The crew chief, who would long remember the incredible poise of the young major, stood on the wing by the open cockpit as the other crew members helped strap Markham into the cockpit. Another crew member ran strips of adhesive tape over the muzzles of the ship's eight .50-caliber guns to keep out dust during takeoff. The chief reported a satisfactory preflight cockpit check. Markham nodded again and thanked

him, then pulled on his lined gauntlets, throat transmitter, and leather
flying helmet. Connections were made for Markham's transmitter and
helmet earphones. Then, the crew cleared the ship and the chief leaned
over into the cockpit.

He explained how Elsworth was an old RAF aerodrome and the runways had not been designed with the weighty P-47 in mind. "Till you
get used to it, the line chief'll be at the runway," he told Markham. "You
watch him. He'll have you crank 'er up higher 'n' you're used to, but
you wait 'n' he'll give you the signal to let her roll. After a coupla times
you won't have no trouble."

Markham thanked the chief for his consideration and said, "See you
soon." The chief clambered off the wing and joined the other ground
crew members along the taxiway.

At 0802 a green flare was fired from the control tower mezzanine.
All along the flight line pilots clicked their ignition switch to "starter,"
energizers whined, then the switch went to "engine," and with a cough
and plumes of blue exhaust the four-bladed propellers began to wind-
mill. Engines caught, roared, propeller blades disappeared in transparent, glimmering discs. Leather-clad heads bowed in the cockpits to check
gauges, fingers flicking at the glass dials to make sure indicator needles
swung freely. One by one, as the engine mercury rose halfway to the red
line, pilots raised a gauntleted hand to signal "ready."

Markham's crew chief would remember his pilot holding his hand
above the rim of the open cockpit, cupping his fingers to catch the prop
wash like a child catching the breeze out the window of a speeding
automobile. "Like he didn't have no care in the world," he would recall.

The crew chief signaled his men to pull the wheel chocks clear. With
a second flare from the tower, the line of Thunderbolts began to slowly
rumble down the taxiway. Each moved in a sluggish zigzag to keep the
following aeroplane from being buffeted by its prop wash. Ground crew
walked along each side of the tarmac as markers for their pilots who
couldn't see the borders of the taxiway over the thick nose of the P-47.

The slightly understrength group—thirty-two ships in all—moved
onto the runway in two-ship elements. Markham and Anderson moved
on together, the fourth pair of the second squadron. They wheeled their
ships to point down the stretch of tarmac and cranked their cockpit canopies closed. They looked for the line chief by the side of the

runway, spied him whirling a small red hand flag in rapid circles, signaling them to rev their engines higher. They moved their throttles to full rich and stood on their brakes as their ships began to shudder and buck with the rising crescendo of the engines. When the line chief was pleased with the pitch of the engines, he brought his flag down in a slash and Markham and Anderson released their brakes and began trundling down the runway. Slowly, each eased six tons of aluminum, steel, petrol, and ammunition into the heavy morning air. The landing gear retreated into its wells and soon Markham and Anderson had joined the fighters above the field, where they circled until the entire group was airborne and assembled.

The group flew east, picking up their B-17 Flying Fortress charges heading northeast over the Channel in just a few minutes. The fighter squadrons separated into their assignments with Markham and Anderson an element in the high squadron. They armed the electrical firing systems for their wing guns, each letting loose a short test burst, then flew well clear of the Fortresses while the bomber gunners test-fired their own guns.

The mission's first Initial Point turned the formation east, the Thunderbolts above and below the Fortresses, jinking to keep pace with the slower bombers. The flight was quiet, with the exception of some scattered and ineffectual ack-ack from the coastal defenses west of Amsterdam. East of Amsterdam, after crossing over the IJsselmeer, the formation hit their second Initial Point and turned northeast. Only a few minutes after their turn, Big Matt Berger's wingman flipped his motor to get the captain's attention. He directed Berger's gaze to the two Thunderbolts slowly pulling away from the formation. The two fighters had the sun behind them so Berger could not identify them. He hand-signaled and then waggled his wings to get their attention, but the fighters continued drifting off. Berger contemplated breaking radio silence to call the ships in, or even flying over to herd the pair back into formation, but his paramount responsibility was to the bombers. He held his position.

A minute or so after Big Matt Berger had been warned about the drifting aeroplanes he saw them both fly into a cloud, a small, solitary nimbus that seemed to be waiting for them. He could hear no noise above the din of his engine, but within the cloud he saw a sudden explosive flash; moments later, bits of shining aluminum rained out of the cloud, fluttering earthward like metallic snow.

Before the incident truly registered with him, "Bandits!" crackled over his headset, and he saw the low squadron dropping their belly tanks and peeling off to engage a gaggle of Focke-Wulfs hurtling upward at the bombers. Berger loosed his own drop tank, his squadron following suit, and followed them into the fray.

It was not until Berger had returned to Elsworth some forty-seven minutes later and made an accounting of his unit that he realized the two aircraft lost in the cloud belonged to Markham and Anderson.

It had been a fortnight since the German raid on Donophan, and one week—nearly to the hour—since the raid on Helsvagen. There would still be paperwork to clear up, formalities to attend to, procedures to execute, but for all intents and purposes the matter was now closed.

I followed the nurse's instructions and found her in a hedged cul-de-sac in a secluded corner of the hospital gardens. She was reclining in a cushioned garden lounger, snuggled deep in a blue dressing gown with blankets over her legs. A magazine lay open and ignored on her lap, and atop its glossy pages sat a teacup. Her cane was propped against the lounger, but the eye patch was gone, her eyes now hidden by a pair of tinted spectacles. Her head lay back, her face turned toward the bright but cool morning sun. She gave no notice she'd heard me come up to her; behind those opaque lenses she could very well have been asleep.

Miles beyond, from someplace below the distant line of trees, came the stirring of aeroplane engines. I could see the first ships arc skyward, small fighters glinting in the sunlight.

I took a moment to study her. Her black hair was straight and a bit matted. I could see the smooth line of her jaw and saw that it would continue round to form a neat oval of smooth whiteness. Black Irish, I thought. The story was the Black Irish were descendants of survivors of the Spanish Armada who had come ashore and never left. Black Irish: bastard children with no native home of their own.

"Yes?" It issued from her as a sigh. She must have heard me.

"Miss Elisabeth McAnn?"

She made a vague motion of her hand in acknowledgment. I walked closer, standing by a bronze sundial. The cement base of the podium was crumbling and the tarnished dial was tilted and unreadable.

"My name is Edward Owen," I said, removing my hat. "I'm a friend of Harry Voss."

She gave no sign the words registered; her face remained turned to the sun. I looked for some record on it of the last days, a sign of sadness, anger, pain. If it had been there, it had been consumed by something deeper, some dark, bottomless pit: *Mater Tenebrarum*. Mother of Darkness.

"How is the good major?" she asked.

"Do you mind . . . ?" and I gestured toward a nearby lawn chair. Again, that vague movement of her hand. I pulled the chair close and sat. "They sent him home."

"How nice for him."

"He wanted me to ask after you. How are you getting on?"

"Did your friend the major tell you why I'm here? They keep asking me if I intend to 'try something foolish' again." There was a flicker of a grim smile, then that dark blankness again. "Curious phrase, don't you think? 'Try something foolish'? You can tell them for me, Mr. Owen, if they ask, not to worry. No more foolishness."

"Harry would want me to apologize for his not coming by. They transferred him quite suddenly last week; the night after, well, after you were brought here. But he wanted me to come by—"

"So you said."

"If there's anything you need—"

"Mr. Owen, I think the major has done quite enough on my behalf."

The sun was losing its summer glare. The warm, humid mornings had given way to dawns of cold dampness and the first touches of color had begun to tint the trees.

"Aren't you chilly out here?" I asked her.

She shook her head.

The wind made dry, rustling noises as it passed through the dying leaves. The sound of engines was getting louder. I turned in my seat and saw the growing circle of aeroplanes over the aerodrome tucked behind the trees.

"Shame, that," I said. "Quite mucks up the view."

"They've only just started," she said. "A new airfield. Opened just a fortnight or so ago, I'm told. Now they seem to fly out more and more. Sometimes more than once in a day. One learns to ignore it after a bit. You're down from London, then? I remember this time when I was a girl, Mum packed a basket with food and we went down to London, made a day of it at the zoo. Is it true about the zoo? I heard they killed all the snakes."

I nodded. "During the Blitz. People were afraid of them getting loose if a stray bomb hit the snake house."

"They killed the snakes. But they kept the lions?" A small flash of a smile. "Queer, don't you think?"

"The main reason Harry wanted me to come round was there's something he thought you should know." I held out the file containing the photostated after-action report. For a moment, she did not take it, as if to say there was nothing I could offer she needed to know, then she reached out slowly, took the file, and began reading.

When she finished she let her head fall back, the closed folder held close to her chest. "They're dead, then?"

"Major Albert Q. Markham and Captain Jon-Jacob Anderson are missing, presumed dead," I clarified. "The Red Cross hasn't reported their capture or that any bodies were recovered. Someone I know in Geneva says that even if Jerry had found them—one way or another—the Germans may just not have gotten round to making the proper notifications. He says they have a tendency to be uncooperative."

"But the Army thinks—"

"I'm told the chances of surviving a midair collision . . . well . . ." I shrugged and she seemed satisfied with that.

She handed the file back. "Thank you for coming by, Mr. Owen."

"May I ask a question? About Dennis O'Connell? Harry . . . he confided in me, you might say. About what he was working on."

She was still, waiting for me to proceed.

"Harry's supposition was that what happened to Dennis was because of something Dennis saw, to prevent him from saying anything when he returned. But the wireless in Dennis's aeroplane was operational until he crashed. If he had seen something, he could've signaled it home. The American Military Police could've been waiting for Markham and Anderson when they landed."

"Really?" She sounded amused.

"Yes."

"Maybe the major was wrong all along. Maybe Dennis hadn't seen anything."

"Then he'd still be alive."

Elisabeth's chin touched her chest in thought, then she laid her head back against the chair. "Maybe he didn't care."

"Didn't care?"

"Or maybe he didn't think anyone else would." The amused quality returned to her. "It is a puzzlement, isn't it?"

I made my good-byes and rose. "Where will you go when you're released? The doctor said you should be able to leave—"

"Soon, yes. I still have family in Ireland."

"Getting a visa for Ireland can be a bit dicey these days."

"Somehow I don't think anyone's going to mind my leaving England. Do you?"

"If I can help, I'm sure Harry would've wanted—"

"I'm tired, Mr. Owen. Would you mind?"

I tucked the file under my arm, returned my hat to my head, and went back down the walk the way I'd come.

She was right, of course, about her leaving. Within days of her discharge from the hospital, she'd be back in Ireland, and the powers that be would follow her lead, scattering the other witnesses to their complicity.

Before his jaw had healed, Armando Grassi would be tucked away at a post at Godthåb, Greenland, a speck you'll find only in the best Britannica, and Peter Ricks would get his combat assignment, coming ashore at Salerno the following month. I understand he lost his left arm below the elbow the next May at Cassino.

The 351st was disbanded. Its duty-fit survivors—like Leo Korczukowski—were distributed to commands in the various combat theaters, while the luckless General Halverson would ultimately find himself commanding six antiquated P-40's protecting bauxite mines in the Amazonian jungles.

As for the unfortunate Greshams, the missus never quite recovered from the attack and Charlie could not persuade her to return to their seaside cottage. She died in London the following year of heart failure,

with her husband at her side, after which Charlie did return to the Sussex meadows. Compensated by the Americans with a new flock, he may
still be tending them to this day.

And poor old Harry? He was posted to Fort Dix, New Jersey, just a
short drive from his family. Perhaps the posting was a bribe, or a re-
minder of what he'd been missing—and would miss again with another
transfer. That was enough to secure his future silence. Or, perhaps like
Dennis O'Connell, by war's end, Harry didn't care any longer . . . or
thought no one else would care.

By 1945, against the complete gutting of such metropolises as Berlin, Cologne, and Dresden and their tens of thousands of civilian dead,
the thousand or so who died at Helsvagen hardly seemed worth the
bother. In the closing act of the war in the Pacific, Curtis LeMay sent
his B-29 Superfortresses, their bellies filled with incendiaries, against a
rota of Japanese cities of paper and wood, burning away sixteen square
miles of Tokyo; a third of Yokohama; two thirds of Shizuoka. Kobe was
torched, Nagoya, Osaka, Kawasaki, and when the great cities were cinders, LeMay worked his way through the smaller ones: over half of
Tsu burned away; two thirds of Aomori; three quarters of Ichinomiya;
nearly all of Toyama. Just a few weeks before the dropping of the first
atomic bomb on August 6, 1945, Fifth Air Force Intelligence would issue the following statement:

> There are no civilians in Japan. We are making War and making it in the all-out
> fashion that saves American lives, shortens the agony which War is, and seeks to
> bring about an enduring Peace. We intend to seek out and destroy the enemy wher-
> ever he or she is, in the greatest possible numbers, in the shortest possible time.

Were anyone to show regrets over such an attitude, the response would
be to look at what had happened at Nanking, or the Blitz, the Bataan
Death March, the Malmédy massacre, the rape of Manila, and Auschwitz,
Bergen-Belsen, Buchenwald, Treblinka, and all those other blasphemies.
After all: War Is Hell.

My cab was waiting where I'd asked, in the hospital car park. The cabbie
saw me and started the engine but I did not climb in immediately. I took

off my hat and let the breeze ruffle my hair. Even over the chugging engine of the cab I could hear the growing din of engines overhead.

I felt tired. Years tired.

Perhaps I had left my stamina back in Singapore with the rest of my leg. Or perhaps watching poor sad, mad Harry fight for the quaint belief that with the world afire from one end to the other, right could still be right and wrong still wrong had exhausted my ability to find amusement in man's self-destruction. The dark humor and condescending remarks no longer anesthetized me against the real pain beneath a catchy headline. Every vessel has its brim and I had filled to mine.

Himself was right. It was time to sit together, chipped teacups in hand, and discuss the possibility of an editor's desk. He was right about something else: Cathryn. I didn't seem to do so well without her.

The fighters were in formation now, climbing, a raft of small, silvery crosses slipping across the sky, off to rendezvous with their bombers somewhere over the Channel, and then on to points east.

It seemed to me I'd never seen quite so many of them before.

ACKNOWLEDGMENTS

There is an idea that writing is a lonely profession, reinforced by the image of a scribbler hunched over his or her keyboard alone with their creative muse. While there is a time in the life of every work when it is solely in the hands of the writer, only the most self-aggrandizing author—or authors—would claim, "I do it alone."

First and foremost among our team would be Kate Miciak, our editor at Bantam. Kate would probably slash through here with her red pencil, urging us to make this short and to the point, but that would be doing a disservice to her. Kate has a remarkable deftness with language, knowing the line between succinct clarity and the perfunctory, between poetry and a writer's indulgence. She shows a wonderful respect for the intent of the author, and knows how to take a writer where he needs to be as gently and in as supportive a manner as one could want. This would not be the book it is without her.

And not far behind her is our copyeditor, Connie Munro. Long after Steve and I couldn't abide another review of the manuscript, Connie was still policing each page to ensure that we would appear as literate as we like to think we are.

There would be no book at all if it wasn't for my agent, Richard Derus, and the support of his colleague, Claudia Menza. Richard literally pulled the manuscript out of a pile, saw the possibilities, and made the first editorial suggestions. That is what a good agent does. A great agent—which Richard is—also provides much needed hand-holding and shoulder-crying services to nervous, despairing authors.

We wouldn't have met Richard were it not for Bob Cope, founder and president of The Writers Foundation. Bob and his annual "America's Best" competition have long been providing a rare venue, as well as moral support, for new writers. Thank you, Bob.

Although *The Advocate* is a work of fiction, Steve and I have done our best to accurately portray the historical period as well as re-create the singular psyche of the time. We would be remiss not to express our appreciation for the talented and diligent authors whose work helped provide us with that basis, as well as those friends and family who shared their experiences:

BOOKS:

Allen, William L. *Anzio: Edge of Disaster.* New York: Elsevier-Dutton, 1978.

Collier, Richard. *Eagle Day: The Battle of Britain.* New York: Dutton, 1980.

Doyle, Edward, and Stephen Weiss. *A Collision of Cultures: The Vietnam Experience.* Boston: Boston Publishing Co., 1984.

Eisenhower, David E. *Eisenhower: At War 1943–1945.* New York: Random House, 1986.

Farago, Ladislaw. *Patton: Ordeal and Triumph.* New York: Ivan Obolensky, 1963.

Gann, Ernest K. *Fate Is the Hunter.* New York: Ballantine, 1972.

Goodwin, Doris Kearns. *No Ordinary Time.* New York: Simon & Schuster, 1994.

Jablonski, Edward. *Airwar.* 4 vols. New York: Doubleday, 1971.

Jones, Ken D., and Arthur F. McClure. *Hollywood at War.* Cranbury, N.J.: A. S. Barnes, 1974.

Katz, Robert. *Death in Rome.* New York: Pyramid, 1968.

Kemp, Peter. *Decision at Sea: The Convoy Escorts.* New York: Elsevier-Dutton, 1978.

Kershaw, Andrew, ed. *1939–1945 War Planes: History of the World Wars—Special Edition.* Hicksville, N.Y.: Marshall Cavendish, 1973.

———. *Weapons of War. History of the World Wars—Special Edition.* Hicksville, N.Y.: Marshall Cavendish, 1973.

Lord, Walter. *Day of Infamy.* New York: Bantam, 1970.

———. *Incredible Victory.* New York: Pocket, 1968.

Manvell, Roger. *Films and the Second World War*. Cranbury, N.J.: A. S. Barnes, 1974.

Nalty, Bernard, and Carl Berger. *The Men Who Bombed the Reich*. New York: Elsevier-Dutton, 1978.

Nalty, Bernard. *Tigers Over Asia*. New York: Elsevier-Dutton, 1978.

Rivkin, Robert S. *The Rights of Servicemen*. New York: Baron, 1973.

Ryan, Cornelius. *The Longest Day*. New York: Pocket, 1969.

Schoenburg, David. *Soldiers of the Night: The Story of the French Resistance*. New York: Dutton, 1980.

Terkel, Studs. *The Good War*. New York: Pantheon, 1984.

U.S. Naval Institute. *The Bluejackets' Manual*. 20th ed. Annapolis, Md.: U.S.N.I., 1981.

OTHER PUBLICATIONS:

Church, George J. "Overpaid, Oversexed, Over Here." *Time*. May 28, 1984: 33.

Dalton, Susan Elizabeth. "Bugs and Daffy Go to War." *The Velvet Light Trap*, 4 (Spring, 1972). Rpt. in *The American Animated Cartoon*. Ed. Gerald Peary and Danny Peary. New York: Dutton, 1980: 158–61.

Gold, Philip. "Courts-Martial." *Insight*. April 13, 1987: 24–25.

Gordon, William. "Victory At Sea." *The Newark Star-Ledger* (New Jersey). May 27, 1993: 85+.

————. "Grand Hotel: Return of an Era." *The Newark Star-Ledger* (New Jersey). June 15, 1993: 37+.

History of the Second World War. Battle of Britain issue. Part 9.

Horne, Alistair. "Breakthrough at Sedan." *History of the Second World War*. Part 5.

Jenkins, Patrick. "Pentagon Salutes Atlantic City WW II Service." *The Newark Star-Ledger* (New Jersey). July 31, 1992: 31.

"The Kaiser Experiment." *Ms. Gazette*. April 1978: 83–84.

Life. World War II special issue. 1985.

Naval Education and Training Program Development Center. *The Law of Armed Conflict*. Washington, D.C.: U.S. Government Printing Office, 1980.

Turner, Patricia C. "War Effort." *The Newark Star-Ledger* (New Jersey). December 9, 1991: 25.

OTHER SOURCES:
The Imperial War Museum, London
The Museum of London

RESEARCH ASSISTANCE:
John Armor, U.S.A.F.
Josephine Esposito
Don Hanle, U.S.A.F.
Lucy Mesce
Marie Mesce
Thomas Mesce, U.S.N.
Faye Palazzo
Mark Peters, U.S.A.F.
Robert Shanahan, Esq.

ABOUT THE AUTHORS

BILL MESCE JR., lives in New Jersey with his wife and children.

STEVEN G. SZILAGYI is a novelist, critic, and journalist living in Cleveland, Ohio. His novel, *Photographing Fairies,* was made into a film. He is at work on a novel about a black regiment in the Civil War.